# Ever My Merlin
## Book 3, My Merlin Series

## PRIYA ARDIS

## Ink Lion Books

Published by: Ink Lion Books, LLC. http://inklionbooks.com
Visit the author website: http://www.priyaardis.com
ISBN-13: 978-0-9848339-5-5
ISBN-10: 0984833951
E-BOOK ISBN-13: 978-0-9848339-4-8
First Trade Paperback Edition, November 2012
Juvenile Fiction / Legends, Myths, Fables / Arthurian

To the boys, always a pair.

# CONTENTS

# ACKNOWLEDGMENTS

It's the last book in the series, so there are a lot of people to thank. First, I'm thrilled to have been supported by my wonderful readers, bloggers, friends, and family! Those of you who have contacted me through the various social sites, I can't tell you how many times I've been picked up by your enthusiastic words and quick note! Those of you who've spread the word about the series via your websites, reviews, and by simply telling friends   I'm floored and very grateful!

A big thank you to my family for putting up with my schedule when I should have been watching movies/at the beach/generally not in front of a computer (I blame the muse!).

A huge thank you to CM at Phatpuppy for her wonderful art and for going out of her way to ensure I was happy with everything—I am! KB at Ink Lion, who's been so wonderfully supportive, for her awesome, awesome, layout design—thank you!

A shout out to my wonderful editors – Teri "the Editing Fairy" G. and Cassie MC—without whom this manuscript would be a mess. Thank you for working your schedules around mine! WM, thanks for pitching in, though you didn't have a choice. Another big shout out to MM, the lone voice of reason, couldn't do this without you! To the remaining yankas, VP, JP, RP, for hanging out and more.

And lastly, I find myself thanking the hands of fate that led me here. As most dreamers and scribblers know writing is a long road and I'm grateful I've had a chance to finish one circle in this winding journey!

# PROLOGUE

I helped my brother up the stairs of our small cottage. We were playing in the woods. He followed me everywhere, but I didn't mind. He had small hands; mine were big. I was the big brother. I would always take care of him.

I turned the handle that latched the back door. Behind me, my brother stumbled on the stairs. I turned back around and caught him before he could fall. The door opened a crack. I helped my brother up the stairs leading into a small storeroom. Across the dirt-floored room, another three steps led up to the cottage.

The Lady sat at a round table and chopped, chopping a potato. I don't know how she managed to hold on to the precious bit of food. Crops liked to grow for her. I'd overheard more than one desperate villager whisper about our bounty, yet no one ever tried to steal or wrest it from us.

Maybe I did know why. One time I took a few leftover bits of food and tried to trade it for a sword. I never saw her so angry.

Her glowing green eyes took the breath from my body. It wasn't until I saw dark spots in my vision that her eyes snapped back to normal and my breath swooped back into my lungs. I knew I almost met my death that day, but in the end, I was simply admonished for possibly exposing us to outsiders.

I was about to fling the back door open when the voice of a man stopped me. We never had a man in our cottage before. We never had any visitors in our cottage before. The Lady was our guardian—I didn't dare call her mother. I had little recollection of anyone before her. For a long time, it had been only the three of us—the Lady, my little brother, and me.

"Are they here?" the man asked.

"No, son. They're out in the woods." The Lady cut another slice of the potato.

I took a few steps into the cool darkness of the storeroom. I could see her above me. My brother started to make a gurgling sound. I put a finger to my lips to tell him to shush. He nodded and repeated the gesture, delighting at the game.

"The elder takes care of his brother well," she said.

The giant of a man sat down in a chair across the table from her. He wore the uniform of a Roman soldier—a breastplate of unusually shiny metal, a leather skirt, and leg armor. His cloak was an imperial purple. On a bare-muscled arm he wore a gold armband in the shape of a fish. Sandals covered his feet. A gold crown sat atop dark-blond hair with a winking green gemstone. "Do I hear censure in your tone, Mother?"

"An observation, Poseidon," she said.

"No one calls me by that name anymore, Mother." The man paused. "Our time is near. You cannot delay much more. We have already lingered too long. Our father has demanded our departure and he is right. We have other places to be."

The Lady continued to cut the potato placidly. "Yet, I am not done. The boys need me."

"Father is not happy with you. What you've done—"

"I've saved this world."

"At what cost? You've brought a plague upon this land. The pandemic will take half their lives in exchange—"

The Lady said harshly, "Better than every single life. There is always a price to be paid when you cheat time. Besides, I will not leave them completely defenseless. I have a plan."

"Oh, yes." The man laughed. "The sword."

"The world will see a dark age, but our garden will flourish again, despite our abandonment."

"It will not be abandoned. Father realizes our time here is at an end. The world has grown, and in time, they will gain their own power. Anyhow, it was not his choice. It was written in the stars. You have only delayed it. The universe will not rest until it finds a balance. Kronos's Fury will rebound."

"I will not give up without a fight." *Chop.* She cut the potato in two neat halves.

In the storeroom, I winced at the hard sound, yet my heart swelled. The Lady would protect my brother and me, no matter the cost.

"They can save themselves, Mother," the man said.

*I didn't like him.*

She answered. "Your father doesn't understand. Sometimes when you see too far, you can forget to look at what is most near.

Fate must be helped along, my son. We must make sure the boys are protected. They will be needed."

"One boy, Mother. There was only meant to be one," the man replied. "I do not know how those idiot wizards somehow managed to cause the conception of two."

In the cold blackness, my grip tightened on my brother. I *really* didn't like this man.

"You can only leave the gift to one, Mother," he continued. "We do not have the strength for more. Who will you choose?"

"I have already chosen." The Lady moved on to a new potato. With one clean slice, she cleaved it open. "However, the two are tied so closely together. This will be hard for them—"

"You orchestrated their conception for this purpose." The man's tone hardened. His green eyes almost glowed as he watched the Lady. "My brothers and I were close once also. You must do what is right as we did."

"I am well aware what is at stake." The Lady paused in her cutting and laid down the knife. "We must all do what is necessary, but it does not mean we should forget our hearts. Are you and your brothers ready to do your part?"

The man stared at the Lady, his mother. I wasn't sure what they were talking about. I knew this moment could change everything. The Lady looked steadily at her son. Finally, he sighed. "You know I would do anything for you. So will Jupiter."

The Lady smiled and picked up the knife again. "And Hades?"

The man shook his head. "*Pluto* does not agree, but is too busy to be a problem. Jupiter has gone to see Father, but you know as well as I that Father will not part with the apples."

"It is merely a ruse," the Lady said. "Your father doesn't know about the ones I sent Hercules to steal."

The man paused. "Are you absolutely certain you want to do this? Father has strict rules against playing with two worlds."

"Sometime you have to break the rules to save what is most important."

"And the other way—"

"It is too risky," she said dismissively, with a wave of the knife.

The man sighed. "I hope you are correct about this boy, Mother. So much hinges on it. I will go to my island after I leave you. I must give them their final instructions."

"You will not be the least bit sorry to leave your son?"

The man's face blanched. "We always knew this day would come. Triton is of this world. He belongs here."

She looked down at the slices of potato. "It will be as difficult for you to let go of the boy as it was for me to let go of you."

"I survived."

"Vivane also reminds me a good deal of you, but he is more vulnerable. He is of this world. He has you in him, but he is not ours. Remember that. Teach him to be a warrior, but do not break him. You must return him in seven years' time. Merlin's training will be completed by then as well."

"Triton knows what he must do," the man said.

In the pit of the storeroom, I stood frozen to the spot. I made an effort to breathe. She was giving me away. She was keeping my brother, but she was giving me away.

My brother would be alone.

A jagged sword of anger surged from inside a deep pit—toward a mother I could barely remember, a father who'd never been there, and the Lady. I remembered the day the Lady came into our hut. My mother cried when she told me to be strong. She told me to always look after my brother. Then, she took a bag of gold coins from the Lady and let me go. The only one who cared about me was my brother. I knew that. And if I cared as much about him, I knew what I had to do.

My hands fisted, a physical reaction to the decision. They squeezed the small fingers laying innocently in mine.

"Vee," Merlin protested.

The day I was dreading had finally come. I looked down at him, his round baby face and big eyes. The Lady wanted him. I knew I had no choice. We never had a choice. Neither of us.

We'd been betrayed.

With a sharp breath, I let go of his hand. Stomping away from him, I went up the stairs. As usual, Merlin ran after me. His little legs stumbled on the first step. I resisted the urge to help him. I kept climbing.

The bright, green eyes of the Lady widened when she saw me at the threshold. "Vivane?"

Behind me, I heard Merlin fall. A thud sounded as his back hit the dirt floor. An angry wail filled the air.

I didn't turn around. He had to figure it out on his own now. He had to be strong. He had to learn to stop counting on me.

The Lady stood up in a hurry. "Vivane, your brother!"

My name wasn't Vivane.

I wasn't needed as an older brother.

I looked at her... I looked at the man. He watched me with steady green eyes, the exact same shade as the Lady's.

I declared, "I am Vane."

And I was alone.

# ENDINGS

Forever. I ached for it. I hurt for it in places that didn't have a name. I wanted it. I wanted it for my friends. I wanted it from my family. The world. Like anyone, I imagined some kind of forever for myself—whether good or bad—then, it was snatched out from under me.

The ghostly faces of seven billion people shimmered in a wall of water that stretched from earth all the way up to the heavens. As I watched the giant wave, I made a wish. I wished to change my fate. I wished to live.

"Ryan," Matt said, taking my hand.

I looked at him and his eyes reflected the same knowledge. We'd come to the end.

*How had I gotten here?*

One word—tsunami. Wave after giant wave of ocean turbulence devastated the coastlines across the world. New Zealand. Australia. Hawaii. California. Indonesia. India. Five volcanoes started it all. Erupting simultaneously, they threw the whole world into a nightmarish scenario. Relief agencies that were strained dealing with just one hotspot struggled to cover five. However, it wasn't just the hotspots that were impacted. The effects bounded out into a radius of pure chaos.

In Hawaii, the Wizard Council summoned the wizards who lived there, a surprisingly high number, to stand on the rocky cliffs and push back the onslaught of water. As the underwater volcano, Loihi, spewed out of control, it gave birth to a new island, a birth that wasn't supposed to happen for another hundred thousand years. The vassal of the Earth Shaker had woken. The Fisher King, and I'd woken him.

I was halfway across the world from Hawaii. My legs were rooted on a flat, concrete rooftop, at the top of a square, white building, in a row of identical white buildings. Other wizards lined up beside me, evenly spread across fifty or so roofs. We faced the ocean, which, just a few days ago, had been a haven of tranquility and peace for the city behind us.

I couldn't see the beach anymore. There was no beach. Wave after wave assaulted the shoreline, overrunning the mile-long expanse of sand that stretched from the buildings to the water's edge.

Squatty steel and concrete buildings, only two stories high, were the last barricade as the water relentlessly tried to inundate the crowded metropolis of Chennai, India.

Its vibrant, noisy city streets, usually packed with three-wheeled rickshaws, bicycles, and cars, were abandoned and silent. Millions of people, a rainbow of brightly colored cotton and spice, had to be evacuated from their homes in the wake of the tsunami alerts. The blare of sirens sounded ceaselessly. Somewhere behind me the static-laden voice of a radio announcer described the panic-stricken chaos caused by the mass exodus.

On the barren rooftop, Matt's fingers tightened around mine. "You can do this."

I looked up into his tired amber eyes, somewhere deep inside a battle-scarred soul, their brilliant depths banked with faint power. Lelex's torture still lingered, and now I was asking for more. My fingers intertwined with his. He inclined his head in tacit support, unruly, auburn curls brushing his forehead.

Grey took up my left. After him, Gia stood holding hands with Blake. The four of us, tied together by our common bond as Candidates to pull Excalibur from the stone, faced a horror from which only the sword could save us. In my free hand, I gripped it. It was King Arthur's sword once, a long time ago. Now, it was mine. Its power hummed in my hand, and sweat filled my palm. It was ready. But was I?

Earlier this morning, Matt, the gang, and I left Greece to fly to Indonesia. Three volcanoes had exploded, spewing smoke, ash, and lava across the island chain. In the northern region of Sumatra, the Toba caldera was the site of a supervolcano. The eruption had caused a massive global climate change about eighty thousand years ago. Only two hundred years ago in 1815, Mount Tambora's eruption, a nearby stratovolcano, instigated a volcanic winter, resulting in a worldwide famine that reached all the way to North America.

No matter which scenario we faced this time, it wasn't good.

On our way, though, we were derailed. Matt and I saw a vision of a massive underwater earthquake farther north in the Indian Ocean. This one occurred near the Andaman Islands, sending shockwaves across the Bay of Bengal to the eastern coast of India.

One call from Matt to the head of the Wizard Council, the First Member, and the private plane carrying us changed course, making an emergency landing at the Chennai International Airport. Several black Mitsubishi SUVs whisked us from the airport toward the beaches. Twelve of us came from Greece—my brother Grey, my best friends Gia and Blake, Colin, three gargoyles, three wizards, and of course, Matt and me. I glanced at my friends. They'd all become my family. After what we'd gone through in Greece, I wouldn't have blamed them if they'd wanted to stay behind. They refused to leave my side.

Blake's words had been memorably British. "Not likely you're going to leave us out of the adventure."

Adventure, this was not.

Sirens started blaring through the city in the middle of our drive as the Indian Ocean disaster warning systems finally caught up to what we already knew. We dodged panicked pedestrians, scooters, and an occasional cow randomly wandering through the dusty streets. The leader of the local underground contingent of wizards, a surprisingly young twenty-year-old named Hari, drove down the crowded streets with a grim expression. Half an hour later, we pushed through the stampede of evacuees to reach the beaches at the edge of the city.

Hari stopped in front of a row of white buildings. I could smell the ocean behind them, and hear the rush of the waves. It evoked memories of cawing seagulls, gentle sunny days, beach blankets, and sweet ice cream. However, this was not that beach. Not today.

Beyond the building, past the solitude of the beach, impending rage simmered in the roaring darkness. I stared up at sulky, grey clouds as we got out of the SUV. Residents hurried past us with bulging suitcases, so focused on their own escape they didn't even give us curious looks.

With Matt beside him, Hari led us into the building and up a narrow, concrete staircase. Hari told him, "I've asked everyone to gather in the other buildings. This house is at the center, so it will be the best for you, Master-*ji*."

"Good work," Matt replied.

Hari beamed under the simple praise, giving Matt the awestruck expression that all the wizards inevitably seemed to get around him. We emerged from a short doorway. I looked out across what seemed like a never-ending sea of rooftops. In either direction from us, men and women spread out in what must have been a mile-long line. Those nearest to us watched the quiet ocean with petrified expressions.

I asked, "How did you gather so many wizards so quickly?"

Hari gave me a curious look. "Keltoi magic originated from here, of course. Many live close to this region."

*Of course.* I knew practically nothing about the origin of magic, or the Keltoi, as the wizards called themselves. As a "Regular," I'd only been taught enough to stay alive.

"Every city along the coast has been readied per the orders of the Council. We have formed a line of defense from here to Kolkotta. We are ready to do whatever it takes."

"I doubt any of us are truly ready," Matt said.

I elbowed him. Unfortunately, he wasn't being dramatic. Whether we succeeded or failed, I had no illusions that stopping a tsunami in its tracks was a task we'd survive. I took out a knife from my pocket and held it up to him.

"*Aayat*," Matt said.

In a faint whisper of blue light, the knife lengthened into a sword. The blade glinted in the dim light, its power throbbing for all to see. Across the rooftops, all eyes turned in my direction.

A slim girl in braids hurried to Hari. Her eyes locked on Excalibur. "You brought her. We are saved."

I tried not to cringe from the expectation in her eyes. Unconsciously, I took a step closer to Matt. My fingers curled around the famous sword. I had to believe I could do this.

Hari put an arm around the girl's shoulder. "Merlin has brought us hope, Sangeetha. He will not let this defeat us."

Sangeetha put her head into Hari's shoulder. Her young face lighting up, she told him, "Neither will you, husband."

Hari grinned and wrapped his arm around her shoulder. The tender look he gave her hit me like a sucker punch. A sudden vision of Vane's smile (arrogant with a hint of reluctant sweetness) flashed in my mind, and I had to look away. It was all too fresh.

I walked to the edge of the rooftop, raising Excalibur in the air, my palms slippery with sweat. Gia, Blake, and Matt fanned out on either side. Grey and the gargoyles gathered just behind. Another string of wizards extended down both sides of me, all looking toward Excalibur. I prayed they would not be disappointed.

"It's coming," Hari said.

The surf on the beach receded. Further out in the ocean, a wall of water, the tsunami, rose up like the giant hand of an ancient god.

Then, it was upon us.

It rushed toward the rooftops. For a moment, its colossal majesty froze me solid and my world became a giant fishbowl. To my right, Matt muttered, "*Sphara,*" and faint blue magic flowed from him. The other wizards followed his lead and chanted along.

I lifted Excalibur higher in front of me. Magic flowed to it from the wizards. I could feel the sword absorbing and magnifying it. The weight of the magic pressed down on me and I struggled to stay upright under the onslaught. A magic veil spread out from the sword and solidified to form a shield, an invisible wall, between the colossal wave and us.

Water bombarded my shield like a hurricane pouring down on a single umbrella. The wizards kept chanting their magic, trying to reinforce the umbrella. The tsunami deluge was ceaseless.

I dug my heels in and braced against the power of the wave that threatened to blow me backward into a watery oblivion. My hand, now squeezing tighter than I ever thought possible, clutched the sword and I hung on for… one second… one minute… one hour… forever.

Finally, an undefined moment in time later, Gia fell to her knees with a defeated gasp. Blake pulled her back up, supporting her. One-by-one, the wizards started to collapse. The shield was weakening. From the corner of my eye, I saw the edge of the rooftop. Hari and about half the wizards struggled to hang on.

My hands, grasping Excalibur, throbbed and I tried not to drop it.

Grey walked up from behind me, grabbing the hilt from one side. I blinked as Excalibur's weight eased. On my other side, Matt stood completely still.

His eyes were closed. "Hold on, Ryan."

"We won't let you fall." Blake moved to the open spot at Matt's right.

The shield held with renewed fortification. I could almost see power draining from them into the blue shield. From the cold weight of the *Dragon's Eye* around my neck, I felt their souls emptying. He and the remaining wizards were going to flame out; and when that happened, nothing would be left alive in the shell of their bodies. Flaming out was every wizard's worst nightmare— to use up your life force to strengthen your magic. I couldn't let that happen. But I wasn't sure how to stop it.

I held onto Excalibur even as my arms throbbed and my muscles burned for relief. The wave continued to beat down on us in a never-ending torrent. The weakened shield started to crack, and water began to seep in. I could hear screams coming from the surrounding rooftops. Water swallowed several rooftops in its merciless advance.

I bit down on the inside of my cheek until I tasted my own blood. The pain helped me refocus my mind. I had to do something. Closing my eyes, I gave all of myself. An invisible hand reached inside my body and scooped out my very insides. My life force enriched the flagging magic—at a price. I could feel a feeble weakness hollowing my bones.

"*No.*" A harsh voice boomed in my head.

*Vane.* He spoke to me through the amulet, the *Dragon's Eye.* A shot of intense longing sped through my veins. At least I would know him one last time, before I knew nothing more at all.

"*Not yet, DuLac. I have use for you still.*" From somewhere in the world—I had no idea where—he yanked open a door between us.

Power flowed to me through the amulet. Vane linked through his brother who linked to me. A surge of magic filled me, green and thick, hungry and strong.

And angry. So very angry.

My eyes snapped open. The new magic shoved me aside to feed Excalibur, sparing my lifeforce. The blue of the shield turned a muddy green and hardened with power. A faint hum filled the air. I caught a taste of the ocean, not the warm waters of the Indian Ocean, but the briny Atlantic.

The cracks on the shield disappeared, and the onslaught of water was stemmed. The thrust of the tsunami now pattered against the invisible wall like the gentle spraying of a spring rain. Another few minutes passed and it was all over. The tsunami subsided; the shield winked out. Magic rippled back into the wizards. Its powerful wave, a backlash, slammed us.

I fell against hard concrete. It took several seconds for me to hear the blood pound against my eardrums once again. Pushing with my palms, I propped myself up. The world around me laid unearthly quiet. Behind me, Grey and the three gargoyles groaned as they stirred on the ground. I dared to look around me.

Strewn across the rooftops, where wizards once stood, their bodies now slumped... unmoving. Nausea spiraled its way up my throat.

Grey pushed himself up and looked around him. Shell-shocked, he said, "Are they all...?" He didn't finish the thought. He didn't need to.

Looking for Matt, I spotted his still form, lying on the concrete, flat on his back. A panicky feeling overwhelmed me. When I saw the faintest rise and fall of his chest, I exhaled a ragged breath. My palms scraped against cold, hard concrete as I pushed myself into a sitting position. I told Grey, "We have to check them all. They might still be alive."

Aside from me, only Grey and the gargoyles woke up right

away. Grey went to Blake. Blake sat up and nudged Gia. She smiled at him weakly. With a shaky grin, Blake pulled her into a protective hug. My chest swelled with happiness at the sight of them—a glimmer of light in the middle of the darkest storm. Hari woke up next. About one in four of the Indian wizards—the strongest ones—woke up. But the rest didn't.

The gargoyles raided several of the flats in the building and found bed sheets to cover the ones who didn't... the ones who were never going to awaken.

An hour later, Blake balanced on a narrow ledge, staring out over the rainbow of bed sheets with a bleak expression.

"Blake, get down!" Gia marched over to him. She yanked him toward her, her body shaking with anger. After punching him in the chest, she asked, "What are you doing?"

Blake ran two hands through his hair. "I-I don't know. I never imagined it could be like this."

"I know," she whispered. Blake pulled her close and wrapped his hands around her waist.

I went to a weather-beaten cot in one corner of the rooftop. Grey laid Matt on top of it. Hari walked up to me and asked, "Is he...?"

"His pulse is weak, but he's alive. I don't know why he won't wake up." I touched Matt's neck, to reassure myself, more than anything. My hand went to *the Dragon's Eye*, the amulet he'd given me.

"*Matt.*" Inside my head, I called for him, but I got no response. Always before, his presence stayed with me, connecting us as long as I wore it. Now, there was nothing but a great void when I called to him.

"This is not good," Hari said.

I looked at him. "What is the word from the rest of the coast?"

Hari smoothed his plaid, short-sleeved cotton shirt. There was a faint tremble in his hands. Sangeetha and another wizard, a younger version of Hari, came up to us. Sangeetha put a hand on Hari's back. The tension in his shoulders eased a fraction.

He said, "Our friends in Kolkotta suffered much worse than we did. Only one-third survived. Over five hundred flamed out."

I sat on a jute-strung cot. My fingers tightened on the coarse, khaki fibers bent tightly around the wooden frame. The rough material dug painfully into my skin. I took a steadying breath and looked out at the eerily quiet ocean.

Hari continued, "That is not the worst of it. I've been in touch with the RTSPs—the Regional Tsunamis of the South Pacific advisors—they are predicting another quake within the hour. They think this one will happen farther south. The Pacific Tsunami Warning Center says the same. This time, they expect it to hit every country in the Bay of Bengal. Sri Lanka, Chennai, Kolkotta. All the way up to Bangladesh and even Thailand, the Andaman Islands, and Indonesia—Banda Aceh—will get the worst of it."

In 2004, the tsunami that hit the Indonesian city of Banda Aceh and its surrounding islands claimed the lives of an estimated one hundred and thirty thousand people. Forty thousand more were said to be missing. I knew because I read the statistics while on our flight to the island country. As strong as that tsunami was, it hadn't even come close to the shores of India. My eyes glanced over the rows of covered bodies across the rooftop. Even at full strength, we couldn't combat such a strong quake.

I looked down at Matt. Our best hope.

"We need him," Hari said, reading my expression. "Without him, you do not have enough magic, sword-bearer."

"He's still weak from our fight with the mermaids." I sat down next to Matt. "Can we evacuate?"

Hari shook his head in a manner that could have been either "yes" or "no." He said, "Chennai is mostly flat, but maybe."

"Then go now," I said. "Try."

"Is there no hope, then?" Hari's youthful face blanched.

"There's always hope." I had to believe that.

"Very American of you to say," Sangeetha commented. "Luckily, we are just as optimistic."

Hari broke into a reckless smile that seemed to lighten his weary features. "I've made my peace. If there's any chance, then I must be here to do whatever is necessary. There are over four million people in Chennai alone. There is no way they could all evacuate. If there is the slightest hope… I will stay. I must." He turned to Sangeetha and took her hand. "But you will go," he ordered. He put her hand into another wizard's hand. "Raj, take her out of here."

In the wind, her black braids swayed with hypnotic calm. Sangeetha tore her hand away from Raj. She faced Hari. "I don't take orders, *Master* Hari. We made a vow and I, for one, took it seriously. I go where you go. I stay where you stay."

Raj protested. "But, Sangeetha, he's right. It's not safe—"

"It's not safe for anybody," she stated. "And don't try to force me. You've never agreed with him before. Now's not the time to start."

With a glare at the two brothers, she stalked off.

"You knew she was stubborn when you married her," Raj told Hari.

Hari watched his wife walk away with a frown. "I should spell her."

"If you do, you'll be eating *gobi* at every meal for the rest of your life," Raj said. He and Hari grimaced at the same time and exchanged an exasperated smile.

I sympathized—with Sangeetha. The two brothers reminded me a little too much of the two who'd recently taken over my life.

Above us, the sky darkened to a forsaken, steel grey. The sharp scent of the ocean permeated the air, filling my nostrils. I knew the advisors were right. We hadn't seen the last wave, nor had we seen the strongest wave yet. I looked around me. Blake and Gia held each other closely while staring out at the ocean. Grey knelt down on one knee, the fabric of his T-shirt clinging to him, to tuck a cotton sheet gently around a fallen wizard. So few of us remained. I looked down at Matt.

The wind ruffled his slightly long hair. His auburn curls fluttered under the soft breeze, framing his face. It was the only movement his body made. I took his icy fingers, wrapping them in mine.

I remembered the day I first met him. It seemed a long time ago, even though it was actually only about five months. The beginning of the school year. Now, we were deep into spring. Almost April. Almost prom. Almost graduation. With all the school I missed in the past month, though, I doubted I could graduate. The stray thought was laughable because it was highly unlikely that I would even survive today.

A slap of wind hit my face, chilling me. Like a boa constrictor tightening around my body, my dwindling hope threatened to squeeze the life out of me. I looked down at Matt's still face and clutched his fingers as hard as I could. "C'mon, Matt, wake up. I can't do this without you."

Closing my eyes, I grasped the amulet. The amulet he'd made. The ruby gemstone heated as I slipped into his mind, seeking him. His name was Matt. His name was Merlin.

***

I noticed him right away. No, it wasn't his lean, rugged face. Or the dark waves of shiny hair that hung just a little too long on his forehead. It wasn't the slim, collarless biker jacket he wore, hugging his lean shoulders. It was the way he stood. The confident way he waited in the cafeteria line to get a slice of pizza. He didn't saunter. He didn't amble. He stood at the center, and let the other people buzz around him. His stance was straight and sure.

He could have ruled the world.

He showed up in my history class that morning. It was his first week. New school year. Our senior year. It was hard for me to believe I made it this far. Hard to believe I was sitting in school as a normal person and not in a padded cell, after what happened. I blinked and reminded myself that I was okay. I got rescued—in a sense. I had begun a new life, and now all I had to do was get through one year of high school. Easy, right?

Maybe I'd even venture out of my comfort zone and actually talk to a guy.

As if he could feel my eyes upon him, the new guy looked up. Amber eyes focused on me, peering into my soul as if he knew exactly what I was thinking. Gads, I hoped not. He smiled with straight, even teeth.

The dull grey of my afternoon lifted. My breath caught.

I almost choked on a half-eaten celery stick.

Coughing, my cheeks heated with embarrassment. I pried my gawking face away from the long, cool drink that came in the form of a six-foot-tall, biker jacket-wearing boy.

His name was Matt. Matt Emrys.

## THE BARGAIN

Matt Emrys. Even the name evoked mystery. I sighed.

Other girls, a mixture of lower and upper classmen, sat at the plain, flat table with me, giving me curious looks. The wide cafeteria of Acton-Concord High School was packed with the usual lunch crowd. Juniors weren't allowed to go off campus, and although I was a senior, several of the girls on the lacrosse team weren't; so here I sat, with my brown lunch bag of a hastily assembled cucumber sandwich and celery sticks.

"Arriane Morganne Brittany DuLac," Alexa said, her model-perfect face reflecting the lines of a keen strategist. "Are you even listening? We're only trying to decide your future."

From across the table, I gave her a look. She rolled her sky-blue eyes. Alexa loved to use my full name to annoy me. Honestly, what was my mother thinking saddling me with that impossibly long name? It was so pretentious, a name for a princess. So not me.

Alexa tapped a manicured finger on the table. Only six months younger than I, she fell pretty fast and quite easily into the role of little sister. My annoyance melted a bit at the words "little sister." I never had a sister, brother, or anything until this year. Now I had both. It was the one bright glimmer in the dark hole I found myself.

My stomach knotted and I pushed the uneasy memories back down. Sometimes I missed my mom so much I wanted to bite my own knuckles until they bled… just to feel the pain somewhere else.

"I think we're all in agreement that Prom was completely awful last year. I don't know how the class went broke by the end of the year, but Ryan won't let that happen to us," Alexa continued. She turned with a fanatical gleam in her eye. "Now that Ryan's been elected student president, she'll fix it."

I sat up straight at hearing this. "What?"

"This is going to be the best prom in the history of Acton-Concord High," Alexa declared.

I grimaced. I never signed up to fix Prom. Actually, I didn't want to be student president at all but somehow got nominated after spending a year coordinating all of the school's charity drives and volunteer activities. Being the new girl at school last year, I thought throwing myself into various school programs would help me make friends. It worked a little too well. Not to mention, when someone asked for help, I couldn't very well say "no." With every "yes" I kept getting asked to do more, and with every "yes" I found it harder to say "no."

Then, my aggressive campaign manager (Alexa) took over, and shortly thereafter, I'd found myself up on the winner's throne after a landslide election. If becoming president was a popularity contest, I'd won because of Alexa's.

She chattered on, "We'll organize fund-raisers. There are plenty of parents we can guilt-trip into spending some extra cash. Sponsorships. I don't care if we have corporate logos as table centerpieces—we can do it tastefully on the sides of vases of white roses—"

"I always thought white lilies would be better for Prom," squeaked a varsity girl from our lacrosse team. The other girls at the table looked at her with surprise and respect. It was hard to stop a steamroller like Alexa after she got started.

Alexa beamed at the girl. "Great idea, Christine. White roses are so overdone."

Ruddy-faced Christine glowed under the praise.

I chewed on my celery stick. "You're a junior, Alexa. Why do *you* care about Prom?"

"Who are you going with, Ryan?" asked Ramanajan, a slender girl with braided, ebony hair, sitting beside Alexa. "Grey?"

"Ew," I replied. "He's my brother now."

"Good," Ramanajan said with satisfaction.

Alexa looked at me, rolling her eyes. I suppressed a laugh.

"But, Ryan, you barely know him and you're going to be adopted, right? No blood relation." Christine sighed. "Grey is so adorable. I slipped in the hallway once and he carried my backpack all the way to class."

Alexa snorted in disgust. "*Never* say that in front of him. His ego is big enough."

But she wouldn't be distracted. Mischievous eyes fixed on me with determination. "Ramanajan is right. We have to find Ryan a date. She never even looks at any of the guys panting after her. How about one of Grey's friends? Brian thinks you're smoking hot."

My stomach twisted. It was okay to look at guys from a distance, but I didn't actually want one in my life. I pictured a boy lying on the floor of my Texas townhouse... his letterman jacket smeared with blood, his head ripped from his body, the cloying smell of iron and meat. He was murdered along with my mother. Somehow, I survived. Guilt bore down on me.

The dark memories must have colored my expression because Alexa reached out with her hand, a calming presence, and held my white knuckles.

I gave her a tight smile. "No letter-jackets."

"Fine," she sighed with exaggerated noise. With a little squeeze, she let my hand go. "But you're severely limiting the pool."

"Maybe you need to take another look at the pool," I said.

"Really?" A perfectly arched, sandy-brown eyebrow rose. Alexa purred, "Methinks the girl may have a Prince Charming in sight. Now who could persuade our Goldilocks to even think about the ball?"

"You're astonishingly bad at fairy tales, Lexa," I muttered. "Goldilocks stole porridge from the three bears' house. She couldn't care less about Prince Charming."

The girls at the table giggled.

Alexa took a big slurp of the lemonade she was drinking. "Well, this bear can tell you're hiding something, sis. Never fear,

I'll figure it out. You can't keep a secret from me—" A shadow crossed Alexa's face for a fleeting second before she masked it with a grin. "I know things."

The hairs on the back of my neck stood up. I turned my head to find Matt staring straight at us from the lunch line across the room.

Following my gaze to Matt, Alexa made a sound. "Ooh, is he new? And way better than Prince Charming."

"Stop trying to dodge the question," I said quickly. "Why are you interested in Prom?"

Alexa sniffed and flipped her shoulder-length hair. "If you must know, Grey's friend, Joey, asked me to go."

"Joey?" Ramanajan giggled. "Maybe you should drive, Lexa."

Alexa elbowed her. "Don't be such a snob."

Another girl laughed. "Yesterday, he started his car and I swear, it let out so much smoke I thought a volcano just erupted."

"It wasn't that bad," I muttered. Although, it was. Alexa was talking to Joey when it happened. We were both sitting in her car. I nearly gagged before Alexa hurriedly rolled up the windows.

"I wouldn't mind the new guy driving me. A friend of mine saw him roar up into the parking lot this morning on this completely hot bike," Christine whispered to me. I followed her gaze straight back to Matt, who now stood at the head of the lunch line. I agreed. I wouldn't mind him driving me either, and I wasn't talking about on a bike.

"You'll never even make it into town in that thing, Alexa," Ramanajan continued. We lived in Concord, Massachusetts, a small outlying city about forty minutes from the heart of Boston.

Alexa's eyes narrowed as she opened her cherry lips to retort. She never got the chance.

"Halloo, sis," Grey Ragnar said as he sauntered over to us. He led a group of his football buddies. Ramanajan beamed at Grey. Her eyes roved over the pack of guys, all in resplendent blue-and-yellow varsity letterman jackets. Grey tossed a bottle of chocolate Yoo-hoo back and forth in his hand. "I need your house keys, Alexa. I forgot mine. I'm going to be late today. Coach has us staying because he thinks some new guy might be worth looking at."

"Hello, ladies." Joey, tall and gangly, rushed forward. His eyes glued on Alexa, he walked straight into Grey. The bottle Grey was tossing around flew out of his hand. The cap must have been loose because it started to erupt in the air. Most of the liquid came spraying straight down at me.

Then, somehow, my chair was yanked out of the way, and I tumbled to the floor. A hand caught me around the waist. The plastic bottle landed on the table with a thud. The lacrosse girls all yelped and jumped up from the table. Gooey chocolate milk ran from it and dripped over the sides onto the floor beside me. At least it wasn't all over me.

Finding myself bent over backwards, resting on his arm, I looked up into the eyes of my rescuer. For a second, I thought I saw a faint glow of blue on the hand before I blinked and the glimmer of blue vanished. I looked up. Matt Emrys.

Amber eyes smiled down at me. He held a palm out in silent question. Gingerly, I put mine in his, and his warm hand closed around mine. A sizzle like an electric shock went through me. A hint of forever blue flared in his dark eyes. It asked me to reach out and embrace its endless expanse, to allow it to wrap around me like a safe blanket.

For a long second, everything stood still. Around us, the cafeteria hushed into whispers as I heard the blood pumping and thumping through his heart along with the accelerated rate of mine. In that moment, I flew like fierce wind across the top of the steepest cliff. So full of life, I burst with it the need to seek expression, and I tumbled off the cliff into the rocks below.

"Grey, apologize!" Alexa patted her shirt where a few drops had fallen.

I blinked and the cacophony of the cafeteria came back into jagged focus. The blue in his eyes ebbed, returning them to a comfortable brown. I wondered briefly if being near Matt Emrys was turning my mind into mush. His hand tightening on me, he yanked me up.

"Th-thanks," I said, wincing. *Why did that sound so embarrassingly breathless?*

"You're most welcome." His words came out in a caress of rolling tones. He had a heavy accent that sounded oddly like a blend of southern US and British.

All my befuddled brain could do was give him a goofy smile back. Alright—so it wasn't really a life or death situation to be saved from a splattering of chocolate milk, but my nerves remained standing on end from the adrenaline rush.

"Ry," Grey started. His hand reached out to as he took a step toward me, but somehow, he slipped on the chocolate mess all over the floor. Matt caught him by his jacket. Grey gave Matt an annoyed look and shook off his hand. Grey straightened up.

"How agile," Matt said, his tone biting. "You could at least apologize to her."

Grey's annoyance turned into a full-fledged glare.

Then, Matt dug his hole even deeper. "If you're an example of agility here, I think I'm going to enjoy this practice."

"You're the new recruit?" Grey said.

Matt raised a brow in a perfect arch. "Figured that out all by yourself?"

Grey's expression bordered on livid. He took a step toward Matt, pulling his fist back in a swing. Matt didn't move or blink.

"Grey Ragnar!" Alexa hissed. "Do you want to get suspended again?"

Grey got expelled last year for fighting. His mother was not happy about it, and it landed Grey in a pricey anger management therapy program. I think the torture of having to attend it was doing more for him than the actual program. Grey controlled himself. "You have a lot of words, Emrys. Let's see how good you are on the field."

Grey turned on his heel as he stormed out. The other football guys shrugged at each other before following him.

Joey looked at Alexa, mumbling, "Sorry," as he hurried to join them.

Matt stared after the group with a strangely speculative expression. He turned back to me, and his eyes cleared. "So that is Grey Ragnar. Rather volatile, isn't he? I hope you don't have to bother with him again."

I suppressed a smile at the new guy. "Grey's my brother."

Matt's eyebrows rose. "I suppose it's going to be complicated, then."

"Complicated?"

Sensuous lips curved up into a half-smile. All-knowing eyes met and held mine. "To know you."

My lips curved up in response.

A shadow crossed over the cafeteria.

Matt's smile froze in place. The whole cafeteria, and everyone in it, froze in place.

Sound stopped, as if someone had muted the scene with a TV remote.

Fluorescent lights darkened.

A loud clapping echoed across the eerily quiet room. I straightened up and pulled away from a frozen Matt. Across the cafeteria a figure stood near the doors. My heart skipped a beat. He watched me with cold amusement. His well-muscled form, clad in a dressy ensemble of form-fitting red shirt and black trousers, leaned back against the wall in a rebel-without-a-cause pose. But this was no rebel. He would never settle for anything less than being emperor.

Vibrant green eyes blazed. God-like green. *Vane.*

I blinked at the sudden appearance of my ex-boyfriend. I never had much luck with boyfriends.

"How adorable," he drawled. "Is this how he became your hero? You have low standards, DuLac."

*What is happening?* I reached out to touch Matt. My hand went straight through his shoulder. I turned to look at Alexa. Her face paused in the middle of a scowl. Beside her, the other girls of the lacrosse team also sat completely still. I walked toward her, stepping right through the middle of the solid wood lunch table.

Either I was a ghost or it was.

"Yes, DuLac, work it out," said Vane. "We are in your mind. This is a manifestation we're seeing through the *Dragon's Eye*. You are on the rooftop in India."

He snapped his fingers. Everyone in the cafeteria disappeared. The tables were empty, and the chairs were tucked neatly back into place. Lights across the wide room dimmed until Vane stood under the lone spotlight, beneath a high window. Outside, the sun faded. The last remnants of light revealed the slanted lines of Vane's harsh cheekbones and kept the shadowy mantle that hovered behind him at bay... for a few more fleeting moments.

I took me a second to recenter. To remember I was no longer that girl in the cafeteria, the one who knew nothing about wizards and swords. The one who didn't ache for the twisted being that stood in front of me.

While I stayed a safe distance away from him, my heart jangled nervously in my chest. My muscles itched with the impulse to leap into his arms. The ice encasing those mermaid-green eyes stopped me. The Vane I knew burned hot. These eyes could have frozen an erupting volcano. My stomach clenched, and for a brief moment, I wondered if I had truly lost him. I dismissed the thought. I refused to believe it. But I also didn't try to move any closer to him.

I demanded, "Why are you here?"

Vane raised a brow. "You haven't found Merlin yet. You only found a memory."

"What have you done with him?"

"You're not going to find him in nostalgic trips to the past. Merlin is not here. Only I am, and you should be glad." Vane straightened away from the wall, but didn't move any further. "Because I am here to answer your pleas, not him. Only I can save you from this disaster."

*Tsunami.* The word brought me abruptly back to the present. I reached up to touch the Dragon's Eye at my neck. I was inside. Outside, I pictured Grey, Gia, and Blake on the rooftop, staring at the ominously calm waves, waiting for it to turn on them. "What are you saying? How can you stop a tsunami?"

"I am the Fisher King, a vassal of the Earth Shaker and all that." His lips curved into a smile. Not the kind that invited play. His promised only pain.

"*I suspect you like a little pain,*" he said arrogantly.

The amulet let him read my surface thoughts. I retorted, "*Get out, Vane.*"

"*Never.*"

"What's the catch?" I asked aloud. "For your help."

A brow rose. "Why should I bother to make the effort?"

"Because you need me. If I die here today, Excalibur will be lost—"

Dark hair glinted in dim light as he inclined his head. "You are right. I do need to rescue... Excalibur. Someone must, I suppose, since you seem to have the uncanny ability to invite danger."

I stared at his smooth expression. It was too easy. One of things that always disturbed me about Vane was how complex his games could be. Now, he possessed a bit of Poseidon inside his body. A destiny he took from Matt.

I picked through his words carefully until I found the flaw in them. "Can you save everyone?" I added carefully, "Not just me. All of us. Sri Lanka up the coast to Chennai. Kolkotta. Around to Thailand and Indonesia. This whole area."

Vane's lips curved into a chilly smile. "I rather hoped you would ask. Alas, to do that, requires a great expenditure of magic, even for the Earth Shaker. I would have to relieve pressure at the fault lines of two massive tectonic plates. You're asking me to move a mountain of rock."

"Can you do it?" I repeated.

"If I do, you can rest assured, this entire region would be safe."

I gazed over the gulf that separated us, merely a few feet in this imaginary hallway, but a grand canyon of ulterior motives. "In exchange for what, Vane?"

Hunger sharpened his smile. "You know me too well."

The smile set my teeth on edge, even as it strung an already tight chord inside me.

"Merlin," he said. "I want his magic. All of it."

# THE LIBRARY

"You are unbelievable!"

He shrugged.

I strove to calm myself. I failed. "It's impossible!"

"I always thought so, but now that I have the Earth Shaker's insight—the answer seems so simple. Imagine magic as one layer of a golden onion. It surrounds us. I have the ability to strip it off him and layer it on myself."

"You want to *skin* him?"

"It won't kill him," Vane said.

I shook my head. "It's not my choice to make. Matt—"

Vane moved so quickly I only had time to blink before he was standing directly in front of me. He caught my wrist and pulled me back until I stood toe-to-toe with him. "Merlin is no longer your crutch. This is your decision, sword-bearer. Do you have what it takes to make it? Do you want to stop this tsunami? Or will you allow millions to die because you can't make a move without Merlin holding your hand?"

He spat the words out and they fell on me like blows. His fingers gripped the vulnerable part of my arm, fingers that, until quite recently, held me with care. The fingers around me now, though, felt like steel manacles. These fingers would just as easily snap my bones as mend them. The truth was, I didn't know. While I did depend on Matt, I'd always thought I made my own decisions. After Vane, I wasn't sure. Had I listened to Matt too much?

I looked at him steadily. "I don't trust you."

Vane dropped my hand as if it burned him. I let out a breath—of relief and sorrow. I missed him so much even his touch hurt. Watching me, his eyes flashed for a brief second. Then, the mermaid hue of green hooded them again and his expression blanked.

"You shouldn't trust me. However, I won't kill him. Taking his magic won't give me Merlin's knowledge so I still need him alive." He retreated, putting some distance between us. "We are on the same side for the moment. Your friends don't have long, DuLac. I need your answer now."

Mentally, I pulled myself away from him and focused on what was happening. "Why do you want Matt's magic? You already have more than enough power." I didn't expect him to reply. Ideas tumbled around in my head until one stood out. "You need his ability. The Lady said the power of the Earth Shaker would show us what is to come. She meant visions. But she meant for Merlin to take Poseidon's power. To enhance it. Only Merlin has visions. Not you. When you took it, Poseidon's power didn't grant you anything new, only enhanced what you already possessed. Therefore, you will never be able to have visions. You have ultimate power, but no ability to use it as we need." My head jerked up to meet his shadowed gaze. "That's it, isn't it?"

Vane said, "Ten points to my star student."

"You're not my teacher anymore, Vane. I'm sure you've been fired by now," I retorted. Vane was the European History teacher at Acton-Concord High. We'd been missing from school for nearly a month. I'd probably been expelled by now too. "Not even you could charm away that long of an absence."

"Is that a dare?" He chuckled a hollow laugh.

My chin jutted out, but I didn't reply. He was a predator, ready to strike at a moment's notice. Could a predator keep his word?

His eyes narrowed. "I see you need convincing that I'm powerful enough. If that is what you require, you shall have it." He walked closer again. "The Earth Shaker enhanced my magic to the extreme. All my magic, but especially the one I'm strongest in—persuasion."

Before I could blink, he took my hand from my side. His hand enclosed mine, our palms touching. As soon as he did, a sizzle of electricity shot up my arm, straight into my chest, speeding up my heart, and beyond my abdomen until it curled my toes. It left me achy, breathless, and completely wanting.

"*Please*," I whispered. I would have done anything to be near him.

"You see—I don't even have to speak anymore," he said in a silky tone.

The *Dragon's Eye* amulet flared against my skin. He pushed past it. The amulet cooled and I realized I had no defense against him. Transfixed, I stared into his eyes and all I saw was a deep abyss. His grip tightened, a thumb pressing into the back of my hand with hard pressure. It filled me with an overwhelming need. I wanted nothing more than to agree to whatever he asked. "*Bend to me*," his voice whispered in my head, a soft suggestion that lingered inside my eardrums until I neither heard nor thought of anything else but him.

I was drowning.

All I had to do was say okay and he would save me. I opened my mouth to do just that. If he'd asked me to drop to my knees and beg him, I would do just that.

Vane let me go. Suddenly bereft, I shuddered a black emptiness left me exposed. I needed him to fill it. I shook my head and backed away. Even though he released me, the desire to please him stayed strong. I gulped, trying to swallow the longing down.

"Convinced yet? Or do you need more?" He took a step toward me.

I held up my hand to stop him. I didn't want him to touch me. I didn't want to be that much out of control. Pulling together my bruised pride, I scowled at him. "You made your point."

"Good." The predator watched me. "We are running out of time. What do you say, Ryan? Will you choose Merlin and allow your friends to die? Or will you give me what I want?"

I stared at him.

In reality, my body was on a rooftop and the tsunami was coming. Within my mind, through the *Dragon's Eye*, I faced the tsunami already upon me. *Vane*.

I bit my lip, debating.

I knew he could fix this. Yet how I could pay his price? To pay with something that was not mine to offer. To give Matt to him when I couldn't be sure that he wouldn't get hurt. I took a slow breath. "Even if I agreed, it wouldn't matter. I came here looking for Matt and he's not here."

Vane's gaze dropped to my amulet. He watched it rise and fall against my chest. "Have no fear, DuLac. I can fix that too."

I ground my teeth. He'd used the amulet to read my thoughts again.

I pictured smacking him in the face.

Shadows deepened the slanted lines of Vane's cheekbones as he gazed back at me with cold expressionless eyes. My insides twisted. The idea that he would want to do this to Matt, his brother, reminded me that he was not the Vane I knew, the one who held on to life with both hands. This Vane wanted to destroy life. He had become a monster, one I helped create. I took a deep breath. "I'll do whatever you want if you save them."

"You'll do *everything* I want."

"Let's see you find him first."

Vane's brow rose. "Do you agree to my terms?"

"As if I have a choice."

"That's my girl. Always eager to sacrifice." The drawl to his accent emphasized the sarcastic edge to the words.

I jerked away and put more distance between us. "I could really hate you."

Vane didn't blink. "Do so. It only binds you more to me."

I ground my teeth harder. Another thing that always annoyed me about Vane—how I couldn't seem to win one single argument with him.

Vane strode to the cafeteria exit. Holding the door open, he

PRIYA ARDIS

crooked his finger at me in command. "Shall we, DuLac?"

Wishing I had something to throw at his head, I trailed after him. We crossed an empty courtyard to the largest of the plain rectangular buildings, the main building of the school. He seemed to know exactly where he was going. It took me a few minutes to figure out. We went down a shadowed hallway lined on either side with tall, metal lockers.

We turned a corner. Vane went straight up to a set of grey metal, heavy double doors and heaved them open. I followed him and paused just beyond the threshold. One whiff of the musty scent of books inside and I knew immediately that Vane brought us to the right place.

The school library opened to a lobby area with ten low tables. Long, waist-high bookshelves surrounded the central lobby and made up three sides of a square. The fourth side, just to the right of the entrance, was a high bar that enclosed the librarian's checkout area. Behind the lobby at the back of the room, row upon row of bookshelves fanned out, filling up the space. The bookshelves extended from floor to ceiling. Glass windows stretched up the back wall and let in a bit of light from one wall to breathe life onto the stacks of dusty paper, wood, and other secret worlds.

While the rest of the school was a cluster of warehouse-type buildings, the library retained the essence of Boston, the birthplace of the American Revolution. History and blood lived inside its closed tomes. Its mark on this world so deep, it escaped the confines of the page and permeated the air. It was the one room in the whole school in which Matt felt safest. His brother knew him well.

"Yes, I do know him well." Vane tugged me farther into the

room. I stopped at one of the low tables. We spent hours in here studying before the one day that changed everything in my life. I sighed.

"We don't have time for sentiment," Vane said, his eyes roving over the maze of bookshelves. "The longer we're in here, the closer the tsunami gets."

"You don't need to remind me," I said.

"This is taking too long," Vane muttered, ignoring me. He extended a hand and pointed it at one of the tables. Making a fist, the table exploded with a loud boom. It burst into a million pieces, sending off a small shockwave that threw its six companion chairs across the room. One chair flew straight at me. I narrowly avoided being clobbered. Moving out of its way at the last second, I body-slammed into Vane.

He caught me. Rigid arms wrapped around my waist and prevented us both from falling. His hot breath washed over my face.

A loud growl filled the room. I turned around in Vane's arms to face the center again. Out of nowhere, a lion leaped from the library stacks and landed on top of a table a few feet in front of us. Rather than terrifying us, the thin lion sported a ragged, auburn-colored mane. Its patchy state gave him a look of desperation... and hunger.

I groaned. "Not again."

I saw him in his lion form once before, after Lelex, the former mermaid king, tortured him. He had to retreat into the form to protect himself.

Vane's hands grabbed my hips, keeping me in front of him like a shield. He pushed me forward. "You're up, DuLac."

I stayed where I was. The lion watched us with tired eyes.

"What am I supposed to do?" I hissed to Vane.

"Get close to him. You're the only one he'll allow. Look for something that shouldn't be there. A discoloration of some kind. When Lelex took him, he planted a sickness inside his mind that's been festering and growing. Like a virus, it keeps reproducing and making him weak. I didn't see it before until I broke through the block on your amulet. It's why he never fully recovered from the ordeal, despite his strength."

I frowned but kept my eyes trained on Matt. "He's sick? You want to help him?"

"I want his power," Vane said harshly from behind me. "Saving him will get me that."

I wanted to look at Vane, but I didn't dare. My heart jangling in my chest, I took a step toward the hungry lion. "Matt? It's me, Ryan."

Enormous jowls moved and he made a low sound in his throat. Yet, a spark lit his gaze. He looked straight at me with unfocused eyes. My heart squeezed inside my chest and I wondered if he was blind. I took another step. The lion's ears twitched. He tensed. Suspicion colored his brown eyes, but he remained in place.

"I'm not going to hurt you, Matt." With another slow breath, I took one last step until I stood directly in front of the beast.

For a second, I thought he would swipe a massive paw and shred me like I was no more than lunchmeat. His hot breath blew in my face and halfway down my body. I tried not to gag. As surprisingly clean as the lion looked—a little fact that told me this was Matt and not a real lion—his breath still stunk. His teeth protruded from the rough, yellow fur on the sides of his mouth. My left arm still stung at the sight of them. Once before, I had reached out to touch him when he was in lion form and the result hadn't been pretty. I had scars up and down my arm to prove it.

I looked down the length of Matt's lion body. I could see most of his back and sides from where I stood, but there was no discoloration.

"Hurry up, Ryan," Vane commanded.

"Stop nagging, Vane," I muttered. Not like *he* was the one standing less than a hair's breadth away from being eaten. Although this was all happening strictly in our heads, the things that took place here would affect our bodies in the real word. In other words, if I got killed here, I would be just as dead in reality. The lion sensed my agitation and his hackles rose. He stood up and let out a great, big roar. I stumbled backwards, falling on my butt.

On his underside, I spotted the discoloration. Vane was right. Lelex had infected Matt. A black grid of veins was visible in the lion's long underbelly.

"It's there," I said aloud.

"Where?" Vane asked.

"From his heart down—" I didn't get a chance to say anymore.

Vane moved so fast I barely had a chance to blink before he reached the lion. The lion roared and raising his massive neck, exposed his belly. With one powerful thrust, Vane plunged a green, glowing hand straight into the lion's chest. The skin ripped open. Blood gushed out. Vane broke through the brittle barrier of his ribcage and tore open the surprised lion.

Matt screamed and started to thrash.

"*Zyayat*," Vane commanded. Green magic spread from his hand to Matt. "Hold still or you'll just make this worse."

The lion froze in place.

"You said you weren't going to hurt him!" I jumped up from the ground, emerging from my own stunned paralysis. I had no idea how to help Matt, but I wasn't going to passively stand by. More than anything, I wished for Excalibur. I had to slay the monster in front of me… and I wasn't talking about the lion. Out of nowhere, the sword appeared. The silver blade fell to the floor between Vane and me. I blinked. Of course, this was all in my head. I snatched up Excalibur and held the sword in front of me.

I had as much power here as Vane.

Vane turned cold green eyes toward me. "Not quite as much power."

"*Zyayat*," he commanded again. A familiar wind buzzed against my ears as his magic wrapped around me and secured me in place. I tried to move and found I couldn't. He'd frozen me, too.

"I told you I wasn't going to kill him. Stop panicking," Vane said calmly.

Matt roared, but under the freeze spell, it came out as a low, desperate mewl. Vane's hand dug deeper into the lion's chest. The metallic stench of iron in his blood made me want to gag. Yet, all I could do was watch. From under a crown of rough mane, the lion's enormous head turned slowly toward me. Huge, amber-brown eyes—Matt's eyes—locked on me for a moment. They were saying goodbye.

Vane yanked out the lion's heart. With a satisfied grunt, he stepped back and the lion fell in a heavy heap to the floor. Without another glance at the fallen beast, Vane turned to me. He held the beating muscle in his hand. Blood dripping, Vane turned Matt's heart over in his hand. He looked at the dying organ with dispassionate eyes.

Still frozen in place, I could only let out a suppressed cry. Closing my eyes, I pictured myself unfrozen. I opened them again and tried to move. Nothing. Even in my head, I couldn't break through Vane's grip.

Vane held up the heart. Black veins crisscrossed the red flesh in a tight web, strangling the vulnerable muscle. "The infection is here. No one would think to pull this out. Lelex was clever."

Lelex, the mermaid king held Matt captive for fifteen days. Fifteen days, which passed as slowly as fifteen years. Days we'd never forget.

"No one who cared about Matt would pull it out," I managed to say despite the freeze spell.

"We have little time for care. It takes twenty seconds for him to die if he has no heart." Vane looked at me steadily, ice chilling his irises. He squeezed the heart with his palm. Green fire flared in his hand and surrounded the organ. Vane opened his hand. The black veins disappeared from the bloodied heart. He strode to the lion and knelt on the floor. Reaching deep into the lion's mutilated chest, he put the heart back in place. Fire flowed from Vane's fingers and he reconnected organ and tissue like it was a broken clay sculpture, not blood and bone. He worked outwardly, and within seconds, Matt's ribs and chest were sewn together. Still, a mark of the trauma remained. A jagged sunburst scarred the lion's chest.

My throat dry with fear, I ached to go to him. I almost fell on my face when the spell winked out with an abrupt "*snap!*" I rushed closer and knelt just above the lion's reclining head. I ran my fingers through his rough, tangled mane. The lion lay still. Too still.

I murmured, "C'mon, Matt."

Vane put a hand to Matt's now-healed chest. He looked at me. "It's your turn."

I swallowed. "What do I do?"

"Nothing." He stood up and snapped his fingers. The Fisher King's trident appeared in his hand. "You do nothing. You will not fight back."

My fingers tightened in Matt's thick mane. The ends bit into my palm. Doubt filled me again.

"Agreed, champion?" Vane mocked.

My palm itched to connect with his face. I took a bracing breath, and said, "I will do nothing. I will not fight you."

Vane's glacial green eyes flashed with satisfaction. It wasn't enough to get his way. He wanted to grind me down at the same time. He aimed the trident at Matt. "*Adhikaram karoti.*"

I jumped a little when a stream of green fire blasted out, hitting Matt directly in the chest. The lion's body shuddered under the attack. A film of blue formed around Matt. Blue was the color of Matt's magic. My hand in Matt's mane burned with such intense heat that I had to yank it away. The fire coming out of the trident intensified. So did the blue. The room vibrated as the two wizards fought, one conscious, the other unconscious. That Matt still had enough magic left in him to fight Vane, even though weakened, filled me with hope. Then, Vane turned the trident on me.

I cried, "What are you doing?"

"It's time." He shouted, "*Adhikaram karoti*," once more.

Green fire blasted me. A blue shield winked around me before it could make contact. Still, I felt the attack like a wallop to the stomach.

I looked at the lion. His eyes were open. Matt's eyes were open! With effort, the fallen lion expended what little strength he had to turn so that he lay on his belly. His massive head rose up off the ground. Blue magic flowed from him to me. Matt was trying to protect me. All I had to do was hold on to Matt's magic.

Vane said, "The lives of everyone, the fate of this entire region, rest in your hands, Ryan."

My body shook under the trident's assault. My eyes locked on Matt's, and I knew what Vane wanted from me. My heart ached with the decision.

"*I'm sorry*," I thought to Matt, and instead of holding on, I let go. As soon as I did, the lion let out a roar. Green magic greedily gobbled blue. It peeled away from me and was reabsorbed back into itself... back into its owner as Vane stripped Matt of his magic. Matt let out another pained roar, but Vane didn't stop.

Seconds stretched into infinitely long moments of time. When Vane finished, my body shook. My palms and knees dug into the coarse fibers of the carpet. Even on all fours, I struggled not to collapse completely. Matt let out a low moan. His head lowered to the ground. I crawled over to him.

With extreme effort, I pushed myself up into a sitting position and cradled the lion's head in my lap. His eyes were closed again. He lay still. I put a shaking hand on rough, yellow cheeks and to my relief, felt a hot, steady breath. He still lived.

"I told you he would," Vane said, reading my mind.

I blinked away the film of tears that obscured my sight. I looked up at him. The Fisher King stood tall. The trident, which he held like a staff, rested confidently in his hand.

"Did you finally get what you wanted?" I spat at him.

Vane crossed over to me. For the first time, the ice in his eyes shrank back. Around my neck, the *Dragon's Eye* heated. Ignoring Matt's head in my lap, Vane knelt down on one knee. He caught the back of my head with one hand, his fingers tangling in the dark blond strands, tugging and straining the follicles on my scalp.

His lips twisted into a small smile. "I haven't gotten everything. I'm working on that part."

He jerked my head so that my face tilted up to his. He gave me a hard kiss, one that didn't promise pleasure, only possession. One laced with icy control, except that it sparked heat wherever it touched me. My body yearned to press closer. It didn't care that there was no respect in the act. It didn't care that he made me betray someone I should have protected. It just craved his touch. The knowledge startled me, shamed me, and quickly sprouted into anger.

I bit down on his lip. Vane pulled back. Fresh blood beaded on his bottom lip.

I had to stop myself from putting a hand up to the cut. "You don't own me."

His eyes flashed. He wiped the blood with a thumb. Reaching down, he grabbed the *Dragon's Eye* gemstone and smeared blood across the gem. Then with casual arrogance, he said, "It's only a matter of time."

I looked at him steadily. "We have a deal. It's your turn. Save them."

He smirked. "As you wish."

With those words, Vane disappeared. I sat in the library all alone with Matt. I closed my eyes. Around my neck, the ruby gem of the *Dragon's Eye* glowed with green magic. I realized with a sinking feeling that the amulet was still bound to Matt's magic; and now that Vane possessed Matt's magic, it bound me to him without any barrier. From somewhere off in the distance, I heard Vane's dark laugh.

"*Worry later, Dorothy*," he said. "*Right now, you need to wake up.*"

***

Opening my eyes, I found myself back on the rooftop. I was smack in the middle of the battlefield with a sudden heart-pounding jerk.

"Sword-bearer," Hari shouted at me. "It is coming!"

Hari, Gia, Blake, Grey and the remaining fifty or so wizards all ran to the edge of the rooftops. The air shifted once again. Another eerie pall fell over the beach. Water receded rapidly in anticipation of the colossal wave. The hand of a higher power pulled back the water and became poised once again to teach us a humbling lesson. I jumped up from the cot.

"Ryan," Matt said weakly from behind me.

I turned back to him. "Are you all right?"

He struggled to get up. I moved to help him. I touched his shoulders. He flinched. Then, with a shake of his head, he hauled himself up. He asked, "What's happening?"

"Another tsunami," I said.

He looked out at the ocean. His body moved sluggishly, like someone who'd just woken from a long sleep or coma. The lines on his face had deepened, making him appear older than he was. His shoulders drooped just a bit from the weight of the world that still seemed to rest on them.

"Merlin!" Blake exclaimed. He, Gia, and Grey turned to us. Gia gave a happy cry at the sight of Matt standing. Blake rushed to us. I felt a little disheartened when Matt quickly moved to lean on Blake for support.

Hari grinned at Matt. "Our prayers are answered. Master Merlin, what should we do?"

"Hold it off," I answered. "We hold it off for as long as we can. It's the only thing we can do. We hold and hope for a miracle."

Hari looked at Matt for confirmation. Matt nodded. Hari took off and shouted across the adjoining rooftops to the other wizards. "Master Merlin says we hold."

They passed the word along, and the thin rainbow of bright cotton shirts and tanned faces turned resolutely toward the impending doom of the ocean. They started to line up again along the ledges of each rooftop.

Matt said to Blake, "Take me to the ledge. We'll line up again to make the shield. We have to hope Vane works fast."

He was pissed. I took in a sharp breath. "You remember."

Matt's lips tightened in an unhappy expression. He didn't look at me. "I remember everything. We'll talk about it later."

He urged Blake to take him forward.

I watched Matt hobble along at his loyal companion's side. Something I could no longer call myself. I closed my eyes. My hand tightened around Excalibur. For the first time since losing Vane, I was completely alone. But there was no time to dwell on the feeling. If Vane didn't come through, I doubted I would even survive long enough to feel guilty about the cruel blow I'd dealt Matt.

It took another minute before we were all in the same position across the rooftop we'd been in before the last devastating wave. I held Excalibur in front of me and waited.

I didn't have to wait long. In an instant, the air turned sinister; the grey in the sky darkened and became black in color. The sharp scent of algae combined with the silent screams of the underwater creatures that were unable to escape. The wave hurtled down on us with ferocity. Unanimously, we all took a step back. We couldn't help it.

This wave looked twice as high as the last one. Where the last one touched the sky, this one penetrated the heavens. It scraped the bottoms of clouds as it threw itself against us.

"*Sphara*," the wizards cried. With clasped hands, the magic whip lashed through me and into Excalibur. A green magical shield rose to block the massive, oncoming wave.

My eyes widened at the color. I glanced at Matt. He had his eyes closed, and sweat beaded on his forehead. Then, I didn't have any more time to wonder. The magic intensified and I had to hold on to Excalibur again with all my strength. My teeth felt as if they would be ground to dust under the pressure. A giant battering ram of water pounded the shield. I felt Excalibur wobble.

"*Hold on*," Matt's faint voice sounded inside my head. "*Just—*"

"*Enough!*" Vane's voice shut out Matt's. "*Are you a champion or not, DuLac? This isn't difficult.*"

I tightened my grip on Excalibur, expending every fiber of my being into holding the heavy blade upright, knowing that any slip was equal to the plight of a million souls. It was the only means of providing protection to the whole city and I struggled to balance it.

"*Hurry up,*" I said to him.

"*I'm underwater now, DuLac,*" Vane replied. "*Need I remind you that you're the one who insisted on me moving around this whole wretched ocean? I'm working as fast as I can.*"

"*So much for being the Fisher King,*" I said grumpily. "*What... are you moving one stone at a time?*"

Excalibur wobbled in my hand once more. My grip loosened. The shield wobbled and the tenacious water closed in on us until the wall of water was brushing our noses.

"*DuLac, shape up,*" Vane shouted again. "*If I have to come rescue you, our deal is off and the rest of these unfortunate souls will drown. Hold the line.*"

Taking an unsteady breath, I pulled myself up straighter. The shield strengthened and pushed back the water just a fraction. I begged Vane, "*Hurry.*"

I closed my eyes. A picture of him flashed in my mind. He was swimming underwater, trident in hand. I felt myself going underwater, almost as if I were beside him, even though I knew I wasn't. Two sides of the sea floor, the fault lines of two plates, slowly met and slipped past each other. To relieve the strain, the ground rumbled. Vane used the trident and magic to suppress the rumble. He aimed the trident at two parts of the sea floor that moved to rub against each other. Then, emitting some kind of warbling song, he extended his hand and let loose a stream of green magic, which managed to move the rock, piling it high. The new rock formation was the beginning of a new mountain range.

"*I'm directing it south,*" he told me. "*Out into the Indian Ocean, instead of at the coastlines.*"

I watched him blast away with the trident in awe.

"*It's like you really are Poseidon.*" The thought leaked out before I could stop it.

Vane laughed. "*How do you think we're going to survive what's coming if not with the power of a god? Now, go away, DuLac. You're distracting me.*"

He blasted another expanse of rock with the trident and simultaneously pushed me away. I opened my eyes and found myself back on the roof, Excalibur faltering in my hand. The giant wave pressed down on us. For a moment, the water pressed so close, a mere breath of wind would have brought the violent force crashing down on us.

Then, as suddenly as it came, the giant wave pulled back. We all stumbled forward with relief as the weight eased against the shield. The shield winked out.

I stood up, panting, my arms heavy with the weight of Excalibur. I lowered it slowly. My body would have easily dropped the burden, but after all the mental energy I invested to keep it upright, it took a while for my mind to let go.

As the first daring rays of sun peeked through the clouds, I glanced to my left across the line of rooftops. To my relief, most of the remaining wizards were either kneeling or standing. I glanced to my right. I said to Matt, "Vane did it. He stopped it."

His expression was unreadable as he stood up. "Hari. Call around. Let's find out if the tsunamis have indeed dissipated."

Hari sat on the other end of the roof, holding a dazed

Sangeetha in his arms. On Hari's other side, Raj took his phone out of his pocket and handed it to his brother. Hari's worn expression cleared. He swiped a thumb across the touch screen. "Kolkotta reports the tsunami has abated. I'll check the other disaster centers."

Wind fluttered and ruffled the wavy ends of his longish hair. He stared out across the rooftops at the long rainbow of faded, colored sheets still covering the wizards who sacrificed themselves in the defense of their city.

Hari typed rapidly on the phone. "The other centers are reporting the same. The tsunami warning will remain in effect, but no alerts are going off. They are only seeing small tremors, no quakes worse than 3.0."

"Vane kept his word," I murmured.

"At what cost?" Matt said.

I took a step toward him. "Matt—"

He didn't look at me. His eyes fixed on the wizards who lost their lives to save the city. "Hari, we will have to leave them."

Hari nodded. "I will inform their families. I'm sure they will want to claim them. The news media will no doubt speculate that it was some kind of suicide pact."

Beside me, Gia got up. "That doesn't seem right."

"I agree." Blake rose and pulled her close. "We can't have their families thinking that of them. They gave their lives for us." Fierce eyes peered over stylish black frames. "People should know the truth. They should know who died while protecting them."

Matt shook his head. "Now is not the time. We don't have the resources to handle such an undertaking and we can't get caught up in the spectacle. We have more important things to do."

"Master Merlin is correct." Hari rose up. "The end is coming. We must ask you to concentrate on that, or none of this will matter anyway. We must prepare."

Grey snorted. "Prepare for what? Do you think if something like this is coming, we can do anything about it?"

I looked out at the ocean. Its waves were soft and tranquil again, disguising the danger that lay beneath them, out of sight and out of mind. My hand tightened on Excalibur. "We can do something about it, Grey. That's why we were given the sword. That's why Vane did what he did—"

"You're being blind, Ryan." Gia snapped as she stood up. "Vane wanted power. Now he has it. If he really wanted to help, he should have allowed Merlin to take it instead."

"What's done is done." Matt sighed, rubbing his forehead. He turned toward the roof access door, a concrete staircase that occupied the middle of the rooftop. "It's been a long day. Right now, we need to get to a safe place. Then, we can figure out what to do next. Vane is too close here—"

"What do you mean close?" Grey asked.

"He pushed back the tsunami," I told him. "He was in the middle of the ocean."

"Yes, but he started off here in Chennai, I would wager," Matt said. "He wouldn't have been able to talk to you otherwise."

Grey frowned. "Talk to her? How?"

The *Dragon's Eye* amulet felt heavy around my neck. No one besides Vane and Matt knew that the small charm linked our minds. Vane and Matt both wanted to keep it secret, considering it too dangerous for anyone else to know that we were thus connected. Now that Vane had turned though… it was also fast becoming our biggest weakness. Still, the time for secrets was past. I opened my mouth to tell Grey, but never got the chance.

"My girlfriend and I have a special connection," a voice drawled from the general direction of the ocean behind us. My head whipped around.

"I doubt you can call me that anymore," I said.

"I can simply call you mine," Vane challenged.

Beside me, Matt gnashed his teeth.

Vane grinned. He stood perfectly balanced on the rooftop ledge. The red shirt I'd seen him wearing earlier, inside my mind, molded to the hard muscles of his chest. It was a posh exterior that hid the animal underneath. In real life, the sight of him felt even more electric and my body reacted just as swiftly. Every nerve stood on end. Not necessarily in a good way. For the first time since we'd met, a sliver of real fear slid through my veins. Fear for myself and everyone around me.

Green blazed from his eyes. Words sounded in my head. "*You wouldn't have to be afraid, love, if you just listened to me. I am only doing what is best for us all.*"

An image of him ripping out Matt's heart swam in my mind. I replied, "*Not going to happen.*"

In the depths of his icy irises, the Minotaur stirred. Vane smiled. "*I rather hoped you would say that. I do so like a challenge.*"

***

He floated off the ledge and landed a few steps in front us.

"Lost your superhero cape, Vane?" Grey said with a small, cynical laugh.

Vane's hand shot out. A flash of green magic flew at Grey. With a strangled sound, Grey dropped to his knees. Four gargoyles rushed to stand in front of Grey. Vane raised an amused eyebrow at them before flicking his hand. The gargoyles sailed across the roof, their heads smacking hard against the ledge. I could hear their skulls crunch.

Grey got up with a livid expression. Matt warned him. "Don't. The gargoyles will heal."

Gia pushed away from Blake's side with an angry howl. "Why don't you crawl back under the rock you crawled out from?"

Matt stepped forward, and Blake, ever the loyal to Merlin, rushed to his side. Hari and the wizards on the other rooftops started to gather. The ones farthest away began jumping across the top of the buildings and closed in on us. Matt smiled. "You're outnumbered, Vane."

"Am I?" said Vane.

Vane raised his hand. A green bubble formed around our rooftop. A wizard, leaping from an adjacent rooftop to ours, hit the bubble and was repelled backwards. I winced when he fell onto the concrete with a hard thud.

The access door blew open. I turned my head to see a line of armed men streaming through its shattered wood. I immediately recognized their leader. Leonidas. My hand tightened in a death grip on Excalibur. I ignored the urge to hurl the blade at him. We'd already spent the better part of a month hacking each other up. He brutally made sure I suffered through that time. I couldn't look at him now without wanting to tear him apart.

The mermaids quickly surrounded us. On the island of Aegae, they wore uniforms that I'd only seen in pictures of ancient Spartans—metallic breastplates, red leather skirts, and helmets with red plumes. Now they wore military-style, black cargo pants and black T-shirts. But they couldn't hide their green-tinted skin. In the dull light, it took on an eerie, ghostly pallor. Dark green gills were slashed across their throats. Vane's throat also bore the gills, firmly establishing him as one of them.

I lifted Excalibur and held it in front of me. Beside me, the gargoyles changed to show their beast—their foreheads extended and fangs stuck out from the sides of their mouths. We all shared the same feeling. With the unforgiving gazes of savage mermaids penning us in, we knew we were well and truly trapped.

I turned back to face their king. "What do you want, Vane?"

"What I always want—more." He looked at Matt. "Give me the snake, Merlin."

*Medusa's snake.* The metallic snake held the blood spilt by Medusa on her death, twenty-five-hundred-year-old blood.

Matt gave him a long look. "It is tied to the past. It will not show you the future."

"You will pardon me if I don't take your word for it. Once again, you've missed the obvious—the Lady led you to it. It worked before, now that I have your power, this will work for me, too," said Vane. "Where is it, Merlin? Or do I have to tear through you to get it?"

"You've done enough of that today, haven't you, brother?" Matt said in a voice laced with bitterness.

Vane glanced at me with a smirk. I resisted the urge to wince.

"Yes, but there is little time for you to wallow. You will accept what has happened eventually. There is no other choice." He raised the trident. "Give me the snake, Merlin. I will not ask again."

Matt crossed his arms across his chest. "I. Don't. Have. It."

"Pity." A shield of ice hooded Vane's eyes. I had a moment of deep foreboding before Vane fired on Matt.

"Vane!" I moved to block the blast.

Matt instinctively put up a hand to shield himself, but no magic came out. Blake made it to Matt first. He held up a weak shield. Owing to the amount of energy the wizards had already used to protect the city from the tsunami, I knew it wouldn't hold against Vane's power. I jumped and caught the blast with the edge of Excalibur's blade just before it hit the shield. The blast slammed into Excalibur's unusual metal. It knocked me backwards to the ground and rebounded into Vane. Vane put out a hand and captured the stream of pure energy into his hand. Somehow, he compressed it so that it formed a tight green fireball and bounced it idly in his hand.

My bones jarred by hard concrete, I forced myself back on my feet and shouted, "What are you doing?"

Thoughtful eyes turned to me. "It seems as if I truly have stripped Merlin's magic."

"You knew that!" I said, seething. "You promised not to harm him."

"I promised earlier. This is later." Frost firmly obscuring any emotion in his eyes, Vane lifted the trident again at Matt. "I need that snake, Merlin. All our fates depend on it."

I strode forward, putting myself between Matt and him, and taunted him. "You'll have to go through me and I know you won't. You still need Excalibur."

"Are you so certain?"

He said it so quietly I felt a trickle of unease go down my

spine. I raised my chin. I hadn't given into him when he was being a jerk before and I wasn't about to now... even if this was a way scarier jerk.

Another figure came out of the door. This one made my stomach clench. He also held a sword. It was the gargoyle king's traitorous son—Oliver, who'd once been my friend. I'd hoped to never see him again. I wasn't so lucky.

Oliver mocked, "Am I late?"

He lined up with Leonidas and the mermaids. Disbelief filled me. I'd lost count of how many times the gargoyle had tried to kill me. I turned to Vane. "You're working with *him*?"

Vane said steadily, "I needed a backup."

"*You sicken me*," I thought to him.

The Minotaur inside stirred and awoke. Green eyes intensified.

Oliver smiled at me. "I will happily take the sword."

I spat, "Try me."

Oliver took a step forward. A barrier of magic blocked his way. Vane said, "We're not here for that today."

"Let's give you a choice, love. Merlin or your friend. Which one will you defend?" Vane's voice said, except it sounded oddly hollow.

A stream of magic sent Gia flying backwards across the roof. She landed on a ledge. Her head and back collided with the wall in a loud "*crack!*" Her head slumped forward as she passed out in a sitting position. Instinctively, I took a step toward her.

Vane raised a brow. "Which one will you choose?"

I hesitated.

Vane barked, "Leonidas, take the red-haired witch."

Sword in hand, Leonidas leapt toward Gia with a feral noise. Grey ran to Gia to intercept him. Everything happened quickly after that. Too quickly.

"No!" Blake yelled. "*Aayat!*"

A knife extended into a sword in Grey's hands. Blake managed to conjure a weak fireball, which he lobbed at Leonidas. He and Grey charged the mermaid prince with a sword. Oliver stepped in against them. Close to the edge of the rooftop, the two clashed. I knew Leonidas too well. Blake and Grey didn't stand a chance.

I ran across the roof to help them. Matt ran beside me.

Out of the corner of my eye, across the long length of the rooftop, I saw Hari, Raj, and about ten other wizards surround Vane and the remaining mermaids. They held swords and fireballs in their hands, with which they bombarded Vane. The small, explosive balls, although magic, lacked strength. Vane deflected the fireballs easily, then imbued them with more strength as he sent them rebounding back. A fast, blazing fireball flew straight back at Hari, hitting him squarely in the chest. With barely a cry, the young wizard sailed backwards. His body collapsed on the rooftop. The sword, now useless in his hand, clattered to the ground beside him.

"No!" Sangeetha, her black braids flying behind her, ran to her husband.

Matt halted midway to Grey. Hari, the young wizard, who was so alive only a few minutes ago, now lay as still as a marble statue. Sangeetha dropped to her knees, letting out loud, harsh sobs. Raj went to her and put an arm around the girl's shaking shoulders.

"Fall back," Raj shouted.

The other wizards backed away from Vane. He let them go. Leonidas grabbed Grey. He slammed his head against the ledge. I turned to go to him.

A few feet away, Blake, black hair wild and wiry in the blowing wind, lunged at Oliver. Oliver struck back at him.

"Blake!" I screamed.

The thick blade connected with Blake's neck with deadly force. Blake never had the chance to make another sound. His head fell to the ground.

## COLD SUMMER

"No!" Matt's cry rung with grief.

I stopped midstride, pole axed and frozen in place. The rest of the world buzzed around me yet it was an indecipherable sound. All I could hear was the stop and start of my heart pounding against my eardrums.

Oliver didn't slow down. With the practiced ease of a trained candidate, he turned and ran at me. I lifted Excalibur in return.

"Enough," Vane roared.

In a flash of green light (Vane's magic), Oliver went flying backwards. But Vane didn't glance at us. His gaze remained fixed on Blake's severed form. Real emotion stirred. For the first time since I'd seen him assume the mantle of the monster, it receded. The green cracked and a glimmer of Vane's hazel irises peered through. Then, Leonidas walked to his side. Shields dropped over Vane's expression and all emotion was buried. The mask of indifference slid firmly back into place.

Oliver got up quickly. "I can bring her down."

"No," Vane commanded.

Oliver lunged at me.

Vane knocked him a few feet away.

"I won't tolerate disobedience." He stood on the other side of the roof. "I'm afraid this association will not work out after all. Leonidas, take the traitor gargoyle prisoner."

Blake's head stared at me from the ground.

My fingers tightened on Excalibur. "No, he's not getting off that easily."

Leonidas blocked my way. The mermaid prince faced me without lifting his sword. I moved to attack him. More green magic blew at me, knocking me backwards. Hard concrete collided with my tailbone. Vane zapped Oliver too. He slumped to the floor, felled by a sleep spell. Leonidas grabbed Oliver and thrust him at the other mermaids.

I jumped up and shouted at Vane, "Did you ever care about anyone? How can you protect him?"

"I may need him," he replied.

While his expression wasn't apologetic, the mere fact that he bothered to explain surprised me. I stared at him through a haze of tears. I didn't move.

Matt knelt beside Blake. He picked up Blake's head and set it against his body. Two young wizards left Sangeetha's and Raj's side and rushed over to us. In a glow of yellow, the young wizards sealed Blake's head back on his body and closed the lifeless, unseeing eyes. They bowed their heads.

The wizards on the other rooftops gathered just outside the green bubble that held us captive. Eyes fixed on the body of their fallen leader, they watched, but could do nothing to help.

Ignoring the pain in my own worn out muscles, I stumbled over to Grey. A cut bled at the hairline across Grey's forehead, and I put my fingers to his neck. His pulse was strong.

"He will be fine," Vane said. "His gargoyle blood will heal him."

I ignored him. Wiping at my wet face, I checked Gia next. She lay on Grey's other side. At my prodding, she sat up slowly. She saw me and frowned. By my face, she knew something was wrong. She looked past me and spotted Blake. As realization hit her, I felt its vicious blow again. Gia made a shrieking sound of horror that pierced the air. Loud sobs wracked her body. I tried to pull her into a hug, but she threw me off and crawled toward Blake. She lifted his limp hand and started weeping.

My insides twisted at the sound of her pain. It echoed mine.

Matt got up and walked to me. He said harshly, "This shouldn't have happened."

I reached out a hand to him, needing his touch, but dropped it halfway when those amber-brown eyes fixed on me. Something profound flickered in those depths. Something hard.

Vane leaned on the trident and watched the scene from a safe distance. Leonidas stood at his right. At a nod from Vane, their king, the other mermaids moved to protectively surround him. Grey stirred and sat up. The gargoyles moved to band together at his side. Beyond the bubble, the wizards on the other rooftops also gathered. All eyes were fixed on the bodies of their fallen brethren, but there was nothing they could do to help.

Vane played with the trident. "Tell me, Merlin, how many more are you willing to sacrifice today before you give me what I want?"

"No one else is going to die here today, Vane." Matt stood up. To my shock, he grabbed Excalibur from my hand. Heaving the blade like a lance at Vane, he shouted, "*Zikara!*"

"*Zikara!*" The other wizards on our rooftop shouted in unison.

Excalibur flew straight and true across the rooftop.

"*Zikara!*" The wizards on the other rooftops echoed. One-by-one, the cry spread out like a wave.

It hit Vane just above his heart. With a yelp, he sailed backwards as the blade impaled his shoulder.

In a rainbow of multi-colored magic, a mist, spreading rapidly from the ocean behind us, attacked Vane's bubble. With Vane now on the ground, the bubble dissipated without much of a fight. Dewy mist solidified into fog as it took over the rooftop. I could barely see the sky above, or the ocean ahead of me. Under its thick blanket, Vane lay still on the ground.

"Vane!" Leonidas said. He knelt down at Vane's side just before the fog obscured my view.

I couldn't help it. I took a step toward him. Matt grabbed my arm and stopped me.

"We have to go," Matt said into my ear.

"No." I shook my head. "Vane. Excalibur."

"I don't want to leave Excalibur with him, either, but we don't have a choice. Excalibur won't slow him down for long. He's too powerful. He was surprised this time, but we can't win against him right now. If we don't go, we won't get out at all."

"He's right, Ryan. We have to go while we can." Grey stepped into view through the thick layer of mist. He held Blake. Gia followed behind him. Her hand stretched out to emit a small bubble of yellow light. It pushed back the mist a few feet from us.

Two wizards carried Hari's body. I glanced back into the grey nothingness that had overtaken the rooftop. It was a very bad idea to leave Excalibur with Vane.

An eerie acapella aria filled the rooftop as the mist started lifting. I saw the mermaids surround Vane. Their mouths were open as they emitted the haunting melody. Vane's body rose in the air. The shroud of mist began to lift along with him.

"They're fighting back against the fog," Matt said. "We leave now!"

We hurried to the broken access door, past remnants of wood still attached to weakened hinges. Climbing through the slats, which hung open like drunken sots, resigned to defeat, we got out.

*** 

*Was this my life now?* I wondered a few hours later as I stood in a secluded clearing just beyond the outskirts of the city. Once you left the main drag, the area turned rural rather quickly. The darkened sky thundered beneath charged clouds and streaks of lightning flashed through small gaps. The first storm of the monsoon season threatened to drench us. Not that it mattered. We were already drowning in our own grief.

The ones whose families would want to say goodbye in their own way, were left on the roof. Placed upon a heap piled high with bent and broken wood, Hari was one of the six in the pyre in front of me. Sangeetha stood stoically beside the pyre, wearing a white sari. She watched her husband fade into ash. They'd only been married for six months.

Raj, Hari's brother and apparently second-in-command, carried the torch, setting the six funeral pyres ablaze. His eyes were red with unshed tears. We stepped back as he said his final goodbye to the dead wizards, his friends, and his brother.

*Six.* It was not a good number, and I had to wonder at life's design, which extracted souls so capriciously. My mother. Alexa. *Blake.*

Blake wasn't included in the pyre. Matt contacted the First Member of the Wizard Council and Blake's body was to be rushed home to England by special arrangement. It helped to have connections in the British government.

Tears fell from my eyes for all of them. I didn't have the energy to brush the drops away. So many had died today, ultimate sacrifices for those they left behind. I pictured Blake's kind eyes and the way he used to fiddle with his geeky, black glasses whenever he was nervous. How he'd always been there for me. He embodied everything it meant to be a knight.

My hands tightened on the strap of the fabric bag I was holding.

I would not forget this day.

Fierce wind blew dust in my face. I glanced at Matt's silent profile next to me. He stared, stone-faced, at the glorious blaze lapping at the sky. Light danced across his high cheekbones, shadowing them, in a remarkably similar way to his brother. Despite Vane being slightly older, they could have almost passed for twins. Except for the eyes. Matt's usually brooded. Today, they just looked bleak.

He didn't return my look. Instead, he stared at the blazing conflagration. I turned back to the funeral. A wizard, dressed in the wrap-around, white sarongs that priests wore in India, stepped forward, muttering a long phrase. He threw a handful of white rice into the fire as part of a last rites ceremony. Nearly a hundred wizards stood in the clearing, a somber crowd all clad in white funeral dress. I took a deep breath, inhaling heat and smoke. It scorched my nostrils and burned the hairs a bit. Its sharp scent went straight to my brain, leaving me a little dizzy; and although it made me feel somewhat more alive, it did nothing to alleviate the cold, hard weight pressing down on my chest.

I turned and began to walk away. My restless legs refused to hold still anymore. Grey, who was standing just behind me, caught my sleeve. He gave me a questioning look. His skin pallor looked like ash, and Gia held him onto him to keep upright. The gash on her head was healed, but she still wasn't okay. She didn't look at me. Or anyone. Instead, she stared off at a point in space, silent tears streaking her cheeks as she looked for something that was now long gone.

I couldn't breathe. I swayed in place. Grey's grip tightened. I let myself draw from his support and straightened. Slipping out of his hold, I kept going. I crossed the edge of the clearing and went down the dirt path to a white concrete house, nestled deep within the woods. The sky darkened over the rectangular house. Two stories high, it had a huge, covered veranda in the front. The SUVs we'd been driving hugged the side of the house. I also noticed a Jeep and several sedans. The place was some kind of safe house for the wizards.

I went up a short flight of steps and hurried past empty rocking chairs that invited you to enjoy the balminess of a sultry evening. I spotted a doorway that led straight into the main part of the house. I stumbled across a tree stump as large as an easy chair and sat down. Inside, open-air seating around a square courtyard revealed more blue sky. Gauzy, white curtains framed the open wall of the seating area. As functional as they were decorative, they would be closed as soon as night fell, to ward off mosquitoes.

Like many traditional houses in India, it was built around a central, square courtyard. At its core, a thick mango tree showed small green fruit starting to emerge from dense branches. I crossed the seating area and went to the next section of the house, where two long, wooden tables took up most of the kitchen. Instead of chairs, benches had been put in place for seating. One table displayed framed pictures of groups of people with garlands around them. I sat down on a bench at the other table and took off the shoulder bag. I stared across the gulf at the smiling faces in the pictures. Most of those wizards were now gone.

I touched my neck. I no longer wore the amulet. Matt insisted that I take it off and I conceded. I reached for the fabric bag and unbuttoned it, drawing out a wadded handkerchief. Matt had wrapped the *Dragon's Eye* carefully after we'd left the rooftop. I set the wad on the table. I peeled off the cloth, being careful not to touch the chain or the gemstone. A simple touch would link me back to Vane.

I was surprised I could take off the necklace. Thankfully, Matt had removed the spell that locked it on me while we were in Athens. He never put it back. Biting the inside of my cheek, I debated what I was about to do. I took a breath. I had no idea where I was. It was as safe as it was going to get. I picked up the necklace and put it on. My body sighed with satisfaction as soon as the gemstone touched my skin. Something about it sent a visceral sigh through me.

Immediately, the gemstone heated. I gasped the intensity of the burn and clutched my forehead. Images flashed through my mind.

*I was standing on a narrow ledge, surrounded by green hills and brown rock. Beside me, a waterfall cascaded from a rock outcropping overhead. The waterfall continued past the ledge and down into a small pool about fifty feet below. From my vantage point, the pool didn't look deep enough for diving. Matt walked into the waterfall. With his palms, he felt along the damp earth of the hill. All of a sudden, a blast of water shot out from the rock, like a horizontal geyser. It tossed him into the air and straight across the ledge. I dove after him, but it was too late. Matt went over the side of the ledge.*

Panting, my eyes snapped open. Vane was seeing a vision.

"*Yes, DuLac, figure that out all by yourself?*" Vane's voice pounded in my head. He sounded out-of-breath and tired. "*I told you it would work.*"

"*Blake is gone, Vane.*"

"*Yes.*"

"*He was your friend!*"

"*Emerson always wanted to be the hero, DuLac. We no longer have the luxury of heroes.*" The words were merciless, but I sensed a trace of regret in his tone. His next words confirmed it. "*It was not planned, Ryan.*"

In the kitchen, I took a relieved breath at the small hint of the real Vane, under the monster's hold. I pushed for more. "*How can you be working with Oliver?*"

"*I agree that was ill-conceived on my part.*"

Ill-conceived. What a massive understatement. But it was also a concession. It wasn't enough. I couldn't let him dismiss Blake as if he meant nothing. "*Vane—*"

Vane interrupted, "*Emerson—Blake, that is. He...*"

Vane trailed off as if he couldn't actually verbalize his thoughts. Yet I could sense the chaos of emotions swirling inside him. In the kitchen, my fingers tightened on the amulet and I dared to have hope.

Vane read the thought. His voice hardened, *"Emerson was one of the first, Ryan, and he won't be the last, unless you stop resisting me."*

A harsh bark of laughter escaped me. *"So this was my fault?"*

*"No."* There was a pause. *"This is but merely a taste of what's coming. We need to figure out what that is."*

*"Is that how you justify attacking us?"*

Vane made an impatient noise. *"I'm not justifying. I'm explaining."*

I pictured the green eyes of the monster. So far, I'd adamantly held onto the belief that I could defeat it. After today, my faith was shaken. *"Is this how it's going to be?"*

*"We don't have to be on different sides."*

*"You can't have it both ways, Vane. I won't let you do this again."*

*"You won't be able to stop me."*

I closed my eyes. *"I will find a way."*

He sighed. *"Then you'll destroy this world. My brother was very clever to use Excalibur against me, but only the sword-bearer may wield it properly. You'll have to do better, if you want to defeat me."*

I didn't want to defeat him. I wanted the real Vane back.

*"He is gone."*

*"Thanks for the tip,"* I muttered.

He paused. *"Why do you still care?"*

The idiotic question didn't deserve an answer. Not that I

would give him one. He'd just use it against me. I only hoped the fleeting glimpse I'd seen of the real Vane meant something good. I rubbed my forehead. "*I'm taking off the amulet, Vane.*"

"*Want to tell me where you are?*"

Matt had one of the wizards put me to sleep so I wouldn't know—a safeguard against Vane.

He groused, "*He is too clever. And making things overly difficult.*"

"*What was that vision?*"

"*How should I know? It's the first one I've ever had.*"

"*Great idea, then, for you to steal them,*" I retorted.

"*Forget the vision. It doesn't tell us anything right now,*" Vane shot back. "*I need you to drink the Gorgon's blood.*"

The Medusa snake. Now I understood why he was still talking to me. "*Why are you so bent on this?*"

"*Time is running out. We still have no idea what is going to happen, Ryan. What good is having the power of a god if you don't know its purpose?*"

I said aloud, "Another thing you might have considered beforehand. I'm sensing a pattern."

"What pattern?" Matt came into the house.

My hand went straight to my neck. With a guilty grimace, I took off the amulet. The gemstone went cold and I knew Vane was gone.

Matt marched up to me, a scowl marring his otherwise supremely aesthetic face. "You're talking to *him*."

I answered evenly, "Yes."

Matt pointed back in the direction of the funeral. "You still want to save him? Even after all he's done! After Blake! Can you really tell me you're happy about how all of this turned out?"

I blinked back tears. Blake's tousled black hair and earnest eyes swam in front of me. "Of course I'm not happy!"

Matt gave a low laugh. "He's taken everything."

I couldn't disagree. Still I tried to explain. "I saw what Lelex left inside you. It was spreading like a virus. He saved you."

Matt thundered, "He *saved* me so that he could take my power. The visions were our one advantage. Now we've lost them altogether."

I ground my teeth. "What was I supposed to have done? Vane didn't give me a choice."

"If I had my powers, maybe I could have changed what happened on the rooftop," he barked. "Maybe we wouldn't have lost Excalibur. Maybe we wouldn't have lost..." Matt raked an unsteady hand through his hair. "So many."

My eyes closed. I forced them open. "I didn't see another way."

Matt looked at me impassively. "You should have found one."

"Really? How?" I took a long breath. "Look, you're upset. I get it. I'm upset, too. I didn't want this." My voice dropped, and I said hoarsely, "It's killing me, what I had to do, but I'm not going to take it back. I made the right choice to save as many as I could."

"The right choice today, without a thought of the cost—"

I stood up, shaking. "I am well aware of the cost!"

A hard glint flickered in Matt's amber eyes. "So it wasn't without thought. It was with arrogance."

I sputtered, "A-arrogance?"

"Yes, Ryan. Everything you do has consequences."

"Is it that? Then, why is it okay for you to make unilateral decisions and not me? I don't remember you asking permission before you took Excalibur." I crossed the floor to Matt and poked him in the chest with my finger. "You say you want me to step up. Well, I did. I made a choice. Me. Myself. I."

"If I hadn't used Excalibur, we wouldn't have gotten off that rooftop."

"You should have found another way." I spat his words back at him. "You could've bargained with the Medusa snake. This battle between the two of you has got to stop. We want the same things—"

"No!" Crossing the short distance between us, Matt grabbed my shoulders. His eyes locked on mine and he stared into them as if he could impress his beliefs onto me by sheer force. "There wasn't another way, Ryan. There is only enough blood left for one more vision. I would never have surrendered that to him."

My jaw jutted out. I said his words back, "At what cost?"

He didn't answer.

"Let me go, Matt," I said evenly.

"You heard her, Emrys. Back off," Grey walked into the kitchen. His arm was around Gia's shoulders, offering her support. "It's been a long day."

Gia laughed. It wasn't a pleasant sound. "Yes, it has."

Ignoring them, Matt released me. "Understand this clearly, Ryan. Vane is not to be trusted. He will do what it takes to save himself. He always has. If that happens to be what we need to do, then all is good. If it doesn't, then we're going to be the ones left paying the price of whatever he does." He pointed at the door, in the direction of the funeral pyre. "Destruction follows him like a plague. Whatever his choices might be, I assure you they will not be the right ones."

"Like yours would be. I'm so glad you're here to save us from ourselves." Taking a few steps, I moved away from him. "You might be upset that I sacrificed your powers, but that's not what's making you so angry. You're furious because you have no idea what to do next. For the first time in your life, you're going to have to learn to live without a safety net."

Matt sighed. "This isn't about me, Ryan. This is about you. You've got to do better."

Gia added softly, "I agree with Merlin."

I reeled back from her words as if she slapped me.

"You shouldn't have sacrificed his magic. We lost too much today." Red-rimmed eyes faced me, but I couldn't meet them. My legs, suddenly weak and rubbery, forced me to sit down.

Grey frowned. "Blake wasn't her fault."

"No, Grey," I said. "They're right. It is my fault."

Without looking at anyone, I grabbed the bag on the table and pushed myself up. Feeling about a hundred years old, I walked slowly into the courtyard. Outside, the sky was colored in ominous hues of purple and dark grey. I could have marveled at its majesty, but all I could focus on was how glad I should feel to even see the clouds... thrilled to see another day... because of Vane. And yet... what he'd done... He was destruction personified.

I put my fisted hand into my mouth and bit down on it. Doubt, an ugly disease, bore down on me. Every insecurity I ever had about being the sword-bearer rushed back. Who was I to make any decisions? But in truth—there was no one else. When Matt and Vane locked horns, they couldn't see past themselves.

I took a ragged breath. I had to hold onto the one truth I knew.

I was the sword-bearer. The burden belonged to me.

My hand pressed down on the side of the fabric bag slung across my chest. Inside was the snake from Medusa's head, a slim bronze artifact about a foot in length. Unbeknownst to me, Matt put it in the bag when Hari picked us up from the airport. The Medusa snake had been in the car the whole time we were up on the rooftop.

Medusa was a Gorgon, who was either seduced or raped by Poseidon, the same god whose power Vane now possessed. Athena, the goddess of knowledge, caught them in the act inside her temple and cursed the poor maiden. Later, after being beheaded by Perseus, Medusa's blood was saved and bottled. Thousands of years later, we found the blood in Athens. The blood held mystical properties and led us to the mermaids. The mermaids—one of the many secrets the sea kept to herself. I looked at the ugly, black scars on my arm. I got them during my last encounter with the snake, and I'd have them forever.

Biting my lip, I took the bronze squiggly metal out of the bag.

Matt ran down two short steps into the courtyard. "Ryan, what are you doing?"

*Probably making another dumb decision.* Taking out the snake topper, I saw he'd been right, only a few drops of blood remained inside.

Matt rushed to me. "Ryan!"

He wasn't fast enough. I put the metal snake to my lips and took a swallow. The last drops of the thick liquid burned as it descended my throat. My eyes watered. I barely felt Matt snatching the snake from my hands. I clutched my throat as I choked and coughed. The blood went down like rotten, maggoty meat. Gagging on it, I spat it back out. And then, spat some more.

I seriously lost respect for all those movies where vampires drank the stuff like sweet nectar. Ambrosia? It wasn't. Matt thumped my back. I coughed again. "That is the most disgusting thing I've ever tasted."

Grey hurried out of the house toward me. A furious expression contorted his face as he barked, "Have you lost your mind? You almost died last time!"

I scowled back. "I had to try."

Matt said, "It didn't work."

"The last two times we had it, you drank it," I said.

"Even in the dungeon?"

I shuddered at the thought of the grisly cell which the mermaid king kept Matt in for weeks. I hoped never to experience that horror again. "You don't remember, but Vane poured it down your throat."

Matt stared at the empty snake. "Since Vane holds my power, only he could drink it."

"Now no one can," I said, waiting to be chastised. It didn't come. Matt's lips curled down, his expression seemingly equal parts anger and desolation. It was much worse than any reprimand. My hand reached out to touch him, but I dropped it halfway. "What do we do next?"

Matt sighed. "We fix this mess."

*Your mess.* I heard the sentiment in his tone even though I could no longer hear his thoughts. Would I ever do anything right in his eyes? I wished I didn't care. Despair jackknifed through my already lowered spirits, and I tried not to let it turn into resentment. It took real effort to stick out my chin. "What brilliant plan do you have up your sleeve?"

"Nothing brilliant," Matt said with a faraway look. "I intended to find the Healing Cup all along."

"The Healing Cup? Do you think it really exists?" Grey asked, his voice hopeful. We thought we'd found the precious item once already.

Matt nodded. "Lelex told us the Fisher King came to him. There is no way he could have survived the wound Vane gave him without it. I absolutely believe it exists."

"Rourke doesn't have much time left," said Grey. "We could spend forever trying to figure out where it is."

My eyes narrowed on Matt. "You think you know where it is, don't you?"

Matt inclined his head.

"But you're not going to tell us," I added.

His expression hardening, he took the now empty metal snake from my hand. "I've found that things work out better that way."

Gia came down the courtyard steps, her long red hair shrouding her face. "Right, Merlin. Nice try. So, where is it?"

"We've been over this before," I said. "This concerns all of us. I'm the sword-bearer—"

"Who no longer has a sword," he pointed out.

"And you no longer have any magic," I retorted before I could stop myself.

Matt's expression froze, closing us all out. Light dimmed above us as night closed down on the sky. Movement sounded from inside the house, and the wizards streamed indoors. I watched the throng of people, their mournful faces as they leaned on one another. Under the expansive sky, however, Matt and I stood alone. Apart.

Emptiness made my stomach hollow. I tried again. "Matt—"

"As you pointed out, I'm sure I will learn to make do without magic." Turning on his heel, he started walking away. "It has been a long day. I suggest you get some rest. You have a flight early tomorrow. The cars are leaving at first light."

In a few short strides, he crossed the courtyard and went into the house, while the rest of us could only stare after him.

"I really want to know where we're going," Grey muttered.

"I'm pretty sure Marilynn made the arrangements for him," Gia said.

She and I both winced at the same time. Marilynn did not like either one of us and she worshipped Matt. We wouldn't get any help from her. For a brief second, I met Gia's gaze and her demeanor thawed. It was fleeting, and a stony mask fell over her face, shutting me out.

Grey snapped his fingers. "I've got it. He doesn't have any magic. Gia can spell him to tell us—"

"Can you spell the greatest wizard in the world?" she murmured.

I let out a small bark of laughter, edged only slightly with hysteria. "You can today."

***

"I'm going back inside," I said, one hour later.

Grey nodded.

Moonlight shone down on the dark house. The power was out. A nightly occurrence in this part of India we were told. The sky still grumbled and rumbled, trying to make up its mind about the storm. In the bubble of momentary peace, we sat out on the front lawn, alongside other wizards. They built a small bonfire in a pit at the front of the house and sat around it, trading stories. Grey, Gia, the gargoyles, and I sat with them.

Sitting on a log beside Grey, Gia continued to stare into the golden flames of the fire blazing before us. In the mystery of the night, in a certain slant of the firelight, I could almost see Blake's ghost, a shadowy form, sitting on Gia's other side. I took a hard breath. There had to be something I could do. Fix this mess as Matt declared.

I listened to the wizards telling some exaggerated and some not so exaggerated tales about their departed friends. It was sweet, really. Matt didn't join us. It made me uneasy. Past an open terrace, a small lamp emitted a yellow glow in the room he'd taken. But I hadn't seen his profile in quite awhile. The hair at the back of my neck stood up. Following my instincts, I left the campfire and walked up the short steps onto the veranda.

"Sword-bearer," a voice called from the shadows.

I stopped just before the front door. Sangeetha walked toward me, a ghostly figure in a flowing, white sari. Tears covered her cheeks. I opened my mouth. She shook her head. "No, you do not have to say anything. I do not think I could stand any more condolences."

I closed my mouth. After a second, I asked, "Can I do anything?"

"Raj tells me the one who killed Hari was Merlin's brother."

My insides twisted. "Yes."

"It is a terrible thing. One brother a savior, the other a murderer." She swallowed hard. "I know not what comes, but Hari told me Merlin thought the earthquakes were just the beginning. You must help him, sword-bearer." She took my hands into her icy ones. "I see the way he watches you. Merlin loves you."

"Not any longer." The words slipped out.

"He does. You must not allow him to push you away. Hari did not choose me at first, either. He said we were too young, but I prevailed. Now, my only regret is that I waited long than I wanted. Merlin will have to battle this brother. It will be difficult, but with you at his side, he can triumph."

"Vane's not himself," I said. "We may yet be able to save him."

Sangeetha's fingers tightened. "You have feelings for the monster."

I lowered my gaze.

"I saw the coldness in his eyes. Whatever he was before, he is no longer. If you choose his side, you will doom us all." Sangeetha dropped my hands. Her voice turned hard. "My husband died to save us, sword-bearer. Do not let it be in vain." In a rustle of white, she seemed to glide off the veranda, like an apparition returning to the shadows. A final warning floated to me through the dark. She whispered, "He was not meant for you."

The words reverberated inside my head. With effort, I forced my bones to walk. Was I really fooling myself about Vane?

I didn't want to believe I'd really lost him. I couldn't believe it. Like I couldn't explain the blackness bleeding into my soul at the mere thought of it. His hazel eyes as they'd smiled arrogantly at me. His cool breath against my skin as he'd held me, promising nothing would touch me.

I crossed the threshold into the house and started to head upstairs. A rustling from the courtyard compelled me to stop. I ventured out into the moonlit yard. More rustling came from a small door at its opposite end.

Silently, I opened it and peered inside. The door opened to the side of the house and to a row of parked cars. At the front stood a safari-style Jeep 4x4. The Jeep was first in a line of cars. Raj and one other wizard wore white cotton shirts that gleamed under the glow of a high-powered flashlight. They stood at Matt's side, with Raj holding keys in his hands. Matt spoke to the other one who held the lamp. "You'll need to give them their flight information. They'll be upset, but don't give them a choice. Knock them out if you have to. They won't anticipate you using magic on them. Make sure they don't know where I'm going—"

In the dark, my jaw dropped open. He held a bag at his side.

He was ditching us.

I took a step to confront him, but stopped. I had no doubt I would be freeze-spelled before I ever got the chance to make a stand. Without the *Dragon's Eye*, I was entirely too vulnerable to magic. I checked out the Jeep. It had no cover. Matt stuck his bag on top of a black tarp, which I figured was the unused cover. Being careful not to make a sound, I slipped into the shadows beside the wall.

"Is everything in place? What is the best route from here?" Matt asked. He, Raj, and the one with the lamp huddled together, studying a map. Raj held his hand over the map and magicked it to show a three-dimensional view of the terrain.

I resisted rolling my eyes. They could have done the same on an iPad, without any fancy spell. I used their distraction to jump from the wall and duck between a set of sedans. I almost knocked over an old radio that was left on the hood of the second sedan. It wobbled, but I caught it before it crashed to the ground. Putting it back on the hood, I went around the side and snuck over to the opposite end of the Jeep from Matt and the wizards.

"Do not worry—the First Member supplied everything you requested. You just need to give them the coordinates. I will take care of anything else that comes up," Raj said.

"Good," Matt said. The wizard with the lamp took a step toward me. I ducked lower, next to the Jeep's back tire and looked frantically for a way to distract them. Grabbing a small rock, I aimed it at the sedan with the radio. The stone hit its target, just as I expected. As a "daughter of Apollo," I had a voodoo sense of marksmanship that usually tended to creep me out, but it also came in handy at odd times.

The radio fell off the hood and crashed to the ground.

"What was that?" Matt and the other wizards turned toward the sound.

I climbed into the back of the Jeep and slid under the tarp covering the trunk.

Raj saw the mess first. "*Sala,*" he cursed. "Someone left a radio on the car. It must've fallen down."

Matt refolded the map. "Let's get going."

"Take care of them all," Raj said to the wizard with the lamp.

He and Raj turned back to the Jeep. I pulled the tarp tightly over me when I heard them walking toward me and held my breath. My nose twitched with the smell of Matt's earthy scent. He grunted, putting his hands on the trunk. He and Raj pushed the heavy Jeep past the back of the house. They rolled it along for a few minutes. Then, coming to a stop, I heard them go around to the front and climb into the seats. I peeked out from under the tarp and saw we'd reached the line of trees that marked the edge of the woods.

The wizard holding the lamp turned back into the house. He closed the door. Raj started the Jeep. The engine rumbled noisily. Under a dull blanket of stars and swaying trees, warm tropical breezes carried the sweet scent of mangoes and other wild fruit as we drove away into the dark.

Grey was going to be so pissed at me.

*** 

I woke up with a start. My head thwacked hard against the side of an unforgiving metal trunk as we came to a sudden stop. I rubbed the sore spot. I had a feeling my head must have hit the side a few times before I finally woke up. The Jeep rattled along an extremely bumpy road. Only the main roads in the cities were smooth. Once you got beyond them, the potholes were everywhere. Rain pattered down on the tarp.

I heard Matt and Raj getting down.

I pushed aside a corner of the tarp and poked my head out. Low energy halogen lights on the sides of large, curved buildings illuminated an airfield. At a faraway distance, I recognized the huge terminals of the Chennai International Airport. We'd come in through a remote entrance, into a section with several small hangars. Raj stopped the Jeep next to a slim, yet long private plane. The clamshell door to the plane was open with its air stair lowered. Matt must have chartered a flight.

Droplets of rain pinged across metal. Matt and Raj walked up to the wing and were talking to a group of men. Two wore uniforms and another five wore jumpsuits. Pilots and aircrew, I guessed.

"Will it be ready?" Raj said in a loud voice.

"Most certainly. The connection is fixed, but we must double-check all the systems. It will only take another half hour, sir," one mechanic reassured him.

Raj protested, "We're on a tight schedule—"

Matt interrupted, "It's all right. I would rather not take any more risk than I'm already taking by even getting inside this steel bumblebee."

I suppressed a smile. Matt hated flying.

"There will be no problems, Master Merlin," one of the pilots said. "We will take off as soon as the systems are checked out. Despite the short notice of your reservation, we have everything in place. We will beat the storm. Meanwhile, we must wait for the last of our crew—your flight attendant. He will be here in fifteen minutes."

Under the tarp, I sighed in relief. With their attention diverted, it wouldn't be hard to sneak onboard. A few minutes and several Bondesque moves later, I was safely inside the plane. The interior was nothing short of spectacular. The front held the cockpit and a serving station. The remainder consisted of three long sections—a front seating area, a dining area, with built-in tables already set up with white tablecloths, and a divan area with sectional doors that looked like they closed for privacy. I glanced at the space under the dining table. The long white drape of cloth made it a decent hiding place, but I chose the divan instead. I opened a small compartment under the divan and pulled out a fleece blanket.

I repositioned the partition, separating the section from the dining area, making it slightly closed and lay down on the bench. I had half a mind to march up to Matt and rail at him for his actions. I didn't think it would work. So I chose the passive-aggressive path and decided to wait until we were actually in the air.

With a sigh, I pulled the dark blanket over me. I was half-asleep when, exactly half an hour later, the plane taxied down the runway and was quickly airborne. As soon as we were safely flying, I peeked out from under the blanket. The neatly dressed flight attendant unstrapped himself and came out of the cockpit area to offer Matt another beer. He took it, and handed the attendant his used sick bag in exchange.

I pulled the blanket completely off my face, but didn't move to get up. Yawning, I lay on the left side of the plane, just a few feet past Matt. Unlike commercial jets, the private plane didn't have row upon row of seats. On the right side of the plane, a group of four seats were arranged so they faced each other with a small built-in coffee table between them. Raj sat near the window, diagonally opposite Matt.

I couldn't see much of Raj, but I had a decent view of Matt's profile as he sipped on his drink. I stared at him and wondered what I was doing.

When did I completely buy into the "greatest wizard in the world" mystique?

I kept trying to prove myself... to be the great sword-bearer... to be good enough. For him. Was that why it had all gone wrong? I looked up at the sterile ceiling, its curves and bumps, and thought of Blake. Vane may not have meant for it to happen, but it did nonetheless. Another debilitating wave of despair hit me. With a weary effort, I pushed it back.

Could Vane be saved? Did he need to be? I may have failed to stop him, but he'd chosen to become the Fisher King. He'd chosen to be alone. In the back of mind, I'd never been able to let go of the thought that I was a game to him.

The *Dragon's Eye* pressed into my skin, piercing through the thin fabric of my linen trousers. Its weight pressed down on my soul even as the cold stone sought to seduce my body. Before I could think about the idiocy of my action, I reached into the pocket and touched the beckoning gemstone. Instantly, it heated.

# LAST OF THE ROMANS – BATTLE OF AD DECIMUM

I had to get home. I had to get to him. The one small face I kept hidden at the back of my mind. The one small face Triton couldn't beat out of me. Triton. The memories of the island began to fade as soon as I thought of them. In a short while, I would forget those bastard mermaids. I'd forget that whoreson of a king. Triton spent years molding me into his ideal of a perfect warrior. He thought he could break me. It took every ounce of my resistance not to let him.

I spent ten years in the military camps with hundreds of other boys. I wore a yellow crystal necklace that bound my magic. So I learned to beat older, bigger boys for clothes and shoes, and zealously defended my place to sleep in the bushes. The trainers only gave enough food for half of us, so I had to become a good thief and avoid getting caught, which meant ruthless beatings and nights in the pit. Succeeding in the camps meant perfecting our hunting skills by slaughtering slaves. As if that weren't enough, I also got singled out for special training. Every once in a while,

Triton would erase my memories—to the point where the only thing I could hold onto was one name, my brother's name. Merlin.

I struggled to remember my name.

Vivane. Vane. I repeated it over and over again in my mind as I hacked away at flesh and bones with my sword. I was on a field. Blood spurted into my face, some of it splattering onto my tongue. I spat it out. I yelled a command and the soldiers behind me advanced a few steps into the onslaught of an army of Vandals.

The grisly battle around me raged. After my final year in Triton's camps, I was released from the mermaid island back onto the mainland. My memories were taken one last time before I was dumped in Constantinople. There, the last of the Romans, Emperor Justinian of Byzantium, sought to revive the bloated glory of Rome. Escaping from slavery was Triton's final test for me. I was bought by a Roman commander who served Justinian's most respected general—Flavius Belisarius. The general had recently cemented his favor with the emperor by squelching a riot against the ruler. He later massacred thirty thousand protesters in a bloodbath inside the city's chariot racing stadium, the hippodrome.

Today, we marched on the African city of Carthage controlled by the very barbarians who sacked Rome—the Vandals. The refugee Germanic tribe took down the western front of the Roman Empire and controlled it from its stronghold in Carthage for nearly a hundred years. On this fall day, we met King Gelimer's forces at the tenth milestone, just south of the city. Our cavalry of five thousand men guarded the front and back of the column. They successfully pushed back the lighter Vandal cavalry. I stood at the front of the infantry line under my commander, Septimus, whom I would have gladly slain, if given half a chance, but I had to survive this battle. I had to buy back my freedom from the snake.

Septimus took one look at the muscle-bound, fifteen-year-old boy, wearing nothing but a simple, white loincloth and a cheap yellow crystal necklace, and paid for me on the spot. I was spared the humiliation of the slave markets only to find myself at the mercy of a man who was capable of much worse. He was also the only man who could remove the necklace binding my powers.

An army of ten thousand should have given us an advantage over the seven thousand Vandal troops, but due to the disorganization of our commanders, our ranks faltered while theirs marched deep into our lines. Septimus led our legion. With naught but a shield, a sword, and a prayer, I wore the crimson cloak of a Roman, the banner of a fading civilization, and struggled to maintain our line. Crude faces adorned in brown and grey fur, a plethora of Vandal barbarians grinned at me through broken teeth even as their blood was spilled under my sword.

Hack. Slice. Pull back. Block. Hack. The barbarians were bigger than I, but not as well-trained. I don't remember how many I killed, but I was never one to keep count. Time passed with only the loud buzz of battle deafening my ears. At one point, I turned and saw no one at my back. Our numbers scattered and a grisly end seemed inevitable. Then, the tide turned. The Vandals, who were winning, failed to press their advantage. Suddenly, their lines began to show large gaps, while in front of us, a beacon of Roman red streaked the sky. It was none other than Belisarius himself who pulled our lines back together. The Vandals retreated, falling into complete disarray. Word spread that a Hun cavalryman, a mercenary under Belisarius, took down a Vandal prince. While they grieved, it was time for us to push back.

The stink of battle finally lessened that night. The broken bodies of men and horses lay strewn across a dusty field. Devoid of even bushes or trees, the usually arid land was finally soaked. Blood fed its parched ground. In the morning, we overtook the city.

Its citizens opened the gates without protest. Belisarius cleverly declared the people of Carthage to be oppressed Roman citizens—which meant they would be spared and not become the spoils of war. Septimus, as many of the other commanders under Belisarius who expected to make their fortune in the aftermath, was not exactly thrilled with the edict. On the other hand, any Vandal and his property, which included his family, could be taken without censure. Rumors of a great treasure, taken during the sacking of Rome and supposedly hidden by the Vandal king drove the soldiers into a frenzy as they ruthlessly sacked the city.

A few citizens protested. Belisarius impaled the head of one such wealthy landowner in front of the townspeople and the protests immediately abated. I looted treasure from an abandoned house before searching for Septimus. With my leash held tightly in his hand, he had no fears that I would try to escape.

It didn't take long to find him. A group of his soldiers were pillaging a wealthy Vandal household near the king's palace. The noble's house stood several stories. As soon as I entered, I knew I found the right place. I tightened the leather strap of the baldric across my chest. The gold, which I wrested away from another soldier, sat heavily inside its pouch. A cohort of soldiers, about sixty, ransacked the spacious house. In the front room, a few feasted on fresh fruit without a glance toward the body of an old woman, possibly a nursemaid, lying on the floor. She was naked, her legs splayed wide, and her stomach was mutilated from the repeated stabs of a sword. Bending down, I drew together her tattered clothes, managing to cover just a bit of her.

"Is she to your liking, Vane?" a brawny soldier, Sergius, said from just inside a hallway. His eyes showed no emotion as he watched me. It helped not to have any in these times. He held a tankard of ale in one hand and an axe in another.

I stated the obvious. "She's dead."

He shrugged. "She's still warm."

I hid my distaste, standing up. "Where is he?"

Sergius's lips curved up. It was not a good sign. "The Vandals have been living like fat pigs. He found much more upstairs."

Not wanting to waste any more time on Septimus's lackey and oft times lover, I headed upstairs. Sergius put a hand on my chest and stopped me before I could pass him. "He protects you, young centurion. You are property and therefore valuable, but if you suddenly weren't, my men and I would enjoy taming a wild one such as you."

Before he could blink, I had my sword at his throat. I may have been a frail boy in comparison to him, but they all knew I had yet to lose a fight. Despite the reediness of my voice, I said forcefully, "Watch yourself, Sergius. You know he won't allow anyone else but him to touch me. He shares you. Not me."

His hardened eyes flared with jealousy, revealing the depth of feeling he had for Septimus. I only suspected their trysts, so inside, I crowed. Now I had the upper hand. My lips curled into a sneer. He didn't resist when I shrugged his hand off me. I added silkily, "Besides, I doubt you would have the... stamina to hold me."

Surprise and a spark of lust lit in Sergius's eyes.

I smiled. I'd learned quickly to play with the enemy. Sometimes I even enjoyed it.

Sergius's rage was unveiled as he spat, "He'll tire of you soon, once you're all used up."

Careful to keep my sword up, I took a step to move past him. "Or you are."

"We understand each other." Sergius smirked. "I would give it a few minutes before you interrupt him. He's busy."

A knot twisted in my belly at his words as I hurried through the house. Beaten servants, the lucky ones, cowered in various corners of the house, trying to hide from the carousing soldiers. I found Septimus in the largest bedchamber. He'd taken off his white plumed helmet, revealing a pretty face topped by black hair, sprinkled with strands of grey. A golden breastplate over a white tunic protected his lean chest. Steel greaves and armor covered surprisingly strong legs, including the knees. His sword was tucked into his belt. Its blade was dirty with blood. In his hand, he casually held a curved knife.

Septimus was standing over a canopied bed. Against my better judgment, I went into the room. A woman in fine clothes sat on the bed. She was bound and gagged. The top of her gown had been torn to reveal a thin shift and bare arms. Slashes covered the length of them. Septimus hadn't taken her yet—he would—but for now, he was simply playing.

His gaze turned on me. I had to stop myself from recoiling. He'd tortured another slave-girl to death just weeks earlier and was wearing that same lust-crazed expression. Boy or girl, it didn't matter to Septimus. Only pain mattered.

Septimus's lips curved up. "Ah, Vane, there you are. Meet my bride, the Lady Aldith. She's a little noisy, but I have been rectifying that quite pleasurably."

"It's noisy everywhere," I commented.

"Good. The men are enjoying themselves, as they should." Narrow eyes watched me. "Did you?"

I returned a pained look. "I prefer things... a bit cleaner."

To my relief, he chuckled. "The barbarians do stink like swine, do they not?"

I crossed the length of the room, eyeing the woman. She wore a resigned expression. At least she wasn't dead. Though, it might have been better for her if she were.

Confined as I was at the time, I hadn't help that slave-girl and I didn't know how to help this one. Septimus made me listen to the slave-girl's horror. He would make me watch the debauchment of this one. I didn't want to think about what he would force me to do... all because I wasn't strong enough to free myself. Frustration gnawed at me. My fingers tightened on my sword, even though I knew it was useless.

For a second, I pictured myself hacking off his head with a blade. I would make it slow. I wanted to hear the satisfying break of his neck. I blinked and the picture receded. Of course, I'd never get close enough. The bind he used to control me was impervious to steel.

Septimus, his Roman face etched with arrogance, grinned at me as if he knew my thoughts. He probably did. Not that he minded. It just excited the twisted bastard.

A whimper drew my attention to the other side of the bed. A delicate-looking boy, a few years younger than I, huddled on the floor with his knees up. Something about his too-old eyes reminded me of my own brother. I glanced at Septimus. He followed my gaze and now wore a twisted smile—no doubt enjoying the boy's terror as much as the mother's. Rage choked me, but I long ago trained myself not to show any signs of it.

Turning an indifferent expression back to Septimus, I said, "You're looking for something."

Septimus beamed with approval. I swallowed my nausea. He put a hand on a bedpost. "The Vandal's treasure. It is rumored that a great bounty was taken when the barbarians sacked Rome. Gold and jewels from all over the world, going back to the time of Alexander of Macedonia. Such treasure would do much for my coffers."

"How do you know it's here?"

Septimus laughed. "A piece of it is here. The Lady Aldith has an aristocratic ancestry. She is related to the royal line through Hildrec, Gelimer's cousin. He was the deposed king who brushed elbows with Justinian himself. While I have no doubt that the bulk of the treasure was taken by Gelimer when he took the throne, these nobles find ways to keep their fair share. Such a share is hidden in this house. I have gleaned as much from Lady Aldith. She is not well accomplished in the skills of guile."

I took off my baldric and threw it down on the floor at Septimus's feet. The coins clinked heavily on the stone floor. "You can add these to your coffers. I believe it will cover what you spent on me."

As I expected, Septimus quickly grabbed the baldric. He opened the pouch and drew out a greedy handful of gold coins. "Nicely done, Vane. Where did you find it?"

"A noble's house. A few doors down."

"From just one house. It confirms their treasures are abundant." Septimus looked at me. "Still, *centurion*, you are much more valuable than a mere bag of coins."

The caress in his tone when he called me by the title he chose for me made my skin crawl.

Septimus smiled, the soft lines of his face disguising the monster lurking inside. "If we were to find such a grand treasure, its worth would be immeasurable…"

A lure. Yet, what choice did I have? Every soldier in this house owed fealty to Septimus. Even if one dared to stand against him, he would surely be skewered for his heroics by the larger army. I touched the threaded necklace at my throat. "Allow me to talk to her."

"Yes, allow him," Sergius said from the door. He stomped into the room. His hulking form stopped just behind me. He put the axe at the back of my head. "I will take care of him if he misbehaves."

"Of course." Septimus laughed. I held my breath as he reached to take off his necklace. He drew out a small green crystal, the bane of my existence, the key to my cage. I yearned to reach for it and yank it from his slimy fingers. I must have betrayed myself because Septimus's mouth curled up. He let the necklace fall back on his chest with a dark grin. Blue eyes met mine. They glinted with the knowledge of the power he dangled over me. They gloated. He said slyly, "No, it would be too easy. I have yet to see anyone withstand *Silvertongue* for more than a few seconds."

I wanted to put my fist into his smug face. I wanted to beat it into the ground until nothing remained but torn flesh and bone. I took a sharp breath. He smiled as if he knew what I was thinking. He probably did. The bastard would probably enjoy it. The morning sun rose higher in the sky. It stained the sky red, a reflection of the battlefield it oversaw. However, the true aftermath of the battle happened in places like these dark, dank little rooms that muffled the screams of horror from within. I stared at Septimus. "What do you want me to do?"

Septimus's eyes glittered. "Ask her nicely."

*Don't damage anything that could be seen.* I drew out a knife from my belt. I walked to the bed. My hands, already dirty with the crimes of the day, were about to become dirtier. Reaching the bed, I put a knee on it. The terrified woman scooted back, trying to get as far from me as possible. Shiny brown hair, bountiful and flowing, curtained most of her face. Eager to get a good view, Sergius moved to stand just below the foot of the bed. I grabbed her ankle. She resisted. Despite my thin frame, she was no match for me. I pulled her forward easily. With the knife, I sliced through the thin membrane of her gag.

Huge eyes locked on me. She didn't make a sound.

If my fingers trembled, I ignored them. With Septimus in my mind, I calculated a dizzying number of scenarios, but none would work where I had no magic. Anger coursed through me and I asked silently for help. Any help. With my eyes on the woman, I gave her ankle a sharp twist. Bones crunched. She screamed.

The boy on the floor jumped up. He held a shaky knife in his hand. Before he could lunge at me, Sergius caught him by the scruff. He laughed. "I think I might take this one, if you don't mind, Commander."

I dropped the lady's fractured ankle and lunged at Sergius, knocking the boy aside. I kicked Sergius as hard as I could in the groin. Letting out a howl of pain, Sergius doubled over. The next thing I knew, I was flying across the room. My back hit the wall hard. Without touching me, Septimus yanked me along the rough stone floor until I landed somewhere near his feet. On the floor on my side, my body curled into a ball and shook with pain. Septimus gripped the green crystal—my chain. It glowed with cruel power.

He walked closer and shoved me with a sandaled foot, flipping me over on my back. "I am disappointed, Vane. You forget to whom you belong to."

My body was shuddering under the pressure of a thousand nails digging into my skin, but I managed to crawl to his sandaled foot. I clutched it. "F-forgive m-me."

Septimus's lips curled into a satisfied smile.

Behind the wall, near the spot I slammed against, I heard a muffled sound.

Septimus heard it too. He let go of the necklace and turned on his heel. The green crystal dulled and so did my pain. I sighed with relief.

Septimus said, "There's something behind this wall."

Only one adornment, a bright red tapestry covered the length of the wall. It depicted a woman, possibly a deity, with a lion's head. The lady wore a bow across her chest and held a cup in one hand. On the lion's forehead a white crescent moon was stitched.

I pushed myself up and forced myself to walk without stumbling until I reached the tapestry. I ripped it from the wall. The jagged stone blocks of the wall gave nothing away. I ran my hands over its rough surface.

"I see nothing," Septimus murmured.

Then, I spotted it. An inconsistency. A layer of dust covered most of the wall except one small block at the bottom, which seemed unusually clean. Leaning down, I pushed at the block hard. It sank into the wall as a line of the door popped open. An arrow flew from within the hidden opening's dark abyss. If I hadn't been crouching on the floor, the arrow would have torn through me. Instead, it sank with unerring accuracy into Septimus's neck.

To my shock, the arrow penetrated. It had no trace of magic.

Septimus didn't have a chance to scream. His vocal chords were instantly severed, and he could only manage a weak gurgle before falling to the floor.

"No!" Sergius cried.

The boy holding him took advantage of the moment to wriggle out of the brawny soldier's grasp. The boy's mother jumped off the bed toward her son. It was a mistake. Another arrow flew from the hidden room. Sergius dove to avoid it. His axe swung and hit the mother squarely in the chest. She fell back on the bed.

I grabbed the green crystal dangling from Septimus's torn throat. I put it against a small, shiny, metal piece on my thread necklace. The metal stayed. I noticed the green crystal had cracked on Septimus's fall. With a loud curse, I slammed my hand into the cold stone floor.

My body shook, rage battling with despair. So close, I was so close to freedom I could taste it. Yet, I couldn't feed.

Another arrow flew with deadly accuracy at my head.

"*Sphara!*" I cried. To my disappointment, nothing happened. No magic. I remained bound. Inches from me, I knocked the arrow away with my sword. Pushing aside the defeat, I stood up and focused my mind. Septimus's key should work. It should free me. The blasted crystal binding my magic should come off. Again, I tugged at the crystal on my neck. It didn't budge. Then, I had no more time to think.

"You are dead, centurion." Sergius grunted behind me. He

lunged, swinging his axe at me. I kicked him again, in his groin. As he doubled over, I lifted my sword. I could have easily sliced his throat. A movement at the bedside caught my attention. The boy, his innocent face, peered at me with wide eyes, and I hesitated for a moment. One moment. Then, I ran Sergius's heart through with the sword. He made gurgling sounds as I pushed him off my blade with a foot. The dead soldier fell to the ground in a pool of his own blood.

I turned to the boy. "It's all right—"

The boy grabbed a fallen knife and hurled himself at me. I flexed my fingers and said, "*Zyayti.*" Nothing happened. I could have cried. Instead, I cold-cocked the kid. He crumpled to the floor. I caught him before he hit the ground and put him on the bed. Mustering up my energy, I grabbed a candle and went into the hidden room.

Light illuminated a room stacked neatly with shining coins and bejeweled artifacts. The amount of gold had me swallowing my own tongue. However, the true treasure stood in front, guarding the bounty. Flickers from the fireball glanced off the flaxen highlights in the hair of a small child, roughly four years of age. Garbed in a dress of fine purple, her tiny, piquant face held a bow with a notched arrow. My savior.

I mumbled, "Rescued by a little girl. I'll never live this down."

The pointed end of the notched arrow followed me as I approached her. It was her last arrow yet her big brown eyes, identical to Lady Aldith's, watched with unworried defiance. Her nose wrinkling, she favored me with a truly adorable frown.

"I'm not a girl, Roman," she spat at me. "I am a princess."

I raised a brow. "Nor am I a Roman, princess. I am Briton."

## GARDEN OF EDEN

A violent downshift of wind caused the airplane to wobble from turbulence. Inside its airy cabin, my eyes snapped open.

"*Dorothy.*" Vane groaned in my head. "*That's enough. I never wanted you to see that.*"

My fingers jerked open and the amulet fell from my hand back into the safety of my pocket. My body shook, but it wasn't because of the cold, sterile air blasting from the vents above me. I dug fingernails deep into the hard bench of the divan. Never had I pictured such vivid brutality in a dream—no, memory. It was a memory. Just as I'd seen Matt's when we shared a link, I had to be seeing Vane's memories. The scenes coated my tongue, leaving a sharp and bitter taste. Their impressions in my mind ran deep, but I sensed they only scratched the surface of a staggering horror. How did he survive it?

How did he retain his sanity?

Well, admittedly, he walked close to the line. Until the trident, though, he was in control. Now, I had no idea what he was. *Dammit.* I shouldn't have let him startle me into dropping the amulet. I wanted to know more... a lot more. Although, I wasn't sure I could handle the knowledge.

The plane dipped and started descending. We had to be getting close to our destination. I pushed open the plastic shutter of a nearby window just a crack. Darkness with a hint of light colored the sky outside as dawn approached. It was a short flight. Under us, blue water stretched out and I wondered where we were.

Raj asked the question for me. He walked down the aisle, having descended from a visit to the cockpit, and stopped in front of Matt. "The pilot says it will be another twenty minutes. Will you tell me where we're going? Or should I read the signs at the airport?"

Matt gave a small laugh. "Your friends tell me you know it well. We'll land in Colombo and take a van to Ella."

"Ella. Colombo," Raj repeated. "We're in Sri Lanka."

Matt's head bobbed.

Raj continued, "This week is the Vesak Poya festival. Buddha Day."

"Rather opportune, wouldn't you say? It's the prefect time to visit the hidden caves."

"That's where you think the Healing Cup is?"

"It's my best guess," Matt replied.

"Good enough for me, Master Merlin," Raj raised his hand, which glowed with red magic. "I will let you know how it turns out."

"What?" Matt said.

I threw off the blanket and jumped up. "Matt!"

Raj's attention shifted to me, eyes widening in surprise. "Sword-bearer. This is a surprise. I am not supposed to harm Merlin, but your death would be worth much." He extended his hand, palm forward, and sent a stream of magic at me. "*Mrayati!*"

Matt threw himself in front of him. He absorbed the blast. It glanced off him. Matt tossed what looked like a glass vial at Raj. A puff of red dust exploded in Raj's face. Raj screamed and clutched his throat before slumping to the floor.

I ran down the narrow aisle to Matt. Grabbing his shoulder, I pulled him down a bit and rose up on tiptoes to peer over him. "Is he dead? Are you all right?" I yanked Matt around to face me and started patting his chest. Raj's blast had hit him dead-on. I demanded, "What was that?"

Matt caught my hands and held them still. A chain dangled from his neck. The topaz gemstone inside it was shattered. "Just because I have no magic, Ryan, it doesn't mean I'm no longer a wizard."

I relaxed. "A charm."

"Better than armor, but only good for one use." Matt yanked off the chain with one hand and tossed it aside.

"You killed him," said a mild voice from behind Matt.

He jerked sideways. The flight attendant, a slim man with closely cropped hair and a hooked nose, knelt down to Raj. Wearing a simple navy suit and white dress shirt, he held a handgun in a casual grip.

Matt's fingers tightened on my arm. "Who are you?"

"SIS. Secret Intelligence Service," Hooked-Nose said. "I was assigned to watch you."

"Assigned by who? The Queen—" I started to say.

"Don't tell him anything, Ryan." Matt stopped me. I blinked when he held up another vial that seemed to come out of nowhere. He demanded, "What do you know of us, Regular?"

"I know that you have about half-a-million pounds worth of magical amulets and potions in that bag." Hooked-Nose pointed to a black duffel bag tucked under Matt's seat.

"Half-a-million," I repeated. I knew that selling magic was lucrative. Grey's family had gotten rich off that commodity for centuries. Having never bought the stuff, though, I never knew how much. I frowned. "Did you buy it here? How did Raj not know?"

"The local wizards don't have enough. Magic may have originated here, but the wizard population is still very low. Every ounce is sold as soon they can make it. I didn't want to take their supply. I took this from Sylvia in Greece as backup."

Sylvia. Grey's mom. My adoptive mother. I muttered, "You brought it this whole way without telling us. More secrets, Merlin?"

"Sometimes discretion is necessary." Hooked-Nose stood up. "I think introductions are in order. My name is Robin Chaucer. I work under the Foreign Secretary. Her Majesty has contacted the prime minister. The MP was called in regards to the threat we now face."

"It's James Bond," I whispered to Matt.

"Who? Never mind," Matt replied. "He's a Regular. We can't trust him."

I rolled my eyes. "You sound like Vane. I'm a Regular. Anyway, just call the First Member and we can confirm everything."

Robin said, "You could, but before you do, you should consider Raj—a wizard of position in this region, difficult to corrupt, yet he was corrupted. The question remains by whom? Who do you trust, Merlin?"

Matt threw a red vial in his face. "Not you."

Robin's eyes widened with a surprised look just before the vial exploded in his face. Red powder puffed in the air. He slumped down next to Raj. I gaped at Matt. "What the hell, Merlin?"

"They're not dead, just asleep," Matt said.

With a frown, I crossed to Robin and leaned down to check his pulse. It pounded strongly against his neck. I checked Raj's. His skin, although still warm, felt different. I checked his neck. I couldn't feel a pulse.

"It's just a sleeping potion. I threw a little bit too much at Raj." Matt moved my fingers directly on Raj's chest and pressed deep. Under the skin, life thrummed.

I sighed in relief and sat back on my haunches. "Why would Raj attack you?"

"Vane—"

"Not everything goes back to him," I exclaimed.

"He convinced the wizards to follow him once before."

I stared at him. "Why are you so bent on hating him? Do you know what happened to him after he was forced to leave you?"

"There was no force. He left," he retorted. Then, his eyes narrowed. "You're seeing his memories."

I said, "They're pretty gruesome. He fought in Carthage—"

"You can't allow the past to affect you. He had a difficult childhood. It happens. So did I. It's what he's chosen to do now that terrifies me. He's bent on power, Ryan. He always will be. His past has made him so, but his current actions can't be excused because of it."

"I know that—" I stumbled when the plane sunk, beginning its final descent.

"We should strap in." Matt grabbed me by the arm and hauled me into a nearby seat. He threw himself into the seat opposite me. His face was tight with a tinge of a sickly glaze to it. He grabbed the sick bag from a side pocket built into the seat and clutched the paper bag like a lifeline. "You shouldn't have stowed along."

"You shouldn't have tried to sneak off." Wisps of hair hung over my eyes. I blew at them. "We're in this together. No matter how upset you are at me."

"I thought we were in it together," Matt retorted. "You're incapable of listening, aren't you? Is it really so hard to understand why I don't want you along for this? You are tied to Vane. I don't want him to know what I am doing."

"Good plan, Merlin." I stuck out a thumb at the prostrate Robin and Raj. "Seems like the whole keeping it secret thing worked really well."

Matt's expression turned grumpy. "Secrets never seem to work well in this century."

"You might consider updating your philosophy."

The amber in Matt's eyes flashed. "Thanks to you, it's all I have left."

His words punched me somewhere low. "Not all."

Matt didn't reply. After we touched down on a secluded airstrip in Colombo, Sri Lanka, Matt threw more sleeping potions at the two pilots upon landing. We pushed the plane's aft door open and extended the stowed air stairs. They slid forward on rails and unfolded outward. We avoided the waiting pit crew fairly easily. After a quick exchange of immigration cards and previously completed forms (from the date Matt filled out on the form, I realized he'd been planning this trip since Greece), we exited the airport. Gloomy clouds hovered over the horizon, yet the sight of them finally eased the tension in my shoulders. With some magical inducement, the men in white customs uniforms inspected the questionable items in his bag. I wasn't keen to be detained in a country where a singular conviction of smuggling resulted in hanging.

Matt pulled me toward a waiting line of taxis. I watched a man in a business suit negotiate a fare with the taxi before accepting the ride, and did the same. I made Matt squeeze into the narrow backseat of a yellow-black, three-wheeled tuk tuk, barely big enough for two. It may have not been the best choice to pick a three-wheeler in the dust and smog of the city, but I'd always wanted to ride one. In the front, where the driver sat on a seat that looked more like a stool, there were no doors. In the backseat, the windows were cutouts without any glass. An unused mileage counter shuddered in the wind as the taxi flew down an open highway.

We sped past white-sand beaches. Hard bits of salty rain peppered us like miniscule bullets. Deep blue ocean and an abundant sprinkling of greenery stretched as far as the eye could see on one side of the taxi (my side). The swaying palm trees attested to the fact that we were traveling the outskirts of a huge island. On the other side (Matt's side), exhaust fumes and clouds of smog that went hand-in-hand with emerging industrialization were his only view. We passed beachfront hotels. Many appeared recently renovated, still bearing the marks of the 2004 tsunami that devastated the region. People streamed through the streets. Street vendors reopened their shuttered shops as the latest threat of a tsunami abated.

The three-wheeler tuk tuk turned off towards the city center and crossed a small lake in the middle. Men in paddleboats rowed casually along it. Huge Buddhist statues hugged the bridges. However, the soothing sounds of the ocean quickly disappeared under a layer of diesel-induced smog and billboards with squiggly writing. Renovated Colonial forts interspersed with glass high-rise buildings. In a cacophony of honking horns and fast-talking locals, the three-wheeler squeezed into a narrow street and through the heart of a bazaar. Shops and department stores advertised various clothing and crafts in rupee amounts. Then, the smell of rice and colored curries hit my nostrils.

My stomach rumbled. Loudly. "Matt—"

He groaned. "We might miss the train."

"We'll get another one." I lowered my voice. "Anyway, I need to get supplies—"

"We'll get them later."

I raised a brow. "In the middle of nowhere? Do you really want to watch me wash my undies every day?"

Matt turned red in the face. I almost laughed, not surprised he was the sort that any mention of the unmentionables would send him into a dither. He scowled at me as if to say he knew what I was pulling, but despite a downpour of rain, he tapped the driver's shoulder.

"Stop here."

A lunch of yellow curried vegetables with a hint of coconut, white rice, and a mango smoothie (called a "lassie" by the waiter) later, I made quick work of gathering a few supplies. Mostly. When a shop full of gorgeous patterned sarongs, waving in the wind like banners, beckoned me closer, Matt adroitly pushed me into a yawn-inducing luggage store instead. I got a backpack—a rucksack, as he called it—to haul around with me.

An hour after our impromptu stop, Matt hustled me back into another three-wheeler. It was a short ride under grey skies and industrial-tinged rain to the Colombo Fort train station. The sudden jerk of the rickshaw, to avoid an unmindful pedestrian, jarred me. I was holding a metal pole on the partition that separated the driver from the passengers, but my hand slipped and Matt caught me as I flew back into him. There were no seat belts. Matt's arm went around my waist to hold me steady. His breath blew warmly against my nape. I grabbed the pole that framed the window and pushed away from him, scooting along the torn pleather seat. He let me go.

But then, he was always letting me go.

Inside the station, Matt managed to get tickets on a departing diesel train for a second-class cabin (only a limited number of trains had first-class cabins)—which meant no air-conditioning during the ride. Inside the train station, beautiful, whitewashed wooden railings and walkways crossed over barren concrete platforms below. Like the rest of the city, old Colonial architecture shone amidst modern industrialized steel.

A khaki-uniformed guard with a long rifle walked in front of me. From passing knowledge, I knew the country had recently ended a thirty-year civil war. The Tamil Tigers, a separatist liberation group in northeast Sri Lanka, continually used suicide-bombers to target civilians, until their defeat by the government in 2009. I was glad we were heading toward the middle of the country, and not the north.

The diesel train pulled forward onto the platform: a long metal snake with stripes of rusty red and blotchy white. Scratches and dents marred its sides, indicating the age of the workhorse engine. Matt and I climbed up steep steps into the railway car. Rows of two seats per side made up the interior. In a few minutes, every seat was filled, and by that time, the train started. A gang of boys in similar short-sleeved, plaid cotton shirts and dark trousers stood at the ends of the compartment just at the exits, presumably poised to jump out if the conductor asked for their tickets.

Once we left the city, the true journey began. Almost immediately, the sights turned rural. The only thing consistent was an on-again, off-again downpour of rain. Sharp ash that caked my nostrils cleared, only to be replaced with the smell of lush foliage. The countryside afforded absolutely stunning sights of verdant fields, colorful flowers, and wet, sloping hillsides. I imagined myself taking a train ride through the Garden of Eden.

We passed farms upon farms, and hills with steps carved into them. There were small villages marked by domed, white temples. Railroad tracks took us across high, Roman-built bridges with arched columns over crisp blue waters. Locals in a mixture of western (shirts and khakis) and traditional (sarongs and saris) clothing chattered with tourists. Merchants passed through the car, offering snacks (very popular) and tea (even more popular).

While I gaped at scenery, Matt studied a guidebook. He bought it at the bazaar in Colombo. It completely captured his interest. A little girl with pigtails, braided and tied at the ends with bright red bows, hung over the seat in front of us. She stared at Matt with huge eyes. I smiled at her and she giggled. Matt glanced at her briefly, then went back to reading his book. The little girl's lip stuck out in a disappointed pout before she flounced around and sank back into her seat.

I could picture Vane laughing with her. He had a soft spot for children. The young siblings of the other lacrosse players back home had loved Coach Vane. (He always found little jobs on the field for them to do. It worked even better than ice cream.) Shaking my head at the unexpected pang the memory caused, I tugged at Matt's sleeve. "You're missing everything."

"I'm not here to enjoy the landscape, Ryan," Matt replied without looking up from a guidebook that must have also contained the secrets of the universe.

"Live a little." We passed yet another towering waterfall nestled in the crevices of a hill.

Matt shrugged. "I prefer to make sure we're not all dead soon."

*Which, apparently, was my preference.* I ground my teeth. "How long are you going to be upset with me?"

"I'm not upset."

*Yeah, right.* I asked, "Then what?"

He stared at the guidebook. "My power in Vane's hands is more than simply not good. It is catastrophic. He'll use what he learns to stack the odds in his favor."

"Stack the odds in *our* favor," I argued.

"If only I could believe that."

I sighed. It was not an argument I was going to win, because everything I'd seen in Vane's memories so far led me to believe

Matt was right. Vane only listened to himself. Unlike Matt, though, I was banking on the hunch that the two end goals were one and the same. Then, I spotted the tight lines at the edges of Matt's lips. He was holding something back. It didn't surprise me, but again, it hurt and I was tired of feeling hurt.

The train crossed a small town. At its center stood a temple with a giant statute of a chubby-cheeked monkey. Matt's head jerked up to study the passing statue.

"That's Hanuman." Matt flipped through the pages of the guidebook. "It says here—in the epic, Ramayana, the monkey god helped rescue Princess Seetha. King Rawana kidnapped her and took her to his home in ancient Lanka. He hoped to woo her into becoming one of his wives. Prince Rama came to rescue her after Hanuman found her. Rama's and Rawana's armies battled across the island until Rama finally defeated the king in battle."

"Why do I care?" I leaned back against the hard plastic of the seat. A gust of cool wind through the open window made my hair dance. I tamed it as best I could. The temperature dropped as the sun sank lower into the horizon.

"King Rawana was said to be a master of astrology. Supposedly, the creator god, Brahma, gave him the nectar of immortality as a celestial gift."

"You think he had the Healing Cup—"

Matt put a hand over my mouth and glanced around the train. People continued to chatter on without paying any attention to us.

"Ease up, Merlin." I pushed his hand away.

"I don't want to run into another Robin Chaucer."

"How do you know Robin wouldn't have helped us? It was Raj who attacked us."

"He's a Regular. He'll only get in the way."

It was an arrogant statement Vane would have definitely made, and yet, coming from Matt, it left me momentarily speechless. "*I'm* a Regular."

"Of course you are," Matt said in a placating tone. His voice lowered. "Listen, I'm not sure how it's all connected, except every instinct I have tells me that the answers we seek lie here. Our foundations go back to this region—"

"What do you mean the foundations? How so?"

"The Council theorizes that the Keltoi emerged first in the civilizations of the Indus Valley roughly in 3000 BCE."

The wizards called themselves *Keltoi*. It was some kind of ancient name.

Matt continued, "Sects of the Indus people migrated across Mesopotamia, Greece, and up into Western Europe. Among them, us. If you follow the derivation of languages spoken in the region today, you can follow the migration of magi—" With another furtive glance over his shoulder, he lowered his voice. "Our people."

He raked a hand through brown, shaggy hair. "But more than that, I get the feeling that we're supposed to be here. That we didn't wind up in this place… at this time… by coincidence."

"What do you mean?"

"The Lady knew what would happen once the Fisher King awoke. She knew we'd come to this region to avert the disaster."

The more I learned of the Lady, the less I liked her. Now, she got credit for my decisions too. "*I* made us come here. You wanted to go back to England, remember? Anyway, Bran of Pellam took the Healing Cup to Aegae."

"I'm not so sure. From what I could glean from Lelex, the mermaids beheaded Bran in Aegae. One version of the Fisher King story says as much—that the head of the king came back and was buried, and its magic protected the Island of Britain from marauders thereafter."

I rolled my eyes. *Boy, had they been wrong about that. The Vikings sacked Britain for a hundred or so years after Arthur.*

Matt continued, "The point is—the mermaids never had the Cup. Galahad and Perceval must have found it. In the legends, it's not clear which one got the cup. They were supposed to bring it back to Britannia, but Galahad never returned."

I blinked. "I thought you sent Galahad after the Cup. Who is Perceval?"

"Actually, three set out after the Fisher King. Perceval, Galahad, and Bors. I didn't mention it before because it was irrelevant. From what I've been able to glean, only one of them seemed to have actually gotten the Cup. Also, Vane and Perceval were close. It happened a long time ago, but I didn't want to remind Vane of him."

I stared at him. He'd just made a small admission that he actually cared enough to spare his brother's feelings. Was I ever going to understand these two? I cleared my throat. "Vane and Perceval?"

"Vane brought Perceval to Camelot with him. Perceval was the youngest son of a noble. He was orphaned and Vane trained him. In turn, Perceval worshipped Vane." Matt muttered, "Seems he has a thing for orphans."

That dig was directed at me. I ignored it since I heard an underlying edge to his tone. He'd been jealous. *Wow, Merlin jealous.* My head swam with the insight. Then, it clicked. "Was Perceval from Carthage?"

"Yes, that is where Vane found him. You've seen him in Vane's memories?"

I nodded.

"As I said, they were close." He went back to reading the guidebook.

My eyes raked over Matt's profile. The straight line of his jaw was so similar to Vane's. Yet, I could never get a good handle on who he was—Matt or Merlin. Matt, I could trust. Merlin, I never had. Matt would save his brother. Would Merlin? After what I'd seen of Vane's memories, their animosity didn't make sense. When had it all gone so wrong? At least the brothers felt so strongly about each other once, it gave me hope that they would again.

It also made me wonder if I made a distinction in my head that wasn't there. Matt or Merlin. Either way, be it Matt and Ryan or Merlin and Ryan, we were at a standoff.

I took the first step. "Matt, I need to tell you something. Vane had a vision about you."

We pulled up into a train station as the train screeched to a halt. More rain poured over the steel roof of a thin concrete platform. A sign declared the stop to be the city of Kandy. Decorative, twinkling lights and bright lanterns were strung across the platform. At its center, a banner celebrated the upcoming Vesak Poya festival. We were halfway to Ella.

\*\*\*

Almost four hours later, I sat, annoyed, in the train. So much for taking the first step—I may as well have not said anything. Beside me, Matt flipped through the guidebook. He'd already read twice. I seriously considered chucking it out the window. His reaction to Vane's vision had been two underwhelming sentences. "It doesn't change my plans. Believe me, I know what I'm doing." Then, he turned back to the guidebook and buried his nose in its pages without speaking another word.

*Boys,* I cursed.

The train took us closer to the mountains in the middle of the island and up into the hills and higher elevation. Outside, the dense foliage resembled a jungle. We passed through a short tunnel, hewn out of rock, and the countryside opened to the sky. Tidy rows of tea bushes layered hillside terraces of a large tea estate. At its center, I spotted a stately white Colonial house.

Matt shut the guidebook and stared out the window in silence.

"No," I burst out. "I refuse to believe that's your whole reaction to the vision. There's more to it. I know it. So do you. So what are you not wanting to say? What are you holding back this time, Merlin?"

He said softly, "I already trusted you once, Ryan."

*And you betrayed me.* The unspoken words reverberated in my head, cutting deep into my heart. I took a breath, and let it out. "I can't change what I did."

"No, you can't."

He was making me crazy. I sighed. "Can you, for one minute, stop feeling sorry for yourself?"

"I might if you'd bother to help me fix what you've broken instead of wasting time admiring the countryside."

I glared at him. "Why do you think I'm here?"

"Why are you? I might deal in half-truths, but at least I haven't been lying to myself."

"What does that mean?"

Matt dropped the guidebook on my lap. "It means you can't have it both ways, Ryan. You can't believe in Vane and me at the same time. Only one of us is right."

I didn't think he was talking about belief.

The train pulled up onto a long platform of another small town. A sign declared it as "Nanu Oya." More old-fashioned oil lanterns lined the platform's ceilings. Colorful hanging baskets of orchids swayed in the cool breeze of the darkening sky. The train pulled to a screeching halt. I watched as those around us jumped up and began to grab bags from the metal overhead shelves that lined both sides of the compartment.

Matt got up and reached for his bag from the overhead rack. His action treated me to a nice expanse of bare skin. He turned to walk off.

I jumped up. "Matt, this conversation is not over."

A few tourists watched us with avid eyes as they took their bags and half-dragged themselves away from the unfolding drama. I flushed under the heat of their scrutiny.

Matt grabbed my backpack and held it out to me. "We're here. This is our stop."

I blinked. "Th-this isn't the stop for Ella."

"I realize that."

Realization hit me, too. I scowled at him. "You lied to Raj."

"Of course I did," Matt said without remorse. "Don't tell me you're actually surprised?"

*** 

Half an hour later, I wondered what the punishment in Sri Lanka was for strangling someone. I hiked uphill, following the bane of my current existence along a muddy trail that squished sticky goo into my brand-new Vans. The tennis shoes managed to survive the mucky streets of Chennai only to be decimated in a hill station full of super-clean, cobblestone walkways. The town boasted Colonial-style bungalow houses with perfectly manicured lawns, a replica of any small village from England. None of which, however, were on the trail Matt wisely chose for us to take... for no other reason than a perverse desire to torture me.

"Nuwara Eliya. Nickname: Little England," I read from the guidebook and trudged along behind Matt. I flipped the page. "In the central highlands of Ceylon, as Sri Lanka was called during its British occupation, the hill country retreat became a private sanctuary for colonists, civil servants, and tea planters where they engaged in their favorite pastimes of hunting, polo, golf, and cricket."

I snapped the guidebook shut. "At least it's not raining."

The valley below showed off another beautiful waterfall, streaming down between the crevices of a green-carpeted hill, which was lined with neatly manicured hedgerows of tea bushes.

"Where are we going?" I asked.

"To the hotel," Matt answered as he continued up a hill of mostly mud.

I took a few more squishy steps forward. "Why didn't we take a taxi?"

"We need to save the cash," he called back.

"Then, why are we staying at a hotel?"

"It's already paid for, and since I made the arrangements myself, I doubt we'll be found."

"You doubt or you're certain?"

"Do you want a shower?"

I shut up… for about a second. "Are you sure we're going the right way? There are no signs on this road."

"It's a shortcut."

The sky rumbled with laughter. Trickles of rain sprinkled, tapping a happy dance on my head. I pulled my rain poncho around me, which did nothing for the cold, while debating whether or not to throw the guidebook at the back of Matt's head. "I'm hungry."

Matt stopped. He waited for me to catch up and took the guidebook from me. He tucked it into his bag protectively. I made a face. He *would* save it from a soaking, but not me.

With a small, internal growl, I pushed ahead. We reached the top a few minutes later. The ground leveled and we passed through a barrier of trees. I almost cried at the sight in front of me. Soft rain kissed the slanted roof of a beautiful white plantation house with a wrap-around porch. Painted railings framed small balconies on the second floor, and halogen bulbs spotlighted a garden with a quiet pond. In the middle of an island jungle, I managed to find a slice of Georgia heaven.

"St. Elizabeth's Hotel," Matt announced.

"Room service," I said happily. Despite aching muscles and an unstable muddy path, I practically ran to the hotel's stone walkway. I tugged off my ruined shoes before rushing into the lobby.

A clerk in a crisp white uniform and thin mustache eyed me with misgiving, but smiled at Matt. "You will be on the second floor. You were fortunate, Master Northe, because of the festival we've been completely booked for months." The clerk's smile dimmed as he turned to me. His nose angled down at the sight of my dirt-caked khakis and bare feet. "If *Memsahib* would like, we also have a full-service laundry available."

I resisted rolling my eyes. "*Memsahib* would like some tea. Can you bring it to the room? Oh, and a dinner menu."

The clerk perked up. "We serve a high tea in the evenings with a variety of casseroles, meat pies, and a scrumptious milk cake for dessert. Of course, our restaurant has some wonderful local dishes the chef's prepared for dinner."

I perked up too. "Really? What kind of dishes?"

"A blend of Indian and Colonial—"

"Tea sounds perfect." Matt took my elbow and steered me away. "Send it to our room. We'll eat there."

"What's your rush, Master *Northe*?" I pulled my arm away from Matt. We crossed the small lobby and bypassed a narrow elevator to go up carpeted, wooden stairs. I lowered my voice and asked, "What's a *memsahib*?"

"I think the translation is 'rich European married woman.'"

"I'm not European," I sniffed. "And right now, I'm dirt broke."

"You're also not married—"

"If you tell me I'm not a woman, I'm going to hit you," I retorted.

"I haven't said anything," he said with a straight face.

I didn't believe him at all. Rustic wooden tables and oil landscapes lined the long hallway on the second floor. The dark color of the wood made the space seem smaller, and suddenly I became acutely aware that Matt and I were essentially alone. To break the silence, I asked, "Why are we using Vane's name?"

"I have a credit card in his name he doesn't know about."

"What? How?"

Matt shrugged. "Just because I don't like to use technology doesn't mean I can't."

I narrowed my eyes. "Grey helped you, didn't he?"

"I don't reveal my sources," he deadpanned, stopping so suddenly I almost ran into him. "Does it bother you, Mrs. Northe?"

It did. Worse, it pulled at me. A gut-wrenching smack in the face of what might have been. And here I was—standing in the middle of a strange country with someone who looked so much like Vane. I said softly, "Would you like to be called by your ex-girlfriend's name?"

"You're my only ex-girlfriend," he replied.

The long hallway had run out of room. "We went on two dates, Matt. I don't think it counts."

Soulful amber eyes locked on me. "It counts to me."

"You texted me to break up!"

"I texted you to say I needed some time."

I moved to enter past him. "It doesn't matter."

He caught my elbow and stopped me. "I apologize if my high school speak is off."

"You wouldn't have done anything differently." I faced him. "You would have still chosen the visions."

"We've been over this. The future—our future—depends on them."

"Not anymore."

I wasn't surprised when Matt didn't reply, although part of me secretly hoped he would. The part of me secretly glad to have this time with Matt. Despite the end of the world looming over the horizon, or maybe because of it, I wanted to find out where we stood with each other.

He started walking. We reached our room in a few steps. Matt used a key—a real iron key, not a keycard—to open the door. I walked past him into the room. The best thing in the grand room was a canopied king-sized bed in the middle of it. A white mosquito net draped the sides of the green fabric bed canopy. Thick, spring-green curtains dressed the sides of the glass-paned windows. In front of the bed, rich red cushions adorned a short divan sofa. Several tartan pillows added to the woodsy Colonial décor. A palm tree swayed just outside.

Matt pulled the curtains closed. "We should sleep soon. We have to be up in four hours."

I threw my backpack on a low wood table. "Huh?"

"We're going to climb up Adam's Peak. It's going to take an hour by car to get there. The guidebook says to see the sunrise— which is the best part of the climb—you should start at one a.m."

"We're going sightseeing?"

"No, we're going to see a shrine at the top of the mountain while everyone else is distracted."

The crumb of information was all the explanation I got before Matt picked up the phone and asked the front desk to arrange for a car. With a sigh, I headed to the bathroom for a much needed shower. The bathroom had no lock and a transparent shower curtain. I grimaced, but decided I wanted a shower too much to be overly concerned. A glance in the mirror made me grimace more. Streaks of dirt covered my face and my hair—well, let's just say that open train windows really miffed the hair-gods, and I found myself with a giant poof of hair that could have trumped any '80s Dallas Cowboy cheerleader's 'do.

Two minutes after I got into the shower, Matt banged on the door. "Food is here."

I turned off the mostly cold shower—tropical resorts don't believe in hot water—and hurriedly got dressed. I pulled on long pajama bottoms—this part of Asia had no concept of shorts (someone might see my ankles and be offended, while bare midriffs on saris produced yawns)—and a long-sleeved top with a tank. I bought the tank separately—an item too shocking to be sold with the pajama set itself. Okay, I sounded bratty, even to myself. I ran my fingers through tangled wet hair and winced as it strained the follicles.

It's just that—I missed home.

I yanked the door open to find Matt standing outside, one hand lifted in the air, mid-knock. His thin T-shirt stretched over his long, lean chest. A soft rumble of want flickered in his eyes. I must have stared too long because he dropped his arm, mumbling, "Let's eat."

I stared after him, my nerves jangling. To my surprise, a small dining table was already set up, the food divided on two plates, and steaming hot cups of tea were poured. Matt sat down. I pulled out my chair and did the same. Vane always waited for me to sit first. Without looking at me, Matt pulled out the same blue guidebook from the train and started reading as he ate. Conversation was not on the menu, it seemed.

I was too hungry to care. I mostly polished off my plate and tea while Matt took small bites of his as he read. Nearly satiated, I paused to chew. "If we have to get up early, should I set an alarm?"

Matt didn't look up from the guidebook.

I waved a hand in front of his face. "Matt, did you arrange for a wake-up call?"

"Hmm…." He flipped a page on the guidebook, taking a bite.

I put down my fork with a sharp clank. "Are you being annoying on purpose? Because it's working."

Matt shut the book and lifted his head to blink at me. He glanced at my finished plate. "The hike up the mountain is long. You should get some sleep. I've asked for a wake-up call."

He was the worst road trip companion. Ever.

I ground my teeth. "Are you going to try to ditch me again while I sleep?"

"I would," he answered bluntly. "If I didn't think you would get into more trouble on your own."

"Thank you. I'm so glad you hold me in such high opinion." I wiped my mouth with a napkin and threw it down at the table before stomping to the bed. "The sofa's all yours."

Matt groaned. "I'm a full head taller than you."

"Don't forget to light the repellent," I said sweetly, pointing to a small plastic burner on the table with a citronella gel pack on top. "The bugs can get nasty."

"They're not the only ones," he muttered.

I climbed onto the large bed, pulling the mosquito net shut. I took off the scratchy pajama top to sleep in the tank. Lying down, I let out a yawn. A hard object jabbed my side. I reached into the pocket of my pajamas and pulled out the *Dragon's Eye* still wrapped in its handkerchief.

Matt yanked the mosquito net open, his expression seething. He tried to grab the necklace, but I managed to hold onto it.

"You are not talking to him," he said with wild eyes. "There is too much at stake."

*He was deranged*, I decided. "I was putting the necklace aside so I could sleep."

He paused, our hands remaining locked in battle. Still, suspicious eyes traveled over me as if he could find some lie in my statement. Then, his brown irises roved on my tank.

My breath hitched.

A flush climbed up to his hairline. "I'll let you get to sleep."

He yanked the white net shut. I fell back against the pillow.

The net yanked open again. Brown, shaggy hair fell over his forehead. "Tell me one thing. Why did you do it?"

I inclined my head on the soft pillow and asked, "Do what?"

"Why did you sacrifice me to Vane so easily?"

Every strand of hair on my arms rose at the intensity in his eyes. He gripped the mosquito net so tightly I thought he might rip it. I sank deeper into the bed's pristine white sheets. "What do you want me to say that I haven't already, Matt?"

"Say you regret it. Say you're sorry. Say you feel something. Anything."

I took in a breath.

"Tell me you haven't fallen in love with him."

The breath whooshed out of me. *So that was it.*

I sat up. I swung my legs off the warm bed and onto cold hardwood planks. I stood up. Desire exuded from his body, but I couldn't touch him. Hollowness made my bones brittle. We remained a few inches apart, not touching. I said, "Would it make it easier if I was?"

"I don't know," he replied hoarsely.

The atmosphere around us seemed to electrify. Two hands slid along either side of my face, cupping it. His fingers tangled in my hair as he crossed them at the base of my nape. Exerting pressure, he turned my face up. In the dim light of the room, shadows danced across his face, obscuring his expression. Hot breath kissed my skin.

He leaned closer and whispered into my ear, "Do you know the one good thing about not having any visions?"

"I hadn't thought about it," I replied.

I hadn't thought about it, but I knew. My daughter of Apollo status stopped his visions. It kept us apart for so long, but now the visions were gone. I flexed my fingers. In this moment, everything could change... if he wanted... if I wanted.

His expression set in brooding lines; his lips grazed mine.

I put a hand against his flat chest. Palm down, my fingers splayed against the surprisingly cool fabric of a soft, cotton t-shirt. Lean, warm muscles contracted underneath. Hot and cold, like him. Part of me wanted to curl my fingers into the invitation his body offered. Part of me held onto sanity. "Matt, we're here to get your powers back."

For the first time since the funeral, his expression held a hint of uncertainty. "Yes?"

I took a slow breath. *It was a question. As in "yes, should I care?"*

My nails dug into his T-shirt. I stood on the precipice. Our lips less than an inch away, all I had to do was lean forward one tiny fraction of space. The ends of the white mosquito net rustled in the breeze. My eyes fell on the bed. The ruby gemstone of the *Dragon's Eye* glinted against a white bedspread.

Matt followed my gaze to it. His expression hardened. "He's not here."

I met his eyes and held it. "You didn't answer—what do we do if you get your powers back?"

Matt blinked. "It doesn't matter right now."

A shaft of air, the same insidious breeze that called my attention to the amulet, chilled my heated skin. Defeat filled me. The answer lay there. I hadn't wanted to see it, but I couldn't deny it any longer. Was I just asking for too much?

I hugged myself. "It matters to me, Matt."

His lips thinned in irritation. "It doesn't mean that I don't care."

"Really?" I forced my gaze off the hard curve of his lips. My heart breaking a little, I asked, "When was the last time you actually smiled at me? A real smile?"

He let out a breath. "Ryan—"

"Think on it, Matt," I said softly. "And then, tell me you still care."

# IN THE FOOTSTEPS OF ALEXANDER, SON OF ZEUS

Adam's Peak. Fifty-two hundred steps. Three hours of climbing uphill to get to the top. It took us four. Not because we stopped to enjoy one of the numerous bakeries or tea shops that lined the trail to enjoy a meal together—no, because it takes two people actually talking to each other to know when the other one has wandered off.

Even though the bed was comfortable, I didn't get any sleep. I always figured when my heart fixed on someone there would be a sense of completion—instead I only got complication. Just the thought of Vane hurt. With Matt, I kept seeing the accusation in his gaze.

The flat steps were packed, even in the middle of the night, and especially during Vesak Poya season. Tourists and pilgrims flocked together up the mountain staircase. In the middle of the jungle, electric lights illuminated our path and chanting blared from loud speakers, creating an otherworldly atmosphere that was also heavily laden with incense.

Matt did a lot of backtracking down the trail to keep me in view as I enjoyed the sights—pocket villages, a few friendly dogs, statues of Buddha and Ganesha, along with small flags hung on ropes over the trail. I spent most of what little cash I had on the young children selling cheap souvenirs. Soon I had a collection of buttons, small flags, and stickers decorating my backpack.

Matt's impatient looks and even the insistent sprinkling of rain failed to make me hurry. It's not as if I was purposefully trying to irritate him, but I didn't feel the need to cater to his wants either. Approaching the top, the rain worsened and I gripped the railings to keep steady on the slippery, wet stone steps. Matt pulled out two plastic ponchos from his bag of tricks. I pulled one over my burnt-orange fleece. The green cargos I wore weren't completely waterproof, so my best hope was for them to dry quickly. Matt's outfit showed more preparedness. He wore a lined, burnt-orange jacket and green hiking pants. Although it wasn't planned, our colors matched. At least we complemented each other on some small level.

A few steps up, the scenery changed from jungle to cloud forest as the mist reflected various diaphanous shapes in the air. Graffiti marked the rocks with names and countries of origin of the former fellow travelers who'd come before us. Just before we reached the top, shivering from the gusts of wind, Matt picked up a few lotus flowers from a street vendor. For a second, I thought he'd bought them for me. When he tucked them into his shoulder bag, I told myself there was no pang of disappointment.

Scores of people crowded the last steps in the misting rain.

Nearly at the summit, a screeching blackbird flew over us as we poured into two narrow buildings. The buildings stood on either side of the steps, packing us in like sardines in a tin.

I could barely perceive the outline of the tiered rooftop on the Buddhist temple clinging to the mountain's peak. The triangular roof was said to match the perfect triangle of the mountain's shadow. I clung to Matt's hand to keep from falling.

Passing the crowd of shivering bodies, we finally emerged onto the narrow steps of a flat, white stone terrace. A huddle of buildings spanned the two levels of the summit. On the lower level were guest quarters for overnight stays. On the second level, just above the stairs, stood a belfry. A pilgrim could ring a tin bell once for every time he or she ascended the mountain.

We took off our shoes in deference to the holy ground. Along the two levels penned in by concrete ledges, people lined up to gaze out at the misty vistas of Sri Lanka. In one corner, a gorgeous view showed a cascade of waterfalls flowing down in faint silver, accenting dense green vegetation somewhere far across the island.

Matt pulled me toward the center of the terrace. A huge rock face marked the highest point of the peak. Over the rock, a concrete walkway supported a shrine and a small temple. The tiny shrine enclosed the sacred footprint, or Sri Pada.

Matt handed me one of the lotus flowers he'd bought.

"For luck," he said, and pointed to the top of the rock at the foot of the shrine. Touched by the sweet gesture, I placed it there. Many other lotus flowers decorated the rock. People crowded the railings, standing on top of small ledges, and taking up most of the free space in front of the temple. Fat raindrops wiggled down from the stormy sky. I looked into the sodden faces of the throng. I doubted we'd be seeing any sort of sunrise. Seeing their dour expressions, I knew they'd come to the same realization about the sunrise.

Matt cursed under his breath and squeezed back across the narrow space between drenched bodies until he reached one corner of the terrace. He drew out an amulet from the magic bag and put it on around his neck, shouting, "*Kavas.*"

People closest to us watched curiously, but thanks to the diversity of cultures and people, no one commented. Dark rain clouds began to clear. People first muttered, then cheered. They moved toward the outward edges of the terrace. Meanwhile, Matt hurried us in the opposite direction, back toward the sacred footprint shrine. He stopped at the base of the stairs that led up to the shrine, sandwiched between several hundred people.

Matt leaned close to my ear. "Be ready. As soon as the sun rises, the priests will start their prayer procession and the mountain will fall into shadow for twenty minutes."

Two minutes later, the beginnings of the most beautiful sunrise ever conceived broke over the summit as the clouds dissipated. An invisible Apollo rode his chariot across the heavens, ushering in the blue sky. The yellow-and-red fingers of the dawn dropped down and fire illuminated the dark island. On one side of the island, majestic mountains, lush green flora, snaked with silvery threads of waterfalls, sprouted from the fertile ground. On the other side, blue and purple lines evidenced a distant ocean.

Beside us, the morning prayer procession started down the temple steps in a thumping of drums. In a parade of saffron orange-yellow robes, monks emerged from the temple and everyone beside us turned to look. Those inside the shrine came out to stand on the steps. They watched the musicians in white muslin. Some banged on drums, some blew on trumpets, and others chanted. Beside us, the pilgrims held up platters of food and rice.

Matt and I snuck up the steps and into the emptied walkway. Plastic curtains kept out rain, protecting the closet-sized five-foot wide shrine. The shrine itself had two open sides, but a wall of people's backs closed off the walkway. Inside the cramped interior of the shrine, a golden half-door hung open above a platform. Curtains of white and yellow cloth draped the opening of the platform. Inside the cubby-like area lay the engraved footprint.

Matt drew out a vial from his bag and threw it above us. A bubble of blue magic surrounded us before it winked out. Without a word to me, he threw another vial at the rock. The rock blew apart, and with an ear-deafening bang, shrapnel flew at me.

"What are you doing?" I shouted, mindful of the people walling us in. They remained with their backs to us, their demeanors unperturbed.

"No one can hear outside the bubble," Matt said calmly.

"I hate treasure hunting with you." I eyed the people nervously, but no mob turned on us. Still, my nerves danced in panic. "Please tell me why you destroyed a sacred relic."

Matt pushed aside the broken rock. Just beneath the footprint he blew up sat another one. "This is the real relic. The top is only a plaster replica."

Outside, sunrise fully embraced the sky. People started to fall out of its trance.

I stared at the footprint. Smaller and rougher than the plaster one, it did look like it could belong to a thirty-five-foot-tall giant or a god. Buddha or Shiva's foot as he stepped on Earth, or Adam's footprint after his exile from the Garden of Eden. "I don't see the Healing Cup."

Matt frowned. "I thought there would be some kind of symbol or something."

"You're insane, Merlin," I hissed. "I thought you knew what you were doing."

"This is the spot. Adam's Peak. All the different legends converge here. The Buddhist's say the Triple Gem, their holy trinity, manifests when the shadow falls over the mountain during sunrise. Alexander the Great thought the same."

"What are you talking about?" I said.

Matt ignored me and continued to mutter, "He came here. He had to be right. This place is marked by the legends of gods. If they hid a secret, it will be here. They wouldn't leave a marker like this for no reason."

"They who?" From the open sides of the shrine, a burst of sunlight streamed onto the rock. I stepped closer to the exposed footprint and the rock started to hum. Out of instinct, I put my hand over the footprint. A shot of electricity from the rock zapped my hand. I pulled my hand back and shook it. "Whoa, what was that?"

Matt's face brightened. "A small portal."

"Like the one at the Seven Gables?"

Matt nodded.

"That was not fun." Watery death surrounded that portal. Matt drew out another vial from the bag. I grabbed his wrist. "You are not going to desecrate a sacred relic."

Matt smiled. "It's just your blood."

I squawked. "How do you have my blood?"

"Blood donations. After you became the sword-bearer, the First Member recovered all the deposits you've ever made."

"That's just creepy."

He raised a brow. "Vane tracked them all down."

"Really creepy," I repeated.

It reinforced my belief that I was just another commodity to the Wizard Council. Nearby us, people groaned. Grey rain clouds started to darken the horizon once more.

"Hurry," I urged.

Matt drew out another lotus bloom and threw it down. He poured the blood onto the footprint, on the heel at the same spot where the sunlight touched. Immediately, the rock rumbled. A small vortex of wind swirled around the room. A single beam of gold light shone upwards. Inside the beam shimmered a square metal cross. It was about a foot long with symbols engraved down one stem, the stipes. A red gem sat at the center of the cross like an ancient eye.

"It's a Greek cross," Matt said.

"How do you know?"

"I've seen it before. The Lady wore this on a chain." Matt reached out to take it.

I stopped him. "No, let me. It was my blood that opened it."

Matt nodded. I grabbed the small statue. It solidified in my hand, and then the shrine started trembling. Lines cracked through the floor around the sacred footprint. It started expanding outwards. The whole rock fell through the crack.

"Oh, crap," I said. "Why do these things always have booby traps?"

People turned to look at the commotion. Gasps of horror followed.

Matt grabbed my hand as he pushed into the crowd. "Because you're not actually supposed to find a relic unless you can prove you're worthy."

"We used my blood to get to it in the first place. How am I not worthy?"

"You don't have Excalibur," Matt pointed out.

I thrust the cross into my pocket. No one stopped us as we squeezed into the crowd. Everyone else wanted to get off the walkway, too. Behind us, the shrine shuddered. There must have been over a thousand people on the terrace who all began to panic. Under the howl of rain from above, the buildings on the summit shuddered and the whole mountain trembled.

"Is it the Total Tremor again?" a panicked tourist shouted.

We made it down the steps of the shrine. People streamed off the top levels toward the exits. The belfry tore apart. The pilgrim bell fell to the ground with a loud clang. Hysterical shrieks became louder. Huge blocks of stone tumbled off the collapsing shrine and temple. They landed like grenades on the terrace.

The charm around Matt's neck glowed, and somehow, a small space opened for us through the crowd of crazed humanity. We made it to one of the two narrow exits—steep steps that led down the mountain. Several people cried out under the onslaught of shrapnel rocks from the collapsing shrine. The river of humanity around us tightened as people shoved and fought to get to the exits.

Matt navigated me through them. I glanced behind me. The whole shrine had fallen into the sinkhole opened by the portal.

For a second, I thought the worst was over. Then, the mountain rumbled once more. A single crack extended from the spot where the shrine had been and out towards the huts in which the priests lived. The whole summit was going to collapse.

Those who were able-bodied streamed down the mountain as quickly as they could. Several elderly pilgrims huddled together, their mouths moving in silent prayer.

"Matt, there's no way these people are going to make it out," I shouted above the noise, yanking him to the side into a small, hidden corner under a rock outcropping.

"There's nothing we can do!" Matt yelled back. "Even if I used every charm I have, there's not enough magic to stop this."

I took hold of his chin and turned it so he could view the collapsing summit. The sinkhole widened. More people shrieked as they pushed forward. The monks were gathered beside the elderly, trying to help them join the fleeing visitors. "We did this, Matt. We have to help—"

Matt pulled away. "There is nothing I can do."

"Not you, but—" I pulled out the *Dragon's Eye* from my pocket and started to unwrap the handkerchief around it.

Matt grabbed my wrist. "No!"

With a quick, accomplished twist, I freed myself. "Do you have a better plan? Because I'm not letting a single person die up here because of us—that's not good enough for me."

Matt cursed. I saw him work over the possibilities before he came to the same conclusion. He took the amulet from me. "You're not doing this—I am."

I watched him unwrap the amulet. He touched its chain and it started to glow. I slapped my hand over his.

"Ryan—" Matt hissed.

I ignored him. I called urgently, "*Vane.*"

Closing my eyes, in my mind, I saw a shut, wooden door. Matt appeared beside me on a grey cloud. He wore his usual grumpy look. Around us, nothing existed but a hazy limbo. Underneath, we stood atop a surprisingly solid cloud. Matt lifted a medieval-looking door latch. The wooden door swung open toward us.

Vane lounged against its thick doorframe on the other side. "Both of you. You must be desperate."

"A mountain is collapsing," I said, trying not to squelch a visceral rush of pleasure at the mere sight of him.

"Interesting." He grinned as if he could read my thoughts—which he could. "And how did you do that?"

"It doesn't matter," said Matt quickly. "Can you stop it?"

Vane paused. "Adam's Peak."

Beside me, Matt ground his teeth. "Yes."

"Now, what could you possibly be doing there?"

"What do you want in exchange, Vane?" Matt ground out.

"Ah, you know me so well, brother." Vane smiled. "The snake, of course."

Matt scowled. He glanced at me. I raised my brow. As if he didn't know my answer.

"Agreed," Matt groused. "We'll leave it somewhere for you to pick up."

The green depths of Vane's eyes flickered. "Or you could take a sip now."

I shook my head. "It doesn't work on me."

"You tried? After I asked?" He smiled devastatingly.

The green in his eyes receded. I ignored my heart when it skipped a beat.

"You shouldn't have," Matt said furiously. "It could have killed her."

The clouds shifted under Matt and me, a rumble of distress reminding us of the mountain's shortening fuse. I stumbled. Matt caught and steadied me.

"Stop being a bastard," said Matt. "We agreed to your demands. Are you going to help or not?"

Green flashed in his eyes. The monster stirred. Its eyes locked on Matt's hands around my waist. Vane snapped his fingers. Matt disappeared.

"What?" I started, stumbling again with my support gone. I caught the doorframe with my hand. It brought me uncomfortably close to Vane.

Vane leaned into me. "He was getting tiresome."

I stayed in place. "Are you going to help or not, Vane?"

He looked at his cuticles with a bored expression. "There's the matter of price."

"Do you always have a price?"

"Always," he promised. Straightening away from the doorframe, he shook his finger at me. "Why didn't you tell me that the Medusa blood is gone?"

Matt had agreed too easily, and Vane had seen right through it. I swallowed. "What do you want, Vane?"

He leaned closer. Lips hovered over mine. Vane's hazel eyes with only a faint ring of green around the irises. He said, "You took the blood."

I was mesmerized. I whispered, "Yes."

His lips pressed hard, crushing soft flesh against unyielding teeth. Lightning in a bottle, electricity crackled across my lips. The ground shifted and I could have cared less, lost in the rapture of the kiss. The sensations spiked, threatening to overwhelm me. Then, he pushed deeper. His fingers tangled in my hair.

"*You're mine, sword-bearer*," the monster whispered.

I shoved at Vane's chest and pulled back, managing to add a few inches between us. "I don't belong to anyone."

Hard green covered his irises like a shield. "Did you kiss him yet?"

"Why do you care?"

Vane's lips twisted into an icy smile. "You're the sword-bearer. The fate of this world rests in whoever controls you."

I gasped. I couldn't help it. The cruel words ripped at the core of all my fears. My hand shot out to slap him. He caught it before I could connect with his cheek. His other hand tightened in the tresses of my hair, making me wince.

He growled, repeating, "Did. You. Kiss. Him?"

"None. Of. Your. Business."

"Good," he replied, seemingly satisfied.

I scowled.

Green receded from his eyes and he released me. "Put on the necklace. I'm not close to you and you don't have Excalibur. Channeling my power is not going to be easy."

"When is it ever easy with you?" I muttered.

A finger slid along the line of my jaw. "It could have been."

He snapped his fingers again and limbo began shifting. Fluffy bits of white cloud rose around me and hardened into forest-green hedges. The world darkened and we stood, once again, in the maze on Aegae. I gazed at Vane. The words we said—the decision I made when I didn't choose him—throbbed within the confines of the hedges. Silent shadows haunted the air, oppressive mournful shapes that threatened to swarm me, sucking the life from my bones.

Vane smiled. He was torturing me and he knew it.

Leaning down, he whispered into my ear, "Do you regret this yet?"

Tears prickled in my eyes, which I closed to hold back. To shut him out. I fought to keep holding on to myself. To survive this. To survive him.

I opened my eyes to find I was back on the mountain.

Matt stood in front of me. The mountain shook. People rushed by. I couldn't hear any sound beyond the pounding of my heart. He silently handed me the necklace. By the odd expression on his face, I wondered how much he'd seen despite being banished by Vane. I didn't have the courage to ask, and as soon as I snapped on the necklace, I didn't have the strength. Vane's magic flowed through the necklace with reckless abandon.

I dropped to the floor with a strangled gasp. My hands touched the wounded surface of the mountain. I shuddered under the onslaught of a foreign power. Unfiltered, raw, angry magic threatened to tear me apart. Above us, the clouds thundered. Lightning flashed between them and heavy rain poured down in sheets. People cried out in further dismay, fearing a living dragon spewed fire off the mountain summit.

"*Help her, Merlin,*" Vane commanded in my head.

I barely noticed Matt drop to his knees behind me. His arms wrapped around my body and Matt took control. Somehow, he directed the magic into the ground, and the earth soaked it up like it did the rain.

I managed to stay strong for another few seconds until the mountain calmed.

*** 

"Vane, I pegged a deer. It's in the woods. Fifty paces in that direction." The little princess stood at the mouth of the cave, pointing outside.

A chilly breeze blew in. Under a warm, fur coat, I barely felt its sting. I'd never worn anything so warm before in my life. I could get used to it. I looked at the tiny girl, her gold-brown hair clumsily plaited and tied to keep it out of the way. I'd plaited it for her after some persuasion. With a sigh, I tossed kindling into the fire I'd just started. "Why didn't you bring it with you? I hope you didn't leave it alive."

She wrinkled a pert nose. "It is dead, but I'm not touching it. You made me do the kill. It's yours."

I stood up, sword held casually in one hand, and walked closer. I loomed over her. "I made you because we have no other food."

"It watched me. Sad and not..." Her piquant face looked down at the ground. "It was an easy shot. It walked in front of the arrow." Lifting her head to glare at me, she repeated, "You clean it up."

I repressed a sigh. "As you wish, princess. Get the bedrolls ready. We get up early."

"I know," she muttered as she marched off. The end of the

bow she slung around her shoulder slapped against the back of her legs. Made for someone much bigger than she, the curved bow had an elegant design, but was very simple at the same time. Considering the amount of gold in the hidden chamber, I had no doubt it was specially made for her.

I stepped out of the cave.

"You're letting her walk all over you," a thin boy said. He held a slim sword in his hand as he stood on sentry duty. I walked to him and silently directed him to correct his stance. He eagerly complied. Worry clouded his eyes still, but they also held a sliver of hope. We were far from his destroyed home, and everyday he grew stronger and the grip on his sword grew more adept.

I asked, "Anything to report?"

"No one."

I nodded. I managed to grab some handfuls of gold and a few other supplies on my way out of Carthage. Through luck, I evaded the other soldiers and escaped the city without drawing attention. Besides the supplies, I also acquired two additional burdens. I called myself twice mad for giving in to their pathetic doe-like gazes and allowing the two children to accompany me. I knew better than to let innocent pair of eyes to affect me. Yet, there was something about the little princess that tugged at me. As if I was meant to know her… I shook my head, disgusted with myself for even thinking such useless thoughts

Nearly one month later, we were camped in the middle of a forest in Gaul. I would not have made it so far so quickly without the aid of a tiny little girl with delicate hands and a royal pedigree. The cave, our rest stop for the night, lay high up. We were trying to remain as far away from the greatest predator that roamed the woods—man.

Septimus. The depths of the man's debauchery, the depths I'd been forced to sink into with him, I would bear on my soul forever. I wished I had the power to heal him, so I could gut the rotting bastard again. I cursed myself for even thinking of him. The crystal necklace sat heavily around my neck. I had its brother, but nothing I tried worked. The crystal held my magic bound without mercy. I remained powerless.

A creek flowed at the mouth of the cave and water thundered down over slippery boulders. A smattering of rocks made the creek easy to cross. Red rays of the fading sun danced off the smooth stones and leaves floated down harmoniously as they fell off the nearby trees.

I had no idea what lay ahead. *First, we must survive today.*

I drew out a knife from my belt. "Stay alert, Lord Perseus. I'll return shortly."

He made a face. "I asked you not to call me that name. Our kingdom is lost. My father is gone. My mother is..." The boy stared up into the setting sun, tears brimming at the edges of his eyes. "I have nothing."

The remark hit uncomfortably close to the bone, but I had something the boy didn't—a brother, one who waited for me to find my way back home.

I asked, "What should I call you then?"

"We travel toward Britannia. I should like a new name for a new home." Then, he bit his lip. Uncertainty fell over a youthful face that couldn't have seen more than ten seasons. "I don't know. I shall have to think on it."

"Keep an eye on your sister," I said, walking into the forest.

"As if anyone could," the boy groused. "She only ever listened to our mother."

I had to agree. The baby princess, with her big, innocent eyes, was a real hellion. Exactly as she said, I found a small doe pinned to a tree, hanging on the shaft of her arrow. She made one clean shot through the side. It didn't suffer. The princess hit the correct spot to cause minimum pain. Lifting my knife, I jabbed it into the deer's tough skin. I got to work. A few hours later, my stomach full of venison, I yawned.

Only small embers remained in the fire.

"*Asana agni.*" I tried. Nothing happened.

With a grimace, I placed dry twigs to keep the low fire burning during the night. A murmur escaped from the sleeping princess next to me. As soon as she lay down, she fell into slumber. One hand was tucked under her chin and the other rested trustingly next to my thigh. The sound of the water relaxed me. Even on Triton's island, it was always the ocean that finally lulled me into sleep. I glanced down at the girl again and wondered briefly if I would ever be able to sleep so well. I doubted it. Life would never be safe enough for me.

She shivered under the cold breeze of the night and the boy pulled his blanket tighter around her. He moved to settle down next to his sister.

"The Vandal king was her father?" I asked the boy.

He nodded and yawned. "I don't know much about it. From the gossip, I know the incident surprised them all. My father chose to ignore my mother's dalliance. What else could he do?"

I glanced at the little girl. "How did he treat your sister?"

"He didn't. He mostly ignored her."

*Not wanted.* I poked at the fire. I knew the feeling all too well.

"And the bow? She's exceptionally skilled."

The boy yawned. "She always has been. My mother had the bow made. She said she had a dream she should."

"A dream?"

The boy nodded. "She said my sister's father spoke to her in it."

"The Vandal king?"

"I don't know. It was a dream."

"A dream," I muttered. My time with Merlin had taught me not to easily dismiss such things. But what purpose lay behind the little princess' gift? I lay down and stared at the jagged rock across the cave's ceiling. Who knew what purpose destiny had in store for me? I was taken from my home. My fingers curled into a tight ball. Whatever my destiny was, I was getting tired of it. I glanced at the two of them. Was it really a coincidence that I stumbled upon them? What game was I involved in now?

"Perceval," I said.

The boy looked at me with bleary eyes. "Hmm?"

"Your new name," I explained.

The boy smiled, the luminous smile of an untouched soul. For a moment, I had to suck in my breath at its purity. It reminded me so much of my little brother. I could almost see his small face in the fire's glimmer. I had to tamp down the pangs of regret. It took every ounce of my will to ease a scant space away from them. I could ill afford to get involved with these two. I had no need for friends. Such weaknesses had surely been beaten out of me long ago. I only needed to survive. The boy had taken one item of particular value. "Perceval," I said. "Where have you hidden the apple you took from the vault?"

## LOVE ME, LOVE ME NOT

I jerked out of Vane's memory when Matt pulled me off the ground. The mountain stopped rumbling. People on the trail seemed to be moving at a less frantic pace. Then, another crackle of thunder hurried them along. Some persisted, lingering to stare at the destruction. In place of the shrine, there was only a deep sinkhole, surrounded by haphazard blocks of crumbled concrete. Down on the second level, the poorly constructed buildings lay in shambles. Yet, despite having just lost their home, the monks continued to help the injured with stoic expressions.

"It can be rebuilt," said Matt, correctly reading my thoughts. He grabbed my wrist and tugged. "We've done all we can."

I stared at him. "You said the booby trap is for people who can't prove they're worthy. Does that mean you knew this might happen?"

Matt's face blanched. "We're disturbing secrets that have been used as protections going thousands of years back."

I ground my teeth. "I'll take that as an affirmative. Why didn't you think to have some kind of plan if it did?"

"I didn't have *time* to come up with a plan."

"You mean you didn't want to risk letting anyone else in on a plan... Say someone who could have blocked off this mountain for us."

"No, I didn't. I couldn't risk it," he said without remorse.

"You're unbelievable."

"I'm realistic. We don't have time to go through the proper channels."

"Says you."

"No one died, Ryan." *Unlike on your watch.*

The words punched me somewhere low and deep. Blake's face flashed between us. Tears stung my eyes, and I took a sharp breath.

Matt raked a hand through his hair. "We should go before anyone starts asking questions."

I reined in the pain. "We wouldn't want that."

"This is only the beginning," Matt said, unknowingly echoing Vane's words.

A crack of lightning streaked above us. Rain came down with a vengeance as we began our descent off the mountain. A sign told us we were in Ratnapura, the city of gems. About a hundred feet down, the stairs became very steep and we clutched the handrails for fear of tumbling over the edge of the mountain. Sheets of rain made the passage even more treacherous. I clung to a set of large chains riveted to the rock.

Matt touched the chains. "These chains were supposedly placed here by Alexander. They could be over a thousand years old."

"So thrilled to know," I shouted back at him. Usually, I loved historical tidbits, but not right now. Not when I was depending on the very thousand-year-old chains with my life. I muttered, "As soon as we survive this mountain, remind me to beat you with that cross."

Matt sighed. "I didn't ask you to come along."

I slipped on wet stone. Matt caught my arm to steady me. I shrugged him off and clutched the handrails tighter. It took three hours of painstaking footholds to get down the mountain. A white dome temple, the beacon of hope, nestled in a valley of mist tucked between the mountains and curtained by crisp, green vegetation came into view. Yet, I didn't slow down to admire the sight. With each step, my anger at Matt grew. I couldn't believe his nerve. He would never trust anyone enough and yet, I was the only one wrong.

I dropped my sodden backpack and collapsed under a covered bit of curb. We'd finally reached the bottom of the trail and a small walkway. The path led off the steps and into a sparse huddle of stores and homes, the last stop to get souvenirs. I even saw a T-shirt declaring, "I Peaked," which would have been funny if I wasn't too wet to smile.

Finally, I asked, "Now what?"

"We get back on the train and find out what the cross opens." Matt peeled off his rain poncho. Wet hair hung over his forehead and the collar of his coat. His T-shirt was soaked against his lean chest, clinging to every hard muscle.

I told myself I wasn't impressed. "It opens something?"

Matt discreetly took out the metal artifact and traced the

curves of the cross. "Looks like a key to me."

"We're looking for a door. Are you telling the truth this time?"

Matt scowled. "Are you going to stop using me as a substitute punching bag?"

My jaw dropped. "I am not!"

"Vane's good at pushing every button and you're letting him push all of yours."

My anger deflated like a punctured balloon. I stared down at my tennis shoes. The previously white laces and rubber lining were stained an ugly brown with mud.

Matt sat down next to me. "You're stronger than him."

"Am I? I never thought so."

Matt's shoulder brushed mine. "Maybe you should start."

I raised a brow. "Maybe you should start telling me why you're following Alexander the Great around on this island."

Matt grinned. "Maybe you should trust me."

I blinked, my gaze snared by his inky, amber eyes. "You smiled."

His expression turned self-conscious. "Yes, I suppose I did."

"Ryan, bear with me a little while longer."

Picking up my cold hand, he squeezed it, and in the middle of the Sri Lankan jungle, surrounded by the smells of roadside egg rolls and hot chai, the clouds shifted enough to allow one single ray of sunshine to shine down on us. Maybe things weren't so bad after all. I didn't squeeze his hand in return, but I didn't attempt to pull it back either.

"Where are we off to next, oh wise Merlin?"

Matt's expression turned sheepish. "Ella."

*****

We never returned to the hotel. Not that it mattered; everything I owned at the moment fit into the small backpack I carried up the mountain. The train from Nuwara Eliya to Ella showcased rolling hills and colorful foliage with enough wild in them to spread out across the land in interesting patterns. Within two minutes of staring at the scenic vistas, I passed out from complete exhaustion.

I woke up with my head on Matt's chest. A bit of drool spilled from the side of my mouth, smearing his coat. I jerked up and the back of my head bumped against the metal side of the train. I winced and wiped my mouth at the same time. My seat was beside the window and Matt sat next to the aisle. I mumbled, "You could have just pushed me aside."

"No worries." He shut the guidebook, his constant companion, or crutch, as I was starting to think of it. "You don't snore… that much."

"So funny," I said, despite the flush spreading over my face. I half-heartedly hit his shoulder. "I thought you were the nice brother."

Matt raised a brow. "Since when?"

"W-well, in comparison—" I stuttered.

"Is that why you didn't pick me?"

This time, my entire body flushed. "W-what?"

"Why Vane?"

"Uh—"

"You like that 'I think I'm so hot when I'm yelling at you'

kind?"

Well, Vane was—hot, that is. And he did yell a lot.

"No need to answer." Matt sank back into his seat. "I see the answer on your face."

"He doesn't lie either," I retorted.

This time Matt flushed. "I'm trying to keep us alive."

"Isn't that what you always say?"

The train screeched to a stop. Someone shouted out, "Ella."

Without a word to me, Matt got up. He slung his duffel bag over his shoulder in jerky movements and marched out of the train. I hurried after him. The Ella train station was one long Victorian-era building with a tiny platform. More red-and-yellow decorations were strung along the platform's ceiling. Matt walked straight to a line of waiting tuk tuk drivers. We clambered into the three-wheeler.

Matt barked, "Ella Caves," and the tuk tuk ambled off.

In a rare bit of clear weather, we passed through the center of town. The driver pointed out a big tent, packed with people. During the festival, rice and jakfruit curry were offered free to any passersby. My stomach rumbled.

"Forget it." Matt handed me a cereal bar from his bag. "Vane knows where we are now. We have to move fast."

I waved away the bar with a grimace (I hated mixed berry) as we zoomed out of the one-road mountain town. The road was fairly well paved, but a bit hair-raising. The tuk tuk flew up the steep sides of the hill country. We must have been going at least thirty to forty kilometers (that's a brisk eighteen to twenty-four miles per hour), yet I was clutching the side of the doorless car and hanging on for dear life. My nose tickled with the scents of damp air and overgrown leafy vegetation. It perfectly suited my new occupation as intrepid explorer in search of ancient treasure, and with the "save the world" badge pinned to me I could ignore all that pesky concern over preservation of cultures and habitats that modern archeologists worried about…

The justification almost assuaged my guilty conscience.

"Why?" I turned away from the entrancing landscape to Matt. He sat stiffly against the opposite side of the tuk tuk, trying to keep as much distance between us as possible. The small interior and rickety ride made this fairly difficult.

"Why what?" he groused.

"Why do you want to save the world? You don't even like people." I flicked a finger at the guidebook tucked in the front pocket of his bag. "All you care about is books and such."

"I care more about seven billion people," he said dryly. "Are you still upset about the temple? If it makes you feel better, I can get a donation together for a restoration project. It will prop up the local economy for decades."

"You can't buy your way out of everything."

"Like Vane tries?" he said.

I frowned at him. "That's not who Vane is."

Matt snorted. "You're right. He doesn't care about money. He cares about power. That's who he is… the kind you like."

I rolled my eyes. "Is it possible for you to find one redeeming quality in your brother?"

Matt's lips thinned. "I've tried for years. Against my better judgment, I tried. I invited him into Camelot and he destroyed it." He stared somewhere over my shoulder. "Vane was taken to train to be a warrior when I was very young. I don't know the exact age. After he returned to Britannia with Perceval, he never answered my questions about what happened to him and I never could ease the strain between us. I always wondered if we'd been too close before he left."

My chest squeezed for them. For the two brothers... they'd been so young and so defenseless. But something didn't sit right. I said, "Perceval and his little sister."

"What?"

"He returned with Perceval and his little sister from Carthage to Britain."

Matt's expression turned thoughtful-Merlin. "You saw her in an another memory?"

I nodded.

"Perceval never said a word about a little sister."

"She was there," I insisted. "If she never made it to Camelot, what happened to her?"

Matt sighed. "I don't know."

"She was just a little girl!"

Matt shook his head. "It happened long ago, yet it goes to show what I've been saying all along—Vane's past gets more questionable with every revelation. Maybe you should think on that."

The tuk tuk stopped before a sign with a mix of squiggly writing and English stating "Rawanaella Ancient Temple and Cave." The sign showed a picture of steps leading up to a jungle cave straight out of Indiana Jones. A little farther up, a small square temple stood to the right of the pathway. It had a raised veranda and seemed to be about one-room deep. Matt paid the driver, but we didn't go into the temple.

A skinny kid, about six years old, ran up to us. His face broke into a toothy smile. He said in poorly accented English, "I can help guide you up, mister. I can get you up fast."

"No—" Matt started to say.

I elbowed him and told the kid, "We'd love some help."

The boy beamed and ran to the steps, gesturing at us. "Here."

"What happened to discreet?" Matt hissed in my ear.

"What happened to helping the local economy?" I snapped back.

He sighed. "With what I have left, we'll be lucky if we can afford our next meal."

We headed up the steep path. Stone steps were carved into the side of the mountain. The path's rock side was overgrown with vines and various ferns. On the other side, a sharp drop-off had no railings to stop you from tumbling into an abyss of wilderness. Because of the free lunch offered in town (I figured), we were the only ones at the site. That way, if we plunged to our deaths, we'd do so without any witnesses.

Our small guide went swiftly up the steps. Matt climbed steadily behind him. I was less steady. My tennis shoes were not designed for hiking. I wondered if Indiana Jones thought about getting better shoes for the girl he dragged along with him. Then, I remembered the snake crawling through high heels in one movie, and decided all guys were pretty much the same amount of clueless. After one terrifying stumble, I chucked my pride and grabbed Matt's bag for some support. "I'm not taking another step until you tell me why we're following Alexander the Great around this island."

Matt glanced at our guide. The boy outdistanced us by several steps. He took a slow step forward. "Al-sikandar. Sikander. Iskander is how he was known here. He conquered every piece of land from Macedonia down to the Gaza strip. In Egypt, he found the sanctuary of the oracle of Ammon-Ra, the sun god. The Greeks believed Ammon-Ra was the god, Zeus. Now, the kings of Macedonia maintained they were descended from Hercules, also a mortal son of Zeus. Alexander's mother believed Alexander to be conceived by the god himself, disguised in her husband's mortal form. Alexander gained confirmation of his demi-god status by the oracle, and thereby declared it to his kingdom."

I took a few shaky steps up the staircase. "Let me guess—he used his divine status to rally the troops to conquer the rest of the world."

"Right," said Matt. "He conquered past the Middle East and India. Alexander's horse, Bucephalus, his most prized possession, was killed in the battle in what is today known as Pakistan. This horse was said to be a gift from Poseidon. Losing this horse had a great effect on Alexander. The oracles at Delphi predicted that whoever should ride the beast would rule the world. It shook his image of immortality. After Bucephalus's death, Alexander came down through India and old Lanka in search of one thing. I believe he employed a wizard to help him climb Adam's Peak, a place said to be protected by numerous deities for this reason."

"Which is?"

"Legend states that Adam's footprint was once encrusted with gems from a grand tunnel."

"Like the gem on the cross?"

Matt nodded. "A tunnel of gems in the mountains holds the water of life."

"Water of life? Or the Healing Cup?"

"I believe so… another name for it may be the Holy Grail. All three legends have one thing in common—they promise immortality. However, Alexander didn't get farther than Adam's Peak. He didn't find the cross."

"But you've figured out what he didn't."

I slipped on wet stone. Matt's arms caught mine. Hooded amber eyes caught mine. I pulled back.

"You stop?" our tiny guide said cheerfully. "We're near, *Memsahib*."

"You heard him, *Memsahib*. No stops," said Matt.

"That's not what he said." I groaned and rubbed my thighs. Already strained from the climb up Adam's Peak, they throbbed in pain.

Matt tugged me forward. "If you want me to tell you any more, you'll come."

I grabbed his bag again with a harrumph. "It better be earth-shattering."

"I'll leave that to my brother," Matt retorted. He resumed the climb. "Alexander should have stopped to listen to the local legends a little more. In the epic Ramayana, King Rawana of Lanka kidnapped Prince Rama's bride, Seetha. King Rawana's ten heads signified his knowledge of the Vedas as well as magic and celestial events. Because of this, he was given the nectar of immortality by the creator god, Brahma. When Hanuman, the monkey god and agent of Rama, discovered Seetha at Ashok Vatica, Rawana's grand palace near our hotel in Nuwara Eliya, Rawana had to escape with the princess. Rawana flew Seetha on a winged chariot to these secret caves. The caves serve as endpoints of a man-made tunnel system built inside these mountains."

"Built by Rawana?"

"No one knows. The tunnels are said to hold many secrets, including Rawana's tomb."

"Rawana. The master of celestial events and holder of the nectar of immortality lies in these caves."

"It gets better," Matt said. "Lord Shiva, the god of destruction, gave Rawana a divine sword much like Excalibur. Prince Rama the avatar of Lord Vishnu, the maintainer god, used a bow and arrow to dislodge the nectar. I believe Rawana's tomb is not here but his body was taken here and sent elsewhere. I sent Bors, Perceval, and Galahad after Bran of Pellam. We know Pellam died on the mermaid island. The stories say while Bors and Perceval made it back to Camelot, Galahad found the Cup and became desirous to leave in this world. Angels carried his body up into the gates of paradise. The place where the Healing Cup originated. I think Rawana's body was taken to the same place."

We reached the end of the steps. At the top, only a muddy path remained.

"I wait for you?" our guide asked.

Matt shook his head and paid him. The little boy quickly pocketed the bills. From the same pocket, he drew out a squashed red flower, handing it to me. "For you, *Memsahib*... Seetha's flower for one as pretty as Seetha herself."

I smiled and leaned down to take the offering. The smiling boy whispered loudly in my ear. "If the thin-lips *sahib* doesn't want you, I'll take you." He flattened his lips, accurately mimicking Matt's sour expression.

I let out a startled laugh and handed him a generous tip. While Matt scowled, the kid hurried off with a wave of his hand.

"Can we go anywhere without you charming the locals?" Matt groused.

"You're just jealous, Thin-Lips."

"Considering we're about to go into a cave infamous for the supposed seduction of Seetha, you might want to reconsider before I feel challenged to defend my thin lips."

"I'm sure you would rather kiss the gates of paradise," I said dryly. "Do you want to tell me what this cave has to do with them?"

Matt walked up the hill to the entrance of the cave. "There have been many names attached to the gates of paradise. One is the Isle of the Blest."

"Isle of the Blest?" I squeaked. "It's practically required for anything with a name like the 'Isle of the Blest' to have a booby trap."

Matt sighed. "It has other names. The Greeks called it the Elysium Fields, a sanctuary of healing, peace, and tranquility. Located past the River Lethe, the stream of oblivion and mortal life, it is the final resting place of all heroes. In yet another legend, a hero was brought to the island by the Lady of the Lake."

"King Arthur?"

"I'm not sure I believe that one, but yes, after his death at Mt. Camlan." With a grin, Matt gestured at the yawning mouth of a cave. "Arriane DuLac, I believe the Healing Cup lies in Avalon and the door to it lies in these caves."

***

Two hours later, I sat down on a slab of barren rock. "Nope, no dead heroes, creepy demons, or supernatural gateways in sight. It's just an ordinary cave."

"Don't sound so thrilled," Matt commented.

The inside of the Rawana Ella Cave had an ordinary dirt floor, barren interior, and endless sloping rock. No writings. No treasure. No Healing Cup. Decently roomy, the front cave expanded to one hundred and fifty feet in length. Other openings, the size of small rooms, could be found here and there as offshoots of the main chamber.

A tunnel opened at the back of the cave. Matt used drops of a magical liquid to mark our trail and a floating orb to light the way. Not that I knew why we needed magic for this. A rope would have worked (Theseus used a plain string to get out of the maze when he went after the Minotaur), and I would have been more comfortable wearing hard hats with head torches.

The tunnel didn't lead us far. Over time, the rocks shifted to block the networked passage. I looked up at the slanted ceiling and inhaled damp dirt and moss. I wondered about my own Minotaur. Was Vane really trailing us as Matt thought?

Matt threw a vial of green potion against a random wall. The hollow chamber shuddered as he blasted a small hole. Rock fragments fell from the ceiling and smacked me on the head.

"Merlin!" I brushed rock bits off my head. "Are you trying to kill us?"

"The dampness has to be coming from somewhere, but the cave just drops off here." He huffed in frustration and drew out a guidebook. "All of these caves around the mountain were supposedly interconnected at one point."

"Don't you have a map? Like one that tells us where to go?"

"I meant to get one from the government, but after Robin, I don't want to contact anyone. Surprisingly, none were marked 'X' for Avalon."

I marched over to him. "You make a terrible pirate."

He flipped through the guidebook. "I'm better at magic—if I had any."

"Poor you," I snapped. "Forced to use ingenuity instead of your easy button. Why don't you tell me exactly why you brought us to this tunnel? Or is that still a big secret?"

"The tunnels lead off into the various places in the kingdom... or they all lead into one place. There are several openings. We're in Rawana Ella Cave. Then, there's Isthripur Cave at Welimada, Senapitiya Cave at Halagala, Ramboda—"

"So why this one?" I interrupted him.

"Rawana came here first with Seetha after Ashok Vatica. It makes sense he would take her to the place he considered the safest." He mumbled under his breath, "And this was the closest to Adam's Peak."

I grabbed the guidebook from his hand. The pages were open to a section marked "Exploring the Epic Journey of the Ramayana." I skimmed over the passage detailing Rawana's hiding of the kidnapped Princess Seetha in the mountain gardens of Ashok Vatica. After Hanuman, the monkey god, discovered her at the gardens, Rawana took her in a flying chariot to the caves we stood inside. The caves across Lanka connected to the same tunnel network. I turned the page.

The Rawana Caves were built inside Rawana Ella Rock. On the other side lay a pool where the princess bathed under a wondrous waterfall. The picture of the Rawana Ella Falls caused my heart to speed up.

"When are you going to figure out you can't do this alone?" I turned the book around to Matt, my thumb on a picture of the falls. "We're on the wrong side, oh wise one. I've seen this before in the vision Vane had."

Two hours later, we stood on a road that ran directly in front of the falls. I pulled my jacket tighter around me. Clouds covered the late afternoon sky, chilling the air. It took us awhile to go back out of the winding cave and down through terraced gardens to get to the falls. I leaned my elbows on steel railings at the edge of the road.

"During the wet season," read Matt from the guidebook, "the waterfall is one of the widest in the country. It resembles an upside-down areca flower with drooping petals—"

"Looks like a palm tree to me." My eye caught one of many pins on my bag of a Buddha, sitting on top of a lotus flower. I pointed to it. "Or this."

Matt gave me a withering gaze. "If you keep arguing with me, we're never going to make it through this."

"I'm arguing because I know what you're going to ask me to do." The waterfall, nestled in a V-shaped crevice in the hill, cascaded from a rocky outcrop above and fell about a hundred feet down over tiered boulders. Green fronds, shrubs, and trees lined the perimeter past limestone bedrock. Water dropped into a pool at the waterfall's base and trickled down onto more rock. Underneath the road where I stood, it became a mossy creek.

Despite threatening grey clouds and cold blustery wind, people stood knee-deep in the legendary pool where Seetha was supposed to have bathed. Against one boulder, level to the road, metal pipes had been installed above the pool to facilitate the flow of water and made a nice shower for bathing. A few women in wet sarongs held tin buckets.

As the blowing wind shifted to a full-on howl, everyone hurried out of the falls.

I played with the zipper of my jacket. "In Vane's vision, we were on one of the ledges above the pool. That's where you get knocked off and plunge to your death. Have you noticed your visions have a nasty habit of coming true?"

"Had." Matt grabbed my hand to stop my fidgeting. "I don't have them anymore."

I resisted rolling my eyes. "What if you do go over the ledge? What then?"

"You can rescue me." His hand tightened briefly before he released mine. "If you care to do so."

*If you care to do so.* In that accent of his, it sounded even more condescending. I ground my teeth. "How about I strangle you now and save myself the trouble?"

"It's always been your choice." Matt walked off toward the opening that led to the base of the waterfall.

*Your choice.* The same words Vane said to me. I bit my lip until I felt the sharp sting of pain. For a second, the teetering edge of my control balanced. It didn't last.

I forced my drooping shoulders to straighten. The rush of the water soothed the jagged edges inside a brittle soul. I hugged the sound deep into myself.

Monkeys balanced on the railing just before it ended at a slanted, grassy area that led up to the right side of the waterfall. The pool stood several feet above road-level. I bought quartz stones from one of the street sellers that traversed the field. By the time I caught up to Matt, he was standing beside the pool. I looked up. On the side of the falls where we stood, tiered boulders stacked uphill like stepping-stones for a giant... or a monkey god who once stood at the top of this rock and scoured Rawana's realm for a lost princess.

"Done shopping?" He tied a rope around my middle and tightened its other end around his stomach. He pointed me toward an opening that showed a rough path up the rocks and started toward it. We climbed slowly up, gripping the surprisingly rough edges of the damp boulders. Several minutes later, I paused for a breath.

"These people are poor. I'm helping them," I said.

"You're helping to create a demand that can't be sustained. What will happen if tourism stagnates, and they've all stopped farming to sell trinkets and become guides? Who will feed them then?"

"Maybe the tourism won't stop. What's wrong with a little progress? It's a new world, Merlin. Embrace it."

"Technology doesn't change people's basic needs or their natures," he muttered. We reached one tiered level above the pool. Matt kept going.

I said to his back, "You're such a pessimist."

"Realist," he answered. "People from this time have a certain expectation from life that didn't exist in mine."

"Did you just call me spoiled? You can't tell me you'd rather go back to the Dark Ages. Starvation. The Plague. No plumbing," I said. "Exactly what is this certain expectation?"

We made it to the second tier. He walked over a thin ledge to a boulder close to the waterfall and tested a small foothold. I tugged at the rope around our middles. It yanked against his stomach. He stilled. "In a sense, life back then was easier."

*Life without you was easier.*

I crossed the ledge to face him. "If I'm so spoiled, then why do you bother with me at all?"

Shadows darkened on his face as the afternoon slipped into evening. "You pulled the sword, Ryan. You're capable of more."

I stiffened. "I can only do what I can. I'm not changing for you."

"I'm not asking you to." Matt took a step closer. Our bodies stood a mere few inches apart. He reached out a hand. It hovered just under my chin but didn't make any contact.

"I'm asking you to make choices, Ryan." Soulful, amber eyes captured mine and refused to let go. He said huskily, "I've told you multiple times how I feel. You've never replied."

For a second, I forgot to breathe. I forgot everything, but us. In this spot. At this time. Roaring water slammed against rocks with the same intensity as my own pulse beat against my eardrums. I whispered, "Maybe because I've never believed you."

Matt let out a small, startled laugh. "You don't believe me or believe *in* me?"

"I could say the same," I retorted.

His head bowed down. "What else need I do to convince you?"

A burning ember lay banked, waiting for me to fan it, to give it permission to blaze. I looked into those hooded eyes and knew he was right. I had to make a choice.

The problem was—if I did, could I live with it?

## GODS OF WATER

I yelped in surprise.

A gush of water surged from the top of the falls and drenched us with buckets of bitterly cold water. The waterfall ebbed into a network of small trickles over the ledge, revealing a small concave curvature to the rock underneath. I gaped at the cleared expanse. I hadn't seen it before because of the flowing water, but I knew this spot.

"This is it. This is the ledge that I saw in the vision."

Matt nodded. He took out the cross from the bag and took a step into the falls.

I caught his hand. "Are you sure? What if the water starts coming down again?"

"That's why I need to go quickly." Disentangling his fingers from mine, he picked his way across the slippery ledge toward the center of the falls. In the sky, a few stars twinkled as the day sought its end. In a déjà vu scene from the vision, I watched Matt run his hand along the wall. He paused.

"There's an engraving here," he shouted past the roar of the water. "A horned deer under a tree. Rawana used a deer to lure the princess to him. The tree is the same size as the cross. I'm going to try it."

*The vision.* I yelled, "Don't, Matt!"

He did anyway.

"Trust me," he said.

I didn't. I gripped the stem of a plant growing in between the boulders. As soon as he put the cross against the rock, an opening showed in the rock and water burst forth. Matt scooted to the side instantly, which saved him from the geyser's direct blast, but it still managed to catch him and he went flying backwards. I caught the rope around my middle and braced myself with the plant. Luckily, the plant held. Under me, Matt swung himself back toward the ledge and crawled back up.

The geyser slowed and finally stopped. Matt peered into the hole.

"What's there?"

"A cave." He tugged the rope to urge me forward.

I inched over onto the ledge. Matt slid into the hole. Above us, the waterfall started to gush once again.

He stuck his head out. "Hurry! I'll catch you if you slip."

No, I really didn't want to hurry. I looked down the long expanse of the waterfall and briefly closed my eyes. Opening them, I ran down the slippery edge. Matt pulled me into the hole. A giant whoosh of water slammed down like a closing curtain behind me. My heart, running a hundred miles an hour, was all I could feel, and it took me a minute to catch my breath and realize Matt was holding me in his arms in the empty darkness.

"Do we have a light?" I said, my voice breathy. Hard thighs braced me, my back against the wet rock of the cave wall. I couldn't see him, but I felt him move against me in the dark.

His lips grazed my ears. "Do we need one?"

I shivered and put my palm flat against his wet, lean chest. His subtle, woodsy scent mingled with the warm humidity of the cave. A trickle of cold liquid dripped on my head and down my back. On my left, a hiss sounded from somewhere down below us. Hard droplets of water shot up in a scattered burst as if we were standing next to a sprinkler.

I startled.

Matt's arms tightened around my waist. "Don't move."

In the dark, I heard him fish around in his bag. A light flared on. I gasped and dug my fingernails into Matt's shoulders. He held an orb in his hand. It showed the sheer edge of a drop-off directly to our right. A quiet stream ran along the cave's edge and dropped deep into a black hole. Suddenly, the pressure of the water increased. Behind us, water gushed down cutting off the hole that led back outside.

I said, "It's going to be tricky getting out of here."

"Let's see what's in here first." Matt let the orb go and it floated in the air. To our left stood a huge chamber. Attuned to Matt, the orb floated a few feet in front of him as he walked beside the stream and followed it further inside the cave.

The creepy cave didn't worry me until I stepped on my first skeleton. *Crunch.*

The orb floated in front of us and I had to stop myself from gagging. Myriad skeletons lay scattered along the interior of the cave. Severed human body parts marked a path across the chamber. Matt knelt down and picked up a broken fragment of a femur. It fell apart in his hand. "These have been here a long time."

"Yay, we'll be its freshest victims," I said with a shudder.

We didn't see anything else until we hit the other side of the chamber. In the wall, ten human-sized heads were carved into the rock. At the center of the heads, on the fifth head, two long vertical stones on the sides and one slab across the top framed a doorway with closed red doors.

"Rawana's ten heads," Matt murmured. "Or ten heads for the four Vedas and six Upanishads, making up all knowledge of magic and celestial events."

I took a breath. "The red doors are just like the ones on Aegae."

"The frame is a trilithon. Two vertical sides and one on top like the ones in limbo. In Aegae, the top slab was triangular." Matt pointed to a golden emblem on the doors in the shape of a lotus. The lotus had a circle with an eye inside.

My brow wrinkled. "Limbo had engravings of the trident—"

"And the crescent moon and the eye," said Matt. "I think we can safely say that those were the symbols of the Earth-Shaker. These are different. Maybe another one the Guides."

"It's Rawana's ten heads. Was he a Guide? That doesn't bode well. Wasn't he called the demon king?"

"By the winning side. In Lanka, he was a great king before he succumbed to his own lust for a married princess."

*Lust and politics.* I'd heard that one before—every time I

turned on the news, it seemed. Matt glanced at me as if he sympathized with the king.

I made a face. Still, had I made things worse between them? Or was I just the latest toy to be fought over by two spoiled children? When I'd been with Vane, I'd been afraid to ask the question. Now, I honestly wanted the answer. "Would you have kidnapped her?"

"No," Matt answered. "Not if she'd chosen. Vane would."

I didn't doubt it. It's why I liked him. I wondered what that said about me.

Matt read the response on my face. "He would have been wrong."

"Someone has to take a risk."

"While someone else pays the price," Matt muttered.

"He knows the line." *At least, he used to.*

Matt glowered. "His line is always further than where it should be."

"Further than where *you* think it should be," I muttered. Matt was like a stone pillar. He wouldn't bend, not on this and I couldn't understand it. Vane was his family. I would have done anything for mine. "He's not perfect, Matt, but he's —"

"I know what he is!" Matt exploded. "Can't you see you're just another one his line of conquests?"

I sucked in a hard breath. "Maybe I am, but why aren't you? You're his brother. You should love him."

Matt didn't answer. My hands shaking, I turned back to the doors. They were easier. The Guides were ancient beings/guardians/gods who'd been around since at least the

Greeks, around 1200 BCE, even further back, if they were involved with Rawana. The question whether the mysterious Guides somehow caused Excalibur to drop into our lives once again remained unanswered. The Greek gods didn't mind interfering in the affairs of mortals.

I touched the golden lotus. "If the Lady of the Lake was Rhea, mother of Zeus, Poseidon, and Hades, and the Earth-Shaker is Poseidon, could this be one of the other three?"

Matt visibly wrestled with some strong emotion, but when he replied, his voice was calm, "The eye points to the future or visions. The lotus means birth or renewal. I'm not sure what the circle means."

Out of nowhere, a thought popped in my head. "The sun."

Matt pondered the emblem. "Or the moon. In any case, like the bull emblem on the Aegean doors was a lock, the lotus must be one also." He took out the cross from where he slipped it in the front pocket of his bag. "The circle looks to be the same size."

He put it against the circle. Nothing happened.

"Now what?" I asked.

"Patience, sword-bearer." Matt drew out the half-used vial of my blood.

"I'd feel better about this if I had Excalibur right now," I muttered.

"I'd feel better if I had my magic," Matt said.

I sighed. He poured my blood on the lock. Immediately, the doorway creaked open, revealing a tunnel, and the whole chamber shook. In a loud whoosh, a vacuum of air sucked us forward.

Matt caught the edge of the trilithon frame with one hand and caught me with the other. Past the doorway, in a burst of orange light, the whole tunnel exploded with fire. If we had stepped in, we'd have been barbequed. Rock from the ceiling fell like grenades in the chamber behind us. Retreat became impossible. Stray bits of shrapnel rock threatened to knock us into tunnel, the mouth of hell.

With a nod, Matt let me go as he tried to dig around in his bag with one hand. Another rock slammed into the ground beside the trilithon. A broken piece hurled itself at the bag, causing Matt to lose his grip. He managed to grab the all-important guidebook, but the rest of the bag flew into the tunnel and exploded. Fire decimated the magical vials in a nice rainbow of color. He cursed. "We can't get through. We'll have to go back."

More rock fell from the ceiling and crashed to the ground. It crushed a human skeleton into smithereens. Apparently, Matt wanted me to die a virgin. I didn't budge from the trilithon.

I shouted, "We'll be pulverized."

"What other choice do we have?"

Water pooled at my feet, almost urging me forward. I looked down. The stream disappeared into rocks under the trilithon. It was funneling into a miniscule opening that ran under the tunnel. Yet somehow, part of it now swam into the trilithon to submerge my feet. Like a snake, it slithered into the tunnel of fire. Steam sizzled where the water fell. I said slowly, "Didn't the stories say something about Seetha going through fire?"

"After her rescue from Rawana, she had to prove her virtue to her prince by walking through fire."

"How virtuous do you feel?" I asked him.

Matt drew the cross from his pocket. Holding it with one hand, he stuck his other hand out into the fire. His jacket started flaming. He stamped it out, using the cross.

He muttered, "Apparently, my virtue has been declared questionable."

More water rose against my feet. It spilled relentlessly into the tunnel. "If my blood opened this door, this is the key past the tunnel. We have to prove we're knights. We have to fully step inside."

"All right, if that's what you choose."

I blinked at his sudden acquiescence. "So if we die here, Merlin, if we never save the world because of what I choose, you'll be all right with that?"

"You were meant to be here, sword-bearer. You've gotten us this far."

Yes, I had gotten us this far, and he had to pick a cave in the middle of nowhere in Sri Lanka, only minutes away from certain death, to tell me such things. *Boys.*

I held out my hand to Matt. He took it.

We stepped into the burning blaze. The flames tickled me like soft feathers, but didn't burn. We passed through them quickly and came out into a smaller chamber. It took me a minute to absorb that we were still alive. I couldn't help it—I giggled. "I was right."

"I could do with a little less surprise in your tone," Matt said dryly. He held the cross up in the air. The metal glowed a faint blue in the dark.

I looked back at the burning tunnel. "Do you think it was the cross?"

"I don't know."

Water bubbled loudly at our feet.

Matt drew another orb out of his jacket and tucked the cross inside. Sparkling with magic, the orb floated up high. Light shimmered on a small waterfall that fell from an opening in the rocks above. I could only assume the stream from the first chamber somehow wound its way to the top here. The water dead-ended into a small pond ahead of us. Three tunnels to its right invited us to explore. Matt sent the light into the first one. The orb illuminated a long tunnel.

Recognition flared through me at the familiar curvature of the rock. My chest contracted. I fought to breathe. Matt took my hand to steady me. A whistle of wind flew through the tunnel and I heard the Minotaur's laugh echoing along with it. My fingernails dug into Matt's palm. "This tunnel. I recognize it. It's identical to the ones in Aegae. The Minotaur's tunnels."

"Good," Matt said.

"G-good? Are you crazy?" He hadn't seen the Minotaur's massive form. My heart pounded at memory of the beast's sculpted human body, its monstrous head and the tail of a horned bull, its eyes glowing green and as cold as the sea. It had chased me and I remembered my heart beating in the dark like a beacon calling to its hunger. I whispered, "Nothing about the Minotaur is good."

Matt looked to me. "I mean it tells us we're in the right place. Which way?"

I shut my eyes. My heart strummed with the anxiety of facing the monster in his home. I pictured it chasing me through the tunnels. Then, I was chasing it. I pictured the lust in its eyes when it looked up after I interrupted it while feeding on the broken body of an animal. I shivered as much from anxiety as a disturbing rush of desire. *Vane.*

A hot burst of musk-scented air, reminiscent of the monster's breath, slithered across my nape. My eyes snapped open and I was safe. I said, "I don't know."

Matt pointed to the first tunnel. "Let's try that one."

Hours or minutes later, it became obvious we were going in circles. We retraced our steps and tried all the tunnels. They led here and there, but the main paths all wound back to the waterfall. There were no markings. No signs. We could wander around here for years and never find anything.

I sat down on a rock as Matt paced in front of the water. I watched him for several minutes before working up the courage to say, "We need to talk to Vane."

Matt continued to pace. "I am not going to risk putting Avalon in his hands."

*He was driving me crazy.* "Can't you see that you both want the same things? Maybe in Avalon we can figure out what exactly we're supposed to do... what we're all supposed to do. Aren't you a little worried about the whole end of the world thing?"

"Don't be ridiculous. Of course, *it's* why we're here, but whatever we find out, we have to be careful. The information can't get into the wrong hands."

"Ugh. Are you never going to learn? We're in this mess because of your pathological need to hoard knowledge. Face it— you're no different than Vane. You want to be the powerful one. The hero. At least he's upfront about it."

"Is that what you think? Was I wrong to not want to unleash the tsunamis on this world? How many died in Chennai, Ryan?" Matt halted in front of me. "Because of Vane."

"There are no easy choices, Merlin." I took the *Dragon's Eye* from my pocket.

Matt snatched it away and tucked it into his. "You're right. No easy choices."

I crossed my arms over my chest. "I'm getting a little tired of you ordering me around. I'm not going to die in here." I kicked the dirt floor. "And I'm hungry."

Matt bent down, his face brushing my thigh as he reached into my cargo pants pocket.

"What are you doing?"

He drew out a crumpled breakfast bar I'd rejected earlier. He sat down on the rock beside me and tore open the package, giving me half the bar. It tasted like soy mixed berry sawdust, but I demolished it in a three bites.

I yawned. "What's your plan, Merlin?"

"Do you think you can stop calling me Merlin?" he exploded.

I looked at him curiously. The orb bobbed above us.

Dim light slanted off lean cheekbones, a princely face. In the dark imaginings of the cave, I saw him riding by King Arthur's side, the shadowy figure behind the warrior. The lion behind the crown. Despite the progress of fifteen hundred years, he hadn't changed all that much. The wizards still gathered around him like he walked on water. They weren't the only ones. Even my teachers at school had done so. I had done so.

What place in his life did Merlin have for a slightly messed up, mostly ordinary high school girl? That was the part I couldn't see. Yet, something inside me reached for what lay underneath. Matt. The one he thought he saw, but still struggled against.

The waterfall rippled in front of me. I got up and moved

closer to it. Matt followed me. Catching me, he turned me until I faced him. Two hands slid along either side of my jaw. I held my breath. Would he finally let go and just allow himself to just be? He turned up my chin and backed me up until we stood just outside the spray of the waterfall. Like the pitter-patter of soft rain, water kissed my skin. Matt leaned down to graze his lips along mine. The waterfall gushed forward, completely soaking me.

Matt stepped out of the way.

"What the hell, Matt?" I yelped.

Water ebbed and I stood dripping wet in the cave. I crossed my arms over my chest and hugged myself. I glared at Matt who remained completely dry.

"I knew it." He pointed to the water. "It's Vane."

My heart thumping, I whipped around. I saw nothing but water. "You've been in here too long. You're having delusions."

Matt grabbed my elbow. "He has Poseidon's powers, Ryan. He's in the water. The Ella Falls must lead back to a river which attaches to the ocean."

I yanked my elbow away from him. "Not surprising, since we *are* on an island."

"I knew he'd react if I tried to kiss you."

"You kissed me to needle Vane?"

"I—" Matt smiled sheepishly. "I'm sorry?"

I gave his back a hard shove. With a grunt, he fell into the pool. Sputtering, he flailed in the water. I smiled in triumph. "Still sorry?"

Matt sank into the water. After he didn't come up for a few minutes, I moved closer to peer into the water.

Matt's head popped back up. He was treading water. "It's deep under here."

I sighed. "A passage?"

"Let's find out." He dove underneath.

Muttering, "Crap," I jumped in.

The orb shot into the water. I sank into the pool. I wasn't a particularly strong swimmer, but a current, like a dorsal fin in the water, caught me and sped me through. Vane's hand, I suspected. Inside a blanket of warmth, the current wrapped around me and sent me twirling and twisting until it spat me up and out at the other end. I landed gently in another rocky cavern, exhilarated by the wild whirlwind ride and disappointed that it was over. The orb floated up and out of the pool just before the water threw up Matt next to me.

He lay facedown on his stomach, vomiting water. "That b-bastard."

I thumped his back and found it icy to the touch. I had to suppress a smile. Vane must have tortured him, it seemed. At the moment, I wasn't feeling too sympathetic.

Matt grabbed my hand. Rolling over onto his back, he pulled me on top of him. Every inch of my body pressed against his. Thin, wet layers of clothing did nothing to hide that we fit together perfectly. He said huskily, "You're warm."

Behind us, the water grumbled. Matt's eyes went to the pond.

I scrambled off him and sat down by his side. "I am not the pawn between the two of you."

Matt sat up, shivering still. "All you have to do is pick a side."

I stood up. "What if I don't want to?"

"Then we may all lose," he said quietly.

"Give me the *Dragon's Eye*."

"Why?"

"To get dry. Otherwise, you're going to catch pneumonia down here." I held out my hand and wiggled my fingers. "He already knows we're here."

"You don't need to keep going to him to get rescued," Matt ground out. He took out the handkerchief with the amulet. Instead of handing it over, though, he took my outstretched hand in his while holding the necklace himself. "*Zusyati.*"

Green magic floated over us. We were dry in seconds.

I arched a brow at Matt.

He shrugged. "This way, I don't have to talk to him."

Issues with a capital *I*. A sense of foreboding went through me. I had to stop this. I had to find a way to stop them from tearing each other apart and taking the rest of us with them. I asked, "Does this mean you can leech off him to do magic?"

"Yes and no. A drying spell takes very little energy. I can't do anything big without his help."

The orb zoomed ahead of me as I moved to step into the darkness. The cavern curved at the top, dotted with stalactites that pointed down at us like sharp fangs. At ground level, neat rows of stalagmites led up to another cliff. The orb danced out over the edge. Light shone down on a valley of nothing but rock, like a miniature Grand Canyon.

"There is nothing here!" I said.

"Are you sure?" Matt took the guidebook out of his pocket. He threw it down at the canyon. Instead of dropping like a stone, the book zigzagged in the air like a kite, descending slowly into the valley.

I stared up at it. "You want to go down?"

Matt went to the edge of the cliff. "These tests were given to the knights to prove themselves worthy. The first test was to prove virtue, and the second test was faith."

I held up a hand. "I am not sky diving without a parachute."

On cue, the pool erupted behind us. A gel-like snake of water rose up and flowed toward the edge of the cliff. Reaching us, the front piece of it shaped itself into a water-gel boat with outstretched wings. Below the boat's prow, the figurehead of a horned deer took shape. Then, the whole gel structure solidified into ice.

"A reindeer pulling a sleigh," I murmured. "Cute, Vane."

Matt set a foot inside the ice-sled to test its sturdiness. It held. He scowled. "Apparently, your chariot awaits."

"Don't look so happy about it," I said dryly. The snake-hand of water squiggled in the air. I gave in to its demand and walked along the edge of the cliff to the boat.

Matt jumped out of the boat. "Dealing with him always has a price, Ryan."

Before I could do more than let out a squeak, he tackled me and sent us over the edge of the cliff. I screamed as I tumbled down a thousand invisible steps of compressed air. Each gust of air hit me with the force of a sledgehammer. Finally, I reached the bottom. The air stopped about fifteen feet up and I slammed into the rocks down below.

Luckily, I knew how to tuck and roll, but the jagged surface of the valley made it impossible to set down gently. Matt fell even less gracefully than I did, landing face-first on sharp rocks. He groaned and got up, looking mostly all right. I stood up with effort. Bruises tattooed my arms and judging by the way the rest of my body ached, I had no doubt there were more. I spat at him, "Are you crazy?"

"We didn't need the sled." He brushed blood off a small cut on his forehead and stalked off toward the hidden island. The orb bobbed happily after him.

*No, apparently, we needed to eat dirt instead.* I yelled at his back, "You better have a plan for us to get out of here."

Nine stone columns held up the rock awning that covered the tiny island. The columns rose out of a moat, evenly spaced across the circumference of the island. We waded through the waist-high water of the moat onto black rock.

I knelt down to touch the odd-looking granite. "Matt, this stone is the same as the one that held Excalibur."

"I'm not surprised." He pointed to a column behind us. On the back of it, a figure of a woman in a toga was carved into the rock. Her arms, like branches of a stone tree, rose up and connected to the awning above. Water flowed out of her mouth and back into the moat. A sentinel, she guarded the island. Matt floated the orb around the island in front of the other columns. "They're all women. Nine women. It has to be the Nine Morgans."

"Nine Morgans?"

"In legend, Morgan Le Fay and her sisters guard the entrance to Avalon." Matt floated the orb to the center. On a rectangular dais lay an enormous stone sarcophagus.

"This isn't an island; it's a tomb," I whispered.

Matt walked over to the casket. I followed. An odd picture had been etched on the top of the stone coffin. In the rough shape of an umbrella, a stick-like body supported a curved line of the ten heads of Rawana. Matt took out the cross from his pocket and held it over the etching. A hiss of wind fluttered through the darkness. I stared down at the casket. "The body could be the stem of the cross and the center head the top."

Matt tried to fit the cross on the center head, but the circles didn't match. "I don't understand. This should be the key."

Another whisper of wind whistled past me, tickling my ears. An intangible memory, fuzzy and unclear in my mind, nagged at me. "There's something really familiar about this—"

Behind me, Matt muttered, "Rawana held the nectar of immortality *inside* his navel. I wonder if that's the answer."

I whipped around just in time to see Matt press the cross vertically down the center head. "Wait, Matt. Don't touch—"

The stone depressed into the slab and swallowed the cross. Matt looked at me smugly, "It worked."

The island trembled. Around us, the stalagmites moved. Not in a good way. They started sinking into the water. The awning began to lower. We were going to get squished.

Matt cursed and jumped up on the casket, sliding over to me. "Run!"

We sprinted toward the edge of the island. We didn't even get close to getting off the rock. A neat row of stalactites fell off the awning and straight down into the moat to form an impassable barrier. We were trapped inside the tightening jaws of death.

"Matt—"

"I'm on it." He drew out the *Dragon's Eye* and unwrapped

the handkerchief around it. The sapphire amulet shone dully under the orb's artificial light. Matt frowned. "I don't sense any magic."

Above us, the awning slipped another few inches. More stalactites fell down around us. Matt handed the amulet to me. I took it, but the gemstone had never felt so cold and dead.

"It's not working," I cried.

"The rock must be interfering somehow." As if he couldn't help it, he added snidely, "You won't be able to run to him to be rescued for once."

The remark broke the last thread of my already battered composure. In jerky movements, I stuffed the unresponsive amulet into the pocket of my pants and turned on him with a vengeance. "Have you completely lost your mind? I know you don't trust him, but ever since you lost your power, you act as if you hate him. You say you care about me, but this whole trip, all you've done is to tell me over and over again how much I've screwed up. If you really cared, you could at least try to be forgiving. Being with you shouldn't have to be so painful." Out of nowhere, tears sprang to my eyes. Annoyed at myself, I rubbed them away. "I thought I knew you, but I'm coming to see that I don't at all."

Matt frowned, but without a hint of any remorse. "Ryan—"

"Forget it, Matt. If I'm going to die here, right now, I want to do it alone." I stalked off across the rock. The amulet jangled heavily in my pocket. I drew it out. The gemstone winked dully. The quiet in the chaos, it sat without life. Vane couldn't help me, yet I still undid the clasp and slipped on the silver chain. I didn't really want to die alone.

A sense of calm filled me as soon as the red gemstone settled against my skin, just above the cleft that encased my heart. A spear of rock slammed down from above just in front of me. The impact knocked me backwards and I landed hard on my tailbone. The stone stalagmite lowered a few more inches. The stone face of the Morgan watched the destruction of the island impassively, but from this angle, I noticed a detail I previously missed.

Matt walked over. "Ryan, listen, please—"

I turned to him, pointing excitedly at the Morgan. "Matt, look at her face. She has pointed ears." I touched my ears. Gia and I got pointed ears when we were temporarily transformed into mermaids.

Matt peered at her, then the next closest Morgan. "It looks like all of them are mermaids. In Greek, the nine water nymphs, the Muses, the daughters of Hesperides, guarded the isle of immortality."

"Look at their mouths," I said. The Morgans' mouths all formed a small O. "They're *singing*. Water nymphs used songs to lure men to their deaths. On the rooftop, I heard Leonidas. The mermaids' power is in their singing. We need a mermaid to sing."

My shoulders drooped. The *Dragon's Eye* sat cold on my skin. There was no mermaid to help us. No Vane.

Suddenly Matt laughed and drew out a plastic vial from his jacket pocket. "We may not have a mermaid, but we do have wind. The sound of the wind will be enough. We only need the key, not real mermaid magic."

I perked up. "What else do you have in there?"

"I keep trying to show you," he said archly, throwing the vial into the air.

It exploded. A wild whirlwind screeched around the island, threatening to send me flying. Matt grabbed my hand and pulled me up close to him. Sober, amber eyes framed by thick lashes held my gaze. Warm fingers shoved back swirling hair from my face.

"Ryan—"

"Later," I shouted.

Matt's fingers tightened on me. "There may never be a later."

More rocks crashed beside us. The wind picked up huge chunks that flew around like bouncy balls. I shouted, "We have to get to the casket. It's our best bet."

The rocks played a deadly game of "whack-a-mole" with us as we bobbed and weaved through them. Just as we reached the casket, a soulful aria filled the cavern. The Morgans sang a poignant melody. Despite my non-wizard status, I swayed in place as waves of magic washed over us. Beside me, Matt fell to his knees. I held myself upright by sheer will. Every bone inside me felt as if it were turning to liquid.

In a haze, I watched the ten heads swirl around in circles. Then, the depressed center head, the one Matt pushed, glowed with golden light. Rays spread over the circling heads, connecting them until they lit up, one-by-one. The Morgans' aria pitched even higher. Matt passed out and fell forward on the ground.

I wanted to lean down to catch him, but couldn't. Gravity seemed to have increased, making my whole body heavier. The sides of the casket rose up and pushed open the top of it. The stone kept rising until they reached past my head. It was the outline of a doorway—two vertical slabs with the lid of the casket balanced horizontally across the top. A trilithon, I realized. Golden light flashed inside the doorway. A portal opened.

I saw mist on the other side.

Then, the wind died down. The aria stopped.

I jerked forward, almost falling on my face as I suddenly became free once more.

I knelt down to Matt. The Morgans started sinking rapidly into the water. More rocks crashed around us. One sharp fragment fell straight down to split my skull. I jumped aside at the last moment, but it sank deep into my shoulder. The awning started to slip-slide down. I had to get out before Matt and I became little more than pancakes. With a cry, I tore the wretched piece out of my shoulder. Blood seeped down my chest. I hooked my hands under Matt's armpits. My shoulder burning with pain, I heaved his shoulders off the ground. Somehow, I dragged him into the mist.

## KRONOS'S FURY

I fell, plunging straight down between the banks of a narrow river. I sank deep into the water and swallowed several mouthfuls before I pushed myself back up to the top. Coughing, I glanced around the water's surface. Matt was nowhere to be seen. I dove under the water again, but I could see nothing in the murkiness. I made several dives before my body forced me to take a rest.

Above me, the darkening sky showed a fading sun and emerging moon. A familiar outline of stars shone from a healthy blanket of blue sky. On the riverbanks, trees swayed under the direction of a quiet breeze. I moved toward the bank. Maybe Matt managed to make it to land.

"One cannot enter Elysium so easily, little one."

I looked in the direction of the voice. Up on a long, slanted boulder, next to the riverbank, a tanned, bare-chested man sat wearing billowing, black Arabian-style trousers. From the middle of his wide forehead, a third eye winked at me. Two gold armlets decorated his beefy arms. Tattoos of heads, five on each arm, were elaborately inked down his upper limbs. A long tongue stuck out of the mouth of each tattooed face.

The giant of a man sat casually on the smooth boulder. Sharp cheekbones on his handsome face gave him an austere countenance. The regal way he held himself reminded me a little of Lelex, the mermaid king—which was not a good thing. He scrutinized me. "Who are you? I wait for the sword-bearer. How did you come to be here, little girl?"

I swam closer to the bank. "I am the sword-bearer."

Rawana guffawed. "I do not believe it. You cannot be the great wizard-warrior the Father said the Lady would dare to send. You are so delicate. Scrawny."

I stared back at him. "How are you still alive, King Rawana?"

"I am not, in a mortal sense," he answered. "You have found a piece of my spirit, left to guard this place. I pay penance for my misdeeds." Rawana stood up. My breath caught. Behind him, previously hidden by his big body, I spotted a black lion. His mane and body glistened with dark fur. Huge amber eyes watched me quietly, yet the lion remained frozen in place.

*Matt.*

I demanded, "What have you done to him?"

Rawana let out an outraged roar. Drawing a scythe from behind his back, he put his foot on the lion's head. "Tread carefully, *warrior.*" He emphasized the last word with a sneer. "I am not one who suffers a slight."

"That much I know," I muttered.

He kidnapped Seetha in retaliation for an insult to his sister.

Sharp teeth flashed at me as Rawana smiled. "Your lover has been changed to reveal his true form."

*True form?* Matt's lion had never been black. My stomach churned. *Had I done this to him?* "We are not here to fight you. We are looking for the water of life."

"Do you not know where you are?" Rawana laughed. "The River Lethe, the stream of oblivion and mortal life. This is the place that heals."

I flailed in the water. "This can't be it. There's so much of it!"

Rawana cocked his head. "If you bathe in the river, you will be cleansed of your mortal suffering."

I looked down at my shoulder. I couldn't believe I hadn't noticed that it no longer screamed with pain. The gash was completely healed, and under the water, fresh skin gleamed instead. I swam closer to the boulder.

A long, thin rock, the shape of an arrowhead, lay at the edge of the bank.

Rawana stared down at me, blocking the path to the quiet forest behind him. "Past here is the final resting place of heroes, but you are not one. Neither is the lion. This one is marked. He has taken a soul from Elysium without permission. It's why he remains frozen where your wounds have been healed." He pulled the lion's head up to expose its jugular and thrust the scythe against the vulnerable spot. "It is time to give another soul in return."

"Stop! Take mine instead." I grabbed the bottom of the boulder and hauled myself up. I slipped the arrowhead into my wet cargos and stood up, dripping from head to toe.

Rawana stilled. The tattooed faces on his arms twitched. The third eye glared at me. He said in surprise, "You would do that?"

I took a step closer to the muscled king. "I would offer myself to the demon king."

Rawana let out a bellow of laughter. "Demon king—"

I threw the rock arrowhead at Rawana's exposed navel. A flash of green burst from the *Dragon's Eye*. On the heels of the arrowhead, it hit Rawana with deadly accuracy in the stomach. A golden apple fell from under Rawana's navel and tumbled down at my feet. Rawana blinked. The scythe dropped from his hand, falling to the ground in front of Matt.

I let out a breath of relief.

Rawana clutched his navel, swaying in place. Then, his legs buckled, and he fell backwards on the boulder. Above us, the sky rumbled with thunder. Dark clouds moved fast to cover the blue sky. I ran to the fallen king. Picking up the scythe, I knelt down beside him.

His three eyes locked onto the *Dragon's Eye*. "You possess surprising power."

Unconsciously, I touched the *Dragon's Eye*. *Vane*. The thought he might be here eased a knot of tension inside me.

From the ground, Rawana asked, "How did you know where to aim?"

"I know your story."

A wistful expression came over his face. "Then, I live on in the mortal realm. I am pleased." His third eye closed. "You do not seem like a warrior, little one, but you have proven yourself worthy. You have defeated me. The apple is yours."

I glanced at the small golden apple. "What is it?"

"After I lost the nectar of my immortality, I was sent here. I was asked to protect this by the Father. It was stolen from him but he was able to retrieve it. He warned me that the great Lady would send someone to collect it, but I could not let them have it."

The great Lady. The Lady of the Lake. Rhea. They were all the same. Excitement shot through me. My fingers tightened on the scythe.

Rawana eyed the blade. "Will you finish me now?"

I laid the weapon down. "Do I need to?"

Rawana gave me a twisted smile. "My spirit is linked to the apple. Now that you have severed it from me, I will not last long."

The river behind me rose higher. Water splashed up the boulder as the landscape turned more violent. I held the apple out to Rawana. "Then, I will not take it. I didn't come here to kill anyone."

He gave me a weak smile of surprise. "You are kind, warrior. You remind me of the one I would have made my queen."

I colored. "I am no queen."

"A title cannot hold a kingdom, while the lack of it cannot lose you one. I lost mine because I took what didn't belong to me." Rawana blinked. He pushed the apple back at me. "The apple is rightfully yours."

"What does it do?"

"I do not know. For my misconduct, I have been denied the vision although I have the Father's Eye. The Kronos Eye." Rawana tapped his third eye. "The culmination of my knowledge of the stars rests here. The great Lady came here once, too. She hoped to see. She hoped to cheat fate, but the time was not right. The event was too far away. Now, you have come. The time is right."

"The Lady called it the day of reckoning." I looked at the eye. "Can it tell us what is coming? If the time is right, can I see what she couldn't?"

Rawana blinked. "You have a touch of the divine, wizard-warrior. It is possible, but you must make haste. My strength fades quickly."

I glanced up at the top of the slanted boulder. The black lion watched, but made no sound. "He should see this, not I. Can you free him?"

"His essence is diminished. His insides are hollow. Only with sheer determination does he continue to breathe. I have not the energy to restore him and accomplish my task." Rawana caught my hand, the one that held the scythe. He stared at the curved blade. "Even if I did, the Kronos Eye would not bend to him. His soul is torn."

"Torn?" Taking his magic tore out his soul? I glanced at the river behind me. "The water of life—"

"Will not heal him. He has defiled Elysium. He has taken a soul back from the dead—"

I bit my lip. *Grey*. Matt had brought Grey back from death.

"The Father does not forgive so easily."

I touched the *Dragon's Eye*. Rawana put his hand over mine. The third eye locked on the amulet and turned a disturbing grey. Rawana intoned, "One to save the world. One to destroy it. Only one was meant to be. Which one?"

The third eye blinked and the grey cleared. Rawana's expression returned to normal.

"What does that mean?" I asked.

The king let go of my hand. Three eyes pierced past my skin

and peeked into my heart. "You are torn, warrior, but deep down, you know the answer. You have always known it. I forced my princess to make a similar choice once. The fate of my world rested on hers. The fate of your world rests on yours."

I told myself the words were overly dramatic nonsense, despite it being uncomfortably accurate nonsense. More thunder clapped insistently at the grey clouds. A flash of lightning struck the river. Behind us, the water churned more urgently.

Rawana's breathing turned shallow. "My time dwindles. You have been kind, warrior, and in the memory of the princess I wronged, I would give you a boon—" With effort, he turned his head. The third eye locked on Matt. "I may restore his soul or I may share my knowledge. I only have enough strength to do one. It will be your choice. Choose wisely."

The lion's chest rose and fell with steady rhythm. Large eyes watched me without a hint as to the direction of his thoughts.

Rawana coughed. "Your choice, warrior… before it is too late."

With a shaky breath, I turned away from Matt. Away from the betrayal I'd chosen once and now, chose again. Away from the guilt. I turned to Rawana and touched the third eye. "Show me."

"As I said, you make a good queen." He coughed again. "Take the apple. You hold the heart of a star in your hand. It will be your guide. Remember that." He looked at the scythe. "Now, take the scythe and cut out my third eye. Hurry, you must do it before I fade."

I balked, eyeing the sharp, curved blade. "You want me to butcher you?"

"If the eye is inside me, you will not be able to use it. You must take the eye yourself and dip it in the River Lethe."

I blew out a breath. "Then what?"

"Take it into your mouth."

"You want me to eat it?" *Eat a slimy, fleshy eyeball? Gross.*

Above me, the sky trembled. Fierce wind sprayed water from the river onto the bank. Rawana's body shuddered. He roared, "Are you a warrior or not? Do not fail now. Once you take the eye, you will have but mere moments. This pathway to Elysium is tied to me. Once I go, it will collapse. If you are still here, you will die."

*Crap.* I grabbed the scythe. He was still alive, but I had no choice. With furious hacks, I began prying out the delicate eye. Blood seeped down my hands. I almost gagged. The eye sat stubbornly attached, and cutting flesh and bone wasn't as easy it sounds. Rawana roared under the brutal operation, but held himself remarkably still. His other two eyes blinked rapidly with pain. Finally, I held the slimy organ in my hand.

He caught my hand and held it. "The Kronos Eye will tell you much, but remember, nothing comes without a price. Our paths are not mapped; they're made."

"Wait. This is the Kronos Eye?" I asked.

It was too late. Rawana's three eyes shut for the final time. On his arms, the tattoos disappeared. At last, his spirit flew free.

The black lion sprang up, also released. Matt bounded down to me. He picked up the apple with his mouth. I dropped the red-stained scythe. He ran alongside me to the edge of the boulder. I dipped the eye into the river. As soon as it touched the water, the organ shrunk and hardened into some kind of crystal. I squeezed the round ball. It didn't give.

The Kronos Eye.

Matt dropped the apple into my hand. The black lion nudged me. I used his mane to climb on top of him. Wind blew furiously around us. Rough waves sprayed us. Above us, the sky dimmed. We had run out of time.

Then, I tried not to gag as I put the Kronos Eye into my mouth and swallowed it.

The crystal hit my stomach. Darkness engulfed me.

I floated in a sea of nothingness. My body had no weight. More precisely, I had no body. Only my soul anchored me to the brightly burning stars that dotted an otherwise black space. Shiny balls of gas and dust spun around the stars. In the cradle of space was a bright spot, a yellow sun, sitting at the center of its children, one of who was a small, blue planet.

Home.

For what seemed like an eternity of time, I watched our solar system spin. It offered a quiet serenity that soothed even the most troubled soul. I sat in a place far away, a place high up on the branches of a celestial tree. The golden apple bobbed happily in front me like a guide.

I didn't see Matt or the lion anywhere.

A sharp light off to the distance drew my attention. Against the canvas of space, bright pinpoints of light outlined a shape in the stars—a hunter with a bow and arrow. On his shoulder, a red star grew dimmer in its last moments of life. Then, in brilliant death, it exploded in a fury of fire and brimstone.

An invisible tsunami spread out of the supernova, shaking the branches of the celestial tree that rooted the galaxy with its tremendous power. The dark hand of the wave sent me whirling along with it. I managed to pluck the golden apple from its spot before being carried off. The wave swept over its closest neighbor, the yellow sun.

Under pressure, the steady sun bared its teeth for the briefest moment in time. Tentacles of fire flared out as it spun. I narrowly avoided the tentacles as they struck out with unintentional wrath. One tentacle, simply and silently one, sent a lash flying at its most fragile child. The flare penetrated the planet's thin barriers, meeting little resistance.

Under me, on the blue planet, the fruit of life—my life—burned.

I fell down into the apocalypse that engulfed my home. Flames consumed the dark land, evaporating the oceans and melting away all civilization. Yet, I didn't see any people. The world stood empty and hollow as if they didn't exist in this plane. I could only imagine the quiet horror of billions of people at the end of existence. The day of reckoning.

I kept falling past the clouds and open air. The stench of sulfur and death scorched my nostrils and throat. Out of black night, I plummeted down to a large island and over a circle of nine stones.

The land widened as I neared the ground. In the middle of the rubble lay the sword inside the stone. Excalibur's metal remained immune to the fiery heat. Its untouched glory clear for me to see as I fell with extreme force onto it. I screamed.

But I never met death.

I hung suspended in the air, the hilt of the sword scraping the unprotected expanse of my stomach. The planet continued to burn around me. I reached out and touched Excalibur. As soon as I did, a bolt of electricity went through my body and I dropped to the ground. I fell scraping my shoulder against the sharp edge of Excalibur's blade. Blood ran from a gash on my upper arm.

The golden apple fell in front of me.

Above me, the sky flared with a rainbow of fire.

I reached out to take the apple. Blood ran from my hand down my fingers.

Out of the night, two hooded figures rode from opposite sides of the burning circle of nine stones. On top of saddled horses, they came together in front of me and blocked the path to the apple. One rode a white horse. One rode a black horse. Both wore brown, shrouded robes.

I recognized the animals—the same ones from limbo. Forever ago, it seemed.

The white horseman started to glow. From around us, an aria filled the air. The buried stones from the circle rose out of the dirt and came together. The white horseman made a structure. Two vertical slabs and one horizontal one, melded together to make a trilithon.

Then he turned. He extended his hand. I took a tentative step towards him. The other horse snorted in protest, blowing musky hot breath in the air. His rider trotted the black horse forward. He jumped down and picked up the apple.

Nothing happened. He walked closer to me. He held out the apple.

I took it.

Blood ran over the apple's gold metal skin. The apple rose in the air. Sparkles of bright lights, tiny stars, glowed inside its dark interior. They bobbed excitedly, becoming charged. Beside me, Excalibur shuddered. The black horseman gestured me to touch the blade. I put my hand tentatively back on Excalibur. Another shot of electricity went through me. I cried out and tried to pull away, but the black horseman grabbed me and held my hand to the burning sword.

The sword absorbed the apple's energy and emitted a blinding beam in return, a lighthouse beacon taming the chaos of the flames around it. It hit the trilithon in front of me, and the structure lit up. White light shone and a rectangular doorway opened.

Inside the doorway, I saw a curved wooden bridge over a thin crisp blue river.

Next to me, the black horseman held out his hand, but not to offer it to me. He reached for the apple. I shied away. Stumbling back, I fell against Excalibur. I pulled the blade and it came out easily from the stone. I held it in a battle stance in front of me. The horsemen threw back his hood. It was Matt. The black horseman was Matt.

The white horseman revealed himself. Vane.

Vane jumped off the horse. In one move, he leapt down. The hilt of a sword gleamed above the belt tied against his left hip. He held out his hand. For me or for the apple, I couldn't tell.

There was only one thing to do. I tucked the apple close to me in a football hold and sprinted past Matt. I tossed Excalibur at Vane. He instinctively reached out to catch it and I used the distraction to leap into the open gateway of the trilithon.

I ran into the mist.

***

I tumbled out, landing facedown in a field of freshly cut grass. Soft earth kissed my lips. I lifted my head. In the distance, a familiar bridge came into focus. The world lay eerily dark. Moonlight reflected off the water. Surrounded by dark, shadowy trees, the shallow river ran under a curved wooden structure. The Old North Bridge.

An unlit lamppost on the bridge, a failed beacon in the darkness, sat silent and without any power. In the distance, nestled between two tree trunks, under another patch of moonlight, the bronze statue of a Minute Man marked the site of the first battle of the American Revolution. Concord, Massachusetts. Wearing a trim waistcoat and holding a musket at his side, the silent soldier welcomed me home.

I pushed myself up on my knees. The apple fell from my hands onto the flat clearing. In front of me, Matt lay on his back on the ground. I started to crawl to him, but a sharp pain made my stomach spasm. Clutching my middle, it rumbled as if a war raged inside. The taste of sharp metal coated my tongue and tainted the saliva. Taking shallow breaths, I rolled over on my back and tried not to pass out. The sky darkened into evening as this side of Earth turned away from the bright gaze of the sun. Stars winked down from a quiet sky.

The *Dragon's Eye* warmed around my neck.

"*Where have you been?*" Vane's voice pounded in my head.

His words hammered my brain, a pounding beat against my temples. I couldn't work up the energy to press my hands against it. I croaked, "*H-help.*"

Vane shouted, "*Hang on, DuLac.*"

"*Where are you?*"

"*Sri Lanka.*"

I almost laughed. Matt was right. Vane did follow us. I

thought back, "*Then, it will be awhile before you get here.*"

"*They have these things called phones,*" he said. "*Help is coming. Stay with me.*"

Another spasm rocked through me. I clenched my teeth at the pain. My mind started to shut down in defense. I told Vane, "*I don't think I can.*"

"*Yes, you will, champion,*" he stated, but I didn't believe him. He couldn't hide the edge in his voice.

I closed my eyes. The *Dragon's Eye* heated.

In my mind, the woods disappeared.

I crawled along the linoleum floors of a grey hallway at Acton-Concord High. I let out a mental groan. My last moments of life were going to be in a high school that had, most likely, already expelled me. Any divine forces watching me had a terrible sense of humor.

The hallway T-boned, and other corridors stretched to the right and left. I stopped, unsure of which way to go. On the cream-colored wall in front of me, a poster advertised tickets to the "Under the Sea" prom. Fluorescent overhead lights blinked on and off, as if powered by a dying generator. The odd lighting made my skin take on a pale, translucent sheen, like the skin of a ghost. At the end of the corridor to the right, Matt suddenly appeared. He stared at me, looking confused.

Another burst of pain exploded inside my stomach. I fell to my knees. Sweat broke out across my skin. I sucked air into my lungs, but couldn't seem to get enough. On the left corridor, Vane winked into existence. He ran down the hallway and knelt beside me.

"I should have known you'd come here." He glanced at the

prom poster. "You missed this place that much?"

"I don't like leaving things unfinished."

Vane pulled me into his arms and squeezed. "You've got a lot of explaining to do."

Pain rocked my body. I took a gasping breath. I voiced the only thought I could hold in my brain. "Vane, take care of my family."

"Take care of them yourself, DuLac," he replied harshly.

The world started turning blue and black. I went limp against him. Vane cursed next to my ear, but the words seemed to come from far away. Matt hurried down the corridor. He knelt down behind me. "She swallowed the Kronos Eye. It's killing her."

"What eye?" Vane barked.

"It's a crystal—"

"Never mind," Vane interrupted. "It doesn't matter. Let's get it out."

The lights shone brightly above me. The corridor started to turn hazy and my field of vision narrowed. I was barely aware when he laid me down on the white linoleum. He yanked up my shirt to expose my distended stomach.

Matt put his palm down on my navel. "I can feel it here, but I can't do any magic."

"*Upari!*" Nothing happened.

Vane exclaimed several expletives. "It's not working. Magic is useless. I can't even make a sword and cut it out."

"This can't happen. It's her world, and she's fading," Matt said.

"Think, Merlin," Vane said. "You always have the answer."

The pain in my stomach intensified. Some kind of foamy drool dribbled from my mouth. I started to take weaker and weaker breaths. My heart rate slowed.

"No," Vane yelled. A hard fist thumped my chest. It pounded unsuccessfully against a fading beat. Vane leaned down over my face. I smiled at him, peace starting to fall over me.

"We can try force feeding power to her," Matt said.

"The *Dragon's Eye*." Vane grabbed the amulet from where it lay against my chest.

His fingers curled around the gemstone, but the ruby remained cold. Vane slammed the stone against the floor. The floor trembled.

"There's still power in it. We only need to figure out how to use it," Vane muttered.

Vane slammed the amulet again. The whole hallway shook.

On my other side, Matt let out a cry, clutching his skull. Blood dripped down from his nose. "Vane, what are you doing?"

"I'm sorry," he whispered. One hand tightened on me. "I won't let you go. I don't care what it takes."

He slammed the amulet as hard as he could. The amulet cracked. Tiles on the ceiling tore open and fell. Vane sent a shot of power burning into the amulet's ruby gemstone. Then, he let out a harsh cry and collapsed on top of me. His body transformed. Instead of a human, the Minotaur rose in his place.

The fissure in the gemstone healed. Matt crawled over to try to cover me with his body. The Minotaur slammed him back with a burst of green magic. Matt flew up high and crashed hard against the lockers. He slid to the ground, totally knocked out.

"*You are caught,*" the Minotaur spoke in my head. The

coldness of the voice drenched my mind, waking me a bit. It was Vane's voice, yet not his. It was a deeper, more inhuman version. The Minotaur's hungry green eyes surveyed my failing body. "*Do you know what I do to those that I catch, my fallen hunter?*"

One of the Minotaur's human hands slid up my thigh. The other pushed down on my shoulder as he pinned me in place. I stared at the unforgiving face of the bull. According to the myth of the Minotaur, many entered its lair, but none came out. All were devoured. Reading my thoughts, the Minotaur smiled—a ravenous smile. The bull bared sharp, white teeth. Without another word, he dove down. Massive jaws clamped on the hard lump under tender skin.

I screamed.

Teeth impaled the sac of my stomach and pulled off skin and flesh in one swift bite. I screamed again. The bull lifted its head. Green-grey mucous and pink flesh mingled with blood on its mouth. The Kronos Eye tumbled out of my stomach.

The crystalized organ clinked as it fell on the hard linoleum.

The Minotaur stared down at me. Blood still covered its mouth. As if he couldn't help it, the Minotaur emitted a small moan as it licked its own mouth. A frenzy rose in its green eyes. Its tongue hanging out of its mouth, it dove for my shredded stomach again. A tongue swept over my torn stomach, licking the blood and broken skin.

I cried.

"Stop!" Matt appeared above my right side. The Minotaur lifted its head and roared. It swiped at Matt. Matt ducked and grabbed the *Dragon's Eye*. He threw it into beast's mouth. "*Upaviz.*"

A flash of blue magic imploded inside the Minotaur, and this time, it was thrown back against the lockers. The Minotaur morphed back into Vane. His face and mouth covered with blood and bits of skin. My blood and skin. Hot silent tears leaked from my eyes, burning my cheeks, and dripped onto the smooth floor.

Matt put a trembling hand on my forehead, his eyes reflecting the horror of the scene. He whispered, "God, Ryan, what did he do to you?"

I didn't reply. Thankfully, I passed out.

## THE GOOD WITCH

I woke up with a start, my vision hazy. Blinding halogen lights shone down from spotlights in the ceiling. In a dreamlike trance, I took in the details around me. I sat in a huge chamber that looked like it belonged inside a palace. At the front of the room, a mammoth tapestry depicted a scene of mythical beasts seated at a round table.

My elbows brushed against cold steel. I was sitting in a wheelchair. Close to the head of a long rectangular table, I was placed behind the Queen of England, the First Member of the Wizard Council.

Grey knelt down beside me, wearing a tailored business suit. The cut of the suit made him look surreally older, shattering the little brother box in which I mentally kept him encased. "It's all right, Ryan. You're under heavy meds. Try not to talk. They're going to ask you a few questions when the time comes. I'll let you know."

*They who?* I opened my mouth to ask, but no sound came

out. A sharp stab of pain pounded at my temples. I lurched in the wheelchair and Grey righted me. The whole room swam circles for a long minute before I could focus again. When I did, I found Matt kneeling beside me with a worried expression. He was all cleaned up, wearing khakis, a button-up shirt, and to my surprise, a striped tie.

"If this hurts her, I'm going to maim you, Emrys," Grey hissed.

Matt took my hand in his, heating my chilled skin. "She'll be fine. She's strong."

I didn't feel particularly strong at that moment, but his amber eyes reassured me. I rasped, "What—"

Matt's fingers squeezed mine. "Just hang on for a little while."

I had no idea what he was talking about, but I couldn't resist a yawn.

He stood up and went to talk to the Queen. Grey exchanged worried glances with Colin. The gargoyle king's enforcer silently flanked Grey's side, cementing his allegiance to Grey. Other adults I'd never seen before occupied the rest of the table. By the distinguished grey in their hair and the grim set of their faces, I guessed they must have been middle-aged or older. Two men in military uniforms with a line of gold stars down their shoulders looked perennially bored. Everyone else, including several women, wore the same homogeneous, dark, expensive suits.

Around the rectangle, everyone held their pens poised over white papers. They fidgeted in place, waiting. It felt to me like we were waiting for a board meeting to begin. I turned my head and struggled against more dizziness. Matt moved to stand at one end of the table. He tugged at his tie as if it would strangle him. Behind him, a long, oval table was built on a level above the rectangular one. Other people sat behind the table with microphones and looked down at us, like judges observing a trial. Beyond the higher table, through an opening in the circle, raised, red-fabric stadium seats were set up in a spectator section.

I eyed the impossibly high ceiling. At the very top of the room, unlit private boxes with glass fronts offered eagle-eye views to the proceedings below. It reminded me of being in the gladiator pit on the mermaid island. Instead of swords, though, I imagined the battles waged here relied on words. However, I didn't see any shapes or movement inside the private boxes and most of the stadium seats were also empty. I gathered this was a secret meeting.

A man seated to the Queen's right leaned close to her, whispering, "Are you sure about this?"

The Queen gave a small sigh. "We have been waiting for this since I told you about the cause of the tsunamis. You would not be here if you did not agree, Prime Minister."

The man nodded reluctantly. A mustached man at the other end of the table cleared his throat.

He intoned, "The emergency session of the Security Council will now come to order."

The United Nations Security Council, I realized. The table quieted.

"Let the minutes show, the participants on this day are as follows…" Mustache-Man started making introductions.

I tuned out as another wave of dizziness hit, making me clutch the rails on the wheelchair tightly. The names of several countries were announced. I only caught the words "the President of the United States" and instinctively turned to look at her. She sat removed from my field of vision so I had to crane my neck to see her. That little bit of exertion rebounded on me, and I had to combat a wave of nausea by staring dejectedly at the boring beige of the carpeted floor.

I must have dozed off for a little bit because when I looked up, the table no longer held bored attendants. The world leaders were talking with Matt, Grey, and Colin. Colin was in his beast form. His forehead protruded like a Cro-Magnon and the elongated incisors peeked out from his lips. Tension screamed from the tight set of his shoulders. Yet, the others around the table seemed unconcerned that a gargoyle roamed in their midst.

One of the men in the military uniforms stood up. "We understand that this Vane person has become a threat, but surely, with your power, you can restrain him."

Matt colored. "He has taken my power."

"This is grave. How are we supposed to defend ourselves from a being that is capable of so much wanton destruction? If they were to learn that the tsunamis were being caused by supernatural wizards... that you even *exist*, the ensuing chaos would be unimaginable," the US President said.

"I'm more concerned about what's happening now," a man in a grey suit beside the President said. "You said Merlin had critical intelligence about the global blackout."

The President added, "Indeed, I can tell you, it's been pure hell trying to keep the people calm. If we can give them answers, is it Vane—"

"No." The Queen replied, "Vane didn't cause the blackout. What happens in the next month will be much worse than a few days of no power and satellites going offline. Merlin will explain the details."

The Queen nodded at Matt. He recapped the events in Greece—the discovery of Poseidon's trident and the mermaids—and I tried to wrap my head around their words. They knew about gargoyles and wizards. They knew about Merlin. And Vane.

Matt took a small, velvet box out of his pocket. "It was after I read about Alexander's quest for the water of life that we were led to uncover this."

He pulled on gloves and opened the box's lid. The Kronos Eye lay inside. He used his gloved hand to take out the crystal. The source of immeasurable pain looked so innocent sitting quietly on his palm.

The Queen commanded, "*Atibha.*"

A bit of blue magic flared. Matt held up the small crystal orb high in the air.

The Kronos Eye lit up. Like a 3D movie, a hologram in full color played out the sequence I'd previously witnessed in person. A star went supernova, causing its younger neighbor, our sun to go crazy and begin emitting huge solar flares. It showed a blue planet. Earth. The sun shot out a particularly massive flare. The bombardment of radiation tore through Earth's thin barrier of defense, the ozone, and attacked the fragile ball's innards. Within seconds, flames cooked the surface of the planet Earth. Steel cities melted in eerie silence.

The hologram winked out.

Matt walked to me and put his hand on my shoulder.

The Queen asked, "Can you confirm, sword-bearer, this is what you saw?"

With effort, I focused on her. "Yes."

A composed man seated by the Queen, the Prime Minister (of

Britain, I assumed), stood up. "Quite fantastic, isn't it? However, it is also quite real. I have taken the liberty of gathering our top astrophysicists to review the vision." He gestured at Mustache-Man, who began passing out a thick set of papers. "You will want to review their reports with your own advisors."

"Pages and pages of calculations." The grey suit beside the US President flipped through the report. "What does it say in actual English?"

"The details are for your scientists, Defense Secretary."

Interesting. The pinched-face man in the grey suit was our Defense Secretary.

The Prime Minister continued, "The report comes down to two simple words—our sun. I will allow Dr. Latimer, who led the report, to explain."

Dr. Latimer, a white-haired man in a too-expensive suit, cleared his throat. "The star identified in… the Kronos Eye… is thought to be a previously unobserved pulsar—a star that has already gone through a supernova. In the reports you will see it marked as MPH2 or Phaethon. The supernova would have been observable fifteen hundred years ago. It sits further out, about fifteen hundred light-years, beyond Orion's shoulder."

*Fifteen hundred years ago.* I sat straighter in my seat.

Dr. Latimer continued, "We've been observing its brother for years. Approximately five hundred and seventy light-years away, the red giant, Betelgeuse, is the alpha star on Orion's shoulder. It has been of keen interest to us, since it will be the closest supernova to Earth in our known history."

"There are two stars going supernova?" asked a military man further down the table.

"Twin stars, we believe," Dr. Latimer said.

"One has gone supernova and one will," the military man said.

*Twin stars. The first one happened fifteen hundred years ago already.* I shifted in the wheelchair. It all sounded hauntingly familiar. Vane's memories came back to me and a chill went through me. *Was this why he and Merlin had waited in a frozen tomb for fifteen hundred years?*

Dr. Latimer clarified, "Technically, they have both happened. It takes light-years for the phenomena to travel the distance across space and be observable. Until then, to us, it hasn't happened—"

The Defense Secretary scowled. "Forget observable. Let's concentrate on the physical effects."

Dr. Latimer nodded eagerly. "Yes, well, as I was saying— the Phaethon supernova, in our terms, happened fifteen hundred years ago from the approximations of the modeling we've done. Now, Betelgeuse will affect us in the not too distant future." He opened a laptop to show a crude modeling of the Orion system. "In the past few years, the scientific community has noticed it shrinking without losing any of its luminosity. There have been no firm conclusions as to what the cause is. According to the Kronos Eye, it is because it is getting closer to a supernova explosion. Or I should say, five hundred and fifty years ago, it was losing its luminosity and we are only observing it now—"

The Prime Minister cleared his throat. "Yes, Doctor, but for all intents and purpose to us this is happening today."

"Yes. Yes." Dr. Latimer added with self-importance, "But I want to make sure you have the facts—"

The Defense Secretary interrupted, "From what I gather, you

cannot confirm the version of events the Kronos Eye predicts with outside data."

"No," Dr. Latimer said. "However, we did run the modeling and the possibility exists. Once the supernova happens it will cause our usually stable sun to start fluctuating for a period of time."

The Defense Secretary said, "What do you mean fluctuating?"

"Increased coronal mass ejections from the suffusion of energy from the supernova explosion."

"A super solar flare," the Prime Minister stated.

"Do we have evidence that corroborates the Kronos Eye?" the US President asked.

"We have previous evidence that coronal mass ejections can reach Earth at an astonishingly fast rate. In 1859, in what was called the 'Carrington Event,' a major solar flare from our sun made it to us in a matter of seventeen hours, thereby retaining much of its energy. At that time, it thankfully resulted in a benign aurora display." Dr. Latimer turned to his laptop and zeroed in on the Orion system. "Secondly, there is Phaethon itself. The simple fact of its existence lends credence to the Kronos Eye. Before nested dust and gas shells obscured our sight around Betelgeuse. Now, we know where to look. Thirdly, we're seeing increased solar activity across the board. The global blackout was the first wave. No one expected a neighboring star to go supernova at the same time as an energetic sun."

The US President closed her report. "What would the supernova mean to us, Dr. Latimer?"

"The supernova itself will be merely interesting—a second sun will be visible in the sky for weeks, we approximate. It is the increased activity from our sun that we need to worry about. The super solar flare will hit our already weakened ozone layer—"

A military man interrupted. "I thought the hole over Antarctica was closing."

"It has been. However, we've been seeing severe storms all over the world this summer—quite possibly due to the turbulence in the oceans caused by earthquakes. It has weakened the layer in major areas." Dr. Latimer continued, "Imagine our ozone, our only protection, as a massive sail with several thin patches that's about to face a hurricane. Mild flares cause satellite disruption and magnetic storms interfering with worldwide communications. A medium flare caused the global blackout. Stronger flares will deplete the ozone layer leaving us exposed to radiation and solar winds—"

There was a pause. Everyone across the table flipped through their handout, not because they were actually reading it, but because they needed something to do.

The Defense Secretary said, "We will make plans to evacuate underground."

The Prime Minister shook his head. "The super solar flare will be like a million megatons of hydrogen bombs being launched on us all at once. Nothing is going to survive that."

Dr. Latimer, his white hair glistening in the dim light, stared at the table. "The universe is in delicate balance, gentlemen. The flare will not only destroy the Earth's surface, but also superheat the core of the planet. It won't take long for the already unstable supervolcanic sites, like Yellowstone, to erupt. This is actually a good thing for the planet. Volcanic eruptions will tear apart the earth and release atmospheric particles trapped in the ground. That will rebuild the ozone layer and ultimately, preempt global cooling. The Garden of Eden will flourish again and the planet will rebuild." He smiled grimly. "However, we will not survive the upcoming chain reaction. Life will be eradicated. We are the dinosaurs."

"Kronos's Fury," Matt murmured beside me. "The day of reckoning."

No one on the rectangular table heard him. The US President tapped her pen on the hefty report. "If it is inevitable, as you say, what hope do any of us have?"

Matt interrupted, "We can do this with the tools we have been given. Excalibur was sent to us for a reason."

The Queen spoke, "Yes, since the Total Tremor, we have known something was coming. We must believe."

With more diplomacy, the US President added, "Sitting back and doing nothing isn't my way."

The Defense Secretary scoffed, "How can some magical sword save an entire planet from a super solar flare? Will you go on top of the Himalayas and knock the flare out of the sky?" He glanced at me and sneered. "Should we helicopter up your precious sword-bearer?"

I rasped, "There's more."

No one heard me.

Matt faced the Defense Secretary with fisted hands. "She is the champion!"

With effort, I grabbed the back of Matt's shirt. I repeated, "There's more."

The Queen's sharp gaze focused on me. "What did you say, sword-bearer?"

With effort, I straightened in the wheelchair. I croaked, "More to the v-vision."

The Queen turned to look at Matt. "Merlin?"

Matt's amber eyes turned to me. "Ryan, what did you see?"

Black dots danced in my vision. I blinked. "I-I…"

"We should use a memory stone to extract it from her. The poor girl is in no condition to speak." The Queen took out a smooth gemstone from her pocket. She floated the seeing stone to Matt. "This is one of the best."

Matt grabbed the stone out of the air. "Ryan, are you sure? This won't be easy."

Grey grabbed his arm. "Forget it, Emrys. I won't let you endanger her anymore."

Matt retorted, "I would not do this if I believed it could hurt her. We've lost enough time to the Kronos Eye. Only a month remains until the solstice. From here on out, every day counts. You know that as well as I do."

"Grey," I whispered. "S'okay."

Grey turned to look at me hesitantly.

Matt stepped around him. "Are you sure?"

A sharp pain focused my attention on my stomach. Fresh blood soaked the loose, dark fabric of my T-shirt. Hoping no one would notice, I nodded.

In his face, I saw the conflict. *Should he believe me? Was risking me necessary?* But we both knew this meeting was too important. This meeting would define how the world reacted. This crisis belonged to us all. It was bigger than him. Bigger than me. And I understood why he'd brought me. He needed me to see what we faced and who it would affect, not a hypothetical "whole world," but the eyes of several billion people peeking out from behind the haunted faces of the leaders they'd chosen to represent them.

Coming to some internal decision, Matt put on the *Dragon's Eye* and held out the seeing stone. I put a shaking hand on it. He commanded, "*Atibha.*"

A heavy pressure pushed down on me. I started to pant, as I was unable to breathe. A bubble of green surrounded me and I inhaled greedily. Vane's magic, I realized.

As he'd done in the Ella caves, Matt was siphoning off Vane's magic.

The meeting room disappeared, but the table full of people remained. The circular table above me also stayed, but the background changed as if we'd suddenly been thrust inside a movie. Still sitting in the wheelchair, I watched myself fall on the nine stones. The horsemen appeared and the scene with the trilithon and the golden apple played over, but at a removed distance.

Beside me, Matt watched it all avidly. His hand linked the stone to me. "This is it. The gates are the answer."

"Or the apple." I yawned. "Or both."

The memory flickered as my strength waned. Matt waved a hand. The meeting room came back into focus.

"That's the plan?" The Queen looked at Matt.

Around us, the table full of world leaders sat in stunned silence.

The Queen cleared her throat. "Merlin, maybe you should explain—"

Matt began to say something. I didn't hear him. The pressure on me was replaced by a loud buzzing in my ears. The door blasted open.

Matt flew backwards across the room. The seeing stone fell at my feet.

"What have you done, Merlin?" Vane's voice boomed through the room.

The military man jumped up. Several others on the circular table above us also rose.

"Who is he?" someone said.

"Vane." The Queen stood up.

"This is Vane?" the US President said.

"How did you get past security?" the Defense Secretary demanded.

Men in black suits and with guns streamed in behind him, but Vane sent them flying in the air. He turned his glowing eyes on the Queen. "I don't have time for this. Stop them or I will kill them all."

Vane's eyes traveled around the room. In front of me, Grey picked up the seeing stone from where it had fallen in front of the wheelchair. Behind Vane, the mermaids surrounded Vane in a protective stance.

"Why are you here?" the Queen demanded.

The other leaders sat in petrified silence. I remembered having the same reaction the day I'd met the mermaids. It hadn't been a good day. I stared at Vane, yet again reminded that he was one of them—their king.

Vane strode straight toward us. Another wave of dizziness overtook me. The room spun and I fought to stay conscious.

The Defense Secretary yelled to the men in black, "Stop him."

"Send more security now!" the Defense Secretary barked into a phone. He leaned down and picked up a gun from one of the fallen guards.

The men in black scrambled up. One fired at Vane's back.

The glow of a green shield popped up around Vane. The bullet bounced off Vane's shield and straight at the nearest target—the Defense Secretary. It hit his chest and the politician fell back on the table.

A stunned assembly watched the trail of blood seep across the white papers on the table. On the floor, Matt slowly rose from the concussion-inducing fall and rushed to the fallen man. The men in black tightened their grips on their guns. Vane glanced at the Secretary without expression and sent a wave of green magic stunned the men in black. They froze in place.

"Anyone else care to test me?" he growled.

Black oblivion stood like a shadow over me. I held it back with a fragile tip of a finger, but it wasn't enough. Pressure squeezed my lungs. I let out silent gasps, trying to suck in air.

Vane turned toward Grey. Grey's fingers tightened on the seeing stone. Colin stepped in front of Grey.

"She's dying, you idiots," Vane barked at them.

Grey blanched. "What?"

Injecting as much vitality into the statement as possible, and with more effort than I actually possessed, I croaked from behind Grey, "I-I'm okay."

His eyes snapped to me. "I don't think so."

Vane shoved him aside. He reached me. Monster green filled

his irises. I couldn't help flinching. Vane didn't miss my reaction. The green receded to leave only hazel-brown. He said softly, "The beast's caged, Ryan. It's just me."

The beast may have been caged, but its door had no guard. Still, I was glad to see him, ridiculously glad.

Vane put his hand against my stomach. Green magic flowed over the cloth, but nothing happened. "Merlin, why isn't this working?"

"It's the same as in the hallway. The Kronos Eye seems to be blocking any magical healing."

Throwing his brother a glare, he ordered. "Ragnar, call an ambulance."

I blinked trying to stay awake as Grey scrambled to get his phone.

Vane grabbed my hand. Real fear rolled off tight shoulders. "If you close your eyes, DuLac, you'll force me to gut my own brother."

I almost smiled. Prince Charming, he was not. Then, my chest constricted. My arm jerked in his grip. Worried eyes, brown pupils surrounded by a ring of green, were the last thing I saw before my heart gave out.

\*\*\*

I woke up to find myself in a sterile, white room.

Everything hurt. Even my eyelids were sore. When I took a breath, my side spiked with pain. My ribs were bruised. My breastbone ached as if it were pounded relentlessly, which it might have been. I remembered hazy bits of an ambulance. Beyond that, I lay immobilized on a metal bed. I looked up. Set against a tiled ceiling, bright fluorescent tubes illuminated the room with crisp clarity. A black-tinted window let in muted, natural light as if too much might be painful. The window showed I lay several stories high in a red brick building, a sign declared it as "Thoreau General."

I stretched out my hand, wincing as something pulled at my skin. Thin tubes slipped beneath the dermis connected to an IV marked "saline." A metal heart rate monitor was wrapped around my index finger on my right hand. Machines beeped steadily behind my head. I pushed up with my elbows on the slanted mattress of the hospital bed and reached for a plastic tumbler full of water. I only had enough strength to swipe at it drunkenly.

The door opened.

"Morning, Sleeping Beauty." Grey walked into the hospital room carrying a handful of white lilies.

I arched a brow, the only action that didn't cause shooting pain. "You got me flowers? You must have been really worried."

"Mom started it." He crossed the room and pulled me into a tight hug. I squeezed him feebly. Weakness made my bones feel like liquid. I tried to drop back against the pillows. Grey held me tighter. "You look better. A lot better. Don't do that again."

With effort, I put a hand on his back. "I know I should've found a way to call you from Sri Lanka, but it was only for a few days—"

Grey pulled back with a strange expression. "It's been two months since India, Ryan. I found you at the old bridge four days ago."

My jaw dropped open. "What—?"

A round, middle-aged woman, wearing blue scrubs, bustled inside the room. "You're awake! I was hopeful when your heart rate fluctuated." With a beaming smile, she crossed to check the beeping machine behind my head. She gave Grey an impatient look and he quickly moved out of her way to the other side of the bed.

I watched her. "What happened to me?"

The nurse stilled, giving Grey an odd look. "We have an on-staff counselor. She will be happy to come and talk to you."

On-staff counselor? That didn't sound good. What story did they tell the hospital? I touched my stomach. Under the cotton blue gown, thick bandages taped my stomach. The Minotaur's sharp teeth flashed in my mind. It was hazy, thankfully so, but I remembered it with more clarity than I intended. I remembered the pain.

Suddenly, I wanted to rip the gown off and examine the horror waiting for me underneath.

Grey leaned over me, tucking a strand of hair behind my ear. "You'll be fine. Mom brought in the best plastic surgeon in the area. It just needs time to heal."

*Plastic surgeon? Since when did I need a surgeon when there were a bunch of wizards running around?* I rubbed my forehead. Memories seemed hazy. I remembered the hallway and the monster. I remembered a strange, yet incredibly real dream of a meeting at the UN. I remembered Vane's fist pounding my chest, fighting for me. Or was it the monster who fought? I didn't know.

While the nurse busily checked my pulse, Grey went to a long tray table beside the bed and replaced some dead daisies inside a crystal-blue vase.

I stared at the wilted brown petals. "How long have I been here?"

"Almost four days," the nurse answered cheerfully.

I started coughing. The nurse handed me the plastic tumbler of water and waited. I lifted the tumbler with shaky hands to my mouth and managed to take a small swallow. My body ached as if it had been run over by a semi-truck. Four days in the hospital. *Two months lost.* My mind struggled to process the numbers. I remembered hazy bits of the hospital. Waking up a few times in a darkened room—probably this room—then quickly passing out again.

The nurse continued to watch me with a critical eye. She waited until I finished drinking before saying briskly, "Excellent. You'll be hungry soon. I'm going to order you some food. I need to alert your doctor and the... others." She pointed to a cord hanging off the hospital bed. "If you need anything, push this button." In a whirlwind of efficiency, she spun around to leave as quickly as she came. She paused at the door and oddly enough, glanced back at Grey. "Are you sure you don't want me to stay, hon?"

I took Grey's hand and squeezed it to show her. "I'll be fine with my brother."

The nurse nodded, but the worried look didn't leave her eyes. This time, when the door opened, I noticed that two men in black suits stood just outside my room.

As soon as the door reclosed, I dropped Grey's hand. "Why am I in a hospital? And why was the nurse looking at you like you're a murderer or rapist? What's going on?"

"Er, a lot has happened, Ry." He paused, giving me a deer-in-headlights look that made me wish I had the strength to toss the tumbler of water at him. "Are you sure you're ready to hear all of this?"

I ground out, "Start at the beginning."

"I got to the Old North Bridge at the same time as the paramedics. You were really torn up and… God, the blood." His eyes took on a faraway look. "I don't think I can ever go back to that park again."

My heart skipped a beat. *Alexa.* We lost her at the bridge. I picked up his hand and squeezed it.

Grey shook off the memory. "Anyway, we made up a story of you being attacked. The police wanted to know how I knew you were there, so I planted a cell on you. Except for a few hours, you've been here since I found you with your stomach ripped open, bleeding to death at the park. Understandably, the nurses have been rather protective of you. They said they'd never seen such a horrific mauling. It almost looked like an animal attack, but some of the bruises they found came from human fingers."

I touched my stomach, pressing in on the heavy bandages, and tears of pain sprung to my eyes. The Minotaur flashed in my head again. I shivered. Even though he tore me open to save me, I don't think I'll ever forget those teeth. "And Matt?"

"He was unconscious when the police came. They think he was attacked first. Which got him off the hook, unfortunately—"

I held up a hand. "What do you mean *unfortunately*? Is he all right?"

"He's fine," Matt answered for himself.

For the first time since I had known him, my heart didn't immediately leap into my throat at the mere sight of him. It could have been because everything hurt too much. Messy, brown hair fell over his forehead as he crossed the room to me. Oh, he still looked mouthwatering in a tight brown T-shirt, lean abs, and ragged jeans, but the faraway, unfocused look in his eyes, which formerly intrigued me so, only annoyed me today.

Grey moved so quickly I almost didn't see him. He punched Matt in the face, growling, "How did you get past my gargoyles? I told you, Emrys, you're not welcome here."

Matt reeled back at the surprise attack.

A clipped accented voice said, "Mr. Ragnar, step back. The gargoyles are fine. Just a minor freeze spell."

"Freeze spell?" the other one muttered, as if he couldn't believe it.

Two men came into the room.

I recognized the first one right away. "James Bond."

"Robin," corrected the British spy from Sri Lanka.

I studied the other man in quintessential Boston wear—black T-shirt, dark jeans, and a Red Sox baseball hat. The whole ensemble was perfect. A little too perfect. Still, he was definitely American. I said, "Is this your friend, Felix?"

"I prefer Frank," the CIA agent confirmed with a warm, you-should-trust-me smile.

I didn't buy it. "What's going on, Grey?"

"Sire!" Colin and five other gargoyles crowded into the small room. Robin and Frank reacted immediately by positioning themselves between Matt and the gargoyles. The spies slipped out handguns with silencers from under their shirts.

Colin sneered at the two. "As if that would hurt us, Regulars."

"No, but it will slow you down enough to take your head," Robin replied.

Two of the gargoyles behind Colin snarled.

I gaped at them all. Nothing in the bizarre scene made sense. I guessed that Matt and the two spies were allied together, and Grey was pissed at Matt. The latter wasn't so odd, after all. Grey lunged at Matt again.

"Grey, stop!" I said.

Colin caught him. Grey spat, "He almost killed you."

"I wasn't trying to kill her," Matt said, rubbing his jaw. "I'm trying save her. To save all of us. She agreed to use the seeing stone."

Grey snorted in disbelief. "You should never have taken her to New York. She had a cardiac arrest."

I squawked, "The UN meeting was real?"

I'd landed in the woods and I'd imagined being back at AC High. I touched the bandages again. The hallway may have existed in my mind only, but the monster had been very real. It had saved me. Then, Matt had taken me to the UN meeting?

I rubbed my head, pushing back the beginnings of a headache. "Can someone tell me what's going on? Why am I in a hospital? Why have I lost two months? Why are the spooks here?"

Matt answered in backwards order, "The First Member asked me to work with Robin. We were in Rawana's realm for a little more than seven weeks. The Kronos Eye poisoned you and you're in the hospital because magical healing hasn't worked. The poison seems to be immune to it."

"The Lady hid the answers in a thing that poisoned her own champion?" I remarked. "Brilliant."

Matt frowned at my assessment. "The *path* to the answers. She didn't have the answers, only the instrument to get them; and I doubt it was her intention to harm you. Rawana said he waited for a wizard-warrior. You're one-half of that pairing. The Lady must have expected me to be there with you. Except I didn't have my magic."

"Actually, you didn't have a pure soul," I corrected.

Grey let out a snort of laughter.

"Because of you, Ragnar," Matt spat out. "Because I pulled you back from death after the trial."

"I remember when I died, Emrys," Grey retorted.

Matt raked a hand through brown hair, messing up the neat style. He explained, "Now that we know what we're up against and—"

"We do?" I interjected.

Matt gave me his long-suffering Merlin look. "You brought the proof, Ryan. This isn't conjecture anymore on our part. The leaders of the world have to know the danger we're facing and we need their help. I've given the apple to be studied—"

My mouth dropped open. "You gave away the apple!"

"Well, it seems I arrived just in time." Vane's mocking voice filled an already crowded space. With one quick flick of the wrist, he sent both groups—the gargoyles and the two spies—flying across the room, parting the way for his entrance.

Vane said silkily, "I find myself very interested in this apple."

He should be. It had been in his memory. Perceval had taken an apple from the vault in Carthage.

The gargoyles and spies scrambled up, drawing swords and guns. They tensed for battle as if the Grim Reaper had suddenly appeared. Vane sneered and marched further into small room.

"The apple is being studied by the world's most eminent

physicists in a secure lab even you won't be able to find," Robin added.

Vane turned cold eyes on him. "Want to wager?"

Frank almost took a step back before he realized what he was doing and stopped himself. Robin gave him a pat of sympathy.

Vane turned to me.

"Forget your minions—I mean—mermaids?" I said lightly.

"They're busy," he answered with an enigmatic smile. He didn't bother glancing at anyone else as he crossed to the bedside. A critical eye swept over me, stopping at my heart, causing it to ache a little. He said quietly, "You could do better than that gown."

I fiddled with the papery green material covering me, sticking my nose in the air. "It works well enough."

"Well enough isn't up to your level," he said huskily.

A sting of tears—happy, unhappy, I didn't know which—sprang to my eyes.

Matt took a step closer to me. Vane's gaze snapped to him. In a blink, Vane caught his brother by the throat and pushed him face down into the mattress at the foot of the bed.

"Vane!" I squeaked.

Matt flailed as Vane suffocated him. Hard fingers squeezed Matt's throat. Vane pushed him deeper into white sheets. He yanked the Dragon's Eye out of Matt's jeans pocket and threw it on the bed in disgust. He railed at his brother, "You've dropped to a new low, Merlin. You can't control something as powerful as the seeing stone with the little bit of magic you're managing to steal. Don't think I hadn't noticed you taking magic from me. You could have killed her."

I forced my fading attention onto the scene. Green encompassed Vane. Although I didn't wear the *Dragon's Eye*, I saw the outline of the monster riding him. A hint of sharp teeth shone from his snarling mouth, and for a minute, I actually believed he might harm his brother.

"Vane, let go!" I said, "I trust Matt. So do you."

"No, I don't," he said.

I grabbed the *Dragon's Eye*. Closing my eyes, I mentally opened the door between us. The monster stood with its back to me, alone in the grey colorless world, of limbo. I went up to its hulking form. Pulling up my courage, I put a trembling hand on its back. Under my touch, hard muscles tensed, as if it debated my sincerity. As if it wanted me to release him and yet was afraid I would.

"Vane," I said.

With a snarling sound, the monster pulled away. He rounded on me, his face furious. Hot breath blew down on me. Teeth glistened with saliva. The wound, my stomach, gave a twinge in response, but for the first time since the maze, I held my ground.

I found myself back in the hospital room.

"Let him go, Vane," I said breathily.

His fingers eased a fraction off Matt. Then, a fraction more. He let go of Matt.

Matt sprang up, swallowing big gulps of air.

Grey stared at Matt with a slight satisfied smile. He said idly, "How did you find her? I used fake names and everything."

Vane raised an arrogant brow. He pointed to a camera hidden at the corner of the room. "I knew you wouldn't take her too far. I hacked the hospital's security feed."

Grey made an annoyed sound.

Matt snarled, "Why can't you just leave her alone, Vane? She's needs time to recover."

Grey said sharply, "As if you care, Emrys."

"Think you've made an enemy of the dog, brother," Vane said with amusement.

I groaned at the amount of testosterone in the room.

Vane looked at his brother. "You didn't find the Healing Cup."

Grey let out a loud breath. Rourke, the gargoyle king, was dying. He desperately needed the Healing Cup. Matt stared back at Vane stony-faced.

"Never mind, I've already found a simulation of Kronos's Fury. I know the endgame." Vane shrugged. "What's the next step?"

"As if I would trust you," Matt retorted.

Vane's eyes flickered over me. "You've never learned to trust anyone."

I rolled my eyes. As if he was that much better.

Vane scowled and moved closer to me.

Matt said quickly, "I need her to keep reviewing the vision in the Kronos Eye. The answers are in the vision. The sword-bearer and I need to work together to see all the nuances."

Each condescending word grated worse than the last one. I was the one lying in a hospital bed and he had the nerve to dismiss me as "*the sword-bearer.*"

My nostrils flared. I snapped, "Fine."

"I need you—"

"I said fine," I repeated, cutting him off.

Matt blinked. "Are you upset with me?"

"I'm not upset!" Of course, I was upset. He was just an idiot. I forced myself to look at the boy with whom I'd been obsessed for what seemed like forever. The boy I couldn't seem to let go. Yet, he certainly had no problem letting go of me. I said in a measured tone, "Exactly when did I not bend over backwards to help you?"

"I-I…" Matt faltered.

"Apparently, she's not upset," Vane said dryly.

"How long do we have to figure out all this end-of-the-world stuff by?" Grey asked. "I missed that part of the meeting."

"So did I." Vane's gaze flickered over me. He answered Grey, "Recall, if you will, on Aegae, the Lady said the longest day of the sun. We have until the summer solstice."

Matt looked at his brother in dismay. "You figured that out?"

Vane's lips curved up. "Afraid?"

Grey took out his cell phone and thumbed the screen. "It's another month until the solstice. A week and a half after the end of school."

I touched my bandages. *Would I be ready?*

Vane picked up my hospital chart, flipping through it. "Your vitals are good. The doctors say you're healing well. You'll be able to walk with a crutch in a few days, I suspect."

I stared at him. "You can read a hospital chart?"

He arched a brow. "I'm a genius and have divine powers."

"Stolen divine powers," Matt muttered.

Vane ignored him. "The last bit about the crutch is in the nurse's notes on her computer. You'll be ready, if you want to be."

"I have to be," I answered flatly.

Outside, the sun shone down with serenity. The giver of life, it was a thing to be taken for granted. Soon, though, it would become the taker of life, a thing to be feared. I lay back on the bed as a rush of fatigue overtook me. I glanced at the motley group. "Now, if you've got what you wanted, can you get out and leave me alone?"

"I haven't," Vane said. The hairs on the back of my neck rose at the edge in his tone, but he wasn't looking at me. "Give her back the amulet, Merlin."

Reflexively my hand tightened. I hadn't realized I'd dropped it. And lost it.

"You have it on you. I feel it. If you'd prefer, I can take it," Vane said.

With a grimace, Matt took out a handkerchief from his pocket. He unwrapped the sides of the handkerchief to reveal the *Dragon's Eye*. For the first time, I got a good look at the necklace. Vane had done something to it in the hallway. A fissure ran down the gemstone. The fissure was a jagged green. Vane snatched the necklace away. He held it out to me. "Put it on."

I recoiled at the heavy-handed command. My bandages seemed to tighten around me at the thought of being tied to the Minotaur.

Matt read my resistance easily. He said with satisfaction, "She doesn't want it."

"Leave her alone, Vane—" Grey started to say.

Green flashed in the room. Everyone, except Vane and I, slumped to the floor.

I gaped at the sleeping bodies. "What are you doing?"

In a velvety voice encased in ice, Vane said, "Do you know how easy it would be to kill everyone in this room? Everyone in this hospital, if you don't cooperate?"

"And I would hate you. Is that what you want? I'm so done with being ordered around by you and Matt. Get it through your head. You. Can't. Force. Me."

His fingers tightened on the necklace. "Then, put it on because I'm asking you."

His voice, sweet as honey, lulled my tongue into forming the word "yes." I resisted the pull. "Why?"

"This is what saved you, Ryan. It saved you in that hell with Rawana. It saved you from the Kronos Eye. You were right to not to take it off in Greece when I asked you." He said hesitatingly, "Now, I'm asking the opposite—just put it back on."

It was a mistake to trust him, yet I couldn't look away from him. I was the captured bird. We both knew he wasn't really giving me a choice. I took a breath. "No games?"

"No games." He held out the necklace.

I pushed. "If I take it, will you leave?"

He sighed. "For now."

I took it and fumbled with the clasp for several seconds, until finally the chain snapped in place. Vane watched me with patience. As soon as the amulet settled on my skin, he touched the chain. A small breeze blew around my neck. The gemstone glowed green as he commanded, "*Arudh.*"

"What did you do?" I squawked, reaching for the clasp. It zapped me.

"I locked it." Vane leaned close to my ear. My body flushed hot, then cold, as his lips grazed the sensitive edge of my earlobe.

He said in a low tone, "No more games, Ryan. I let you toss me away once. This time, I will hold what's mine."

A hint of teeth showed between bared lips. His eyes met mine. The fiery intensity in them made me catch my breath, but I didn't see any hint of green. This wasn't the Minotaur talking, this was Vane, and I had no doubt he wasn't playing games. The angry intensity in his gaze, in a sick way, turned me on.

"You came to find me at the UN meeting," I said.

"I will always come." Then, as if admitting too much, he stepped back. Putting distance between us, he added, "Sword-bearer."

I let it go. At the moment, I didn't have the strength to fight him. He knelt down beside Matt and started going through his pockets. It took me a little while to figure out what he was doing. "You haven't seen the seeing stone."

"I was a little busy saving your life." Not finding the seeing stone on Matt, he stood. His lips lifted into a small grin. "I will, though."

I looked at him curiously. "I could tell you."

He stilled. "Would you?"

I hesitated, glancing at the limp bodies on the floor, glancing at Matt.

Vane read my expression. His own tightened. "Still can't make a move without Merlin."

"You could take it from me."

His eyes flickered over my amulet. "Yes, I could."

I touched the quiet gem. "What's stopping you?"

"You're not strong enough. Yet."

For a second, I stared at him speechless.

He continued, "You'll be useless if I make you a vegetable."

I raised a brow and baited the monster. "Or you're not *able* to take it."

Icy green pupils hardened. Internally, I winced. Why was I waving a red flag in front of the bull? On my neck, the *Dragon's Eye* heated. A pressure built inside my head. The monster reached inside my mind. It dug its hand into the black mess of my memories. I let out a small cry. I slammed the door shut in its gleaming face. To my surprise, the door held. The gem turned cold under my command. I looked at Vane in shock. "I can shut you out."

"You're welcome for the lesson," he said dryly. "Don't get used to it. I'm being nice."

I bit my lip. "I know."

He glanced down at Matt. "Anyhow, I will know soon enough."

"You're going to use me to spy on him."

"He works better when he thinks he's not on a leash." He shrugged. "That's the side benefit."

"What's the main benefit?" I retorted. *Why was I asking a question to which I knew I wasn't going to like the answer?*

His lips twisted in a strangled smile. "You work better on the leash."

"That's what I am to you? Work?"

Emotion flickered in his eyes. His right hand fisted. "That's what you chose to be. Get some rest, Dorothy. You're going to need it to face the wicked witch."

My eyes raked over his green-tinged ones. *"You are the wicked witch."*

Vane arched a brow. *"In an alternate version, the green witch was the good one trying to save Oz, and Dorothy was duped into killing her."*

*"Is that what you think you are? The good witch?"*

A hungry smile curved his lips. *"I can be flexible."*

## ACTON-CONCORD HIGH

What does one do when the world is about to end? I went back to high school. One weekend back at home convinced me.

I left the hospital on Friday and felt almost alive by Sunday. Vane was right about the crutch. My strength returned quickly, but then, I was the sword-bearer. Vane also said the mermaids were busy and he wasn't kidding. While Matt and I were traipsing around Sri Lanka, interesting things were going on at Avalon Prep.

Vane took over the whole school and most of the Council. The wizards were split. Those loyal to Vane remained. Those who disagreed, left. Some went home, but most went to where they thought Merlin might be—Ragnar Manor. In the past month, the elegant, gothic manor had transformed from my home to a halfway house for wizards, candidates, and even gargoyles. Next, I kept expecting to run into a bald professor in a wheelchair in the corridors.

Rows of simple cots lined Grey's gym. Grey informed me they

were taken up during the day for training. What kind of training? Grey wouldn't tell me. So I asked Colin. And I didn't like the answer. While I was gone, they went back to the plan of finding replacements for me. Since they didn't have Vane as a trainer anymore, Grey was chosen. I didn't doubt Vane had a similar replacement hunt going on at Avalon Prep. It irritated me, but didn't devastate me. Too much. If only I could lose the sword-bearer title so easily...

The manor was also turned into a high security stronghold. I thought it was bad when Vane had a few wizards patrolling the woods in dark SUVs. Now, about a hundred or so gargoyles, wizards, and hired military muscle guarded the perimeter of the manor's five-acre plot.

The strangest thing, though, was finding out that I hadn't been expelled from school. In fact, I was probably going to be in the student president hall of fame (no, there was no such thing) for pulling such an amazing prom together.

Grey drove me to school Monday morning. He pulled the Land Rover out of a three-car garage annexed onto the side of the manor sometime during this century. Water spilled over the turrets and rounded corners of Ragnar Manor. Ordinarily, I wouldn't have noticed the unusual amount of rain, but after the discussion at the UN, I was keenly aware of the turbulent weather.

A circular driveway held a broken fountain, one that would never get repaired. Nestled in a clearing, surrounded by towering pine trees, the manor had one visible path from the woods. The other way was well hidden. Grey turned onto a one-lane street past a red mailbox that marked the long road home. The narrow streets of Concord ebbed and flowed like gentle waves.

Behind us, Tommy, the school bus driver, lumbered along in

the big, yellow bus. About half the kids in the school bus boarded at Ragnar Manor. It was one of a handful of vehicles still allowed in the manor's new security force. Acton-Concord High had received a big infusion of students these past few months. I wished I could have seen them that first day. A bunch of wizard kids from England going to regular school. I snickered at the image of them standing in line at the cafeteria, instead of the sit-down dining hall at Avalon Prep.

"What's so funny?"

I giggled. "There's no potions class at AC High."

Letting out a groan, Grey said, "It's Marilynn's fault. She transferred all their records so they could go. Wanted to keep them busy. You should see them in math. It's pathetic. Their little wizard brains can barely handle two plus two." He muttered, "At least the gargoyles are more or less normal."

"Did you really just say that?"

Grey turned red. "Are you sure you really want to go to school?"

I stared out the window, without seeing. "I want my life back."

He said matter-of-factly, "We're never getting our lives back, Ry."

"Then, I'm holding on to whatever I can have."

Grey made a face. "You know the Council ordered Marilynn to take—"

"She doesn't want to talk about it, Grey," Gia said.

She sat in the backseat. I was in the front passenger seat. In the months I'd been gone, she'd cut her hair super short again. It framed her face in jagged red lines. Turning, I smiled at her. She didn't return the full smile, but her lips uncurled just a little. The small thawing left me happier than I thought possible. I sank back into the Land Rover's cushioned seat.

*Marilynn. Ugh.* I hadn't planned on going to school this morning. After Matt's little speech about needing all my attention, I intended to spend the day reviewing the Kronos Eye. Then, I had gone into the kitchen for breakfast.

*** 

Six a.m. My eyes snapped open under the command of my internal clock. It took me a minute to realize I was actually on *my* bed, in *my* room at *my* house. I stretched and winced. I pulled off the cami I slept in. Black and blue bruises covered my ribs. The darkest one lay right over my heart.... where Vane had given me CPR. Grey told me he'd done so at the UN Meeting before the paramedics arrived. He'd kept me alive.

I touched the breastplate. The knowledge left me in an odd place. By my count, this was about the tenth time he'd rescued me. Funny, because I was hoping to rescue him.

My hand slid over the thick bandage around my lower abdomen. I could keep down solid foods since Friday, my last day at the hospital. The doctors refused to release me until I had a bowel movement, the best indication that my insides were healing. I shuddered at the memory of that experience. As well as I was treated, I hoped I would never have to step inside a hospital again. With effort, I swung my legs off the bed and stood.

Too quickly, I fell down with a solid thump. The door flew open.

"Are you all right?" Gia stomped over to me.

"Fine." A draft slid across my bare back. I lifted myself on my elbows. "Um, can you shut the door?"

"Sure," she mumbled. Long bangs fell over her eyes. She avoided looking directly at me. She hadn't forgiven me. Not that I blamed her. If I let myself think about Blake too much, I would become paralyzed.

I hoisted myself up on my elbows. "It's early. Why are you up?"

Gia's eyes widened at the extent of my injuries. "I couldn't sleep. Grey snores."

"Really?"

She blushed. "Yeah, well…"

"Don't worry I won't ask for details." I picked up the steel crutch lying by the bed. It zigzagged at the top and hooked around my arm in an innovative way.

"My room is the one next to his!"

"Sure," I said lightly. Grey had given her Alexa's old room—something I doubt he would have done if he didn't care a lot about her. Even if she wasn't ready to admit it, I was happy she and Grey were supporting each other.

I hobbled to my closet. I pulled on a bra and shirt fairly easily. Garments below the waist were a different matter. I stared at them, trying to figure out how to stretch, without inducing too much pain. Gia walked over to me silently and took the undies and skirt. With minimal help from me, she slipped them on me.

"You look terrible," she muttered.

"It's my special gift."

"What? Causing pain? There we agree," she snapped, walking to the door. "I have to go get ready for school."

*Monday, right.* I called, "Gia."

She paused, her hand on the doorknob, but didn't turn around. I wanted to say a million things. About how sorry I was about Blake. About how much all this sucked. I noticed how white the knuckles of her hand became from her death-grip on the doorknob and got out just one word. "Thanks."

The death-grip eased off the knob. "I hope this is over soon."

She slipped out of the room before I could answer.

"So do I," I said to the closed door.

I moved slowly down the hallway, trying to keep the rubber sole of the crutch from slipping on the manor's slick hardwood floors.

Colin came out of a room near the end of the hall. Through an open door, I glimpsed Rourke, lying still on a large, four-poster bed. Sylvia's bed. Despite it being the middle of summer, a thick comforter covered most of his body. On a large easy chair beside him, wearing a T-shirt and yoga pants, Sylvia lay asleep. From what I understood, she rarely left his side.

Colin shut the door with a quiet click. "I didn't expect to see you about, sword-bearer."

"I've slept enough," I told him.

Colin nodded. He hovered behind me as I made my way down the stairs. We parted in the hallway. He headed to the gym, while I stumbled a few feet to the kitchen. I swung open its silent door. As soon as I did, I wished I'd never gotten out of bed.

Raindrops streaked down the wall-to-wall windows in the drafty kitchen. The smell of fresh scrambled eggs and toast filled the air. In the middle, next to the island, two people ate breakfast and shared a laugh. Matt and a girl.

It was so normal.

We traveled all over the world and I couldn't remember him looking so relaxed with me. The grey hue of the kitchen made Matt's dark brown hair shiny. Next to him stood a delicately framed girl. She was half a head smaller than him, reaching just past his shoulder. From this angle, I saw her profile—high cheekbones, slender nose, and angled jaw.

She had annoyingly white teeth. She twirled a strand of dark-blond hair around her fingers. The last straw was when she lightly slapped Matt's shoulder as he made another comment. She smiled, showing more white teeth, and I wanted to smack her.

I would be smacking myself. Through the kitchen's open door, I watched myself.

A duplicate me.

I squinted at her. Well, not quite duplicate.

There were slight differences. She appeared completely the same, but also not. Unlike me, she was uninjured and whole. No black scars on one hand. No bandages. No crutch.

I stepped into the kitchen and said lightly, "I can see I've been missed around here."

Matt jerked away from the duplicate as if he'd been caught with his hand up her skirt.

The duplicate turned to face me. Her lips curled into a small, tight smile.

"I've been keeping up appearances for you because you're so important." From behind the kitchen island, she took out a duplicate crutch. She glanced at Matt. "Don't worry, I'll continue to serve as needed."

*Serving who as needed?* I bit back the mean-spirited retort.

Instead, saying, "Well, you can stop stealing my identity. I'm back."

It was surreal. Like talking into a mirror, except that this reflection talked back.

Matt sighed. "Marilynn, please take off the glamour."

The duplicate shifted back into her true form—a college-age girl with a svelte figure, straight black hair and long legs. Marilynn. The wizard school's administrator. The one who had been crushing on Matt ever since I first met her.

"Why the clone?" I demanded.

Matt answered, "She's a decoy. To protect you."

*Right.* "Exactly how was she protecting me when I wasn't here?" I held up a hand. "You know what? I don't care. There's no need for this act anymore. You can go."

Her eyes hardened. "I don't have anywhere else to go. Your boyfriend saw to that."

My eyes flickered over Matt. I muttered, "As if Vane is the reason you're at Ragnar Manor."

She stalked towards me and the door. "I should get ready for school."

I put a crutch out to block her. "*Ryan DuLac* will be going to school today. The real one."

Marilynn looked down her nose at me. "You're supposed to have a two-hour meeting after school to finalize everything for Prom. Think you can handle it?"

She knew I couldn't. I had no idea what she'd been doing for two months, but I wasn't about to cave. "I'll figure it out."

She smirked and sent me a "just try" look.

Once the door closed behind her, Matt pounced. "I need you to work on the Kronos Eye with me this morning."

I ground my teeth. Standing in front of him, leaning on a crutch, looking like death warmed over, and he couldn't bother to ask how I was doing. God, I needed a break. I said simply, "No."

"Why?"

My appetite gone, I turned to head back to my room. "Because I need to remember why I *should* help you. I need to remember what's at stake."

*And I need to remember it away from you.*

\*\*\*

The Land Rover swerved into the student parking lot, nearly hitting a smaller sedan. Very quickly, I was thrust back into reality. I shouted, "Grey!"

"Sorry, I was thinking about something," he muttered.

"So was I." I shook off the morning's aggravating encounter with Matt.

Lately, it was one aggravating encounter after another with him.

Grey pulled up to the curb. I slid out of the SUV. Gia emerged from the back. Weighted drops of rain pelted us. Grey handed me my crutch and drove off to park the car. Gia and I hurried to get under a roof. Well, Gia hurried. I went slower to avoid stretching the muscles too far and tearing the stiches. At least my bruised ribs were healing quickly.

During first period, I watched an indoor lacrosse practice from the bench. The new coach wasn't too thrilled with my latest injury. The team wasn't doing so well. The co-captain's performance (my performance) plummeted after winter break—

almost as if she played like another person—and they had a brand new coach. The previous coach (Vane) had been yanked out of the country due to visa problems.

Two girls, one grunge and one cheerleader, smiled at me with too much teeth as I hobbled into history later that morning. Neat rows of desk-chairs ran from the front to the back. I took a seat at the back of the class so I could lean the crutch against the wall. My hand against the bandages on my stomach, I maneuvered myself into a seat. The girls watched me with wide eyes and whispered to each other. I was pretty sure they never talked to each other before today, but everyone knew about the attack. The local news had been quick to pick up on it.

Ramanajan, the captain of the lacrosse team, sauntered into the class. She stopped short when she saw me. Giving me a small, forced smile, she quickly took a seat at the front, far away from me. Another girl on the team, Christine, walked in and sat down in the row beside me. She leaned bulky shoulders against the steel back of the chair.

"You have the worst luck. First, a sprained ankle in winter break and now, attacked…" She colored and ducked her head, her eyes filling with tears. "Sorry, that was dumb. Are you okay? I hope they catch the psycho."

A picture of Vane flashed in my head. How many times had he been called psycho? At least once or twice by me. Although his methods got results, the label still seemed to fit.

Everyone at school knew of the attack. Concord might lie on the periphery of Boston, but it wasn't the big city. Communities in the suburbs remained insular, and maniacal knifings weren't supposed to happen here. I put a hand on Christine's arm and squeezed. "Hey, it's okay. *I'm* okay. The doctors say I'll be off the crutch in less than a week."

As I said the words, it actually felt true—which was a little depressing on its own. It meant I was getting used to life as the sword-bearer. Ironic, since the end loomed closer and closer.

Christine beamed. "Just in time for Prom. You've worked on it so hard. I checked out the Park Hotel during the break. We took some family into the city. My cousins were so jealous. It's like having Prom at a palace—the huge ballroom, the upstairs balconies, and the view of the city. I can't believe you pulled in enough money to book it."

"We did it," I reminded her. Christine was part of the Prom committee.

She nodded happily. "Oh, I can't wait."

I smiled. "Who're you going with?"

She colored. Her eyes sought out a boy in tinted glasses and bleached hair lounging in his seat at the front of the class. "Taylor asked me last week."

As if sensing her gaze, he turned to look back at us, giving her a shy smile. She grinned back. Their happiness hit me like a brick.

I forced myself to smile brightly. "That's great. I'm thrilled for you."

And I was. Still, I was floored. This was how I imagined my life. Shy exchanges. First love. Prom. Happy graduation ever after. Instead, I let this fairy tale slip away, and with time swiftly running out, I had little hope of recapturing it.

Students streamed into class and took their seats seconds before the bell. Grey slipped into a seat beside me. Our history teacher hurried to her desk. Back from maternity leave, she didn't look as if she'd gotten more than a few hours of sleep. The bell rang. One last student walked in.

Matt Emrys.

His sudden appearance instigated a new wave of whispering across the room.

"They let him out?" someone hissed beside me.

"I heard he got a lot of therapy," another girl replied.

Someone giggled. "Does he still think he's Merlin?"

Ramanajan sighed. "I wonder if that means Coach Vane is back, too."

I watched Matt move with controlled grace to the teacher's desk.

"Matt? You're back," Ms. Bedevere said happily.

He handed Ms. Bedevere a slip of paper. His rolling accent washed over the room. "Just returned."

"That's wonderful," Ms. Bedevere said, all smiles. "You look so… fit."

Wearing his usual jeans and T-shirt, he modeled both as biker and hippie professor. Instead of his usual shaggy hair, though, he styled the brown locks so they emphasized the lean slant of his high cheekbones. His jaw looked freshly shaven. He hadn't looked this neat at the UN meeting.

A boy in front of Grey commented, "Those padded, white rooms make nice getaways."

Grey kicked his chair. "You should know, Joey."

Matt's gaze zeroed in on me. He walked to an empty seat on the other side of Christine. At the front of the class, Ms. Bedevere went to the chalkboard and started writing. My pocket vibrated as I got a text on my cell phone. It was a new one from Sylvia. As far as I knew, only she and Grey had the number. I snuck a look at the screen. The text listed a blocked number.

*You should be resting.*

I glanced at Matt. Sure enough, he'd snuck out his phone and was typing away.

A second text buzzed. *You look hot.*

I wondered briefly if he'd been body snatched. I stared at the words, unable to make sense of the sentence. *Hot?* I didn't even know the word existed in Matt's vocabulary.

I wrote back. *What are you doing here?*

An answer zinged back. *Couldn't leave you alone on your birthday.*

My head jerked up. A calendar next to the chalkboard confirmed what I had forgotten. Eighteen. Happy birthday to me. I snuck another glance at Matt's profile while he played with his phone. He'd remembered.

As if sensing my gaze, his head turned and his eyes caught mine. A certain glint in them left my throat parched. With unsteady fingers, I thrust my phone deep into my pocket, although I felt its heavy weight at my side.

"World War II. Last week we started the final section we will be covering before the end of the year. Today, I'd like to start off with a quote from your readings." An open book in her hand, she pointed to the words she'd written on the chalkboard. "'*Now this is not the end. It is not even the beginning of the end. But it is, perhaps, the end of the beginning.*' November 1942. Who knows who said this? Matt?"

Matt didn't reply, but returned to fiddling with his phone.

Ms. Bedevere waved to get his attention. "Matt, do you know

who said this quote?"

Matt focused on her with visible effort. "Ah, what?"

Ms. Bedevere's smile dimmed. "It's all right, Matt. You probably need a few days to catch up."

Matt's gaze fell on the chalkboard. "Winston Churchill."

Ms. Bedevere beamed at the reemergence of her star student. Then, she started lecturing. The rest of the class passed quickly, primarily because I kept glancing at Matt. He spent most of the time fiddling with his phone. Twice, Ms. Bedevere noticed his covert actions and reprimanded him. Twice, he blasted her with such charm she became flustered and began averting her eyes from his general direction.

As soon as the bell rang, students rushed out of class. Matt didn't wait for me. I hustled to catch up with him in the hallway. Luckily, his attention still glued to the phone, he wasn't walking too fast. I came up behind him, and used my crutch to block his path.

He stumbled, grabbing me to regain his balance. The action tugged at my stomach and I let out a pained gasp. He released me quickly. I wobbled and dropped a crutch. He picked it up, but didn't return it. Instead, an arm slipped around my shoulders to steady me. The touch, surprisingly conscientious, made my pulse skitter.

He pocketed his phone. "I'm beginning to think you like pain."

"No, but I don't mind things a little rough." My bare knee brushed his leg.

Desire shot through his eyes. He muttered, "Ryan."

*Ryan.* I looked into pretty amber eyes in confusion. I was sure the boy standing in front of me was not Matt, but Vane never called me Ryan. I leaned closer, debating whether to glare at him or rub my cheek against the soft jersey T-shirt clinging to his chest. A spark of raw desire lit up his eyes, causing my knees to knock together.

*Okay, forget intimidation. Seduction was way better.* I said throatily, "I thought you'd be holed up all day at the manor doing research."

"I remembered something during our last sojourn to the library. I came to see it."

"Why did you go to history, then?"

He shrugged. "I don't know."

I bit the inside of my cheek to suppress a smile. "Did you miss high school?"

"I simply wanted to remember what's its like to be in a place where you have all your possibilities in front of you."

"Uh-huh." I didn't believe him. He had fun here. I could tell from his voice.

He made an irritated sound and grabbed my crutch. His arm around my shoulder propelled me forward. We went up a short flight of stairs and down another hallway that led to the front of the building. Decorations and glittery signs advertised various clubs and activities. One banner shouted out at me. It was the same one I'd seen in my head when I came out of Elysium. The one I focused on when the Minotaur was attacking—correction: saving—me. Prom Tickets on sale now! With a black marker, someone had scribbled underneath, "Still available! Best Prom at ACH ever!!"

I must have stared at the banner for too long because

Doppelganger-Matt waved a hand in front of my face. He asked flippantly, "Dreaming of ball gowns and flirty dances?"

I kept a straight face. "More like mini-dresses and dirty dances."

Doppelganger-Matt's cheeks puffed. He halted in the middle of the hallway and turned to look down at me. "Is that why you're wearing that minuscule skirt?"

*Miniscule?* I smoothed down my skirt even though the hem fell just above my knee—close enough for regulation length. Maybe it wasn't such a bright idea to wear a skirt while hopping around on a crutch, but after Sri Lanka—I had no desire to pull on cargos for a long time. Besides, May was one of only three months in Boston when I could wear something that wasn't seven layers thick.

Doppelganger-Matt smirked at the self-conscious reaction. I stopped fighting with the skirt and decided to play. Putting my hand on his waist as if to steady myself, I fluttered my lashes. "Maybe I'm wearing it to get a date. Know anyone who'd want to… dance with me?"

His eyes narrowed. The bell rang. Students rushed into class around us.

I pushed away from him and reached for my crutch. "Time to go."

"I don't think so." He caught my wrist, his brows set in a deep V across his forehead. Before I could do more than squeak, he picked me up, as the crutch swung wildly in the air.

"W-what are you doing?" I sputtered.

"Calling your bluff." Doppelganger-Matt carried me a few steps to a closed door on the wall next to us. A placard on the door designated it as the student store. He leaned my back against the door as he twisted the knob. It opened. I felt pretty sure he used magic, but I didn't see the telltale green spark to absolutely confirm him as Vane.

As soon as we crossed the threshold, he kicked the door shut, flipped the light switch, and set me down. Under the dim yellow of a single overhead bulb, he stared at me. The student store was actually a converted walk-in closet. I leaned heavily on my crutch and listened to the loud sound of my labored breathing in the enclosed space.

Doppelganger-Matt's eyes glittered with some unnamed emotion. From the rapid way his chest rose and fell, I couldn't tell if he was simply pissed or far beyond pissed. Not that he had a real reason to be.

He said silkily, "So you want to dirty dance with Merlin?"

*Merlin.* I almost laughed. His eyes may have been amber, but the green flame of jealousy couldn't be hidden. Metaphorically and literally. At the thought, more nervous laughter bubbled up inside me. I tried to squelch it, but my lips twitched.

"Are you laughing at me?" Doppelganger-Matt scowled.

I giggled. "A little—"

I never finished the thought. He yanked me to him. I dropped the crutch. His mouth swooped down on mine. The kiss, layered with hunger, half-punished and half-begged. I tasted the rage of a turbulent ocean. Unlike Matt's scent of fresh soap, Doppelganger-Matt wore cologne. Dark wood mingled with coarse tobacco—it was uniquely Vane. I wrapped my arms around his neck and held on. Even though I responded, the kiss wasn't gentle. He moved away from the door. Without breaking contact, he adjusted my legs to wrap around his waist and carried me a few feet to the cashier's stand.

My pulse beating to the pounding rhythm of a DJ's thumping dance mix, I tongued him with every ounce of breath I had. When he lifted his head, I moaned in protest.

His lips grazed the pulse throbbing at my neck. Teeth bit the spot lightly. "Do you know how badly I want you?"

He leaned away to reach under the cash register, yanking out a condom. My eyes went from the shiny wrapper to the shelf behind his head. Beside an array of candy bars, white notebook paper, and baseball hats, a baby's bib hung from a hook. The words "AC High" had been embroidered on cute white terry cloth.

The fog of hormones clouding my brain evaporated, and it all became too real.

Doppelganger-Matt's styled hair had become shaggy under the ministrations of my desperate fingers. Brown waves fell over his face. Still it was *Matt's* face. Amber eyes, *Matt's* amber eyes, locked on mine. But I didn't want Matt.

Doppelganger-Matt pushed the hair back from my face. He traced the line of my jaw. Our lips met again in a gentle press. Not content, his mouth devoured mine. With a silent gasp, I closed my eyes and pictured Vane. His tongue explored my mouth sending little shivers of electricity through me. Heat pooled between my legs. My chest burrowed into his, strong arms tightened around me, arching me against him.

From the way my body throbbed for a release, I was tempted to allow the charade to continue. As messed up as it was, it would be so easy to let him pretend. Dealing with Monster-Vane was complicated. This way, we could ignore the problems between us. We could simply be a boy and girl.

My fingernails dug deep into his shoulders. The temptation was strong.

If I let him do this, it would only last for this fleeting moment in time. Not a bad thing. The end of the world was coming. I didn't really want to die unloved. Yet, at the same time, I knew if we did this while he pretended to be Matt, we'd never recover. This twisted game wasn't fair to us. It wasn't fair to Matt.

And deep down, I still believed there would be more.

My fingernails detached from his shoulder. My legs let go of his waist.

I tore my mouth away.

Doppelganger-Matt blinked at the release.

Defensive shields rose and his lips curled into a sneer. "You were bluffing."

Even if I had been, I wasn't ready to throw in the towel. "Tick-tock" the hands of a clock in the corner of the room chimed. I gambled, making my last play. I laid my palm on his chest, above the solid thump of his heart. "I'm not bluffing. I'm just not letting you get off so cheap. I should at least get some roses or dinner or something before my deflowering."

I let the words sink in. Startled, he drew back. He raked a hand through brown hair and grinned sheepishly. "I forgot. How about that dance instead?"

I arched a brow. "Is this your way of asking me to Prom?"

He bristled. "It's one week from now. I doubt you'll get a better offer—"

"Will you please shut up?" I sighed. "My answer is yes."

He stilled. "Good."

"Good, you're picking me up. I want a limo." Actually, I could have cared less about a limo, but I did enjoy ordering him around.

"Fine," he said in a low tone. "I'll even bring a corsage, if you bring the skirt."

Translation. *You bring the sex.*

For show, he took out a few more condoms from under the register.

I flushed at the sight of more plastic wrappers. "How did you know those were there?"

He stuck them in his pocket. "Kids talk."

"They don't talk to me," I muttered.

Husky laughter soothed over me. "Your reputation is too clean."

"And yours isn't?"

"I never claimed otherwise." He glanced up. A small mirror hanging down from the ceiling (to keep an eye on potential shoplifters) reflected his face—Matt's face. His expression shuttered at the glimpse of his appearance.

Mentally, I sighed. *Oh, the games we play.*

He pulled fully away from me and went to pick up my crutch, which had fallen near the door. I jumped down and tottered over to him. He thrust the steel crutch at me. "If you're done distracting me, shall we proceed to the library?"

Without waiting for a reply, he stalked to the door. I saw him fumble with the doorknob, muttering curses under his breath. I watched him, chewing my lip, but not saying anything. Finally, the knob turned and he banged the door open. He hurried off down the hall.

I caught up a few minutes later. Down the hallway, around one turn, I found myself in front of the closed double doors of the library. As I struggled with one heavy door, it flew open. Doppelganger-Matt propped it open and pulled me inside with a look of exasperation. The musty scent of books hit me immediately. No one sat behind the high bar that enclosed the checkout area. Glancing around, I saw no one in the library. A low barrier of bookshelves separated a study area from bigger shelves extending from floor to ceiling that filled up the rest of the room. Not a soul roamed the stacks.

I wondered if Doppelganger-Matt had broken in while the librarian was on a break. He led me into the study area of neatly lined tables. I paused, picturing the lion on top of them. My throat dry, I swallowed. The memory of what happened came rushing back, and even though it was only in my head and not physically here, the details of the library were too accurate for my mind not to replay the scene.

Doppelganger-Matt stopped just before a waist-high bookshelf directly at the library's center. He let out a breath. "It's not here."

"Maybe it's below?"

He knelt to run a finger through an ordered stack of coffee table books.

"What are you all fired up about?" I moved closer to his side and propped my crutch against the shelf. When I leaned against his shoulder, he stiffened.

I yawned. "I'm getting a little tired."

Grabbing me by the waist, he hoisted me up and set me on the shelf. "You shouldn't have come to school at all."

I said in a throaty voice, "Think of all the fun I would have missed."

Without commenting, he knelt back down and eyed the books. A soft blush covered his cheeks. I bit my lip to stop a smile. It was cute.

"This is it." He stopped on one book and pulled it out. I leaned over, but I couldn't see its title. His body effectively covered it. He pulled up his shirt, showing Matt's lean abs, and tucked the book into his jeans. Lucky book. I caught a glimpse of the back cover—an illustration I didn't recognize, soft hues of red, cream, and blue—before he yanked his shirt down.

"What's in the book?" I asked.

Doppelganger-Matt stood up. Keeping the book out of my sight, he leaned closer, as if he were going in for another kiss. My pulse spiked. He slipped my phone out of my pocket.

I tried to grab it back from him, but he moved away. "What are you doing?"

"Texting Ragnar." His fingers flew deftly over the touch-screen phone.

Another reason Doppelganger-Matt could not be the real Matt. The real Matt picked at the screen with excruciating slowness. He handed the phone back to me. I glanced at the screen. The text read—*In the library. Sick. Take me home.*

"High-handed, aren't you?" I remarked.

"Yes." He pulled me off the bookshelf. A hand snaked around my neck and drew me in for a quick yet heartfelt kiss. My other hand curled in soft, brown hair. His hand slid up my bare leg. I caught it before he reached too far up. Squeezing my thigh, he pulled away. "Happy birthday, Ryan."

My mouth was freed, yet I remained breathless.

Before I could manage more than a blink, he loped halfway across the library.

"Wear something pretty Saturday," I called out.

"Get a longer skirt," he replied, without turning around.

He left through the open door. I looked down and made a face. He'd left my skirt hiked up. I smoothed it. I heard a shuffling at the door. My head jerked up. Mild unease filled me at the thought that someone might have actually seen us.

Matt, the real Matt with pensive amber eyes and sober expression, came into the library. Marilynn trailed him. My mild unease turned to full-blown embarrassment.

"It was Vane," I said.

"I figured." Matt walked toward the bookshelf. His eyes flickered over the low tables. The memory of the lion washed over us. Matt held my gaze. "Why me?"

Why did I kiss Vane while he looked like Matt? Or why did Vane take his form? Either answer was one Matt wouldn't like. I chose another safer one. "He snuck in to get something from the library."

Matt wasn't fooled. His gaze fell on my mouth, puffy lips that still tingled.

"It's not him anymore, Ryan."

"You're not giving him much of a chance, Merlin."

"I've given him plenty. So did Blake. He can't be trusted." He glanced at the bookshelf. "If he could be, then why sneak in here? Why the disguise? Which book did he take?"

I played with my bottom lip. "He didn't want me to see—"

"Typical," Marilynn muttered from behind Matt.

I tamped down an urge to stick my tongue out at her like a five-year-old. "I saw a picture on the back cover. I can search for it in the library database."

"It gives us something, at least," Matt said. His unhappy expression didn't waver. He gestured at Marilynn. "Take over for her this afternoon as we planned. Ryan's had enough time to be normal."

I shook off the weariness sapping my strength. Stubbornness straightened my spine. "Stop thinking you can run my life, Matt. I'll be home after school." I scowled at Marilynn. "I don't need the duplicate to fill in."

"We should follow up on this right away," Matt shot back. "Stop being so childish."

*It was the worst possible thing to say.* My hackles rose even more. "We can work on it this afternoon." I told Marilynn sweetly, "You can cover the afterschool Prom meeting."

Matt raked a hand through his hair in frustration. "Everyone is depending on us—"

I didn't waver. "They can wait a few hours."

Matt's lips tightened. Turning on his heel, he walked out.

Marilynn shook her head. "You're an idiot, DuLac. He says it's for everyone, but he only looks at you. He's doing this for you."

I stared after Matt. If that were true, it would have been him taking me to Prom. It would have been him who remembered my birthday. I said softly, "No, he's not doing this for me. He just hasn't admitted as much to himself."

## THE TEMPEST

I went home early. After five hours of sitting still in class, I was beyond exhausted, so I decided to skip last period. A.P. Chemistry. I abandoned the idea that I would be taking any of the advanced placement tests. Not that it would even matter anymore. I had to survive the apocalypse first. It took all the motivation out of studying.

Anyway, I spent most of my other classes surfing the Internet for information on the book Vane took. The library database had no pictures. Once or twice I got caught, but a sob story of how worried my mother (Sylvia) was after the attack let me off the hook. One morning with Vane, and I'd already turned manipulative. He was not a good influence.

I pushed down the guilt, telling myself it was for a higher purpose. If only high school gave extra credit for save-the-world projects. I looked out the window. Furious clouds hid the radiance of the sun. I wondered if the planet wanted to fight back. I hoped so.

Annoyed that I hadn't found anything, I decided to talk to Matt.

Yawning, I forced myself to make the long walk down the hall to Sylvia's study at the back of the house. It was past a front foyer, various living rooms, and the kitchen. More rain pelted the thick-paned windows. The manor was built in a flat clearing, but the land was on lower ground than the rest of the woods surrounding it. In winter, the school bus couldn't make it up and down the path. Today, the weather didn't seem much better. Inches of water rose around the manor's foundation. The house would soon become an island if the rain didn't abate.

Grey stood outside the study. His hand clutched the doorknob and he was in the middle of opening it, but instead of going in, he pulled it back shut. Then he stood staring at the block of wood with a flabbergasted expression. When he spotted me, the tips of his ears turned red. "Ah, maybe we should get a quick snack first."

"Did you remind Marilynn she needs to go to school for the meeting?"

His arm went across the doorframe, effectively blocking me from it. "I called ahead earlier. I was going to bring you home anyway after last period. She said she'd be ready. It's still a little early."

I yawned again. "Okay, well, I need to talk to Matt. Is he in there?"

"Uh, you should get some rest first. You look pretty tired," he said quickly. "I can tell him whatever you need."

I frowned at his odd behavior. "It's complicated. I'm trying to figure out which book Vane took from school."

Gia came up behind me. "What's going on? Why are you blocking the door?"

"Uh." Grey turned to answer her.

I took advantage of his distraction. In his haste, Grey hadn't clicked the door fully shut. I flung it open with my crutch.

"Shit," Gia muttered.

My eyes immediately found what Grey wanted to hide. Past a huge, mahogany desk strewn with papers, books, and two open laptops, on a one-armed sofa framed by huge glass doors, long slender fingers tangled in shiny brown hair, girl's fingers in a boy's hair.

In return, Matt's hands wound around long, dark-blond strands of hair. My strands. As I watched, he caressed apple cheekbones. My cheekbones. She straddled him while he lay back on the soft cushion of the sofa. He gripped her neat waist to grind her narrow hips closer to his. My waist. My hips.

At least they had their clothes on. Mostly.

Matt was shirtless, showing off a bare expanse of skin and short fine hair. Hair I'd been sliding my fingers through earlier this morning. *On Vane.*

For a minute, all I could do was watch Matt kiss me. Watch him kiss Marilynn... in my body. It was surreal, beyond disturbing, and— narcissistically hot. I don't know why I wasn't more upset... maybe because I was guilty of the same misdeeds.

I pushed past Grey. He grabbed my elbow before I could go too far.

"Grey," Gia said warningly from behind us.

The two on the sofa jerked apart, finally noticing they had an audience.

"Ryan." Matt scrambled up. Marilynn almost fell off the sofa on the floor. Matt distanced himself from her by going behind Sylvia's huge, mahogany desk. He wiped a hand across his mouth. "You're back early."

"Yeah." *Duh.* I stared at the two of them. Their mussed hair and blotted lips... but I couldn't actually articulate another response.

Marilynn stood up quickly. Two red spots flushed her cheeks. My cheeks. She glanced at Matt, but he stared down at Sylvia's desk. Biting her lip, she ran out of the room.

Grey came up from behind and put his hand on my back. "Ryan?"

I shook my head. "I want to talk to Matt alone."

For the first time since the rooftop, Gia looked at me as she'd done before—as my friend. "Are you sure?"

I exchanged a girl-to-girl look with her. "I'm fine. *Really.*"

Gia nodded, pulling Grey out of the room.

As soon as the door shut behind them, Matt said, "It wasn't planned."

I glanced at the curved sofa, the cushions still flat from its recent occupation. Dark rain continued to paint the glass of a set of French doors. It outlined Matt's form, lending him a soft aura of melancholy. "Is this because of this morning? The library?"

"Maybe." Matt's shoulders drooped and then straightened. Amber eyes pierced through me. "You're not upset."

I walked farther into the room. "I wasn't kissing you. I was kissing Vane."

He blinked. "I wasn't kissing Marilynn. I was kissing *you.*"

I bit back a semi-hysterical laugh. It was a freaking Shakespearian tragedy. Or comedy. Honestly, I couldn't tell which. With more bitterness than I wanted to express, I stated, "I don't think you know what you want."

He picked up his T-shirt from the floor and pulled it on. "That much seems to be true."

"I can't keep doing this back and forth with you."

"And I can't help myself from wanting you even when I shouldn't."

Soft amber eyes watched me in silent question. The yearning look asked me to take Marilynn's place on the sofa. He stood on one side of the desk. I stood on the other. The distance wasn't far, but the gulf between us had become infinite. While it made me sad, it didn't devastate me. Somewhere along the way, somewhere along the circular road back home, had I learned how to let him go?

"You shouldn't have to help yourself," I said slowly. "It shouldn't have to be so hard, Matt."

Matt slammed his hands, palms down, on the desk and leaned against its sturdy wood as if he needed the support. A hard glint entered his eyes. "If it is, it's because you made it so."

*Bastard.* How did guys flip the switch from nice guy to jerk so quickly? I didn't say the thought out loud because, although it stung, he was partially right. I had made it complicated or rather Vane had. Yet, I couldn't lie to him like he wanted. That would have been worse. "I don't know what's happening between Vane and me, but I haven't given up on him—"

His whole body stiffened. "Is he the better catch now that he's the greatest wizard in the world?"

The question left me speechless for a minute. It was insulting on so many levels. Tamping down my temper, I ground out, "I don't need to *catch* anyone, Merlin. Your magic, or lack thereof, had nothing to do with this until you made it so."

"Well, I intend to get it back." Matt yanked open a drawer on the desk and took out a small metal box. The Kronos Eye.

An ominous wave of foreboding rose in my stomach. "What are you doing with that?"

"I've been studying it since Vane pulled it from you. I hoped to use it to save Rourke." Matt shook the crystal. "It's hard to see, but beyond its hardened shell, there's water inside. The water of life. It's why you were poisoned."

I shrank back from the Eye. "I thought you couldn't hold it."

Matt closed his fist around it. "My theory is that the shell became porous when it was in your stomach. It's harmless until then."

"It reacts to stomach acid?"

"Yes, although not as well." He walked to a console table hidden in the shadows of the room. The thin table against the wall held a small chemistry setup of glass beakers and distillation equipment. Matt picked up a tiny blue vial hanging on a clamp. "I was able to extract a few drops, but no more. I tried several variations—increasing the amount of acid, other chemicals, yet this was all that came out."

I stated, "I'm not swallowing that again."

"No, I've asked Rourke. If it is the water of life, it might work differently on him than you. He's already been poisoned. This might cure him."

"Or it might kill him quicker."

Matt hung his head. "Yes, that is the main objection."

"Whose objection?"

Matt cleared his throat. "Sylvia, Deirdre, Grey, Colin… pretty much everyone but Rourke himself."

"You mean the one person who's desperate for whatever suggestion of a miracle you throw at him? You're batting average as bastard has become particularly high these days."

"No reward without risk."

I arched a brow. "You sound like Vane."

"We've got a month before we lose several billion people. Do you have any better options? Rourke is dying."

The laptop on the desk beeped. An incoming call sprang up on the screen.

Matt looked at the username. "It's the Queen. I have to take this."

It was a dismissal. I nearly screamed.

The Queen appeared on the laptop screen. "Merlin, we are making good progress. If this continues, we will have the rocks mined long before we anticipated. Your plan is unfolding perfectly."

Matt beamed under her praise.

"Have you gotten the sword bearer to agree to her part?"

I stomped to the laptop and slammed the lid shut. "What part?"

The door burst open.

Grey flew inside with a wild look. "Emrys, come now."

I hurried to him. "Grey, what is it?"

"Rourke," he said. "He's having another stroke."

\*\*\*

We ran upstairs. Colin, Deirdre, Sylvia, and five other gargoyles held Rourke's shaking body still. Marilynn (minus the glamour) and a few other wizards muttered a chant as they tried to heal him. Fluctuating auras of light bounced off him. It wasn't a good indication.

Rourke gave a violent jerk. The gargoyles drew back the layers covering him. His entire body was soaked with sweat. Blood spilled from his nose. His eyes flew open. The healers increased the amount of magic, their auras getting brighter.

Finally, he quieted and fell back against his pillow.

Deirdre, on the far side of the bed, put a hand to his forehead. "He's sleeping."

"For how long?" Grey said. Lying against his side, his hands shook. He fisted them. "He's getting worse much more quickly than you said. I thought we had months."

I went to Sylvia, who stood on the opposite side of the bed from Deirdre. She bit into her nails, her face pale. "Should we call an ambulance?"

"The Regulars have nothing that can help him." Deirdre shook her head. As if unable to help herself, she glanced at Matt.

He said quietly, "It's his choice."

"We barely saved him—" Marilynn interjected.

"No." I grabbed the vial from his hand. I held it up and shook it at each grim face in the room. "This is poison. Not a cure. We keep looking."

"For what?" he muttered.

I gave him a pointed look. "For the right answer, not the desperate one."

No one contradicted me.

The rest of the evening passed quickly. Despite the somber edge in the air, Grey and Sylvia surprised me with a huge cake— Bavarian vanilla decorated with purple roses. The young wizards cast a small spell that made the kitchen sparkle with twinkling lights and the floor mist to look like clouds. We walked on them for one evening. With all the people in the house, the entire sheet of cake disappeared before dinner. The Land Rover officially became mine. The best present, though, was an awkward hug from Gia and a moment to enjoy simply being with my family.

I didn't see Matt.

He disappeared into the gym and I heard from Colin he spent the night training with the gargoyles. ("Getting beat up" was Colin's exact phrase.) I kept the vial with me until bedtime. Bone tired, but happy, I found myself crawling into bed at eight o'clock.

I don't know how long I slept.

A voice whispered at the edge of my dreams, prodding me to wake up.

*"Dorothy."*

The door in my mind creaked open. A shadow slipped through to where I slept. A hand smoothed back my hair and traced the curve of one ear. I sighed contentedly and snuggled deeper into the bed. The hand slipped down over my shoulders, under my cami, and delved between my breasts. I moaned.

A chuckle washed over me. The all too real sound snapped me into consciousness.

My eyes flew open and I sat straight up in bed. I glanced

around. No one. Only shadows danced in the darkened room.

The *Dragon's Eye* was hot against my skin. Vane's voice purred inside my head. *"I knew that would get your attention."*

"What do you want?" I said irritably.

*"Something is happening."*

It was then I noticed the sliver of harsh yellow light coming from the hallway. My door was slightly ajar. I knew I closed it before bed. Someone had been in my room. I glanced at my dresser and the empty spot that should not have existed.

Someone had stolen the vial of poison. And I knew who.

*"Something wrong?"* Vane said, sounding interested.

With a curse, I threw aside the bedcovers and pulled on clothes I left lying on the floor. I grabbed the crutch and hurried out of the room. The stitches across my stomach protested as I rushed down the hallway. As I'd feared, the commotion came from Sylvia's room. A gang of gargoyles milled around the doorway, blocking the path to the door. I started weaving my way through. My stitches protested more. Through a crack in between two sets of massive shoulders, I saw the entire bed tremble as Rourke's body shuddered.

"Help him!" Sylvia clung to a bedpost and tried to catch one of Rourke's flailing hands.

Marilynn and six wizards stood at the foot of the bed. They sent a wave of magic onto Rourke. It sank into his body, but it did nothing to slow the shudders. He started mumbling incoherently. Marilynn said in defeat, "I don't know what else to try."

Deirdre grabbed her son's hand and hung on. "Merlin, do what you must."

"No!" I shoved past the last line of gargoyles, ignoring the shooting pain across my stomach. It was too late. Matt poured the vial down the gargoyle king's throat.

"No!" My crutch went flying as I pitched into the room. Colin caught me before I fell on my face. He handed me the crutch. I took it. I hissed at Matt, "What have you done?"

"He's out of time," Matt said stoically.

Blue veins popped out along Rourke's throat as the water of life entered his system. The shudders stopped. Calm reigned for several seconds. It stretched out into a minute.

"It's working," Grey murmured. He stood toward the head of the bed.

I bit my lip, hoping against hope that I'd been wrong.

Then, he coughed, and that hope died. More shudders rocked his body. Blood leaked out of his eyes. His face transformed. His forehead extended, fangs elongated, and the gargoyle came out. He let out a tremendous scream. It was the last sound he made before he collapsed back to the bed. This time his body stayed still.

Sylvia put a hand to her mouth. Her strong face ravaged with tears, she stared down at Rourke as if she couldn't quite understand what had happened. And didn't want to. Grey let go of me to walk to his mother. She turned into him and started sobbing.

Deirdre sank down against the wall. Her eyes dry yet devastated. Around us, the gargoyles transformed. All of them, including Colin and Deirdre. All except Grey. They let out a beast-like howl unlike anything I'd heard from an animal. The glass windows of the room cracked as if it had been made of tissue instead of thick panes. More howls sounded from the gym. They spread through woods as other animals picked up the call of mourning. It continued until the howl was all that could be heard under the waning moon.

I watched a star shoot across the sky.

The gargoyle king had passed.

Matt stared down at the still body, his amber gaze flickering with uncertainty. His shoulders drooped. I knew how much he'd been counting on this working for Rourke and for himself. For a second, I thought of going to him and offering support. Yesterday, I might have. Today, I couldn't help but wonder if I knew him at all. He'd become so desperate to regain his magic he hadn't hesitated to use Rourke's broken body as a human experiment.

I left the room. I slipped through the gargoyles and found Gia just beyond them in the hall. She sat huddled on the floor against a wall. Her head down, her arms hugged her knees to her chest. Ignoring the pain under my bandages, I sat down beside her, my shoulder against hers. She lifted her head to look at me with dry reddened eyes. I put my arms around her shoulders and we huddled together.

She said, "I can't do this anymore."

"Yes, you can."

"Why should I?" She gave a small hysterical laugh. "The world is going to end anyway."

"Because you have to. Because we need you. Grey needs you." *Now more than ever.* Until Grey transitioned, the gargoyles were leaderless. It was too soon to think about it. *Rourke. Blake.* Their silent faces pressed down on me. I leaned my head against Gia's. "Because there will be a tomorrow."

And as I said it, I wondered if I believed it or simply

pretended. Or if that mattered.

It was nearly morning by the time I crawled back into bed. My body ached fiercely and I couldn't sleep. The pain left me trembling. I should have called for help. Instead, I touched the *Dragon's Eye.*

I opened the door inside my mind and said, "*Vane.*"

He answered swiftly, "*What have you done to yourself?*"

I groaned. "*Everything hurts.*"

"*I'm coming over.*"

I jerked up in bed and fell back down. "*What? No.*"

"*I'm know I'm not wanted—*"

"*They'll freak out! Anyway, there's nothing you can do to fix this.*"

"*I might have found a way. Let me try.*"

It was tempting, but dangerous. Too dangerous. The monster was unpredictable. *Rourke—* I broke off, not sure if I should tell him about the king's death. So I said lamely, "*It's not a good time.*" Through the link, I felt him roll his eyes. I yawned. "*I just need to sleep. Tell me a story.*"

"*I don't know any stories,*" he grumbled. "*Close your eyes.*"

Leaving the door between us open, I did as he asked.

***

"Time to sleep." I tied the final knot on a pliable piece of bark I'd shaped into a small circle. I stamped out the small flames of our campfire. It was too dangerous too keep it going for any longer then absolutely necessary.

"Vane, can you tell another tale?" Big brown eyes blinked sleepily on a delicate face.

I shook my head. "I've already told you one. We start early again tomorrow."

She pouted. I ignored her, steeling myself against those big eyes. We'd traveled far in a few short weeks. We'd remained well fed and undetected through wild lands. With her bow and arrow, she'd kept us in plentiful supply through this barren terrain. I'd never been so completely useless.

"Are we there yet?" Perceval asked.

I glanced out at an expanse of gently rolling hills and small shrubs. Above us, a short tree swung its leafy reddened hair. We were almost home. We'd crossed the short stretch of sea from Gaul and into Britannia. However, battlefields of territory remained before I reached home. We'd made it through the men of Kent and were deep into the territory of the Saxon barbarians. A few more days would lead us to Domnonia. Keltoi territory. Merlin.

"Soon," I told him. I stamped out the last of the fire. Uncertainty filled me the closer we got to home. I'd hung on to a dream for so long. I wondered what would become of it. I glanced at my unwanted companions. The little princess jumped up. Lopsided braids flew in the air. Braids I'd been forced to make.

"Here." I thrust a small circle of bark I'd made from the rowan tree at her when she neared me. Taking it, she looked at it curiously. With a sigh, I slipped the band onto her wrist. "Three knots on a circle made from the bark of a rowan tree. For protection."

To my surprise, she flung herself against me. Little arms tightened around my sides, hugging me. "Do not worry, Vane. You're never going to be alone again. I will wed you when I am grown."

On the other side of the dead fire, Perceval laughed. I felt myself turn red in the face.

I stuttered, "W-we'll see when you're grown."

"I will be very pretty like my momma." Huge brown eyes smiled and the dark world lit up for a moment.

I believed her.

Sticking out her tongue at her brother, she skipped off to her bedroll. Under the slope of a gently rolling hill and a lone rowan tree, the little princess closed her eyes.

Perceval looked at me with pity. "She gets what she wants, you know."

I pointed a stick of bark to the top of the slope. "You're on watch first."

Perceval laughed again and rose. He trudged off up to the top of the hill.

Some time later, heavy footsteps pressed into soft earth, tearing into brittle fallen leaves. I rose swiftly from my bedroll, ready sword in hand. The muted sounds of deep night had gone unnaturally silent. The round shapes of the hills lay in peaceful deceptiveness... for they were not empty. Hidden danger walked over their slopes. The rowan tree's bushy leaves swayed in the wind. A wind carrying the musty stink of an unwashed body I didn't recognize.

An intruder.

A hill fort stood off in the distance. I'd avoided going near it. Apparently, I hadn't taken us far enough. I cursed the fact that I didn't have any magic and kicked at the embers of the fire. I had put it out to hide us. Now, its shadows hid the intruder. A few flames flared. From the shadows cast down by the sloped hill, a man lunged at me with a gleaming sword.

I barely had time to raise my blade and block his strike. His breath close to mine, I recognized the face beneath the beast. It was no barbarian. Nearly unrecognizable in brown peasant-wear, this was worse.

I pushed him back. "Sergius."

"Vane!" The little princess scrambled awake.

Sergius sneered at the sight of her. "I see you kept a few prizes."

"Run, now!" I told her. The simple command proved to be a distraction. Sergius got close enough to kick me in the stomach. The power in the kick sent me flying to the far side of the small camp.

To her credit, the little princess acted swiftly. In half a blink, she grabbed her bow and sent an arrow flying at Sergius's head. It hit him squarely. He snarled. His face transformed into one of a beast with a distended forehead and gleaming fangs. He plucked the arrow out of his head as if it was nothing. The wound started healing on its own.

"You're a gargoyle," I said in surprise.

"Unfortunately for you, boy. It took a while to recover from the heart wound. I'm not as quick of a healer as others, but I vowed to make you pay." He stalked towards me. "You managed to travel far."

*Because of her.* I'd never met another person like her. "You've been tracking us since Carthage?"

The little princess shot another arrow. Sergius knocked that one down while still in flight, like swatting down a buzzing fly. "I'll deal with you next, little one."

"What did you do with my brother?" she yelled.

Perceval had been on watch just above us on the hilltop. I glanced at the spot where he should have been. It was empty.

Sergius smiled with broken teeth. "He's a bit tied up at the moment."

Internally, I sighed with relief. At least he hadn't killed him. No doubt saving him for a bout of prolonged abuse later. Except that wouldn't happen. Now I knew how to kill him. My hand tightened on the leather hilt of my sword, I smiled back at Sergius. "Good. We can finish this without distractions."

I leaped back up. He ran at me. We dueled with our heavy swords, but despite his strength, he was no match for my training. One well-aimed thrust sent his sword flying. One stomp on the knee brought him down. Following the steps to a deadly dance, I moved behind him. One kick sent him sprawling facedown to the ground. With a yell, I hacked down at his neck. Blood spurted at me. My blade met skin and bone, but I didn't stop its descent. Sergius's head severed in a last cry of battle.

The crunch of more footsteps broke the quiet night.

"*Agatya.*" A command came from above.

The sword went flying out of my hands. I looked up. A band of soldiers on horses stood on the hilltop. Two stood slightly in front—an older boy about my age and a younger one wearing dark robes, about Perceval's age. A sword sat comfortably on the older boy's right hip. He held a heavy shield with ease. The emblem of a flying red dragon covered it. A dagger lay tucked in his leather belt. Though he wore plain trousers instead of the skirt of a Roman soldier, I knew by his stance he'd been trained as one. I knew by the austere lines of his privileged face and unbroken teeth, he was also this band's leader.

The little princess shot off an arrow from her bow. It almost nailed him between the eyes. A black-robed boy beside the soldier let out a stream of magic and the arrow dropped harmlessly at the soldier's feet. The little princess swiftly notched another arrow.

"Stop!" Perceval shouted, his head poked out from behind the robed boy. "They untied me. They mean us no harm."

Perceval scrambled down the black gelding. The boy carrying him threw back the hood of his robe. A single shaft of moonlight hit the robed boy's face.

I nearly dropped my sword—something a soldier would rather die than do—yet my suddenly damp hand and fingers struggled to hold on to the bloody blade. I took a few unsteady steps up the slope. I whispered, "Merlin."

The boy blinked, a frown falling over an otherwise expressionless face.

"Merlin, it is I," I said, louder this time. Happiness filled my chest. I swept one hand across the face, wiping away the blood that shadowed it. "It is your brother. Vivane."

Merlin's expression changed. It was the tiniest of movements. If I hadn't been watching with such desperate intensity I would have missed it. His mouth twisted at the ends. Not to one of happiness as I hoped. He grimaced. It was fleeting. Merlin quickly smoothed it away. Yet, I saw it. I lowered my sword. The hope to which I'd been clinging—the hope he'd understand why I left him—faded. The blade sank deeply into a maiden earth. It was all I could do not to sink down with it.

I'd come home. Such as it was.

The older boy lowered his red dragon shield. "Is it true?"

Merlin nodded. "He is my brother, sire."

A jaunty smile stretched across the boy's narrow face. "Will you not introduce us?"

"Vivane—"

I interrupted. "I am Vane."

Merlin nodded. "Vane."

To my dismay, he said the name easily... acceptingly, and my hopes plummeted even more.

"Vane," repeated Merlin. "This is his highness, Prince Arthur of Cambria, Demetia, and... Domnonia and—"

"Other surrounding lands." Arthur interrupted. "We've been thinking of picking one name."

My eyes flickered. Prince of Domnonia. The Roman ruled my homeland. My magic may have been blocked, but I didn't sense any Keltoi blood in him. I said, "You've been busy with such a small band of men."

"Our camp is on another hill." Arthur inclined his head. "And it is my father who has been busy."

There was an edge to his tone that caught my interest.

"I seek to hold what we've gained," he said. "The Saxons continue to press on us."

I didn't entirely believe him. Ambition colored the prince's face. I played to it. "I would say you haven't dealt them a big enough blow."

"I mean to." Arthur's light eyes traveled over me with calculated thoughtfulness. They lingered on the bloodstained sword I still held loosely. "I'm glad to meet someone else who understands such things."

Under his interested scrutiny, I relaxed my fingers on the

blade even more. *Never let them know how much you want something.* Arthur urged his horse down the slope toward me. Merlin rode down after him. I fought back a smile. Renewed hope filled me. Maybe home had a place for me after all. I glanced from Merlin to Perceval and his sister. A place for all of us. I turned back to Merlin. And a second chance.

A wave of light sparked the dark night. It hit us with the strength of a thousand cavalrymen. The men on the hilltop slumped in their saddles. Arthur and Merlin followed. My head jerked to the little princess. The wave hit her first. She fell onto the bedroll.

*No.* My head screamed. The wave hit me. I held onto the sword.

Under my tunic, the crystal necklace, the shackle that bound magic, burned. I let out a cry and fell to my knees. My palms hit dirt, but I managed to stay awake. Long moments passed. I hung on, my body shaking under the pressure. Just when I thought I would break, the wave finally passed.

The crystal necklace unclasped and slipped off my neck. I was finally free.

Over the hill, a shadow appeared. The figure walked down the slope and stepped into the camp. The firelight illuminated his face. Septimus.

## PROM

The week passed swiftly. Marilynn was only too happy to get away from the house (and Matt). She covered the first half of the week while I slept most of the time. Sylvia managed to get a doctor to make a house call, but I didn't really need one. Vane had done something while I'd slept. I didn't know what, but it helped. Although I was tired, my body seemed to be finally healing.

I made it to school Thursday and Friday. They were easy days. No one really wanted to concentrate. Most of the talk centered on prom and who had gotten accepted to which college. Bennett, our valedictorian, got early admission to MIT. She was staying nearby. Many of the kids decided to stay close. Ramanajan was going to Boston University. Nearly a hundred colleges lay scattered through Boston and its surrounding areas. I hadn't even applied. Neither had Grey, but Harvard held a reserved family seat for the Ragnars.

It depressed me a little that I wasn't thinking about the future. So I decided to go home and pull out the stack of brochures lying forgotten at the back of my desk. I'd filled out one online application when a thought struck me. I searched for the keywords 'King Arthur' and 'Boston.' Pages and pages of results returned for the Total Tremor and rumors about the inevitable end of the world. I decided not to read the conspiracy columns. I wondered how many of them were put out by the government.

The Security Council had decided not to go public. One, there wasn't an immediate solution to offer. Two, they were working on a secret project with Merlin to which I hadn't been able to get the details. (Matt refused to tell me in case Vane gleaned it through the *Dragon's Eye.*) Three, it was decided the chaos such an announcement would cause would undermine what efforts they could make to find a way out.

On impulse, I added another keyword 'illustration' to the search. One link immediately stood out—a series of murals hanging in the Boston Public Library. I clicked through websites that detailed the murals. My heart sped up. The series was titled *The Quest and Achievement of the Holy Grail.*

The drafty glass doors of my room showed a clear night sky. The clock on my cell read midnight. I wouldn't be able to get into the library tonight. I glanced at my room's closed door. If I wanted to do this tonight, I had to ask Matt for help. We'd barely spoken since Rourke's death. He remained holed up in his study, doing who knows what. He didn't ask for my help and I didn't volunteer. Again, I found myself unable to cross the chasm between us. It was becoming a pattern.

But I couldn't ignore this. I trudged down the stairs to Sylvia's study, deciding not to take the crutch. The hallways were eerily empty. The house had been emptied of gargoyles. Grey, Gia, and Sylvia would return tomorrow morning from the funeral. Apparently, Rourke owned a brownstone in New York or an estate in Long Island. No one wanted to mention the inheritance of the throne, but I noticed Deirdre and Colin staying very close to Grey. As for Grey, I knew he wanted nothing to do with it.

I couldn't blame him. I hadn't touched Excalibur for months. I didn't miss it.

Okay, that was a lie. I tried not to miss it.

I passed by the living room. A group of twenty or so young wizards sat together eating popcorn. Marilynn was on the couch at the center of them. A few girls sighed and pointed to the giant flat screen. I immediately recognized the ultimate prom movie (a personal favorite of mine which I would only admit to under pain of death)—*Pretty in Pink.*

A girl with long braids spotted me hovering. She gave me a beaming smile. "Will you be going tomorrow, sword-bearer?"

The question blindsided me. I doubted Vane would actually show. "Uh, I don't think—"

"Merlin is taking her," a boy next to her said. "I heard it at school."

Marilynn's gaze locked on me. "Is he?"

"He hasn't asked and since it's tomorrow, I doubt it."

Marilynn nodded as if I told her nothing she didn't already know. The other witches and wizards gave me pitying looks. I asked quickly, "Are all of you going?"

The whole group nodded.

"Don't you have dances at Avalon Prep?" I wondered aloud.

"Um, not really," said the girl with braids. "We used to have a Yule Ball, but they gutted it after someone made the decorations explode."

"They were trying to magic them to dance," murmured the boy beside her.

The girl with braids took his hand and gushed, "Tomorrow is going to be so much fun. I heard the hall is grander than a Parisian opera house."

It was. I'd seen pictures of the venue. Marilynn had outdone herself. I glanced at her. She was grinning at the girl. For someone who had to be twenty-something Marilynn was oddly obsessed with prom. I groaned internally and forced myself to do the right thing. "Since I'm not going, Marilynn, you ought to go. The head of the committee should show up just in case."

Her head snapped up to look at me. I returned the suspicious look with a steady gaze.

"Just in case," she agreed quickly.

She jerked her head back toward the screen as if to stop me from changing my mind. I bit my lip to suppress my smile. The group shushed each other as the big prom finale started on screen. I watched for a few minutes and slipped away. The study, it turned out, was empty.

No Matt in sight.

That's how I found myself at the library the next afternoon.

I spent the morning on the phone dealing with a last minute prom crisis over parking. Marilynn disappeared somewhere (sans cell phone, I suspected a prom hair emergency). After solving said crisis, it took two hours to drive to Alewife, catch the Red Line train into Boston, and switched subway lines to get to Copley Station.

The Boston Public Library took up two buildings. A harsh sun heated the wide concrete surrounding a patch of grass called

Copley Square. The McKim Building resembled a three-story palace with arched columns and giant entrance. From the first floor, I climbed up to the mezzanine level. Below me, children played in an open courtyard complete with fountain. Resisting an urge to linger and watch their laughter, I followed the signs up to the second floor. I crossed past librarians milling with researchers and other patrons and reached the other side of the building. The ornate grandiosity of Bates Hall caught my eye. Coffered ceilings and arched windows had been architected as a Roman cathedral. Rows of low desks with lamps lined the length of the hall as if waiting for class to begin. Bookshelves lined the sides but didn't reach high enough to touch the domed ceiling. To the side of the grand hall lay Abbey Room where Edward Austin Abbey's murals covered the walls, floor to ceiling. The gallery held five paintings. I read aloud, "The Vision, the Oath of Knighthood, the Round Table, the Departure, and the Castle of the Grail."

"About time you found them."

Matt's voice made me jump. Except it wasn't Matt. My pulse went from normal to skyrocket speed in less than a second. Doppelganger-Matt stood casually just inside the gallery. He wore pristine black formalwear with easy confidence. The tailored tuxedo fit him perfectly and the freshness of the material indicated it had been made recently. He'd gotten it made for me, I realized. For today.

A shiny deep-green vest, reminiscent of the sea, fit snugly across his lean chest. A matching green tie was tucked neatly under the vest and shiny black shoes completed the ensemble. Longish brown hair was tamed into submission—something that confirmed Doppelganger-Matt's true identity.

"Going somewhere?" I asked.

"I have an engagement." His eyes swam with calm waves and the way they watched me… I could have melted right on the spot.

A glance raked me from head to toe. "You look better."

"I feel it. No more ugly crutch." I raised and lowered my hands. "See."

His gaze lingered on my T-shirt as it stretched across my chest. "I agree. Not ugly."

I lost the fight to not blush. "How did you find me here?"

"I'll always find you," he replied with a roguish grin. He lifted his wrist to glance at a heavy silver watch. "It's early. Would you like to walk around with me?"

He stuck out a tuxedo-clad elbow. I found myself taking it. A charming Vane was impossible to refuse. Walking around in jeans and T-shirt with a guy in fine formalwear made us strikingly conspicuous, but I found it easy to ignore the occasional passerby's odd looks. He led me to the first painting in the series. I read a plaque near the painting. "In the Vision, a white-robed nun holds up the child, Galahad. An angel visits. The angel carries a dove, a golden censer, and the Grail under a red shroud. What's a censer?"

"It holds burning incense." His arm slipped out of the elbow-hold and a warm palm settled on my back instead.

I struggled to concentrate as we walked to the next painting. My voice had a slight waver as I read the next description. "The Oath. The nuns bring Galahad to Sir Lancelot and Sir Bors, who fasten spurs on him."

"Getting him ready for his journey." Doppelganger-Matt leaned close.

All too aware of his proximity, I tried to ignore the sweet, clean breeze of his breath as it traced the curves of my ear. Finally,

I couldn't stand it. I jerked away from him and walked to the next painting. He chuckled behind me. I leaned down to read the next plaque. "In the Round Table, the leaders of Arthur's realm are seated at a full table with only one empty seat when the palace becomes suffused with light and Galahad comes in with an old man to take the empty seat."

"The one pure of heart is found," Doppelganger-Matt said softly.

Pure of heart. I paused. Vane had once said that only one pure of heart could pull Excalibur. Also, the picture seemed familiar. Much like the tapestry in the UN Security Council room. I went to the fourth painting. "In the Departure, the knights attend mass with Galahad, who is now a knight."

Doppelganger-Matt stared at the painting. "It looks to me as if they're waiting at the altar."

"In Castle of the Grail, the Fisher King, the King of the Grail, has been wounded by an act of unlawful love and lies under a spell. Although the Grail appears in front of them, they cannot see it. Until Galahad, the most blameless knight arrives. He sees a damsel with a golden Dish, two knights with the candlesticks, a knight holding a bleeding Spear, and the bearer of the Cup. Galahad must ask what these things denote. The first time, he does not, and the Castle continues to suffer for his silence. On his second visit, many years later, he asks the questions and is finally rewarded."

I traced the painting in the air. "The golden dish— doesn't that look like the sun? It's a golden circle. The bleeding spear is the Fisher King's trident. The Cup—we already know that's the apple—"

"We do?" Doppelganger-Matt said.

"It's under a red shroud in the first picture. Red for apple."

"And the candlesticks?"

I squinted at the painting. "Don't candles mean divine light?"

Calm sea-eyes fixed on me again. "Divine light or celestial light… a sign of Kronos?"

I frowned. "What does all this tell us, though? Why these paintings?"

"The paintings are not the point. It's the story they are telling. It's been told over and over again… for a reason."

I tilted my head to look up at the straight line of his jaw. "Tell us what?"

"I had hoped you'd have that figured out for me by now."

"I've been unconscious for most of the week."

"A sorry excuse," he deadpanned.

I stuck my tongue out at him. "Do your own work."

Before I knew it, I was being yanked to him. My tongue captured by his mouth in a wild kiss. It didn't last long. A loud harrumph by an elderly man had me pushing him away, despite being nearly blinded by my own hunger.

"Do you want to eat?" he said.

"Uh" was all I managed as a reply.

"The library will be closing in five minutes, please take your selections to the checkout desk," intoned a voice above us.

"It's later than I thought." He grabbed my wrist and led me out of the gallery. We dodged a few slow-moving strollers on the stairs.

I went willingly until we reached the mezzanine level. "Wait, where are you taking me?"

"There's this dance."

I halted. "I don't have a dress."

He tugged me forward. "It's in the limo."

I stared at him. "You hired a limo."

"You asked."

I bit my lip. This didn't seem like the smartest idea. Under his fine suit and civilized glamour, an untamed monster lurked.

I didn't get a chance to refuse. Doppelganger-Matt hurried me along an open balcony toward stairs to the first floor. I went while still debating the question. I gave myself until we reached the front of the building to make up my mind. In the courtyard, a toddler broke away from his family and hurled himself into an outgoing stream of people. They surrounded him, cutting him off from his family. His face screwed up to let out a wail. I moved to go to the boy, but Doppelganger-Matt beat me to it. If I hadn't been so aware of him I wouldn't have noticed the slight movement of his hand. A subtle breeze parted the wave of people, creating a clear path between the boy and his frantically searching parents. The father spotted him first and ran to his son with a happy cry.

"Stop dawdling," Doppelganger-Matt told me gruffly and led me out.

I didn't say a word when we came out of the building. I also didn't turn and take off toward the subway. A white limo pulled up to the curb to meet us. Doppelganger-Matt didn't wait for the driver. Opening the door, he quickly packed me inside.

Inside the limo, he handed me a wrapped sandwich. "Eat."

"I can't go to prom—" *With you, Vane.*

"Don't worry. You'll look fine. You have an appointment at a salon in a few minutes." Taking the sandwich from my hands, he unwrapped it and thrust the bread under my nose. "It's your favorite."

It was. Hummus and cucumber on wheat. My stomach grumbled, reminding me that I'd forgotten breakfast. The smell of crisp cucumbers took me back to Sri Lanka for a second. Matt had only fed me under protest. I took a bite of the sandwich. It tasted hot and sweet and freshly made. "How did you know?"

"It's not hard to remember a sandwich," he said dryly.

I took another big bite. "What are you eating?"

White teeth flashed briefly. "I ate. Something more substantial than the deer food you like."

"You like deer," I commented. Sharp brown eyes fixed on me, and I realized I'd slipped. I wondered if Matt didn't like deer. The deer was in Vane's memories. Mentally, I kicked myself. Keeping up the pretense was hard, but I wasn't ready to confront him. Not yet. I was enjoying having Vane without the baggage. We both needed the charade to continue.

I pointed to three giant, white boxes lying on the seat on the opposite side of the limo. "What's in the boxes?"

The ploy worked, or he let it. He answered, "Your dresses."

"Dresses?"

"Three of them. I didn't know which color you'd like."

He got me three dresses because he didn't know which color I'd like. It took me a minute to absorb this. I finished the sandwich in a few quick bites. "Can I see?"

Skeptical eyes swept over the crumbs scattered across my T-shirt. The limo pulled to a stop. He commanded, "Let's go. You can look at the dresses inside."

The salon was tucked into the bottom of a brown-brick building. Inside, posh marble floors hummed with busy energy as Saturday evening neared. It took forty-five minutes to do hair and makeup. Doppelganger-Matt spent most of his time tapping the screen on his phone.

"What's so important?" I asked him.

"The end of the world," he quipped back without looking up from the screen. "I've been trying to get a few things in place for days and it seems to be all coming together today."

"Everything happens at once." I stared at myself in the mirror as the makeup artist fluffed my eyelashes to twice their size. "Do you have to leave?"

Part of me wanted him to go. A bigger part of me, the selfish part, ached for one night of normality. I wanted to be with him and told myself one night would be enough.

He didn't get a chance to answer. The artist put down her brush and swiveled me around to show me off. "She's a princess."

Doppelganger-Matt's head jerked up. Stormy brown eyes fixed on me and widened.

He muttered, "Yes, she is."

I resisted an urge to undo my tied-up hair. "I want to see the dresses."

He smiled. The makeup artist led us to a large dressing room tucked at the back of the building. Doppelganger-Matt followed me.

"I'm not going to run out the back door," I murmured. *I might have thought about it.*

"You'll need help buttoning up," he replied innocently. "You're still recovering."

"I'll manage." I shut the flimsy dressing room door in his face.

The three boxes were stacked neatly across a bench seat. I opened the first one. A flirty gown of deep green chiffon, the same color as Vane's vest, lay waiting inside. I tried it on, enjoying the short flowing hem that ended just at the knees. The next box held an equally stunning off-white gown with a corset top and billowing taffeta skirt. I pulled it on, only to yank it off when I heard myself unconsciously humming the wedding march.

I lifted the lid of the last box and tried not to gasp. Carefully, I slipped the slim gown over my head. A low décolletage trimmed with gold emphasized the lines of a purple high-waist gown. Soft silk-faced satin made up a straight skirt. The hem, also trimmed with gold thread, peeked just above the ankles. I opened the door to the dressing room and locked eyes with Vane. He sat in a metal chair just outside.

I smoothed my hand over the front. "It's gorgeous."

"Imperial purple with gold trim." He tucked his phone into his pocket and walked to me. "Why this one?"

"It reminded me of you," I said simply. *The real you. The one I've been seeing in bits and pieces of old memories. The one who asked me to choose him.*

"Did it?" Desire sparked his eyes, but he didn't touch me. His hands fisted as if he didn't dare. It was then I noticed that he'd already changed into a matching purple vest. I frowned. "How did you know?"

I touched the *Dragon's Eye. Had he been peeking without me knowing it?*

"I had a feeling," he answered enigmatically.

I raised a brow. "So you were just testing me with the other colors?"

"Does it matter? You always pass."

*I hadn't in the maze.* My throat dry, I said, "This gown doesn't scream 'Under the Sea.'" *More like Roman empress.*

Instead of replying, Doppelganger-Matt went into the dressing room and returned with a gold mask with a curved fish-scale pattern in one hand. I laughed. "And yours?"

"I have a matching one and a trident."

*I know you do.* I took the mask and put it on. I looked at myself in another mirror just outside the dressing room. The mask almost completely obscured my face. Doppelganger-Matt stood behind me and, for a moment, we stood together, both lost in a picture that didn't reflect either one of us. It should have been sobering; instead it only freed.

From behind his back, Doppelganger-Matt drew out strappy gold sandals and pointed me to a spindly chair. I sat and lifted the hem of the gown. Kneeling down, warm fingers skimmed my skin as he tied the heels to my feet. They fit perfectly, of course.

I stared down at his bent head. I wanted to say something, but the moment felt too delicate for words. Then, he looked up at me. His hand still wrapped around one foot. The skirt fell away from my hand, and from the stormy depths of his eyes shone all the emotions he couldn't quite bury, the light of his soul that wouldn't fade and asked for redemption.

From that moment on, I was ensnared. Captured by his spell, I found myself being drawn deep into the night. The limo took us past Fenway Park into historic Back Bay. Darkness descended over the city by the time we came to a stop at the Boston Palace Hotel. Tucked to the side of the hotel, the Imperial Ballroom overlooked a bean-shaped pond framed by weeping willow trees. Five hundred or so kids milled inside the majestic domed ballroom. A photographer clicked a picture of us in front of a life-size painting of a pirate ship with billowed sails.

Blue, green, and yellow strobe lights sparkled off the crystal chandeliers. Two curved staircases led upstairs, where kids leaned over royal-style balconies on a second story. Floor-to-ceiling windows canvased a midnight-blue sky on one side. On the other side, decorations of sea nymphs and big-eyed mermaids lined the walls. (After all I knew about them, the pictures made me smile.) Circular tables covered with white linen showcased glass centerpieces of pink-and-purple sea anemone.

Half the kids wore masks. Half didn't. In my daze, I barely noticed the crowd. I smiled and waved, having no idea who was who. Friend and foe, tonight—on this one night—they all mingled together.

On a grand stage above us, the very appropriately named band, *The Neptunes,* thumped out fast-paced music and lyrics that screamed not to stop until the world ended. Vane drew me out into the middle of the dance floor. A laughing Christine and her date danced on the outskirts. I spotted Ramanajan with one of the young wizards who invaded my house. Gia gave Grey a tentative smile as they moved to the beat. Various friends— Regulars, wizards, and gargoyles—made up the odd crowd, but none of them looked out of place. Their happiness surrounded me.

Then, as if on command, the music slowed.

And all I saw was him.

Beneath the twinkle of a lone chandelier, I pictured Vane's actual face under the mask. I'd worn a mask at the music festival in Glastonbury. We'd kissed for the first time that night in a smoke-filled basement surrounded by blood-spattered walls. Today, he held me in the middle of a glittering ballroom. Yet, I clearly recalled how he'd taken me into his arms that terror-filled night. How safe I felt in them. The hunger in that first tentative kiss and promises it suggested.

Around us, the song whispered about two souls fated to meet. In the lullaby of the moment, suspended from the present and unmindful of the future, I laid my head against his chest. My cheek pressed into the cool silk of his vest. I listened to the steady rhythm of his heartbeat. And there I understood why prom had become so important to us. Something about the last dance before the final act spelled the end of all things and the beginning of new ones.

Matt's words came back to me.

I stilled in the middle of the dance. The words sounded in my head with desperation. *Tell me you haven't fallen in love with him.*

But I had.

## OF KINGS AND MEN

*Crap.* I yanked off the mask and stared at myself in the mirror in the girl's bathroom. Thanks to black kohl, my eyes looked raccoon wide. Smeared gloss plumped my lips, leaving it a vulnerable pink. My hands shook as I rested them on white marble and took heaving breaths. I left the ballroom for a hidden restroom, closer to the lobby. The rush of music vibrated the old walls of the historic hotel, making it come alive. Too alive.

I left him in the middle of the dance floor.

*I'd fallen in love with him.* There, I admitted it. The one thing I'd been denying for months. I was only seventeen—no, eighteen. I wasn't supposed to be in love. Real love. The kind that changes you type of love.

Lust, definitely. Like, it's what I thought we had.

But this… not him. Not Vane. He was the wrong one.

I didn't want to be broken.

*Matt.* I hadn't believed him when he'd said the words. I hadn't dared. I hadn't been ready, and now, I was in the same place. God, it was awful. In the mirror, my reflection grimaced and replied with a silent mocking, '*You're screwed.*'

"I love Vane," I said, hoping it would sound less painful out loud.

"You what?"

My head jerked to the opening and wanted to sink into the floor. Matt slipped inside. I cursed the lack of a door. Only a curved wall barred the view from outside. He wore a tux identical to Vane's, except for the color of his vest and tie. Buttercup yellow matched sober amber-brown eyes. I didn't need the color change to tell who he was. The lion burned in his eyes, and while I loved him too, I wasn't *in* love. He didn't have the same power over me. I didn't feel as if every breath I took was for him. He couldn't break me.

"Matt," I started and stopped. I didn't know what to say.

He looked ready to explode. "Is it true?"

I winced at the bite in his tone and mumbled, "Yes."

"Have you told him?"

*I'd rather eat nails.*

"Have. You. Told. Him?" he ground out when I didn't answer.

"Of course not!" I snapped. With a sigh, I faced him. "Listen, Matt, I'm sorry—"

"You should tell him."

*He's lost his mind.* I said, "What?"

"This was inevitable," he muttered to himself.

Inevitable. I stared at him. I didn't understand. *Unless...* "You had a vision."

It wasn't possible. Vane had taken his magic, but I knew Matt. His shoulders drooped with the secret, the weight of the world pressing down on him once again.

Matt muttered, "You won't understand."

*Meaning there is something to tell.* "How?"

He confirmed it by closing his eyes. After a long second, he opened them. "I had the vision a long time ago... shortly before Vane returned from Carthage. I had just freed Perceval. But I never thought it would come true. I never thought I could actually lose my magic."

"Losing your powers was the trigger." All this time, was this the real reason why he got so upset with me? Because I triggered a chain of events. It took me three steps to reach him. I put my hands on his shoulders. "What have you seen about Vane?"

Matt stiffened. "What makes you think this is about him?"

I gave him a slanted look. "With you, everything goes back to him."

Matt straightened away from me. "Not true—"

I grabbed his arm. "For once in your life, forget about strategizing. This is about your *brother.* Just tell me."

"It's not just about Vane. It's about us all." Matt's eyes became unfocused as he stared off to a point somewhere in the past. "It happened after he came from Carthage. The first time I saw him. He'd changed so much. By sight, I didn't even realize it was Vane when Arthur spotted his small camp."

Vane's memories replayed in my mind. "And?"

Amber eyes refocused on me. "It's why I wanted desperately to find the Healing Cup."

*A cup that doesn't exist.* I pushed. "Why?"

"I saw myself take my magic back. I didn't understand that bit of the vision until Chennai."

"But that's not all."

He took a strand of my hair and wound it around his finger. A yearning look softened burdened amber eyes. He said quietly, "I saw myself kill my own brother, Ryan."

I took a step back. Hair slipped through his fingers. I said emphatically, "You wouldn't do that."

"Wouldn't I? What if it's the only way to save everyone?"

I had no good answer. He was capable of it. Instinctively, I reached for the *Dragon's Eye.*

"Is he here?" Matt asked sharply.

"I told you I could shut him out." *I think.* Knowing I was playing a dangerous game, I let go of the gemstone. "Describe the vision exactly."

"We were standing in the middle of a circle. Everything around us was hazy. The skies above seemed to be dotted with fire. They shimmered with all kinds of different colors. Vane lay on the ground. I knelt beside him. His eyes glowed green, but he was sick. I saw the blackness tearing through his insides. He was dying. I had Excalibur. I put my hand on his chest, but instead of healing him, I stabbed him. Magic flowed into me more powerful than I've ever felt and I sent it back out. To this."

Matt pulled out a phone from his suit pocket and clicked on the touchscreen. It showed a circle of stones with standing trilithons.

"Stonehenge?" I said.

He nodded. "Kronos's Circle. It's torn apart, but we're taking steps to rebuild it as we speak. From your horseman vision, I figured out that the Lady was leading us to quarries that hold the metal used to construct the trilithons. The government is mining them. The mermaid song, the aria you heard in Elysium, is what constructs the gates."

"Vane controls the mermaids."

"I can replicate their magic using the Fisher King's trident."

I gave him a skeptical look. "How will rebuilding Stonehenge save us?"

"I don't know yet. The Lady has a plan. We have to figure it out. But that's not the bit involving Vane. Constructing the trilithons isn't enough. We need energy to power them—"

"The apple?"

Matt shook his head. Lips tightening, his expression became bleak. "I would have thought so, if not for the horseman in the Kronos Eye and my vision."

"What is more powerful, then?" I knew the answer. I couldn't say it.

"Vane."

"You're going to rebuild the trilithons in Stonehenge and then you're going to take his powers to open them? For what?"

"I'm going to take back my powers."

I whispered, "You're going to kill him."

Matt's gaze didn't waver. "Yes."

"You'll let yourself flameout."

And I would lose both of them. His placid expression made

me want to hit him.

He continued. "Poseidon's power must be released back into Kronos's Circle. That's why it was left for us to find. The Kronos Eye confirmed as much when the white horseman opened the gates. This is why the Lady meant the power for me. When the time comes, Vane won't be able to do what is needed."

"To be the sacrificial goat?" I said, almost shouting. "I don't know why he wouldn't want another way. Why haven't you looked for another way?"

"The Lady has been training me since I was a toddler to be the greatest wizard in the world. For this. So I could do this."

"Maybe the Lady is wrong, Merlin. *You* chose not to take Poseidon's power in the maze. Can you for once not follow the path you think is laid out for you and make your own?"

He shook his head. "Don't you think I want to? But I can't take that risk. I won't. Not with so much hanging in the balance."

I wanted to throw something. "Vane has Poseidon's power and your magic and he's not going to give either one up easily. Meanwhile, you have none, Merlin, and since you gave away Excalibur, neither do I." I stated with certainty, "You couldn't kill him even if you wanted to."

The vial of poison was gone.

"I wouldn't be too sure. You gave me the answer, remember?"

An ominous wave of acid rose in my stomach. "The Kronos Eye."

"You can get close to him. The poison won't kill him, but it will weaken him." Matt took out the Eye from his pocket and held the poison out for me to take. "If you want to save everyone, all your friends here tonight… if you want to save your family, the billions of this world, you're going to have to do this."

I shrank away from him. "How can *you* even think of doing this?"

"It was meant to be me!" Matt slammed a fist into the marble countertop. I winced as the long sink wobbled. The sound reverberated inside the small bathroom. "Just me! Whoever took Poseidon's power was meant to die. I was meant to die! Only me." He closed the distance between us. His hand wrapped in my hair. "You should have only been mine."

Then, he kissed me. With desperation. With finality.

It was the finality that left me nonplussed for a second. I didn't like the feeling of giving up. My mind ran. There had to be another way. I had to find another way. I pushed away from him, but not quickly enough.

"I seem to have lost my date," Doppelganger-Matt said from the opening.

Marilynn, doubling as me, gaped at the real Matt and me. She wore a buttercup-yellow gown that matched his vest. Purple looked better, I thought. She gave Doppelganger-Matt a glowering look. "Which one of those wizards put you up to this? Who are you?"

Doppelganger-Matt said dryly, "Much like you, I'm the extra."

Glowering at him, she turned her attention at me. "What are you doing here?"

I ignored her. I couldn't take my eyes off those green-tinged eyes. "Vane—"

"Vane!" Marilynn screeched and practically leaped halfway across the room to hide behind Matt.

"You knew," Doppelganger-Matt said with a small smile.

My heart in my throat, I walked toward him.

The smile tightened. He said, "I don't think you want to come near me right now."

"I always knew it was you," I whispered.

Light flared in his eyes. "Quite frankly, that makes it worse."

As I struggled to come up with a reply, his cellphone vibrated loudly in the pin-drop silence of the room. He took it out and stared at the screen for a second.

"It seems our time is up." Without sparing me another glance, he turned on his heel and stalked out of the suddenly claustrophobic bathroom, but not before I saw the monster coming alive within those stormy eyes.

*Shit.* I took a step to go after him.

Matt caught my arm. He thrust the Kronos Eye in my hand. "Remember what's at stake, Ryan. This is not the right time—"

With a quick twist, I broke away from him. I slapped the offending crystal back at him, refusing it absolutely. "If you keep waiting for the right time, it may never happen. Sometimes you have to make the most of the time you have."

I plunged back into the party after a pissed-off animal—Vane. The hallway pounded with the music's loud bass. He disappeared into the ballroom. I ran into the crowd and stopped at the edge of the room, my heartbeat pumping along with the frantic music. I scanned the crowd for a trace of him.

I touched the *Dragon's Eye* on my neck. A purple vest on the stairs flashed under the swirling lights. I cut through the middle of the dance floor. Weaving and twisting through shimmering silk and satin that invited you to gyrate wildly in the night. Around me, the song urged everyone to take off their clothes along with their inhibitions. I'd lost mine on the first dance.

I made it through the dancers to the curved staircase. The pads of my fingers slid up cold marble of an elegant balustrade. I went up past lingering bodies, laughing and drinking and teetering precariously on the flat steps. Upstairs, curved balconies like numerous theater boxes gave a voyeur a full view of the glittering celebration below. With the *Dragon's Eye* to guide me, I stalked the monster down the long mezzanine as I'd stalked him once through the maze.

I stopped near the center of the row of balconies on an abandoned one. In the shadows, past a circular table with wilted flowers and crumpled linen, I sensed the lurking animal. I walked deeper into the dark. The balcony gave an expansive view of the ballroom below, but I saw no one in the shrouded space.

Cursing, I turned and ran straight into the wall of Doppelganger-Matt's chest. I caught his arms to keep from stumbling. His hands went around my waist. A lone ray of light shone down on his face, a closed off face. The scent of a stormy ocean-blue surrounded me and I was caught in its waves. The thumping music from below muted and sank into the background.

"Looking for someone?" He leaned down. His voice rumbled against my ear.

My body flushed hot and cold. My fingers tightened on him. "Only you."

Green rose in his eyes and the monster snarled. "The wrong only."

The same words I said to myself. It sounded more devastating when he said them, and it was then I knew I'd been wrong. I put my hands on his face. "Only you. Vane."

The monster watched. It reached for me.

I resisted. "Drop the glamour, Vane."

He did. Doppelganger-Matt disappeared and the hard lines of Vane's body took its place. My mouth watered at the sight of him—the hard lines of a warrior's body. The fighter versus the scientist. His lips crashed down on mine. Teeth parted and his tongue slipped inside. His taste, a sweet, clean spring, overwhelmed me. He pulled me into the shadows. My back met the smooth column that separated the balconies. A hand tangled in my hair and another down my side. The heat of his hand penetrated the thin silk of the dress. His tongue plunged deeper into my mouth and he arched my back, pulling me closer against him.

His phone vibrated loudly.

I slipped off the offending jacket that contained it. It fell to the floor in a heedless mess, the phone along with it. My fingers tightened in his hair as he continued the kiss. I don't know how much time passed. All I heard was the music. All I tasted was his breath as I swam in the tides of moments for as long as the song would allow me. He pushed me deeper against the cold stone of the column. His leg slipped between mine.

A loud harrumph finally brought us back to land.

"Sire." A voice came from somewhere beside us.

Vane tore his mouth from mine with a groan.

"You have the worst timing, Leonidas." He moved off me and turned to face Leonidas, who stood on the outskirts of the small circular balcony.

"You did say to notify you immediately." Leonidas's stoic eyes locked on me. I could imagine what he saw—a rumpled gown and bruised lips and more...

We stared at each other for a second. Sizing each other with mutual distrust. Neither one of us would forget the gladiator pit. Vane picked up his jacket and I moved back into the light. I leaned on the balcony's railing and tried to catch my breath.

Looking past the heat of the dancers, my gaze swept over the windows to the cool serenity of the pond outside. I stilled when I spotted a face that shouldn't have been there. Under dim lamplight, I spotted a face I'd hoped to never see again. *Oliver.* Once a candidate for Excalibur, now he was only a son who'd murdered his father.

Oliver stood near the pond. A group of mermaids with swords in their hands surrounded him. I swiveled back to Vane. "What is Oliver doing here?"

A flash went through his eyes. His head jerked to the windows and he spotted the mermaids outside. He crossed to me in two steps. His hand slipped around my waist, gripping the curve of my hip.

"I'm sorry, Ryan," he murmured before turning me to face the ballroom. Green magic sent a loud boom across the domed hall. There was a moment of stunned silence as the music cut out.

"Grey Ragnar." Vane's voice exploded across the suddenly quiet hall. He put his hand around the back of my neck and brought me close to him in a mark of clear possession. "You're needed outside."

"What are you doing?" I demanded.

"Coach Vane?" a girl from the lacrosse team cried in recognition.

In the crowd below us, a young wizard pointed up. "Vane!"

"Get Merlin," someone hissed.

Vane waved his hand. Music filled the space again and drowned out the charged chatter. It couldn't diminish the sudden tension prickling in the room. The regular students murmured amongst themselves in confusion.

Vane turned to me. "Come with me."

I shook his hand, a manacle, off my neck. "I don't think so."

He lifted his hand and turned it palm up. A small green fireball spun with hungry eagerness. "This is a very crowded ballroom, Ryan."

I narrowed my eyes. "Are you threatening me? Because I don't believe it."

A hand clamped on my bare shoulder. "Actually, everyone but you." He looked out over the ballroom. Ice green filled his eyes. "I suggest you believe that."

I did. The answer showed, because he grabbed my elbow and led me downstairs. It didn't take long to cross the dance floor. The crowd parted for us without even noticing, and we left the imperial room to the dark green lawn outside.

Vane marched me to the group of mermaids. Dressed in black cargos and T-shirts, they could have passed for a SWAT team. Except their skin was tinged with green, two men sported pointed ears, and angry red slashes—their gills—poked out from under their collars. Vane barked at their leader, "Does he have it?"

Leonidas, the hulking mermaid prince, said slowly, "Of course. It's as you thought, sire. He was lurking around the hotel. Waiting for a moment to get her alone."

Leonidas held up Excalibur. I gasped. My arm instinctively

reached out for the blade. It swung toward me, also seeking my hold. Vane stepped in between and took the blade. He turned to me with an impassive expression. I dropped my arm.

"How did Oliver get my sword? Why is he loose?"

Vane's brow arched. "*Your* sword was stolen."

I scowled at him. "You let him steal Excalibur? You let him escape?"

"I didn't *let* him. He did. And I was… otherwise occupied." Impersonal eyes traveled over my bare shoulders down to the plunging neckline. My body tightened even under the cold perusal.

Two other mermaids held Oliver at swordpoint. On the ground lay several dead gargoyles. Vane stared at them. "The dissension among them is intensifying. Rourke should have declared his heir."

"You know he couldn't," I said. Since Grey hadn't transformed, only Oliver was eligible to take the throne. Rourke wasn't about to name the son who'd poisoned him as his successor.

"More's the pity," Vane murmured.

"I am the king!" Oliver snarled. He lunged past the mermaids at me. They quickly subdued him. One pressed the tip of a sword into his chest, breaking skin.

"Stop," Vane said. "He is still useful."

I didn't like the sound of that statement. "Useful how?"

Oliver laughed. "To replace you, sword-bearer. Why else? If I kill you, I can claim Excalibur."

"Is that right?" Leonidas's mermaid green eyes flickered over me. I could see his mind turn as he glanced at Excalibur. He'd beaten me several times in the pit, if only I hadn't survived. A flash of green magic zapped the prince. He fell to his knees with a pained grunt. Leonidas's sword flew into Vane's hand. He put it above Leonidas's bent head. Blood formed at the edge of the blade.

Still holding Excalibur in one hand, Vane pressed the second sword into the back of the prince's neck. "Remember your place, mermaid."

Leonidas took a heavy breath. "I beg your pardon, my king."

Vane dropped the sword at Leonidas's feet. Leonidas quickly grabbed it and stood up.

I faced Vane. "This is why you took me to prom. To use me as bait."

He shrugged. "I knew he was lurking close. A trap is better when you're the one who's laid it."

He'd laid it, and I'd fallen right in. My hands fisted at my sides. Anger coursed through me. "And coming to school? What was that about?"

His lips curved into a wistful smile. "A small ruse—"

"Ryan."

Grey strode up the slight slope from the ballroom. Colin and a huge gang of gargoyles took up his left. On his right, Gia, in a flowing white dress, a group of younger gargoyles, and a surprising number of wizards dressed in formal suits flanked him.

Vane glanced at me. The thin strand of a weeping willow swung between us like a pendulum. Light flickered across eyes dotted with more hateful green. He stated, "There can be only one king."

One gargoyle king. I went cold. "What are you doing, Vane?"

My heart sank when the green in his eyes intensified. He said softly, "What I have to."

With sharp fingernails, I gouged my own palms. "There's nothing you have to do. It's always been your choice."

He inclined his head. "I've never seen it that way."

"*Vicarati,*" he said. A green breeze covered me briefly. I tried to move, but found my body locked in place. I grimaced. At least I could move my face. The *Dragon's Eye* heated my neck as I began to fight against the spell.

Vane chuckled at my persistence. Drawing my hand up, he kissed it.

"Leonidas, keep an eye on her." Even though I couldn't move, Leonidas grabbed my shoulder and thrust a sword in front of my stomach. It dug into the bandage under purple silk, sending shooting pain up my abdomen. I hissed, the only thing I could do. Leonidas grunted in satisfaction at the sound of my pain.

Vane faced Grey with Excalibur in his hand. "I need the gargoyles, Ragnar. You're standing in my way. The problem is if I kill you, I'm not sure the gargoyles will wholly fall into line. You've made some powerful allies." His eyes settled on Colin. Then shifted to the dead gargoyles beside Oliver. "Unfortunately, his claim to the throne is stronger. He is Rourke's direct descendant. Which leaves me one way to solve this."

Vane crooked a finger at Oliver. With a snarl, Oliver shook off the mermaids holding him. He stalked forward, transforming into his gargoyle face—protruding forehead and elongated teeth.

"A duel," Vane told Grey.

"No," Gia and I cried at the same time on opposite sides of

the field.

Vane faced the gargoyles. "He hasn't changed. I thought he would after Rourke died. We all thought so. So did you."

Colin and the gargoyles behind Grey shifted.

Gia protested, "There's time—"

"No, there isn't." Vane pointed up at the sky. "The gargoyles must have a leader. I don't know how we're going to live through what's coming, but I do know the gargoyles must stay united. Now is not the time for us to splinter. If you fall into a civil war, none of you will survive."

"He's right," Grey said. He walked up the slope. Gia and Colin walked up with him.

Colin drew out a knife. Uttering a small command, he changed it into a sword. He handed it to Grey. "We follow him."

"Not if I win. Then you will bow to me. You will have no choice." Oliver laughed from beside Vane. The hierarchical nature of the gargoyles demanded it. It physically hurt them to refuse a direct command from their king or even their clan leader. It was the downside to being part of a super-strong, nearly indestructible beast.

Gia gnashed her teeth. "I'll happily kill you. That will take care of the problem."

"You're nothing but a coward, Oliver," Grey sneered.

Vane held up Excalibur. The shining metal blade sword gleamed in the darkness, catching the light of the moon. It glowed with banked energy.

The most powerful sword in the world, and Vane handed it to Oliver.

Oliver took it with a gleeful smile.

For a second, I simply couldn't believe it. He'd betrayed us. Truly betrayed me.

My stomach turned. In protest and in denial.

Grey, too, stilled at the unexpected development.

I begged, "Vane, no."

Vane ignored me. I fought against the freeze spell. Desperate for freedom. Desperate to help Grey. Furious at the prison forced on me. It was all a lie. The hope I carried was based on one belief—that he'd never deliberately hurt us. That belief lay shattered with one single act. Mentally, I pulled hard on the *Dragon's Eye*. One arm broke free of Vane's magical stronghold. It wasn't nearly enough.

I shouted into his head, "*If he dies, I'll never forgive you.*"

The answer that came back was succinct and edged with sadness. "*I know.*"

The sadness made it that much more chilling. Tears prickled at my eyes and spilled. A mournful symphony traveled from the ballroom to wrap around us as the dance hurried to a close. Under the soulful cry of the moon, knowing there was nothing I could do to help him, I watched my brother go to his death.

## I WAIT FOR YOU

Swords clanked and hacked at each other. Excalibur moved with ruthless precision, but Oliver couldn't seem to figure out how to command it. Grey and Oliver fought furiously, even for skilled swordsmen. Both attacked each other with desperate determination. Both knew there wouldn't be a second chance. In a surprise twist, Grey punched Oliver with his free hand.

The powerful blow sent Oliver reeling back. Grey knocked Excalibur out of Oliver's hands. Oliver fell to his knees. Grey's sword swung at Oliver's neck.

Oliver panted. "Stop. You win."

Grey stopped it just at his skin.

Vane shook his head. "Only one can remain, Ragnar."

"I'm not a murderer." Grey lifted his sword and stepped away.

Oliver retrieved Excalibur.

"Grey, watch out," I cried in warning.

An amulet glowed around Oliver's neck. A fireball formed in his hand. He threw it at Grey. Gia jumped in front. It hit her squarely in the chest.

"Gia!" Grey raged as he caught her.

The wizards among the gargoyles ran forward. Grey thrust Gia at them and grabbed the dropped sword. He snarled at Oliver. "You're dead, Oliver."

Something changed in Grey. The fury I'd seen him repress several times blazed forward. The shadow of the beast slipped over him as he thrust Gia's limp body at Colin. He raised his sword and met Oliver. He knocked Excalibur away. His blade sank into Oliver's stomach. He pulled it back out. Oliver fell forward and landed on his knees. Grey swung his sword. As he did, his face changed. The beast took over. A Cro-Magnon forehead protruded and his teeth elongated as he transformed.

Frozen in place, I watched my brother become the gargoyle king.

"No one move." A voice came from the shadows farther down the slope.

In a few seconds, a contingent of soldiers, about a hundred or so, dressed in black cargos surrounded the pond. They all held long black rifles. Robin and Frank, the two spies, stepped out of the shadows with Matt. Intermingled among the Regular soldiers were several young wizards in prom-wear. Two wizards and Marilynn, still looking like me, rushed to Gia. Relief went through me as they began healing her.

Their eyes took in Oliver's decapitation.

Unperturbed by the soldiers, Vane locked eyes on Matt. "New

friends?"

"They're a little upset at you for killing the Defense Secretary."

Vane shrugged. "Convenient for you that I do all the dirty work, isn't it, Merlin?"

"Because you're so altruistic," Matt said. "What are you thinking, Vane?"

Vane glanced at Oliver's severed head. "You know we needed this decided. Tonight happened to be the night the fates chose."

"I'm not talking about the gargoyles," Matt said.

"I know," Vane replied.

The soldiers pressed closer. Vane watched them with a derisive curl of his lips. Matt picked up Excalibur from where it had fallen beside the corpse of Oliver.

Vane signaled Leonidas. The mermaids turned to face the pond.

"*Upari*," Vane commanded, raising his hand. Fierce wind blew, shaking the willow trees. Gusts howled across the small clearing, surrounded by a tall forest of high-rise buildings. The water on the pond rippled wildly. Mist rose and mingled with Vane's magic to become a thick fog of mossy green.

"What is he doing?" Robin yelled.

"I think you'll want to see the little discovery I've made. Your secret is no longer, brother," Vane said lightly. "I had it brought here especially for you this morning. I have to say the gas accident to cover up digging was played quite well by the Regulars. I don't think the townspeople of Derbyshire like the reopening of their quarries after all those years of protest. Your friends are nothing if not overbearing."

Matt asked, "How did you find out?"

Vane took the seeing stone out of his pocket and held it up. "I convinced a spy of my own." He grinned wolfishly at Robin. "Their allegiance was remarkably easy to buy. Something about surviving the end of the world."

With a growl, Robin took a step toward Vane. The soldiers behind him gripped their guns and aimed at Vane.

"Wait," Matt said to Frank, who motioned for the soldiers to hold.

Under cover of the mist, a truckload of black metallic rock in all different shapes and sizes emerged from the pond. Vane directed the rocks with his hand. Taking them from the water, he dropped them on the grass. The mermaids started singing. The soulful aria filled the air and increased in pitch. The sound became painful. Soldiers, wizards, and gargoyles alike held their hands to their ears. Some sank to their knees as the pressure became too agonizing.

The aria heightened even more. The windows of the ballroom rattled and then completely shattered in a booming explosion. Screams and yells followed as glass shrapnel scattered. Most of the blast went outward, directly at us.

As the mermaids continued to sing, the blocks of broken rock seemed to change state and become gel-like. They formed into the shape of the trilithon—two giant vertical lines and one horizontal slab. The structure reminded me of the *Arc De Triomphe* in Paris, on a much smaller scale. The vertical slabs stretched nearly two stories high, the horizontal as wide as football goal. The song stopped.

A mermaid took out the Fisher King's trident and handed it to Vane. Leonidas went to a plastic bag tucked behind a willow tree. The label 'MIT Bookstore' marked the bag. Leonidas drew out a metal box from inside the bag. He opened it and held up the golden apple.

Matt stalked toward him holding Excalibur. He stopped close to me.

"Hand it back," Matt ordered Leonidas.

The soldiers got to their feet and trained all their guns on Leonidas. With a bored glance, Vane sent a green wave through the crowd. The soldiers and Matt froze in place. Leonidas handed Vane the apple.

In one hand, Vane held the apple and in the other, the trident. He slammed the staff of the trident against the ground. The ground rumbled. A crack formed on the ground and ran along the green lawn. A tremor went through the area. Buildings around us shook and shuddered. Everything quivered as the power of the Earth Shaker was called.

The trilithon shuddered, but nothing happened.

Vane slammed the trident to the ground once more. The crack grew wider. Under us, the ground woke like a sleeping giant and growled. The lights of every building in sight flickered and burned out. With a cry, Vane fell to his knees. The monster rose.

Green flowed into Vane, but for a moment, the shape of the bull solidified. Around us, the mini-earthquake he was causing under the ground grew more intense. The high-rise buildings shook harder and for a minute, I was afraid they would crumble. People rushed out of the ballroom and the hotel. They stopped to stare at the imposing trilithon and the wide crack in the ground that seemed to be extending from it.

Under the moonlight, Vane glowed like a charged battery.

Green colored water from the pond rose into the air and soaked him. He went to the trilithon and touched the empty space. As soon as he did, the charged air crackled with contained lightning. The door opened.

Vane's power ebbed. Although exhausted, the monster remained.

"Take him." Vane pointed two mermaids to Robin. "Leonidas, get Ragnar."

"Vane," I gritted out. I thought to him, *"Are you going to leave us frozen?"*

Through the *Dragon's Eye*, in my mind, I searched for Vane. The monster sent me flying back to reality. On the ground, I found I could move. I took a shaky step.

The two mermaids picked up a frozen Robin. Leonidas picked up Grey.

The monster's cold green eyes watched me. He held the apple casually in his hand. "It appears I must take my leave, love."

"I don't think so." I moved to take Excalibur from Matt, who remained frozen just a foot away from me. When my skin grazed his, Matt drew from the *Dragon's Eye*.

"*Anuzyayati,*" he muttered.

I swayed, momentarily dazed, as power flowed from the amulet and the freeze spell broke across the crowd. Inside my head, the monster made an unhappy sound.

I grabbed Excalibur from Matt.

With somber eyes, Matt held out the Kronos Eye. I blinked, but my hands closed around it. I palmed the small crystal and dropped it into the top of my dress.

Vane and the mermaids were a few steps from the gate. Two mermaids were in front holding Robin. I sprinted toward them. Matt followed behind me. The two mermaids went in. Vane took a step into the mist. I hurled Excalibur at his shoulder, the side that held the apple. With my spot-on accuracy, the blade sank into him and the apple wobbled. He dropped the trident to grab the apple closer. Vane fell through the gate. Matt scooped up the trident.

I reached Leonidas, who was last. He carried Grey over his shoulder. I grabbed Grey's feet as Leonidas entered the mist. I pulled him out of the doorway. Grey toppled to the ground. A hand caught me and yanked me through instead.

***

Tumbling, I found myself on the other side. I landed hard on a neatly manicured lawn and fell flopped onto my stomach directly on top of Leonidas. Beside us, Vane pulled Excalibur from his shoulder with a pained grunt. It fell beside me. I rolled off Leonidas to grab it.

Early morning birds chirped as Apollo rode his chariot to bring in the dawn.

Another trilithon stood behind us. Between its columns, the light was gone.

The doorway had closed.

I instantly recognized where I was.

Buildings ran around a football field-length rectangle all connected by a ten-foot wall of grey stone. On one end stood a plain English manor. On the other end, a long, pointed tower with beautiful rose-and-ivory stained-glass windows stood attached to a majestic medieval cathedral that shimmered softly with morning dew. Behind the trilithon, a large fountain with several lion heads spouted water.

I was back at Avalon Prep. I was in Vane's stronghold.

Mermaids and wizards started to crowd the square at the sudden appearance of the newcomers. Leonora came running out between them and almost tripped in her Grecian white gown. She stopped between Vane and Leonidas. Her eyes widened at Vane's sword wound. She moved to heal it, but Vane waved her away.

He handed her the apple and stalked to me.

Glacial green still coloring his eyes, he knelt beside me. "Miss me already?"

My hand tightened on Excalibur. I hurled myself at him. Vane's eyes widened before I knocked him over and straddled him. I brought Excalibur crashing down on him. The blade never made it anywhere close to him. Green magic bent my wrists backward. I let out a pained gasp. His magic handcuffed my hands in the air in an invisible steel grip.

"You're upset," he said.

"What reasons could I possibly have? You used prom to draw out Oliver. You used me to get to Grey." I spat. "You left Gia lying across the field, dying."

He'd crossed the one line I never believed he'd cross.

"You gave Excalibur to Oliver," I ground out.

"It was necessary," he replied without apology.

My insides lay in shambles while he stood in cold isolation—completely unaffected by the goings on of mere mortals.

"*I hate you,*" I whispered in my head.

"*You'll get over it,*" came the calm reply.

I dropped the blade, hoping it would sink into his neck. It didn't. With god-like arrogance, he simply shot me with a sleep spell and knocked Excalibur aside.

Vane sat up as I pitched forward. He put a hand under my knees and rose to his feet while still holding me. My head flopped against his chest.

Leonidas pushed Robin forward. "What do you want to do with him?"

"Set him free," Vane replied. Shifting me, he took the seeing stone out of his pocket and tossed it to Robin. "Return it to your superiors. Tell them they've lost. Merlin can no longer help them. It is time to admit the world is lost."

The cryptic statement was all I heard before my eyes shut.

*\*\*\**

*I am Vane*, I said to myself and asked for strength.

My nightmare walked closer. The hill seemed to tremble with every step he took. I tensed. Deadened eyes swept over the camp until they found Sergius.

Septimus sighed. "I am proved right again. If you want something done, you must do it yourself."

I pushed myself off my knees. "I'm not going with you."

"I'm not here for you." Septimus smiled, a very different smile from the lascivious one he usually gave me. This smile was calm, neither friendly nor unfriendly, yet at its edge I sensed a dangerous cliff. The earth trembled under his every step. Nervous sweat broke out down my back... something that never happened with Septimus. Whatever stood in front of me, I realized, was not Septimus. I very much doubted him to be a man at all.

"Who are you?" I dared to say.

Septimus's lips curved into a chilly smile. His eyes glowed a furious green. "You are correct. The true spirit of this body has already crossed realms. I am merely borrowing it. However, I am disappointed. Have you forgotten me already, Vane? Have I not always treated you like a favored son?"

The sweat on my back chilled my skin down to the bone. I couldn't say the name out loud. I didn't dare. *Poseidon.*

He strode to the little princess and picked her up.

It was the only thing that could have made me move. "What do you want with her?"

Poseidon glanced at me with mild amusement. "You ask a lot of questions. I shall forgive your impetuousness since you have served me well. You found the little one, but her destiny lies not in this place."

I stared at the princess. "Is she yours?"

Poseidon laughed. "No, she is not mine. I leave such things to my brother."

I swallowed. "She is one of you?"

He shook his head. "A mere mortal with just a touch of the divine and thus, entirely vulnerable. I meant for the gargoyle to protect her, but it seems I chose poorly. I admit we have allowed their numbers to dwindle, but perhaps with the dark times coming they will have room to flourish again." Bright green eyes fixed on me. His voice warbled with suppressed power as he demanded, "Now, where are the apples?"

Unable to resist the compelling voice—a gift I always enjoyed using on others and didn't enjoy having used on me—I glanced at our bedrolls. A whip of power rose in the air. The apple tore through the bag of hidden gold we buried and floated before us.

Poseidon plucked it from the air. He opened his mouth and a strange song filled our ears.

I jumped as the ground ripped open. Clumps of dirt mixed with stone rose up. The dirt fell back to earth, leaving only stone. Poseidon re-shaped it into a three-sided bluestone structure. I recognized it. The Domnoni knew the stone circle of the giants. *Caer Sidi.* Saturn's circle. The Roman god, Saturn, known to the Greeks as Kronos. The stone monolith was one from Kronos's Circle of time.

Poseidon took the sleeping girl and tucked the apple in the crook of her arm. "Time for you to make your journey, little one."

"No," I cried out in protest.

Green eyes softened. "She is not meant for you, Vivane."

His eyes made a movement. If I hadn't been watching with petrified awareness, if I hadn't been trained to look for every weakness, I would not have noticed the slight movement of his eyes that sought out my brother. *Merlin.*

What could my brother have to do with her? They just met.

"She has another purpose. You must let her go. My mother has chosen." Poseidon answered the question I hadn't formed.

His words nagged at my spotty memory, but I couldn't decipher them. Yet, the way he said it, I knew I'd already lost her.

"Do not worry." Poseidon inclined his head at the sleeping bodies across the hill. "Limited strength remains in me, but I will make certain none of you remember her. You will all forget until the time is at hand."

*Forget her.* I would not even have that much. The meager pieces of my life, leftover scraps sown together with flimsy ties and desperate need, would once again be torn apart. I didn't know if I had it in me to bear more. I said hoarsely, "Why?"

Poseidon's gaze flickered over Prince Arthur. "Because the threads of fate are held in delicate balance. We can only interfere so much before they start unraveling."

He waved a hand at Sergius. The wrenching sound of breaking bone filled the air as Poseidon tore Sergius's body apart. Blobs of blood floated in the air. Poseidon held up the apple. It absorbed the gargoyle blood; the gold color turned luscious red. He mingled his own energy with the blood and walked to the bluestones.

"A bit of the monster and the divine," he murmured.

He neared the bluestones, and empty air inside the monolith flickered with a flash of light. The light calmed and a deep mist appeared inside the stone doorway. Through the hole he'd opened in the cosmos, I saw the dawn of a morning sky in some distant land.

Poseidon walked toward the mist.

I didn't understand it, but I knew what he was about to do.

I sent magic hurtling toward him… magic I knew would be useless against a god. Yet, I didn't care. I yelled, "She's not yours!"

Poseidon raised a hand.

I went flying back to the ground. Wrenching pain went through me at the impact and at the loss. In Poseidon's arms, the little princess murmured, echoing my silent cry, and stirred. The movement caused Poseidon to catch sight of the rowan bracelet I'd put on her wrist. For the first time, he smiled truly. He seemed to be stunned, yet not displeased.

He laughed. "It seems she has chosen. My mother may have underestimated you, my son. Who knows? All may not be as lost as it looks today. As my father says, the stars are not mapped."

He put a foot into the mist.

I asked, "Where will you take her?"

Poseidon watched the mist. In the trick of the light, the expression on his inhuman face seemed almost wistful. "To her home. To Camelot."

## TELL ME YOU LOVE ME

I woke up on a sofa inside the common room of the teacher's residence.

Out of a set of four, it was the only sofa remaining. The common room had been converted to be a command center of sorts. Instead of a piano, only a bench remained. Leonidas sat on it and ate something while Leonora paced in front of him. Occasionally, she stole glances at Vane. I tried not to roll my eyes. She'd developed a major crush on him on Aegae and apparently it hadn't abated. Beyond them, two mermaids practiced sword forms in the far corner that I knew led off to the elevators.

The sofa lay at one end of a rectangle, along with a low coffee table. Beyond it, two rows of long tables held computers and extended across the width of the room. Several wizards hunched over the ten flat-screens with intense concentration. One monitored news footage. One scrolled through street maps of different cities. Some watched what looked like security feeds of different people. I saw Matt on one screen.

At the other end of the rectangle, Vane sat behind a massive desk. A tinted window behind him diffused the bright sunlight. I had no idea what he was up to and at the moment, I couldn't find the strength to demand the answer. Everything inside me lay broken. I'd lost... again.

He was gone. The Vane I loved was gone.

Matt was right. I hadn't listened to him and he'd been right.

"She's awake," Leonora said.

Vane's head jerked up from a computer screen. He left the desk and crossed the empty middle of the rectangle to me. I didn't move. I couldn't. I was barely holding on. He sat down on the coffee table, his eyes no longer green, but a normal hazel.

"Feeling calmer, sword-bearer?"

*Sword-bearer.* Inwardly, I shrank further into myself. Outwardly, I made myself sit up. My stomach rumbled.

"You're hungry. I'll take you to the dining hall."

After ripping me to shreds, now he wanted to feed me. I wanted to cry, but had no tears. "I'd rather starve than eat with you."

Vane's eyes flashed with annoyance. "*This is getting old.*"

"*You're right.*" I stood up. "Do I still have a room here?"

"Always," he said.

I ignored the caress in his tone. I took a step toward the elevators.

Vane caught my hand. "I haven't given you permission."

I tried to twist my hand loose. Vane held it in a manacle-like grip. Having taught me how to escape such holds, he also knew how not to let me. He tilted his head. "Why?"

I retorted, "Because I never want to see you again."

Beside him, Leonora gasped. She watched us with avid attention. Leonidas gave me a bored look. The wizards at the computers gaped at us. Vane glared at them and they quickly turned back to their screens.

"Because you hate me," he said mockingly.

I stared steadily into hazel eyes, saying simply, "Because I don't care anymore."

His eyes shuttered, a cold green covered them again. He stood up.

"Then, you won't care if I do this." He pulled Leonora to him and kissed her. It wasn't a mild kiss or a small gentle peck. It was a full-on, mouth-to-mouth, not-coming-up-for-air kind of kiss. The *Dragon's Eye* warmed with his desire and it washed over me. He yanked open the door between our minds. He deliberately juxtapositioned her with me. If I closed my eyes, I would have seen us back on the darkened balcony. Instead, I watched him kiss her.

The musty smell of desire filled the room. His. Hers. Mine.

It made me sick.

Leonidas, recovering from momentary shock, jumped up with a roar. He lunged at Vane. Vane flicked him away like a bothersome mosquito, but he released Leonora. She stared at him with a dazed expression, lips bruised in the same way I imagined mine had been just hours ago. Vane's heated eyes turned to meet mine. He dismissed Leonora with a casual wave of his hand, disposing her as easily as a used tissue.

Leonora's face crumpled. Tears springing to her eyes, she ran out of the common room. On the floor, Leonidas sat up with a furious expression. I pointed Leonidas to follow in her direction. "Go get her, idiot."

Leonidas gave Vane a final disgusted look and hurried after her.

"How could you do that to her?" I demanded.

He raised a brow. "I thought you no longer cared."

"I don't care about *you.*" I turned on my heel and stalked off. "You're not worth it."

I made it down the hall and into the residence hall's tiny elevator. I barely stepped inside when Doppelganger-Matt slipped inside behind me, a hulking form crowding me inside the small space. He punched a button and the door jerked closed behind him and the elevator creaked up. I faced the back of the elevator and refused to turn around.

Unfortunately it didn't help. Mirrored panels all around the elevator box surrounded me with Matt's calm reflection. The illusion didn't fool me. Under the civilized expression, he couldn't hide the monster. The Kronos Eye sat heavily atop my chest, inside the gown.

Doppelganger-Matt looked at me in the mirror. "Is Merlin worth it?"

"Yes," I replied honestly.

"Why?"

I stared at his reflection. Matt's reflection. "He doesn't think everyone is collateral." *Blake. Gia.*

He heard me. Doppelganger-Matt punched a hand against a panel. It cracked the mirror. I watched as blood streaked down from his knuckles into the mirror's shattered glass. It was how I felt.

"They *were* collateral. And necessary. Everything I've done has been necessary."

I stared at the red mess on the glass. "Necessary for you."

"I'm trying to save you!"

"You're trying to save yourself."

He raked his clean hand through his hair. "I see you've started to believe my brother."

"Isn't he right? You got everything you wanted."

"You know the answer to that better than anyone." He leaned into his bloodied hand, digging it farther into broken glass. "When have I ever gotten anything I wanted?"

"It was a long time ago. I'm talking about now."

"It will never be long enough." His clean hand touched the nape of my neck. His palm flattened on the bare skin exposed by the sleeveless gown and a thumb traced the length of my spine. "Because there is only one thing I will ever want."

He would never understand—there were lines you didn't cross if you wanted to keep your soul. I asked hoarsely, "Is Gia alive?"

"She is."

I could hear the truth in his words. He didn't lie. He played games. He manipulated, but he had a core integrity that didn't waver. No matter what it cost. It made it easier to forgive him, but I couldn't. Still, relief washed through me.

I closed my eyes. "Why Grey? Why tonight?"

"I didn't choose tonight. Oliver did. I merely anticipated he would." Over my shoulder, he looked at his own reflection. "As for why—the end is close and we're going to need the gargoyles to make the journey. They're strong. I want them with me on the other side."

"Other side?"

"Of the gate."

"What does that mean? What you said to Robin… why is the world lost?"

In the mirror, Matt's image arched his brow. "Hasn't Merlin revealed his final secret? What do you think the trilithons mean?"

"He said he was working on it. It has to do with Stonehenge."

"Kronos's Circle is the center link, but it is not the whole of it. There is no secret machine that will shield us from the Fury. The trilithons are doorways, as you know. You saw my memories, Ryan. Merlin hasn't admitted it, but it's time we all must. We're not saving the world. We're evacuating it." He added the detail I didn't want to hear. "No, not all of us are going."

I turned to face him. "Explain."

"There's simply not enough time. We can only build so many trilithons. Gates. Since you came out of the Kronos Eye, we've been fighting for one thing—control of who goes. Control of the gates."

The elevator reached the top. The door opened. I didn't get out.

"Wizards and mermaids," I answered for him.

"The gargoyles will go too," he added.

"And everyone else?" I said.

"There was never going to be an everyone else. Why do you think this hasn't gone public? Why do you think Merlin is working with a select group of people? There's a short list of who's taking this journey. A very short list."

I pictured the prom. Every one of the young faces. The hope in their eyes. The future that lay ahead of them. Ahead of us. The future that was being snatched away. The garden destroyed.

The door tried to close. Doppelganger-Matt held it open.

I moved past him in a daze. I made it halfway down the hall, before the pounding in my ears forced me to stop. Doppelganger-Matt stepped out of the elevator, but didn't follow me.

I whirled around and demanded, "That's the best you can do? You and Merlin. The greatest wizards in the world with the power of gods behind you. This is supposed to be our great destiny?"

He took a few steps toward me. He pulled out his phone and pulled up the pictures of the paintings from the Boston Library. "Remember these? It is not so much the paintings as it is the story, and the key is to work backwards. There are four items of importance. Three players are at the heart of the quest—two knights and a damsel. One knight holds the spear. One knight holds the cup. Both together hold the divine light. The one proven pure of heart must stand before the altar. Two others must assist him. The one crosses the altar with the help of the believer and reaches for the angel on the other side."

"What's on the other side?"

"It doesn't really matter. The point is that it is away from here. We're to cross the altar to meet the angel on the other side." He pointed to the first painting with the red cloth. "Whatever is under the cloth provides sustenance for the journey. Meaning it's the guide. The apple is the guide. The dove above the angel means two things—the mournful call of a soul passing from earth, and it's also a symbol of the Lady. The censer marks the angel as one of the apocalypse. Behind the angel, you see another golden halo that could mean the sun. To sum it up, during the apocalypse caused by the sun, use the apple to pass from earth."

"So that's it." I shook my head in disbelief. "You and Merlin want to abandon this planet—our home—like it's so much trash?"

"We're trying to save as many as possible! Did you imagine we were going to find a giant shield to stop the sun? Or maybe build several billion umbrellas? This is the only option. And it's not that certain either," he said. "It's going to take everything we have to open all the gates we can build. It's going to take more to get where the apple will take us. At this point, we only know how to open one. Only know how to go somewhere close."

"You don't know even know *where* you're going!"

Doppelganger-Matt smiled grimly. "Haven't you been paying attention? We're going to Camelot."

The connections, his memories, all threaded together in my mind. The reality of it all hit me. This was the Lady's plan. I wasn't going to help save the world. I was just a navigator, a Noah, to guide them off a doomed planet.

I couldn't breathe. I sat on the hard stone floor.

I reached in my dress and pulled out the Kronos Eye. It replayed the scene of the supernova. The following super flare. It replayed the burning planet, the melting cities, the death and destruction. This was the fate we were going to leave everyone to while a privileged few moved on to better pastures. God, I was dumb. Why hadn't I asked Matt these questions? Why had I assumed he would find a way to magically save us all? Why had I been so naïve?

I believed in Merlin. I believed in his plan. I had been wrong.

PRIYA ARDIS

"No," I said.

"Ryan—"

"No." I looked up at him. I made myself stand up. "There has to be another way."

A hint of admiration flickered in his eyes. "There is no other way."

"There has to be!" I shouted. The words echoed down the hallway. It wasn't enough. My emotions ran too high. I punched the wall with a fist like he'd done. It hurt. Tearing up, I cradled the abused hand. It looked much easier when Vane did it. The skin bled, the sting worse than I believed possible.

Doppelganger-Matt walked to me. "Let me heal it."

I pulled back, shaking my head.

He took off his T-shirt. His expression mild, he wiped away at the blood. "There isn't another way. You need to help with the way we've found."

The irony of it struck me. Vane looking like Matt and talking like Matt.

I squelched a hysterical giggle. "You *are* Merlin."

It was the wrong thing to say. He closed the distance between us. I was pushed against the wall. His body covered mine, but I refused to look at him. Vulnerability echoed in his voice as he asked against my ear, "Is that what you want? Who you want?"

I searched, still not looking at him, through the *Dragon's Eye*, but I couldn't see through the fog of his chaotic emotions. "*What does it matter what I want? It's over.*"

"It's not over. It's not what any one of us wanted, but this is what remains." He added, "Deal with it."

My head bent forward and I rested it on his shoulder. My lungs squeezed with difficulty. My own breath choked me. "*Why should I?*"

"Because we have right now. Right this second. We're alive and we're going to fight to keep living. It's what we do."

I took in one breath. My teeth dug into his bare shoulder, into skin, into something solid and alive. He winced. Then I took in one more breath. He traced the naked length of my shoulder above the gown. A strong hand slid down my arm to the Kronos Eye I held in my palm.

He didn't take it from me. "Did you come here to kill me?"

I angled my head and finally met his gaze. "Yes."

"Do you still want to?" His lips grazed mine.

I didn't bend to them. "Why did you give Excalibur to Oliver?"

"Excalibur is yours. It's magical and it's tied to you. You love Grey. As long as those ties are in place, I knew Excalibur would not deliver a fatal blow to him."

"Oh." I stared at Doppelganger-Matt. I said huskily, "Take off the glamour. You're not him."

Need shone in his eyes, sending my pulse skittering. He pressed closer, letting me feel his body against every inch of mine. "I can be whoever you want."

I met his eyes. "Why?"

"Because it's who you want." His hands took mine and held them against the wall. Lips skimmed the racing pulse at my neck. He sucked on it. "I would give you anything you want. Everything I have is yours. Even this. Whatever it takes to have you."

"*Because nothing else matters but you,*" whispered in my head. Aloud, he said, "Tell me you don't regret dancing with me last night, Ryan."

I stared at his bent head against my skin. The fire under Matt's skin he couldn't bury. Didn't he realize it? I would never have mistaken the two. "Vane—"

Firm hands kept me pinned in place. "Tell me."

"I don't regret it," I said honestly.

"Good." Fingers tightened, digging into my skin, and for a moment he held me as if wanted to keep me there forever. But I didn't want to lie to myself or to him.

"Vane," I said. The word came out as a sigh.

He stroked a finger down my cheek. "You keep turning me down. I thought it was Merlin, but it's not, is it?"

"The monster has its hold on you—"

"No, that's not all," he said.

Green-tinged eyes traveled over me, dissecting me to the bone with a razor-sharp scalpel. Suddenly I was very aware of the solidity of his body, his arms pinning me in, his presence surrounding me and leaving little room for escape. He could hurt me. Yet, I knew he wouldn't.

He read my thoughts. Leaning down, he touched his forehead to mine. "DuLac, you're more than you think. You always have been. It's the first thing I see when I look at you. You're the last thing I want to see when I close my eyes. Someone stronger than I can ever be."

The yearning in his voice made my insides melt.

"Take off the glamour, Vane," I asked again.

His shoulders drooped. Eyes closing with a defeated expression, Doppelganger-Matt disappeared. Letting go of my hands, Vane stepped back.

Cold air took up space between us. Too cold.

I leaned forward, a few inches away from the wall.

I put my palms against his flat stomach. I traced the line of Vane's well-defined chest, his bare skin rigid with sculpted muscles. The differences between him and Matt were small and yet so stark. His eyes stayed clear and focused while Matt's held all the secrets. His purpose, whether I agreed or not, was etched in the hard lines of his body. The waves of his slicked-back hair added a touch of wild that would never be completely tamed, but it could be softened. I ran a hand across his shoulders—they could bear a surprising amount. The scar on his chest, the Fisher King's wound, seemed smaller. It melded into his skin rather than stood out from it. My fingers slid across tight pectorals over to a flat male nipple. I tweaked it.

With a strangled smile, he groaned. "*Ryan*—"

I whispered, "Tell me you love me."

"You know I do," he said without hesitation.

Hazel eyes flickered with green. The monster and the man waited, both in agony. I should have been afraid. I wasn't. I had been wrong. Vane and the monster couldn't be separated… but maybe they didn't need to be. With the monster inside him, Vane teetered on the edge of control, but I knew deep down he would not become one. He'd fought that battle fifteen hundred years ago. He didn't enjoy pain and that made all the difference.

He leaned down for a kiss. I let him in.

I expected it to be brutal. It wasn't. He gently explored my mouth. A hand trailed the length of my jaw. A finger traced the length of my breastbone and down to bare skin along the top of my cleavage, just above the tapered edge of the gown. He murmured, "This dress is a dream. I'm going to enjoy taking it off."

*Dream. Vision.* A thought penetrated the fog of desire. I jerked back.

Vane arched a brow. "I have a condom."

I bit my lip.

Tensing, he said, "I won't ask. Not again."

*Not after the maze.* I flushed at the memory. Of me straddling him. Of him asking me to choose him. Heat pooled inside me, an ache begged for release. With strained effort, I subdued it. A turbulent sea swam in Vane's gaze. I pushed further away from him. "You don't understand. You have Matt's magic. The curse. You'll lose the visions if we… you know."

Vane let out a bark of laughter, eyes twinkling in the low light of the hallway.

"How is this funny?" I said in exasperation.

Hands grabbed my hips, pulling me against him completely. "If you think I'm going to pick visions over having you, you don't know me."

With just one sentence, the clawing insecurity I was carrying inside me shrank. I finally let go of the want I'd been holding in check and gave free rein to the rampant hunger he'd woken during our first kissed in a dank basement.

My arms wrapped around his neck. My legs wrapped around his waist.

I said against his ear, "I know you pretty well."

Vane's breathing deepened. Rough fingers tightened on me, digging deep into skin and soul. He pushed away from the wall.

He took me to his room.

***

I got there too late.

I don't know why I came at all.

*You came for her.* My insidious mind laughed at me. Fifteen hundred years later, like a fool, I still sought that one girl. The one to truly see me.

Blood soaked the room. Soft moonlight shone down on the townhouse's dirtied white walls. The once pristine kitchen ran with streaks of red. The red didn't bother me. It hadn't bothered me since I made my first kill at the age of eleven.

I walked past the boy in the school letterman jacket—a headless boy. His head had tumbled off after I hacked it from his shoulders, and his youthful face, its invisible beast underneath, lay lifeless under a cheap wooden table with sunny yellow placemats.

I ran the sword against my leg. I don't know why I bothered to clean it. Any sword I touched got dirty. This one wasn't mine. It belonged to the dead mother and the girl on the floor. I didn't look at the mother, another casualty in a silent war. *If only I got here a few minutes sooner...* I clamped down the thought. It never paid to look back.

My eyes sought the girl. She looked broken; golden-brown hair splayed around her still face like a torn halo. She wasn't, though. She was strong, surprisingly so. Her name was Ryan. Odd name. A man's name, not a princess's. Yet, I liked it.

I liked the way she laughed, freely yet with a hint of yearning. The way the light caressed her profile when she stared off into space, almost as if she could sense me in the shadows.

For weeks, I watched her. I shouldn't have after I found out she wasn't a candidate to pull the sword. She wasn't anything special. Just a regular girl.

Then why did I linger? Why did just looking at her make me want to forget every purpose and every vow? Why did I feel as if I waited more than a thousand years for a chance to know her?

I gnashed my teeth, shutting out such pointless thoughts. I couldn't get distracted. My brother needed me, although he'd never admit it. I'd failed him too many times. I was a wizard and I had a destiny to bend.

I laid the sword beside her. In a small burst of magic, I melded the fabric of her torn shirt. I touched her pink lips, just one touch. A bit of blood smeared where my finger pressed, marking her. She would never even know I was here. She wasn't mine. For one eternity of a moment, though, I wanted her to be.

But then, I was selfish that way.

*After all, I am Vane.*

***

*My name is Merlin.*

I knelt on the ground beside my brother. In one hand I held the trident. The instrument of Poseidon hungered to make the earth rumble. Vane lay still on the ground, his green eyes closed.

"Matt!"

Of those who knew truly knew me, only she called me by that name. Only she really meant it. The one who should be mine. She sat on Vane's other side. Wind lifted the dark-blond curls around her head like a halo. Tears streaked her eyes. She clutched his hand.

Around us, the giant stones of Kronos's Circle watched quietly.

Stonehenge.

I glanced up. Red bled across a part of the sky where only yellow should have shown. A round ball of fire burned through the protection of blue-blanketed clouds. The celestial map, rearranged, and a giant gas ball, previously hidden, blazed out from its spot on the hunter's shoulder. Orion. It was the death of a star. In the sky, it blazed as a fleeting second sun. It would be the death of us. As with any passage, it caused a Fury.

The skies above us turned hazy and shimmered with streaks of color. The Fury bore down upon us. Around us, the refugees waited. Trucks and helicopters readied to speed through to an unknown place. They readied to escape the inferno hurtling closer. The inferno would strip away everything and everyone they knew. Only they, the lucky few, would survive this terrible day.

Brutal wind pelted us with hard bits of stone and dirt, the earth aware of the upcoming inferno. Above us, the sky screamed.

"It's time," I told her.

Her reddened gaze lifted from Vane to meet mine. "I can't," she said.

"It's the only way," I said.

The green gemstone of the *Dragon's Eye* glowed on her neck.

My brother had to die. And so did I.

And she would be the one to kill us both.

## THE LION AND THE TIGER

*Everything had changed.*

I opened my eyes. The latest vision (it was of the future) had been through Matt's eyes. I didn't know what happened to transfer it from Vane... Well, actually I could guess. I buried my face deeper into a fluffy pillow and inhaled the clean scent of Vane's cologne. Resisting the urge to go back to sleep, I yawned and pushed up on my elbows. Muted rays of a setting sun streamed in through a window in Vane's bedroom. I'd never been inside it. At least the double bed was bigger than the one in his Boston apartment. That one could be more aptly described as a pallet.

I sat up. White sheets caressed my bare skin.

The bed was empty.

A note lay on top of a book and an iPad. I picked up the note to find it was a postcard. I read the bold strokes of Vane's handwriting.

*Find another way, if you can.*

I turned the card over, expecting to find a picture of a tropical island. I'd seen a picture of one in Sylvia's office of Alexa and Grey as kids on surfboards against a backdrop of rainbow-covered mountains, high-rise hotels, and the pristine sands of Waikiki Beach. Instead, the postcard showed the House of Seven Gables with an old-fashioned sailing ship in the harbor. A cartoon witch rode a broom across the top. Ghost-shaped letters declared— Salem, the place for witches.

A command, a dare, a sly bribe, and nothing more than the one line.

I oscillated between screaming and melting at the same time. It was so Vane. I thought back to his memory—that horrific night in my mother's townhouse in Texas. My grip on the postcard tightened. I hadn't wanted to see that. A raw wave of sadness went through me. Today of all days, I wished I could talk to my mother. I focused on the one part of the memory that didn't hurt. Had Vane really harbored such strong feelings for this long? How could he not tell me?

He thought he was selfish. I'd never met anyone who'd given me so much. Not even Matt. I glanced down at the iPad. It was pulled up to a countdown app. I grimaced. So much for a thousand years. We barely had three weeks left, but we were finally together and I refused to spend even a minute more without him.

I picked up the hardcover book. It had a plastic covering and an AC High label on its spine, the one he'd stolen from the school library. I hugged the book to me and let myself hang on to something tangible from home.

The door burst open. Matt strode inside. Grey followed on his heels, a sword in hand.

Matt halted at the sight of me in bed. "This is Vane's suite."

I nearly died from embarrassment. At least the sheet covered me. I pulled it tighter up against my throat, while gaping at them. "What are you doing here?"

Grey smirked at me. "Rescuing you. Not that you seem to need it."

I asked, "How'd you get in here?"

"I brought a whole army," Grey said.

"Where is he?" Matt demanded.

Gia walked up. She paused at the threshold when she spotted me. "It seems Merlin was right. I was looking for you in the wrong place." Behind her, the living room stretched out. The suite was made up of two rooms and identical to the one across the hall. The one Gia and I shared.

"Are you all right?" I asked.

Her voice edged with anger, she said, "Your boyfriend hasn't managed to kill me yet."

"It was Oliver."

"Vane's still responsible."

I sighed. She was right. Yet, it wasn't entirely fair. There were no easy answers.

An incoming text buzzed on Grey's cell. "Colin says he found Vane in the cathedral!"

He, Matt, and Gia rushed out.

I cursed. I threw on one of Vane's shirts and ran across the hall to grab some clothes I left in the room. I ran down the stairs (not wanting to wait for the ancient elevator) and out into courtyard.

A firefight was going on. I wished I had Excalibur. Vane and a contingent of mermaids and wizards faced Matt, Grey, and their army of gargoyles. Fireballs flew across the pristine green lawn. They ricocheted off the lion's head fountain, destroying it. Blue and green magic battled each other. Matt formed one huge fireball and tossed it at Vane. His eyes glowed with blue brilliance. I barely had a chance to register that Merlin had his magic back.

Vane caught the fireball and tossed it back. He had Excalibur tucked in his belt. The ground trembled where Vane walked, the power of the Earth Shaker roaring within him. Leonidas grappled with Grey. The green-skinned mermaids clanged swords with the beasts.

On the sidelines, I stood frozen. I had friends on both sides. Matt's brown mane caught the light of a red sky. It bounced off him to his counterpart. Red highlighted Vane's graceful muscles as he faced off with his brother. The lion against the tiger... in a fight that could have no winners.

Over us, the sky rumbled, echoing my pained bewilderment. The Minotaur rose. I saw its shadow rise above Vane. Green glowed from him. My anxiety increased. Blue began to burn around Matt, and the anxiety became full-blown panic. For a minute, I wondered if it was all over. We'd end up obliterating ourselves before Kronos's Fury ever got the chance.

I had to do something or I would lose them both. I weaved and bobbed through the battle, straight into the middle.

Green magic surrounded me. I met Vane's eyes. The monster colored them. It startled when it saw me, but it couldn't pull the magic back. It was too far gone, drunk on the fight. Blue magic slammed into it. Around my neck, the *Dragon's Eye* let out a scream. It echoed mine.

I held onto it. The explosion cratered the earth under me. The impenetrable stone buildings of the rectangle shuddered. The great grey-stone wall cracked and fell like rubble. The cathedral's rose window shattered with a loud pop.

I felt myself fall.

In the dust, I saw everyone go down as the dueling magic sprayed out.

I lay dazed on the ground.

Only Vane and Matt remained upright. Vane stood, while Matt was on his knees. Vane watched me without moving, his eyes back to a normal hazel. As if he couldn't move. As if he didn't dare. Matt ran to me.

I tried to open my mouth to say something, but no sound came out.

His face covered with dust, his eyes tinged with blue, Matt picked me up. He shouted at Vane, "This is your fault."

"Yes," Vane agreed readily.

Around him, the mermaids started to get up. Behind Matt, so did the gargoyles. The wizards still lay on the ground. I flopped in Matt's arms. I told my limbs to move. They refused.

With a flick of his wrist, Vane called Excalibur to him. "She's mine."

Matt shook his head. "I'm not letting her go."

"I could take her."

"You're never going to be the right one, Vane," Matt spat at him. "When are you going to understand that?"

"When I stop breathing," Vane replied.

"Then you'll have to stop my breathing," said Matt.

The sky rumbled again. The clash of magic swirled in the clouds, turning them a muddy mess of colors. Vane stared at it. "Will you not work together?"

"You chose your path a long time ago. It's never matched mine."

"Then, I will leave. For now," he said with finality. "Take care of her, but don't get used to it."

*** 

I woke up in my room. Grey snored on a chair beside the bed. I sat up stiffly and he jerked awake. With a yawn, he raked a hand through his hair. "This is becoming a pattern."

"The perks of being the champion," I said feebly.

"You're up." Matt and Gia walked in from the living room.

"Vane?" I asked.

"Gone," Gia said flatly.

I sank into the bed, wishing I could just hide away, knowing I would never be able to hide from myself. I looked at Matt. "You have your magic back."

"*Upari.*" Amber eyes lit with the brilliant blue of his magic. The entire bed, chairs, nightstand—every piece of furniture in the room vibrated and lifted off the ground. He let it hang in the air.

"How?"

Matt lowered the furniture. The bed landed with an uncomfortably hard thunk. "Apollo's curse. My magic reacted to it, but instead of just disappearing, it rebounded from Vane back to me." He gave me an ironic look. "I didn't need the Healing

Cup. All I needed was for you to sleep with him."

I tensed. Not from awkwardness, but from worry. "And him?"

"As you saw, he's still the Fisher King." Matt glowered.

"He has Excalibur."

"And I have his trident."

I confronted him. "Is it true, Merlin? Is your whole plan to run?"

He blinked. "My whole plan is to make sure as many survive as possible."

"I'll take that as a yes."

"What are you talking about?" Grey frowned.

I explained about the evacuation plan—the gateways, the trilithons, and the apple. Gia turned green and crumpled against the doorframe. Grey sank into a chair beside the bed.

"I'm not giving up. As I see it, we have less than a month to figure this out," I said with determination, foolish or not. I looked at them. "I would rather not do it with a team of one."

Grey leaned over and put his hand over mine, the one clutching the sheet with a death grip. He squeezed it. "I'm all for saving the world. Joey owes me money for the limo we rented."

"I just got into college," Gia said with a small smile. "My mother used to smack me and call me stupid when I was a kid. I'm not going to miss my chance to show her up."

Smacking wasn't all it had been. I'd seen her memories when she drank lake water. Her mother had beaten her black and blue. Matt's eyes lingered on the *Dragon's Eye*.

He spoke in my head. "*You're not a team of one, but your refusal to pick a team hurts us all.*"

"I did pick, Matt," I said softly.

"You didn't pick well." With those words, he stalked out.

Grey's cell buzzed. He took it out of his pocket. "It's Deirdre. I should take it. If you need me, I'll be downstairs."

He ambled out.

Gia watched him go. Folding her arms, she leaned against the doorframe. Red hair fell around her face. She smirked. "So, champion, what does it feel like to get bagged by a douche?"

I threw a pillow at her.

"A hot douche," she corrected.

"Why is this so hard?" I asked her morosely. I already missed him.

Her expression sobered. "He won't change, you know."

"I don't want that." I met her gaze. "I just need him to bend enough to accept I love him."

She tilted her head. "Why him?"

*Why not Merlin?* Was her real question.

The answer came from deep in my soul. "With him, I'm always home."

***

One week passed faster than I could have thought possible. Gia and Grey went back to Boston to finish school. I wasn't going to make it to graduation. I refused to let Marilynn walk across the stage in my place and would get an incomplete for my senior year. Sylvia sent the notifications to the colleges where I was accepted. More notifications than I thought—she filled out several applications for me. I cried when she told me... that she cared enough. Oddly enough, in that moment, I felt the spirit of my mother hovering over me.

Not unskilled with computers, I quickly found Vane's schedule in his command center. There was no effort made to hide his plans. He planned on traveling the world and building a trilithon in every major city. Each one a hundred times the size of the one he built in Boston. With his core crew of mermaids and wizards, his calculations indicated he could make thirty-one gates.

Matt wasn't going to take that lying down.

Believing he could build the gates with the Fisher King's trident, Matt drove me to the quarries. The long-dormant quarries opened under a storm of environmental protests. The protestors, who'd spent years living in tunnels and tree houses to protect the national park and ancient monument of the Nine Ladies, had only recently packed up and left, thinking their long-standing battle won.

Near the town of Derbyshire, under grey English skies, Matt showed me the stone circle of nine. The upright sandstones sat in gothic silence on a mossy green clearing in a hilly area dubbed Stanton Moor. A tenth stone, the King Stone, sat out of the circle and looked down on the Nine Ladies. It struck me as a little creepy how identical the stones were to what I'd seen in the Kronos Eye. It legitimized the rest of it. The exploding star. The furious sun. A burning sky.

No place to run.

As we drove to the quarry site, I saw a uniformed guard wrestling with a protestor trying to storm past a heavily guarded gate at one of the reopened tunnels. We went past a chain-link fence to the front of the tunnel. We found a fairly isolated area with a giant pile of mined stone. Matt handed me the trident. We spent the next few hours with me trying to open a gate with the trident while he used magic to pull together the trilithon. Translation—he spent hours muttering, pacing, and shouting hocus pocus spells at weird metallic stone blocks.

I spent hours waiting around and getting hungry in between bouts of shooting at said weird metallic stone blocks. I didn't mind, though. More gates meant more people saved.

However, the metallic rocks never changed state, from rock to gel-shape back to rock as the mermaid song had done to the blocks in Boston. The trident only broke up the stone into little bits. Not ready to give up, Matt got us rooms (separate rooms) at a local inn and we went back to the quarries day after day.

Meanwhile, because they had little choice after Matt's failure to build a gate, the governments conceded and bargained with Vane. He got resources, cover stories, and however many seats he wanted on the evac trucks. (I had no contact with him. My info came through Matt and Grey. The Queen acted as his go-between. She refused to give me his number on his demand, and the *Dragon's Eye* remained firmly quiet. He'd locked me out.) The Council regrouped to help the wizards with the preparations. The wizards flocked back to the school from various parts of the world, knowing Merlin was there. Vane had taken Leonora and Leonidas with him.

To build a giant gate took about a day. It became a game with me to figure out which cover story they used in which city. Not wanting to admit the pathetic stalking I was doing as Vane traipsed around the world, I only did this on the iPad when I thought no one was looking. I'm pretty sure Matt knew anyway. He would test me by casually asking which city was next on the schedule and then grimace when I replied from memory.

I researched the golden apple frantically.

Something about Vane's memories nagged at me.

Matt finally admitted defeat in Derbyshire, and we returned to Avalon Prep. He and I often worked in the school library together... Neither one of us wanted to be alone. We worked, but we didn't talk more than absolutely necessary. I didn't know what to say to him—*I'm sorry I may possibly kill you soon. I'm sorry I slept with your brother.* (I wasn't.)

*I'm sorry my brother ditched you after one night.* I imagined as his reply. Followed by, *I told you so.* He didn't say it, but when I met his gaze, I knew he'd read my thoughts and I knew he agreed with them.

Help also came from other sources. Marilynn took detailed pictures of the Boston Library paintings and whatever other research bits she could from Boston. Grey tried to help, but was called into organizing the gargoyles for the evacuation. Gia got pulled into helping him. The excruciating part for everyone—the governments, gargoyles, and wizards alike—was picking and choosing who would be told about the evacuation and who not. Who would live and who would die.

I researched more. I slept very little.

But mostly I just missed Vane. As I watched the numbers on the countdown clock become smaller and smaller, my uncertainty grew bigger and bigger. The old insecurities crawled back. Was I just another in a long parade of infatuations? As Gia said, had he wanted to bag the sword-bearer? Was it another ploy for control?

Outside, the sun shone with excruciating heat as Kronos's Fury neared.

Even the nights were hot. The airless atmosphere made everyone restless.

Then there was the constant anxiety at what was coming. Mark, Gia's ex and one of the wizard candidates Vane recruited to try his hand at pulling the sword, convinced me to resume training. We had no teacher, but it helped keep the crazy in check.

Two weeks passed.

One afternoon, I stumbled on Matt watching a secure web feed.

"You don't want to see this," he said.

Of course the declaration made me want to see it more. So far all anyone had told me about the evacuation was "you don't need to know" and "concentrate on getting better." I sat down next to him. It didn't take me long to figure out I should have listened to his warning. A group of world leaders sat around the rectangular table at the UN headquarters. From the limited number of people in the room, I guessed it was another secret session. I asked, "Is the Queen there?"

Matt shook his head. "Not for this."

A mustached man, who I now recognized as the current president of the Security Council, came into focus. "Merlin, have you confirmed how long the gates will be open?"

Matt cleared his throat. "We will build as many as possible until the last possible moment. Since there is only one apple, we must open all of the gates at once from a central point."

On the video chat, numerous faces stared back, waiting for a final number.

"Using the Kronos Eye as the model reference and extrapolating for the level of activity, the current data model sets the time at seventy-six seconds. We can last for seventy-six seconds before the Fury overwhelms us."

*Seventy-six seconds to evacuate our whole planet.*

Murmuring broke out in the meeting room. Questions started coming at Matt about who made the determination, how it was made. I listened, but got lost at the names of experts being thrown around. I tuned back in when mustache-man steered the meeting along.

"...let us proceed to today's topic of discussion. We have come down to these proposed criteria. The first is a lottery system. Second, standardized school scores..."

I took a harsh breath, finally understanding why Matt had not wanted to involve me.

They were coming up with a way to pick evacuees. As I listened to them define a system to designate a number rank to sum up a person's worth, the overwhelming guilt I'd been keeping at bay threatened to choke me. Midway through the arguments my mind rebelled. I stumbled into the nearest bathroom, the nearest toilet, and tossed up the entire contents of my stomach.

I don't know how long I stayed in there, but by the fading light in the window, I figured it was most of the afternoon. I alternated between rocking back and forth on the floor and hurling offerings to the porcelain gods. Finally, my stomach emptied.

I stayed on the cold floor, too weak to get up. Sometime later, Matt walked inside. Arms went around me. He pulled my back against his chest. The simple touch was all it took to open the floodgates. I turned into his chest and cried. Not the soft kind of weeping, but the kind where I expelled huge amounts of snot and tears until his T-shirt became soaked with fluid. He held me for what seemed like forever. I fell asleep on his shoulder.

I woke up later in my bed. He slept in Gia's bed a few feet

away, his face turned toward me. Hugging a pillow to myself, I stared at him. His eyes opened.

"Do you think we can be friends?" I asked.

He stared up at the ceiling. "Probably not, but we can pretend."

"I don't want to pretend." I tilted my head on the pillow. "Why did you tell Vane you wouldn't let me go?"

"You know why."

I chewed the inside of my cheek. "You have your magic back." *And the curse.*

"He's the wrong one."

"Maybe I am too."

He continued to watch the ceiling. "Do you know I used to wait for him? After he left, I used to sit in the woods outside and wait for him to come. I made a secret satchel, so we could run away. I waited every day for two years. Then, one day I missed going out. A few months later, I missed two days in a row. Eventually I stopped. He never came."

"The Lady forced him to leave."

"I know, but I waited. I thought he could do anything." His head turned on the white pillow. Shaggy brown hair fell over his eyes as he gave me a tired smile. "When I turned five, I started having dreams. They were horrible dreams. Of what he'd done... what he'd been forced to do. How many he'd killed. I saw them all. Then, he came back and I had the vision of me killing him. I wished he'd never come back."

It hurt to hear him say it. It made me even madder at the Lady for tearing them apart. "Matt, he loves you—"

"I don't think so."

I couldn't believe my ears. He didn't think his brother loved him. I wasn't sure how to convince him.

"It doesn't matter, Ryan. We've got bigger worries." Matt flipped to his side. "Didn't I tell you it was going to be complicated to know me?"

"A swoon-worthy line." I smiled at the memory of our first meeting. "I didn't realize you were being literal."

"Neither did I."

After that, I tried not to think about the evacuation.

After that, things became less awkward with Matt.

Three weeks after Vane left, my mind swam with the details I collected from researching, but a silent hand seemed determined to keep it all in separate boxes, and I couldn't make the connections I desperately needed. Finally, I ditched the library in defeat and went to work out. I hoped pushing my body to exhaustion might push my mind to flow.

I walked into the converted cathedral to meet Mark and a few other candidates. Past stained-glass windows and white-stone walls on the ground floor, curved archways led up to a turret with a winding staircase. On the second floor, the large gym had gleaming wood floors, intricate wood moldings on its windows, and rustic racks of weapons along the walls. Inside the medieval training room, a very modern gel mat outlined a workout space.

It was hard to be in the room. Every single time I stepped in I expected to see Vane, and every single time I didn't, I felt a little broken. His office lay down below another winding staircase, off the side of the gym. I did sword forms with Mark and four others. Two friends of Blake and two more of Vane's candidates. Three girls and three guys. Mark and I ended up being the mismatched pair since we pushed ourselves the hardest.

The arrangement had been working fine until Mark whacked me across the stomach with a sword. It wasn't a practice sword. We were the last ones left. The others had already gone off to dinner. Mark dropped his sword. I sat down hard on the mat.

"Shit, DuLac." He dropped down beside me and tried to heal the wound. Unfortunately, the cut exacerbated the healing wound and he wasn't strong enough to combat the widening gash.

"Get Merlin." I lay down on the mat, holding my stomach. My hands quickly became wet with blood.

Mark ran to his duffel bag. He cursed. "He's not online."

"He's probably in the library."

Mark hurried off. I closed my eyes.

Around my neck, the *Dragon's Eye* heated.

I lay on a beach. Soft blue waves rolled gently into a curved cove. I hadn't been there before. It wasn't the same one from the Medusa visions. This one boasted smooth yellow sand. A lush green mountain with a hint of black on its peak served as a backdrop. Rain clouds misted the top, but down on the beach, the sun shone brightly. No threatening clouds hovered in the horizon. Warm blue-green water tickled my toes as I lay just above the surf.

I could have stayed forever.

"*Leave you for a bit, DuLac, and you wind up with blood on you.*" Vane's voice washed over me. I blinked. The door between our minds gaped open.

"Nice place for a rest," he said. The ocean turbulent behind him, he emerged from its furious waves. The mermaid walked on the beach. His hardened torso glistened under the soft rays of the sun. His hair wet and coarse with saline, I wondered if his lips would taste salty too. The wondering made me angrier.

Vane knelt down on the sand beside me. On top of my stomach, my hands curled into fists. Green ringed his pupils. He looked exhausted. I told myself I didn't care.

I was not happy with him.

He gave me a wistful smile as if he read me, but offered no explanation.

"I'm going to put you to sleep," he said.

"Not a chance!"

"You're going to bleed to death if I don't heal this."

He'd healed me twice before while I slept. I didn't know how or what, only that it worked. I had a feeling I didn't want to know. That was before. Before he left me in pieces for Matt to pull back together.

"So do it." It couldn't be worse than what he'd already done to me.

"You don't want to see this. Trust me—"

"You're right. I don't. Trust. You. At all. Because you're a big egotistical jerk." I stared off into the blue sky and waited.

After a few seconds, he growled, "Fine. Be stubborn."

Green intensified in his eyes. It overtook him. The monster snarled free. A shadow fell over Vane. Against my will, my eyes fell shut. Red eyes, horns curling out of his head, and the face of a bull melded into Vane's sculpted chest.

The Minotaur sat on the beach. I lay spread out like a bonfire buffet before him. I took in a panicked breath. The monster I helped bring to life would be the end of me.

## FAITH IN WESTMINSTER

"*Don't move,*" the bull's mouth commanded. Its hands pushed aside mine to reveal my stomach. It lowered its mouth. My nails dug into my fists. The agony of the bull tearing through my stomach still sat fresh in my mind.

A thick tongue extended and licked my wound. Saliva coated the gash while the bumpy tongue swept away the blood in slow whorls, much as the warm ocean bit and nipped at my toes. I lay still through it, oddly and completely content.

The monster gave a final lick and started to fade.

"Wait," I told it.

The bull looked at me curiously. I put a hand up to its cheek. It crooned into my palm and snorted hot breath that tickled my skin.

"I need to ask you something."

Its red eyes watched me calmly and waited.

"Who am I?" I asked him.

I didn't think he would answer. He stared off into the volcano. A shadowy figure moved behind us that caught his attention.

"*Daughter of the sun and sky. The Preserver,*" Vane said in a low, rougher voice. "*The one for whom I waited—the one to free me.*"

The one to free me. It didn't sound good. "Hercules defeated your father on Crete. Do you know the story?"

It snorted with displeasure. "*Poseidon resurrected me with my memories.*"

My heart sped up. "Do you know how many apples Hercules stole from Elysium?"

"*My mother said three.*"

The shadowy figure stepped onto the beach behind us. It was Matt.

The bull vanished and in its place, Vane sat beside me once again.

Vane gave me a considering look. "You didn't panic."

"You did."

I wasn't talking about the wound. He knew it.

He glanced at his brother. "Merlin is right. I'm not the one meant for you."

"I'm not the little princess from your memories, Vane. I don't need to be protected."

Taking my hand, he jerked me up into a sitting position. "Then, why do I keep having to rescue you?"

He winked out of sight, leaving me alone.

"Jerk," I repeated.

I opened my eyes to the bright light of the cathedral. The salty scent of the surf still lingered on my senses.

Matt sat on the floor in Vane's place. "You talked to the monster."

Mark hovered behind him. Thoughtful amber eyes flickered over my healed skin. I touched it gingerly. "I've always been afraid, but this time... I wasn't." I looked at him. "We have to go to London. I figured out how to save Vane."

"That's going to be difficult," Matt said.

"Why?"

"The story just broke. The Queen conferenced me to formulate a response." Matt held up an iPad. It was stopped in the middle of a news clip labeled 'Breaking News – End of the World Tomorrow.' A reporter sat with Dr. Latimer, the physicist who'd written the supernova report for the UN.

He said grimly, "Kronos's Fury has gone public."

I wished I could close my eyes and go back to the beach.

***

Later that evening, I stood beside King Henry V's tomb inside the gothic grandeur of Westminster Abbey. The main hall of the monastery boasted pointed arches, rose windows, gold filigrees. Statues of knights, kings, and memorials to the famous and not-so-famous departed lined the stone floors as well as the walls. Tucked past the main hall, in the tomb, the coronation chair of Edward the Confessor, and all subsequent British monarchs, stood upon a stone pedestal.

The simple wood chair with a high back and plain finials didn't seem all that grandiose, more befitting the simple stone frame of the monastery than its layers of accrued adornments over the centuries. The chair had a simple seat and small wooden legs. Sometime in the sixteenth century, a base of gold with four gilt lions serving as its legs was attached at the bottom of the chair.

I ran one hand over the stone pedestal and gripped the strap of a bag I'd picked up at school with the other. "This is it, Mark."

"What are you doing sneaking in here?" a furious voice asked me. "You set off about a million intruder alarms. They have a wireless security system. At least that made it easier."

I jumped about a foot in the air. I turned to see Vane striding down the silent monastery. Somehow he fit in the cold walls of the church, and yet, he also fit in the ultra-modern black suit he wore. Mark had broken through the security gates, but with brute magical force. I hoped it would take care of any other alarms in place. I arched a brow at Mark.

He returned a tight smile. "Vane told me to let him know if you tried anything."

Great. I recruited a spy.

"Get back to the school and cover for her," Vane barked at Mark. I'd snuck a van out of the Avalon Prep garage, and convinced Mark to come with me.

Mark jumped to do Vane's bidding.

"Don't even think about it." I glared at Mark. It took several hours to drive back to Somerset from London. "How am I supposed to get back?"

"I'll take her back," Vane said.

Mark shrugged. "You needed a wizard, DuLac. Vane's a better

one."

*He is also a bastard.*

*"I never said otherwise."* The words shot back in my brain.

Mark rushed off without a backward glance, leaving me alone with the one person I didn't want to be alone with. I muttered, "I need to enlist better help."

"Merlin's caretaking skills are abominably lacking," Vane said with exasperation.

I glanced around. No minions lurked in the shadows. Vane was alone. For once. I scowled at him. "The schedule has you in Paris."

He inclined his head. "You memorized my schedule?"

I glowered at him.

Stormy green eyes turned smug. "I finished in Paris early. Others are working here."

"And your usual entourage?"

"Getting ready," he replied cryptically. He tilted his head. "Why are you here, sword-bearer?"

"You told me to find another way." I turned back to the Coronation Chair. "Do you remember Glastonbury Abbey? During Arthur's time, it was considered one of the wealthiest and most well-endowed churches in the country. Said to supposedly house the tombs of Arthur and Guinevere."

Glastonbury was the town outside Avalon Prep, otherwise known as 'the mystical land of Avalon.'

"So?" Vane walked closer to me. He put a hand on my back, and my loose T-shirt suddenly felt tight.

However I refused to jump when he called. Stiffening, I took a step away from him. "Legend has it that Joseph of Arimathea, one of the three brothers who went on the quest for the Grail, found it and brought it with him to the abbey."

"I thought it was Perceval, Bors, and Galahad," Vane said.

I shrugged. "Different names. Same story. Anyway, after 1066, William the Conqueror commissioned the Doomsday to take a census, but everyone knows he was also evaluating wealth. During that time, everything truly valuable was taken out of Glastonbury Abbey and brought to Westminster to keep near the king. William was the first king crowned here."

Vane tugged at a strand of my hair. "What does it have to do with the chair?"

"A panel under the seat used to enclose the Stone of Destiny. Today that stone sits in a museum in Scotland, but I think the whole 'Stone of Destiny' is a cover story to keep track of what's truly hidden here."

I turned to look at him. The shadows played over the hard lines of his cheekbones. In the silent peace of the church, he only appeared more vivid. Being near him sent a shaft of agony through me. Why did he keep running away?

"What is hidden here?" he said huskily.

I swallowed and resisted the urge to touch him. My fingers ached to confirm he was real. He was here. "The Lady sent Hercules to steal the apples from Kronos. Matt and I found one apple in Sri Lanka. In a place she directed Matt to go. In your memories, you, Perceval, and the princess found another apple that Poseidon took. Well, what happened to the third apple? Why do we have these stories of the grail? What if the last one was brought home? Taken back to Glastonbury Abbey—to Merlin, to Arthur. During the dark ages, the churches were the only places of light. If a treasure of such importance had to be kept, it would be kept by them."

Vane turned to the wooden chair of kings. "And later William the Conqueror put it in his chair?"

I nodded. "The real stone of destiny. Hiding in plain sight."

"Not quite plain." Vane waved his hand and shifted the chair forward along with the waist-high modern pedestal. It butted up to Henry V's casket. The movement in the already tight room pushed me up against Vane.

He caught me about the waist. "Ryan—"

"You left, Vane. I'm pissed. Just let me stay that way. It's easier."

"I never had a choice about leaving." *Since I was a boy.* His arms tightened around me. "Someone had to build the gates."

"You could have taken me."

"I didn't think you would want to come."

"You didn't ask."

"You were injured, sword bearer, and your protector took over. You needed to rest."

I pushed him away, sputtering, "And I should be grateful? You are the most conceited... pompous... idiotic..." I broke off to grind my teeth. "Don't worry. The sword-bearer will do her part tomorrow. You don't have to seduce me into it."

Vane stared at me. "Is that what you think? That I want you because of Excalibur?"

"What else am I supposed to think? You and Matt have been going back and forth over me since we met; and it's not because I'm so awesome that you can't live without me."

*Even though I want you to think so.*

Vane snorted with laughter. "Yes, sword-bearer, I don't know how we've managed with such burdensome baggage like you."

"Shut up." Humiliation colored my vision red. I confessed my deepest fear and he was laughing at me. I pointed him out of the room. "Just go away, Vane. I can do this by myself. I don't need you."

"I know you don't." His expression tightened. "I've been given away too many times to not know that."

"So instead you'll just push me away first?"

Green flashed in his eyes. "You made your choice in the maze—"

"And you chose the Minotaur!"

Vane caught my wrists and held me against the pedestal. "I did it for you. To save us."

"Then you have no idea what I want," I said. "If all we're going to save is us, then we haven't done anything. Why bother with the gates, Vane? Why bother saving anyone? Don't tell me the mermaids matter to you."

"The ones who care about me matter to me."

"When are you going to learn that it's not enough to protect the ones that matter to you? It matters what mark you leave."

Vane let go of me. "If you want sanctimonious, go back to Merlin."

"At least he has a heart, Vane. You've cut yours out."

He recoiled as if I struck him. "It was cut out."

*By his mother. By the Lady. By Merlin. By me.*

It was the way he saw it. He was wrong.

"We're human. It's what we do." *Hurt each other. Then glue each other together again.* I put my hand on his chest. "You can grow another one."

"It's not that easy." Vane turned away. He stared at the floor of the church.

He flexed his hand. "*Khand.*"

The floor exploded. The panel was thin, as I'd predicted. The perfect hiding place. Vane leaned down and reached in past the rubble and cleared it away. I put my hand on his neck; my fingers slid through his hair.

He sat back on his knees. "There's nothing here. It's gone."

"No." I dropped down and dug into the rubble. It was a hidden compartment—an empty one. I clutched my chest. "It can't be."

Vane tucked me to his side. "I told you, love, it's not that easy. Nothing ever is."

Vane led me outside. I walked in comatose silence. It had been my last-ditch effort. I'd failed again. We went through the narrow buildings. My whole body shook, a bundle of nerves. The streets were eerily silent. London, a ghost town. I never would have imagined it.

We crossed into the more residential sections of the city. Many of the windows looked to be boarded up. Even if people didn't quite believe the end of the world alarmists, they were taking precautions. Not that it would matter.

A black truck screeched up to a small building.

Vane pulled me out of sight into the alley.

A family rushed out—a mother, a father in military uniform, and three children. Under the cover of the night, they snuck onto the street, obviously trying to stay quiet. The mother had tears running down her cheeks. She clutched the smallest of the three, a toddler boy, to herself. A Superheroes backpack dangled from her arm. The other children, a teenage girl and a preteen boy, wore heavy backpacks. Another man in black uniform stepped out of the truck.

"Tom Drust, ready?" he said in a clipped voice.

Tom, the father, nodded. "These are my eldest, Maura and Max. They're on the list."

"Mum!" the preteen boy cried. The father picked him up in his arms. He and the teenager, who also started crying, stumbled to the truck. The father hustled the two kids inside.

"We have others to pick up," the military man prodded the father.

"Anyone not show?" The father's voice broke. "We have Mark."

The military man checked a smartphone he carried. He shook his head. On the street, the mother burst into loud sobs. She held the toddler tighter in her arms. The Superheroes backpack dropped to the ground.

In the alley, Vane's front pressed against my back. His arms went around my waist.

I heard the father's whisper down the quiet street.

"I've been assigned to guard the London gate. The gun is in the safe. Two bullets for when you need it." The father's face streamed with tears. He wiped it, gave the younger kid a pat on the cheek, and turned away, his shoulders drooping with failure.

*Evacuees.* This was real. This was all there would be. I put my hand to my mouth in the alley. Nausea rose in my stomach and climbed past my throat. I choked it back.

Vane's arms tightened around me. "What will you give me to save him?"

*The toddler?* I blinked. "What do you want?"

"A favor."

It was a demand and a plea. The last favor in Chennai hadn't worked so well, but I replied, "Anything."

On the street, the military man's phone beeped. He looked at the screen in surprise. "Wait. I've been given an extra space."

The father straightened. The mother didn't wait for him. She rushed up with the last child. She thrust the kid into the truck. Her daughter quickly grabbed him and the Superheroes backpack.

"I'll take care of them," the teenager sobbed.

The mother put a fist to her mouth and nodded. The father jumped in the truck.

The truck roared away. The mother cast a furtive look around her and then rushed back into the small house.

I turned around and faced Vane. He deliberately slid his phone into his pocket.

For a minute, I wanted to hit him. What kind of bastard was he? Then I noticed that bit of wistfulness in his hazel eyes again. The same wistfulness with which I'd caught him watching me. Acting on impulse, I grabbed the phone from him.

I ran down the street, clutching the phone like it was a lifeline. He chased me. He could have felled me with a simple spell. I don't know why he didn't. As I ran, I tapped the screen. It had a password. *Vivane.* I rolled my eyes at the tremendous security.

Vane stopped me. A manacle went around my wrist. He

snatched the phone back. I stumbled back against the side of a random car. He caught me and pulled me to him. I grabbed steely shoulders. The details of the webapp selected on the phone. He'd added a space for the little boy. The webapp recorded the time of the transaction. He'd done it several minutes ago, before I agreed to the blackmail, probably as soon as he'd found out the boy's name.

"Why?" I demanded.

He said, "There's always a price, isn't there?"

"Whatever the price, I'll pay it," I said.

"I know. That's what scares me."

I understood. And I hurt. I looked up. Clear skies belied the coming storm. The stars above shone too brightly. The moon looked mournful and no help was coming. My arms went around Vane's neck. I let all my weight hang, my knees too weak to hold me up. I listened to the beat of his heart, a good heart, even if he didn't believe it. I couldn't look at him as I whispered, "I don't want to lose you either, Vane."

He took my chin and forced me to meet his gaze. His lips curled up into an arrogant smile. "You won't. I'm like a god, remember?"

A fire hydrant opened behind us. Water gushed out of it. It fanned out around Vane and soared straight into the sky, stabbing it with determination. I watched the watery spectacle.

That's what *I* was afraid of. He and Matt thought they knew what they were doing. I wasn't so sure.

Even gods weren't infallible.

## FOREVER AND EVER

During the drive back to Glastonbury, I kept glancing at him.

Vane let out a breath. "What, DuLac? Spit it out."

I wasn't sure I could. Any hope I held for a miracle had died. It reminded me of his memory. *Never let them know how much you want something.*

Well, I wanted. Now I was paying for it.

I crossed my arms and hugged myself. "What happens tomorrow?"

"I bring Excalibur. Merlin brings the apple. Once the Fury starts, we can use Excalibur to open the gates. I will use the trident to extend the energy to all the gates from the central one at Kronos's Circle. All of us, including the evacuees, will go through the gate. We take the apple through. Because the gates are tied, I believe it will lead us to the same place."

"Why the circle?"

"Poseidon touched the stone in the circle in my memory. In the Kronos Eye, the same stone appeared with Excalibur in it. The stone is still there."

I ran out of things to say. The impending doom pressed down on me.

We drove along the road.

Finally, Vane spoke. "If he didn't have the curse, would you be with him?"

"I fell for him first," I said honestly.

Vane let out a hiss.

I added quietly, "But I fell for you harder."

The car swerved. Vane cursed. "Don't say things like that when I'm driving."

"Then don't ask the question."

"If I wasn't already late, I'd pull over and take off your pants right now," he muttered.

I smiled. "I like you too, Vane."

We sped down the winding one-lane roads of Glastonbury. We passed a stately manor estate with a sign declaring its modern-day update to bed and breakfast. Closer into town, we passed cottage-style townhouses and narrow streets interspersed with bushy green trees. The van ambled down the narrow streets until we reached an open, well-preserved area.

Vane stopped the car in the parking lot in front of the remains of Glastonbury Abbey. Due to the late hour, it was empty. The park had already closed for the day.

Beyond the fence, the ruined abbey's impressive stone arches still stood tall. Behind the arches on a clear stretch of lawn a

Roman chapel built in the eleven hundreds remained. A mist of blue, the color due to the local stone in the rolling hills had settled over the abbey, lending it an otherworldly air. A figure popped up next to me, just outside the window. I let out a small shriek. For a minute, I thought I was hallucinating. I rolled down the window.

Grey's face peered down at me. He, too, wore a formal suit.

I pushed open the door and jumped out. I threw myself into his arms. "What are you doing here?"

"This place is seriously creepy." Gia tugged on a strappy pink gown.

Vane got out of the car and came around the front. The small Avalon Prep van Mark had taken was parked beside us. Several wizards got out. They all wore formalwear. Mark climbed out of the driver's seat. "I brought everyone she wanted from the school."

I frowned. "Who wanted?"

Vane walked to the fence. A breeze blew around us. He handed me a box. "You'll have to change in the Rover."

I opened the box. It was one of the three prom dresses—a flirty gown of deep green chiffon.

"You got the green one!" Gia made a face. She touched her hair. Its brilliant red clashed with the soft pink of her dress. "This blows."

I glanced at Vane. I noticed he wore the same color vest.

He leaned close to me. "Someday I'm going to put you in a white one."

I blushed. "What's going on?"

"We're going to a wedding."

"Whose?"

"Change and you'll see. They're waiting for us inside."

It took me five minutes. Everyone except Vane was gone by the time I emerged from the car. Vane leaned against the hood. "I was thinking about coming in to help."

"Help me with the zipper." I turned around to show him my bared back. The dress opened down the length of my spine.

Vane made a growly sound and stepped up behind me. His fingers traced the knobs of my spine as the zipper slowly slid up. "Want to see if the Rover's backseat has as much space as is advertised?"

I turned around to face him. I took his lips between my teeth and bit gently. "I might let you if you're really good."

His eyes heated. "I'm better than good."

With a shake of his head, he yanked me toward the park. "C'mon, they're waiting."

Instead of going to the entrance, Vane went up to the fence. He hauled me up and bent his knees. He jumped with me into the air. Not at all what I was expecting, I squealed and flung my arms around his neck. We sailed over the iron links and onto the other side. Vane landed on his feet.

My heart hammered from the impromptu flight. He chuckled into my ear. "Surprised?"

Surprised was a mild word for his flair. He loved to shock me and I loved... I curled my fingers into his hair.

"Save it for later," he said.

As if there was going to be a later.

He let me down. We walked into the ruins of the stone abbey. In between its ruins, a crowd of mermaids, some wizards, and a smaller set of gargoyles stood waiting. As we neared, Vane took a crown out of his jacket. The last time I'd seen it had been on Lelex's head before Vane had killed him. The simple gold band had a large emerald embedded into a curve at its center. The crown's ends curled up in the shape of a fish. Vane also took out two armbands. He put on one fashioned like a snake. On his right, the armband was of a mermaid holding a trident.

"The king," announced a mermaid near the front.

The mermaids sank to their knees.

There were no chairs. It wasn't necessary. Pink, white, and green flowers decorated the ruined walls of the ancient abbey. Two monuments of crumbling stone, the ruined front face of the once-tall monastery, made the perfect arbor. There were no attendants to the bride and groom. A line of stone in the short green lawn marked the aisle.

Vane walked me down the aisle and deposited me next to Grey and Gia, who stood toward the front. The happy couple already stood at the head of the crowd.

Leonidas and Leonora both knelt on the ground.

They wore white. Her long ethereal gown offset by his kilt-like uniform. A gleaming sword lay strapped to his belt. The slight tinge of green to their skin sparkled with life.

Vane stepped past them to take his place at the front. I realized the king would be officiating the wedding. He gestured and everyone rose.

"Before we begin, I have one order of business." Vane took off his crown and handed it to a shocked Leonidas. "Tonight, I abdicate the throne to Leonidas. He is the rightful king."

My jaw dropped. I saw a similar stunned expression go

through the rest of the crowd.

Leonidas found his voice. "No, you are our leader. The line of Lelex cannot get us through this dark time. If we make it, it will be because of you." He thrust the crown back at Vane. "You are a mermaid, Vane. You always will be. Even before you were the Fisher King, you won your throne."

The mermaids cheered. Several raised their swords high. Metal clanged in the air.

For the second time in my life, I saw Vane completely flummoxed. The first had been at Buckingham Palace when I asked him to kiss me.

"Now, if you do not mind, Majesty." Leonidas's gaze fixed on Leonora. "I would really like to be married."

After that, the wedding ceremony was brief. Pretty much a do you/don't you affair. I doubted the happy couple could have said much more. Leonidas's 'I do' had come out broken. Instead of rice, dew drops pelted us as they kissed.

I cried.

Beside me, so did Gia.

Grey pulled us both close.

And that small hope, the one I thought snuffed out, flickered once more.

***

He found me beside the water. On the grounds of the park, past a square plot of dirt behind the ruined abbey marked as the grave of King Arthur, a small pond celebrated life. The spot hosted ducks, fish, and a canopy of weeping trees. I stood under one tree and watched the moonlight dance over serene ripples. A mother duck shepherded her ducklings into the quiet water.

He came up to the tree. He raised his hands and grabbed a low branch. He leaned on it, and I watched the water reflect off his long torso, its well-defined muscles honed by an unrelenting life. He watched me.

"That was an interesting twist to the ceremony."

A brow arched. "Did you approve?"

I titled my head. "Do you care?"

"I do." He sounded surprised. "Think there may be hope for me after all?"

I played with the drooping branch of a weeping tree, tracing its ribs as if I were tracing his. "You make it hard, but I think so."

Green fire lit his eyes. "You like hard."

I smiled. "Do you know me so well?"

He replied seriously, "I will never know you well enough. I will always want more."

The words full of yearning melted every doubt inside me. I blinked back tears. For the night stretched deep but dawn lay waiting to pounce. I peered through the branch swaying between us, a seductive veil. I asked softly, "How can we survive this, Vane?"

*Because I don't think I can live without you.*

Watchful eyes fixed on mine and read the unspoken thought. He sucked in a breath, yet stayed entirely still. "There's another story I know. This one doesn't have any swords or visions. This one is about a boy who found a girl during a terrible time."

"How did it turn out?"

"I don't know, but I do know the boy doesn't regret it. Not a minute. No matter how it turns out. Because he's been waiting for this girl from the time she was born, and if it takes another thousand years to meet her again, he'd wait again. Whatever it takes."

Tears, which had gathered, spilled from my eyes.

Finally, he walked closer, coming behind me, and wrapped his arms around my chest. We watched the ducklings float in circles in the water.

A sight in the distance caught my eye. A triangular terraced hill, a short distance from town. The tower on top of the hill could be seen for a hundred miles. The ruined church seemed to be a beacon promising hope, but giving no real answers.

"Glastonbury Tor. Two thousand years ago, the sea washed right up to the hills. The tower on the hill is called St. Michael's tower, the warrior saint who beat back the darkness. Some say that Avalon is where sea met the land and became the meeting place of the dead, the point at which we pass to another level of existence."

Lips grazed my ear. "Another apple can't help us with the evacuation."

I bit my lip. I looked up at the airless sky.

I hadn't told Vane about Matt's vision, mostly because I'd been in denial. The thought of losing him was a physical ache. The thought of the horror coming up... and I didn't know how to stop either.

My hands tightened on his. I brought them up to my lips.

A cell buzzed in Vane's pocket. He ignored it. It buzzed more insistently the second time.

"It could be important."

Vane took the phone out. "It's Leonidas. He says to come to the front."

I let go of him. "I'll be here."

Vane turned me in his arms. Piercing eyes saw right through me. Need rose in them. He said, "Tell me you choose me."

I met his eyes. They were tinged with green, but they didn't scare me. Maybe they should have. The monster had me now, but I'd already laid down my weapons.

"You know I do," I said.

In the moonlight, the monster smiled. "Good. I'll be back."

Vane hurried off.

I turned back to watch the ducklings for a little while longer.

Matt stepped out of the shadows. The lion tread softly down the slope.

I raised a brow at him. "Crashing the wedding?"

"Am I to assume that Vane's gained permission to use the park?"

I shrugged. "A wedding will bring us good luck. We need it."

"I take it you didn't find the apple in London."

I shook my head. "You knew I left?"

Matt's eyes flickered over the *Dragon's Eye.* "I believe him. He would wait forever to meet you again." He added, "So would I."

A sudden chill made the hairs on my arms stand up. I rubbed my arms. Resignation, chilling and merciless in its inhumanity, hooded Matt's eyes.

He asked, "Do you trust me?"

I took a step toward him. "Of course."

"I've found the one thing he can't win against." Matt's eyes flashed with pain. "I'm sorry, Ryan."

I didn't see the sleep spell coming until it hit me.

Matt caught me before I fell to the ground. He whispered in my ear, "He loves you, Ryan, and that might just save us."

## BEGINNINGS

I woke to the middle of the battle.

The sky sparkled in muted hues of red, purple, and pink. I only saw it through tinted glass. My head pounding, I jerked up from where I'd been slumped asleep. Instead of a gown, I wore a thin jacket and black cargos and found myself stuffed among a group of people inside a moving truck. They were all Regulars from what I could tell. Men, women, and children, but not complete families. Seeing their torn faces left me sucker-punched once again.

We sat in one of those trucks transporting prisoners. It had metal walls and a bench seat. From my vantage point, tinted windows showed the sky outside and nothing else. A thick metal wall separated the back from the drivers. A porthole allowed them to observe us in the back.

Bodies packed every inch of space, standing room only. Cold

artificial air blasted us, probably to keep us from rioting. I doubted anyone would dare. After all, we knew we were the lucky ones.

Disoriented and pissed, I stood up on the bench seat and peered outside. Hordes and hordes of black trucks roared along the road. Over one gently rolling hill, Stonehenge came into view. At first, I only saw the wide plain and the lonely stones as I'd seen countless times on TV. I'd been around wizards long enough to recognize magic. I squinted my eyes and made out a faint barrier of bluish magic. Merlin's magic. A shield blanketed an enormous umbrella so that the casual observer wouldn't see the parking lot of mismatched vehicles surrounding the stone circle in a wide radius.

Besides the black trucks, there were double-decker buses, hummers, and even army helicopters. This had been planned well to maximize every bit of space the gate offered. I turned back to Stonehenge. It had three main circles. The outermost circle was about three hundred twenty feet in diameter. The ground around it had been cut into a ditch.

Much smaller than the outer circle, the inner circle contained two rings. The inner circle was the famous picturesque view of the monument. The bigger ring of the inner circle reminded one of giants playing blocks. The ring of sarsen and bluestones, vertical slabs topped by horizontal ones, although broken, stood like giants. The trilithons ranged from thirteen to twenty-four feet in height. The inner most ring was made up of three trilithons.

An altar of unusual green sandstone sat at the center of the monument. It faced the grand trilithon of the inner ring and reached sixteen feet long. Outside the circles, a heel stone sat far out past the outermost circle. The layout of the monument reminded me of a pocket watch where the heel stone would be the stopper at the top.

The mermaids had straddled a giant trilithon directly over the heel stone. The new trilithon did look like a square version of the enormously huge *Arc De Triomphe*. It would be able to accommodate the organized onslaught of vehicles. It stood about a hundred times bigger than the one he'd built in Boston, A chill went through me. Vane had barely managed to open the small one. I had no idea how he planned to harness the Fury.

I reached for the *Dragon's Eye*. It was gone.

Matt had broken through Vane's lock. I was completely on my own.

I glanced down at my wrist. A faint scar marred it. Matt had taken my blood. He drained me like I was nothing more than a blood bag. Apparently, I wasn't needed for anything else.

I had no idea why Matt put me in the truck.

Was he hoping to avoid the vision or fulfill it?

We reached the fence just outside the famous monument. Stonehenge was generally shut off from the public. It made it easier for the barricade the soldiers and wizards had erected. Cars and people jammed the fence. I saw sparks of magic fly when an unauthorized car tried to ram the barricade. It was all going well until the earth started rumbling.

Around me, everyone let out a shocked cry and started pointing to another window. I fought my way past them to look and saw a second sun, a circle of flaming red, poke through the sky.

It was the first sign of the end.

I had to get out of this truck. I crossed to the closed door and tried the handle. As I suspected, it was locked from the outside. He'd hidden me well. Among the numerous black trucks, I could be in any one. I looked for help.

I found the three Drust children. It took me less than a minute to enlist them (knowing their names convinced them). They, in turn, persuaded a few to help me kick down the door. Never underestimate Regulars.

I jumped down from the back of the moving truck. The door slammed shut behind me as the evacuees huddled back inside. I started running. More sparks flew across the sky. A rainbow of colors swirled as the first soft volley came from the sun.

The Fury was coming.

A soldier spotted me among the slow-moving trucks. He gave a warning shot. I ducked and turned. His shocked face never anticipated my tackle. I knocked him down and grabbed the gun. Then I ran. The soldier didn't stay down. I heard him radio for help, but didn't stop. I kept running through toward the inner rings. The number one rule in Vane's training book was that slowing down equaled dead and gone.

The closer I got, the number of soldiers increased. Luckily, so did the number of vehicles. They shot at me but were limited in their range. The soldiers were careful knowing the precious cargo the trucks carried, several with their own family members—the bargain they'd made to save them. With a few shots (my aim was fairly good with a gun), I managed to dodge the soldiers by rolling under a few moving trucks. Dirt, grass, and scrapes covered me.

I saw the famous ring of the Stonehenge. I ran straight into a wall of muscle and a gun aimed straight at my head. I slumped in defeat. The back of a truck burst open. The soldier's eyes flickered. I knocked the gun from him. Grey and Colin jumped out.

I'd never been so glad to see anyone. Grey carried a limp Gia over his shoulders.

"Ryan, what's going on?" Grey yelled. "Emrys drugged us. We just woke up."

More gargoyles jumped down from the truck.

"I don't know. Let's find out." Although we had no weapons, it was a lot easier to get to the front using the gargoyles as shields. Thanks to their super-healing abilities, shots didn't faze them too much. Once Gia woke up, she started throwing spells and mowed the path.

When we reached the inner circle, I signaled Grey to approach silently. I had a clear view from the altar stone to the mammoth trilithon at the heel stone. Excalibur lay embedded in the green sandstone slab.

In front of it, the golden apple lay silently on the stone.

Blood covered it. My blood.

At the center of the chaos, two colossuses faced each other. Green magic swirled around Vane. Blue colored Matt. It was the same fight. Fifteen hundred years ago they battled over one kingdom. Today, over the world.

The mermaids stood quietly behind Vane, their swords at their feet. Soldiers surrounded them. I spotted Robin near a military man with an iPad for a clipboard. Matt paced, glancing at the apple. Everyone watched the metallic apple, waiting for it to signal the time.

And the evacuation would begin. At the end of all things.

Vane watched Matt. "I'm not opening anything until I know she's safe."

Matt dangled the *Dragon's Eye* in front of Vane. "You'll have to take my word for it."

"We need her here."

Matt gestured at Robin. "I can get her if we do."

"We had a plan," Vane said.

"This way, I know you'll stick to it." He looked up at the sky. More light streaked it. The wind rose and kicked dirt around the plain. "Open the gates and everyone, including her, will go through."

Vane let out a small laugh. "Still don't trust me, Merlin?"

Merlin stopped pacing. "I won't take the risk. I've seen it—"

"You can't hide behind visions forever. This has always been about me leaving. I don't know why I didn't see it. Maybe because I never believed you could care that much. I had no choice, Merlin. The Lady picked my destiny."

"She separated us for a reason," Matt said.

"Because you were meant to kill me," Vane said. "You don't need to lie anymore, Merlin. It finally makes sense."

Matt stilled. "What do you mean?"

"I keep having to remind everyone that I'm a genius," Vane said lightly. "The reports on the apple hypothesize that the exotic particles inside will keep the gates' wormhole open and large enough to accommodate everyone. By opening them at the same time, we will be able to bind all the gates into one bridge. However, to go off-planet, as we think the apple will take us, requires a tremendous amount of energy. We must use the power of the Fury, and the monster must harness it."

"The Lady chose me for this," Matt whispered.

*Chose him to die.*

Behind the stones, I glanced up at the burning sky. The apple wobbled.

The time was close.

Vane smiled. "She chose you, but failed to take one thing into account. I never stopped being your brother. Ryan wouldn't let me. It's amazing what we will do for those we love. What we will sacrifice."

Matt's eyes hardened. "It's why I'm keeping Ryan in the truck. If you want to save her, you'll have to save everyone. No matter what it takes."

"I'm not talking about Ryan. I didn't come here to evacuate, Merlin. I took the monster because I knew whoever took it would die today. I took it so you wouldn't have to. For you. For her. She was meant for you."

Matt gaped at him.

"I am sorry, brother. You will have to be alone once more." Vane drew the Kronos Eye out of his pocket.

"No!" I did the one thing I could. I used the gun I'd taken and shot Vane's hand. The bullet grazed his hand. The Kronos Eye rolled on the ground.

Matt grabbed it. He shot his brother with a spell. "I'm sorry too, Vane."

Vane went flying back. I realized he went down too easily. He coughed, letting out blood on the ground.

Everything inside me stilled. I stilled.

He was dying. Blood pounded the chambers of my heart, but couldn't flow. My body refused to pump it.

"Ryan," Vane croaked.

Blood forced its way through my arteries. I ran from my hiding place. More soldiers tried to tackle me. Grey and Gia fought them off, but they kept coming. I dodged past them to reach Vane. I dropped down next to him, my cheeks wet and dirty.

Matt held the Kronos Eye in his palm. "The water's been drained from the crystal."

"I took it earlier." Vane laughed weakly. "Once the monster gathers enough energy, I'll let go. Then, you can take the monster without flaming out."

On the slab, the apple stirred.

"It's time, Merlin," Vane said. "Just like you wanted."

Matt knelt down on his brother's other side. "This was never what I wanted."

It was the vision. The sky burned above us, displaying a magnificent and deadly aurora. Wind swirled through the stone circle.

We sat on either side as Vane closed his eyes.

The apple rose fully in the air.

Matt picked up the trident from Vane's side. He leaned on it. I snatched the *Dragon's Eye* dangling from Matt's pocket.

"*Vane*," I sobbed. "*Why didn't you tell me your plan?*"

"*Ryan*." The word, my name, held a wealth of longing. Then, it sharpened. Vane's voice reverberated in my head. "*Tell me you trust me, Ryan.*"

"*You know I do*," I said.

"*Then, look for the answer. Inside Merlin. Look now. You're the only one he'll let in. His defenses are low. He won't stop you. And remember, whatever you find—you can bear it.*"

I looked. Using the *Dragon's Eye*, I walked into Matt's mind. I had no idea what I was looking for, only that I desperately sought it. A vision of a cottage stood before me. It was the same cottage as Vane's vision. Only this time, I saw it through Matt's eyes. I saw the Lady. She had green eyes. She smiled at me. She sat at the table with a knife and a potato.

"Which would you choose, Merlin?" she asked. "To save your brother or save everyone."

"My brother," I answered without hesitation.

"I know," she said softly. "That's why I did what I did. Why I had to send him away. I hope you will understand someday."

She put the knife on the potato. "Remember this, Merlin. Whole, it can keep one full. Cut it and it will feed us all a little bit. Cut it and the risk to you is great. Keep it whole and the risk to everyone else is great. Either way a choice must be made."

The Lady cut the potato in half. Only it was no longer a potato.

*A choice must be made.*

And I had my answer.

The secret the Lady had unconsciously revealed to Merlin. The one Poseidon had known.

I opened my eyes.

Above us, the sky turned red. The Fury would be upon us soon.

Matt picked up the trident. He hit the ground with it as I reached Excalibur.

The ground cracked and rumbled. A mist began to form around the gates.

My hands closed around Excalibur.

"Ryan," Matt yelled. "What are you doing?"

"I'm finding another way." I grabbed Excalibur out of the rock.

The mist died. The gates never opened. The apple fell.

"No!" Matt lunged for me.

It was too late. I brought Excalibur smashing down on the golden apple.

In that moment, I risked us all. The entire human race on one belief—for a few to survive wasn't enough. To simply survive wasn't enough.

The apple exploded. Spots of black and white sparkled out of the apple's hollow middle like fairy lights.

The sky screamed as the Fury neared.

"Matt," I cried.

He stood frozen, looking at the destroyed apple.

The *Dragon's Eye* heated in my hand. I called to the monster. It rose.

Vane's body shuddered as the monster took over.

"It's time," I told the monster.

It roared. The fairy lights floated all around us. The exotic particles from the apple spread farther and farther up in the air. It took seconds. Precious ones while no one evacuated. The gates, the passage out, remained silent and closed. Far away energy spiked in our yellow sun, causing the monster's energy to spike and spill. Around us, the fairy lights changed. The whole planet stood suspended in space for a moment.

Then in the span of a wink, the earth disappeared.

Like a two-dimensional character suddenly thrust into a three-dimensional world, I saw beyond myself. Where once the blue planet had stood, only empty space remained. I held onto Excalibur as we shifted to another phase of existence, one made only from our consciousness.

Instead of creating a passage connecting two endpoints, the exotic matter from the apple created a hole in one spot, a hole big enough to fit one planet.

The Fury hit.

The sun flared and its tentacles slashed at us. The inferno passed straight through, only meeting with empty space where the earth should have been.

We watched from outside it, like holograms who saw but didn't feel. Seventy-six seconds passed. Precious seconds. And in those seconds we changed the fate of all and saved our souls.

The Fury continued.

The fairy lights danced with increasing brilliance as the Fury intensified and I had to close my eyes at the lights' twinkling ferocity. Beside me, Vane's body shuddered harder. The monster struggled to hang on. I could do nothing but watch as bit by bit the monster burned away under the onslaught of eternal fire.

The Fury passed.

Inside Vane, the monster roared mournfully, a blistered husk. It sighed when Vane finally let go, his body stilling completely.

I choked back a cry.

Matt put his hand on Vane's unmoving chest. He took the

monster into himself. Green colored Matt's amber eyes.

I held onto Excalibur, the lone tether back to our physical existence. Matt's arms came around me. He used Excalibur to focus. Green swirled around us in huge waves, calling the fairy lights back to the sword. He commanded them into the broken pieces of the apple. They refused.

Excalibur stayed hot in my hands.

I threw the sword at the gate. As soon as Excalibur neared, The middle of the trilithon lit up. Mist flared inside the gate and Excalibur sailed through the doorway between worlds. The fairy lights, like bees to pollen, swarmed after the sword. As the fairy lights receded, around us the world began to solidify.

The planet reappeared in space, winking back into physical existence. I looked up from the ground. A translucent sky became colored with a thick blanket of homogenous blue. But it wasn't over.

As soon as the last of the fairy lights passed and the world fully materialized, a sonic boom blasted us from the open mouth of the gate. A tremendous tornado churned in the sudden vacuum. Like the mythical whirlpool, Charybdis, it tried to suck us into the gate.

The broken pieces of the apple flew though the gate and to the other side.

Matt stuck the trident into the ground. His arm still around me, we held on. Vane's still form flew past and I grabbed him with one hand. Matt helped me pull him close.

Trucks and busses flew around us like huge asteroids of metal. Some passed through into the gate and disappeared past the mist. Some tumbled off onto the plains on this side of the gate. On the ground, many others hung onto the trilithons. Grey, Gia, Leonidas—all held onto rough rock. The wind got worse. It buzzed loudly against my ears.

Matt held on to me.

He dug in his pocket and took out the Kronos Eye.

I shouted past the wind, "What are you doing?"

"I should have believed in him more. Believed in you more." Amber eyes smiled sadly at me. "You saved them, Ryan. I know you can save him."

"Matt, no!" My hands tied up with Vane, I couldn't stop him from swallowing it.

"It's time for me to let go," he said huskily. "Take care of him."

The monster cried out one last time. Matt put his hand against Vane's chest. Green flowed from him into his brother. The green in Matt's eyes snuffed out. He slumped over the trident. But Vane didn't wake either.

Fiercely, I held on to them both.

I pulled the trident from the ground. Matt, Vane, and I went flying into the gate. In the mist, in between sea and land, the hole in the cosmos gaped opened. I saw the shadow of a kingdom and its castle, high up on a cliff, its turrets boasting with flags of a red serpentine dragon. But I sought another place. I pictured where I wanted to go. I held Matt close, the Kronos Eye within him, and I said, "*Elysium.*"

We landed on its banks. Above me, blue sky winked in and out. The power of the monster was fading, the gates closing. I didn't have long.

I used the trident to make a jagged cut across Matt's stomach.

I tore out the Kronos Eye. Then, I dragged him and Vane to the edge of the bank. They floated in shallow water.

For several heartbeats, nothing happened. Serene waves of the river flowed without disruption. I remembered Rawana saying Matt had defiled Elysium.

I refused to give up. I yelled into the air. "They've done everything you asked! You owe them a life."

The wind took my words, examined them, and tossed them aside.

I picked up the trident and slammed it down on the bank. A wave jerked in the river. I slammed the trident again. The river reacted angrily, more waves rose. I slammed the trident a third time. Before me, the waves rose high like a hand until it towered over me. The watery hand came rushing down with furious speed. It crashed onto the riverbank.

Water slammed into me, threatening to drown me.

I struggled to stay afloat. I lost track of Vane and Matt. Behind us, the trilithon gate opened. The river washed me toward it and dumped me into the mist.

A whisper came out of the dark. *Camelot.*

## CAMELOT

He was a conqueror, fashioned by the sea. Arrogant and merciless, yet also containing the essence of life itself, and he'd saved us all. Gentle surf tickled my feet. I recognized the beach. It was the one where I'd let the monster heal me. I didn't know quite where we were, but I knew we hadn't gone far.

We were still on Earth. I knew by the two suns hovering in the sky, one yellow and one red, one to stay and one to fade. Kronos's Fury had passed. Yet, the blood spot of the supernova would remain in the sky for months until like a scab it healed. The memory of the Fury would remain burned in our minds, until it, too, would wane. But for today, the world was saved.

We'd done it. And we'd come home.

I hoped my family was all right. Grey. Gia. Matt.

I looked down at Vane. He lay still on the beach. I lay on top of him. Where I wanted to be. I watched the breeze play with his hair. I watched his chest rise and fall and I hoped.

He was alive. We were together.

"*Together, does that mean you have a thing for me?*"

I nearly shrieked when his voice sounded in my head.

Hazel eyes popped open. I smiled. Probably a really idiotic smile, but I couldn't help it. My fingers dug into his shoulders. His slid into my hair.

"Am I alive?" he said huskily.

A cold wave slapped our feet to answer. I moved to sit, my knees dug into the sand. Vane pulled me back down to cover him. "*Don't go. Ever.*"

"*How are you talking to me?*"

Vane reached into the pocket of my cargoes. A hand tickled a small hole in the pocket. I squirmed. With a wicked grin, he pulled out the Kronos Eye. Its odd shape had solidified into green crystal. Vane's hand glowed with faint green, and it shrank even more.

He held it out in his palm as a promise. "I always wanted to make you an amulet. It seems as if you could use a new one."

I touched my neck. The wind had taken the *Dragon's Eye.* Like Excalibur, it lay somewhere between the mist and the stone circle. I moved to take the Kronos Eye. With a baiting smile, he tried to close his palm on it. I was faster. I snatched it to me, giving him a triumphant look. He returned my look with a smug one of his own.

Life would never be dull with him. I sighed, though all I really wanted to do was smile even more idiotically. I asked, "How did you make this? The monster…" *Is gone.*

Vane inclined his head. "A bit of him remains. It's not tangible, but I feel stronger. I doubt I'll be able to move mountains, but a bit of Poseidon will always be within me. I am a mermaid, after all."

Behind me, a wave rose up high and danced as if it agreed. It hurtled forward onto the beach. I tensed. The wave stopped suddenly, as if it hit an invisible wall. It dissipated and fell harmlessly back into the ocean.

I looked down at Vane. Amused hazel eyes watched me.

Godlike powers. He was going to be trouble.

"Oh, yes." Sensuous lips curved. "You could use some trouble."

"Matt gave the power back to you. To save you." A tight feeling came over me. I glanced around the beach. We were in a cove. In front of us, a rocky hill rose into woods. On either side, black lava rocks formed sheer cliffs. I saw not one person.

Vane tugged at my hair, drawing my attention back to him. "He's alive. I would know if he weren't."

"Then where is he?" I scanned the cliffs.

The shadows remained dark.

Vane stared at the same cliffs. "It's done. The story is done. Merlin has to find a new one. Seems this one was meant for me after all."

I looked down at him. "Will you ever call him Matt?"

White teeth flashed unrepentantly. "It's one and the same." His grin turned wistful. "Will you always love him?"

"Almost as much as you will."

Vane gave me a very male look. "I don't think I like you

knowing me so well. I will have to work harder to distract you."

I repressed an urge to melt onto him, and instead traced a finger along the hard length of his jaw. "How did you know the Lady accidentally told Matt about the other way?"

"I didn't. I remembered what Poseidon said and I took a chance. She was with Merlin a long time."

Took a chance. As I had done. "But why did you do it? Why let me take the risk with the apple? Matt wouldn't."

"It was what you said in Westminster. We're human. It's what we do. And I finally realized, it's what you would do." Vane smirked. "I told you I would save you."

"*I* saved you."

Mischief danced in his eyes. "Don't get cocky."

He'd said the same thing the night of our first kiss in the basement. I had no intention of listening to him—then or now. I arched a brow. "Then, don't fall for me."

"Too late, Dorothy."

*Dorothy.* The name rolled off his tongue like the sweetest caress. My lips curving up, I turned to gaze out at the ocean, an open expanse of never-ending water. "Where are we?"

"Home. Camelot. As long as I'm with you, I don't care."

Catching my hand, he brought it to his lips and kissed the back in an old-fashioned gesture. Just when I began to surrender, he shocked me by sinking his teeth lightly into the skin. I shivered and looked up at the yellow sun. Our sun. Vane understood me well. Camelot had always been here. At Home.

A figure lurked in the shadows. It pushed back green fronds at the base of the cliff and walked slowly down to the beach. He came closer. I cried out happily. Grey. He waved at me.

I moved to get up. Fingers wound tightly in my curls. Vane's legs tangled around mine, holding them in place. "Will I ever be allowed to have you to myself for more than a minute, sword-bearer?"

"Probably not," I said readily. "Though, I'm not the sword-bearer anymore." The sword had done its duty and thus, disappeared into legend once again.

"You may no longer have Excalibur, but you will always be the sword-bearer." With a tug, he flipped me over. I sunk into damp sand. His muscled body completely enveloped mine, and lips grazed up along a tender column of my neck. "You belong to me."

"Yes."

He bit an earlobe, causing me to buck under him. "Tell me you love me."

My heart filling at the hint of urgency in his voice, I said, "You know I do."

He added, "Vane."

I put my hands on his stubbled jaw, reveling in the way the rough bristles prickled the soft skin of my palm. It was real. He was real. I replied, "I love you, Vivane."

He smiled, a sweet smile. It held a hint of the boy in the cottage, the one beneath all those red-stained layers who still survived. I pressed closer to him.

He would never be alone again. And neither would I.

\*\*\*

I lost her. I watched them from the shadows.

I got my brother in return.

That I didn't regret the exchange may have been why I lost her. I shrank back when she glanced in my direction. Under me, Grey walked from the base of the cliff and onto the beach. He'd go to her instead.

Beyond him, I saw others. An upside down truck—its passengers shaken but unharmed. Regulars, wizards, mermaids, and gargoyles wandered the woods. I suspected some of those drawn into the tornado had crossed the mist to another world, while the rest of us were dumped here. Back on Earth.

Ryan had risked it all to save... well, everyone. She'd done what I could not. Unearthed the memory. Made the decision I could not. By taking Vane away, the Lady had believed she ensured I'd never take such a risk. As I watched those wandering below, I knew the Lady had been wrong. Love didn't weaken me. If we'd evacuated, what kind of half-life would we have led always missing those we'd left behind? I'd been so sure of my path, my purpose. I'd been so wrong.

Like lost ducklings, some of those below would seek the beach and wait to be shepherded back. Others would turn and find the city on the other side. There was always a choice to be made. I glanced over rainbow-covered mountains, painted surfboards on crowded sand, and a resort's well-maintained beaches. I recognized the spot. A picture of this place hung in Sylvia's study. Ryan looked at it sometimes with wistful eyes when she thought no one watched. I did.

I was up on the cliff. For the moment, I was alone.

She had Vane.

And I was free. The weight of my brother was lifted.

He forgave me for planning his death. I forgave him for being the source of my guilt. As much as it killed me to see him with her, I also wouldn't have her with anyone else. The two who filled me, but completed each other more.

I would miss them.

I would see them again. Someday. When the time was right. When I could be with them without this savage jealously wrenching through me.

Vane understood.

I saw his piercing eyes fix on my spot. He knew time healed. It would be slow. Turning on my heel, I walked into the tropical jungle. Just beyond the stretch of green trees, the outline of a high-rise resort rose above the horizon. On the other side of the gate, after we'd left Elysium, I'd glimpsed the kingdom in the mist. More than anything I'd wanted to fling myself toward it. Ryan wouldn't have gone. Her Camelot would always be here. In a sense, she was right. This was the moment. Camelot had to be made. Every day and with every fight.

As much as I'd wanted to, I hadn't crossed the mist to the other world. My place was still here. With her. With my brother. Our lives finally together. I looked up at the twin suns. It would pass and the Earth would have one sun again soon. We saved the garden. The cradle of life.

I would live, too. Someday I would breathe again.

Until then there would be a lot of questions. The Queen would need me. I was not meant for obscurity. I had a lot left to do. A world to right.

And maybe I would look for the second apple.

After all, my name has always been Merlin.

But now, I was Matt too.

\*\*\*

## EPILOGUE

Much later, I asked Vane what was next.

A wicked gleam shone in his eyes. "A university in New Haven keeps begging me to accept a tenure. It has a penchant for secret societies that intrigues me. It's a stone's throw from Boston. You'd be close to home. Think of the fun, Ryan." A hand reached around to lightly touch my back. He added low into my ear, "I know my way around a ruler."

I let out a small moan. College with Professor Vane. Oh, Greek gods.

—THE END—

## AUTHOR'S NOTE

I hope you have enjoyed the conclusion of the My Merlin Series! I will miss these characters as I go on to new stories but at least I can always open the page and re-read their adventures as I hope you will!

Please look for more on my upcoming books by staying connected at the following sites or signing up for notifications of new releases at my website (http://www.priyaardis.com). To read deleted scenes, articles, and listen to the soundtrack, follow my Blog: http://blog.priyaardis.com.

Talk to me at the following hangouts!

Twitter: http://www.twitter.com/priyaardis

Facebook: http://www.facebook.com/priyaardis

Goodreads: http://www.goodreads.com/priyaardis

## ABOUT THE AUTHOR

Priya Ardis loves books of all kinds—but especially the gooey ones that make your nose leak and let your latte go cold. Her novels come from a childhood of playing too much She-Ra and watching too much Spock. She started her first book at sixteen, writing in notebooks on long train rides in India during a hot summer vacation. Her favorite Arthurian piece is *The Lady of Shalott* by Lord Tennyson. A hopeless romantic, she is a longtime member of the Romance Writer's of America.

When not living in her character's world, she might be found at the local coffee shop—her nose buried in a book.

Made in the USA
San Bernardino, CA
05 June 2015